18/3 DMH

Little Woodford

CATHERINE JONES lives in Thame,
where she is an independent councillor. She
is the author of eighteen novels, including
the Soldiers' Wives series, written under
the pseudonym Fiona Field.

Also by Catherine Jones, writing as Fiona Field

Soldiers' Wives
Soldiers' Daughters
Civvy Street

Little Woodford

The Secrets of a Small Town

CATHERINE JONES

HEAD
of ZEUS

First published in the UK in 2018 by Head of Zeus Ltd

9 7 5 3 1 2 4 6 8

A catalogue record for this book is available from
the British Library.

ISBN (HB): 9781784979799
ISBN (E): 9781784979782

Typeset by Adrian McLaughlin

Printed and bound in Great Britain by
CPI Group (UK) Ltd, Croydon CR0 4YY

Head of Zeus Ltd
First Floor East
5–8 Hardwick Street
London EC1R 4RG

WWW.HEADOFZEUS.COM

To Fearne Lace Stibbs – 16th February 2017

1

Olivia Laithwaite, resident of Little Woodford, mother of four, town councillor and general do-gooder, was on her way to her hair appointment when a car zipped across her path, over the pavement and through the gate of The Beeches. So, thought Olivia, maybe this heralded the new owners who were moving in at last. She took a few more paces then peered round the gate post and saw the estate car parked on the gravel drive. A youngish blonde was getting out of the driver's seat and a sultry-looking teenager with raven hair spilling down her back emerged from the front passenger seat. Out of the back tumbled a couple of small boys, both fair-haired like their mother. From the way the four interacted, chatting, laughing, the girl holding hands with the smaller of the boys, it seemed as though this must be a family, except that the girl bore no resemblance at all to the others. Maybe she took after her father. And where was he? wondered Olivia. Not that it was any of her business.

She strolled on towards Cutz and Curlz, the lone hair salon in the town, passing, as she did, an estate agent. She examined the A4 cards with the house details, pasted in the window. She liked to see what prices houses in the area were achieving – not that she was planning on moving but it gave her a sense of smug satisfaction to know that, if some of the smaller houses round and about were hitting the half-a-million mark, her huge barn conversion, at the top end of the town, must be well into seven figures. She recalled that when The Beeches had gone on the market the previous owners had wanted an eye-watering amount but it had been up for sale for so long that Olivia doubted they got what they'd been after. She remembered that the For Sale sign had gone up way before Christmas and now Easter had come and gone and, in under a fortnight, the schools were due to start the summer term. She longed to know what the final price had been – she expected it to have been north of a million and a half, but not the nearly two million they'd wanted. Which begged the question: how could such a young family afford the place? She was still mulling this over when she reached the hairdresser's and pushed the door open. At the ping the receptionist looked up. Olivia didn't think her blue hair did anything for her – made her look quite sallow. What *had* the girl be thinking of when she'd dyed it that colour?

'Mrs Laithwaite. Mags is just finishing off another client. She'll be with you shortly. Can I take your jacket?'

As Olivia shrugged off her navy blazer and handed it to the receptionist to hang on the rail in the alcove behind her desk, she looked across the salon to where Mags the proprietor was working. Mags was little and dumpy with bright auburn hair cut short and brushed into artful spikes. Olivia was in no doubt that both the artful spikes and the colour were courtesy of hairdressing skills and had nothing to do with nature. She sniffed. And wasn't Mags too old to have that shade of red? If she was any judge, the woman had to be pushing sixty – wouldn't a slightly less garish shade be more appropriate?

She sat on the sofa and picked up a magazine. Across the salon, she could see Mags puffing spray onto Belinda Bishop's newly styled hair – at least Belinda's shade looked more natural. The two seemed to be discussing some reality TV show or other. Olivia sniffed again. Really, she thought, she could understand Mags watching such tripe but Belinda? And when did she have the time? Surely as the landlady of the Talbot, the local pub, she would be better off running her business than slobbing in front of rubbish. Ah well, each to their own. Olivia shook her head. Belinda and Mags were laughing now. Maybe if Mags got on with her job instead of chatting, she wouldn't be running late for her next appointment. Olivia stopped trying to eavesdrop and instead immersed herself in an article about Carole Middleton. Now *that* was a family to envy.

Mags's daughter Amy glanced across the street at her mother's hairdressing business as she walked to one of her many part-time jobs; this morning she was cleaning for the vicar's wife. She needed to ask her mum if she'd do her a cut and colour sometime soon; her roots were starting to show something terrible. Maybe she'd pop round tonight to fix up a time. Actually, maybe she'd do it right now. Amy crossed the street and pushed open the door. Oh, gawd, there was Mrs Laithwaite, another of her ladies that she 'did' for.

'Morning, Mrs L,' she said with fake cheer.

Olivia barely looked up from her magazine as she acknowledged the greeting. 'Morning, Amy.'

As usual the old bag looked like she'd swallowed a wasp but her mum said she was a good tipper and Amy herself always got given a bonus at Christmas, so she wasn't all bad, just a bit heavy going. Mind you, thought Amy, it wasn't like she couldn't afford the odd show of generosity, not with living in the big house and everything.

'Hi, Janine,' she said to the receptionist. 'Love the colour.'

'Ta,' said Janine, picking up a lock and staring at it. 'Thought I'd try something a bit different.'

'Good for you.'

'Hi, love,' called Mags. She put down the mirror she'd been using to show Belinda the back of her new hair-do. She swished a brush over Belinda's shoulders to get rid of the last of the stray hairs and then helped her take off her gown. 'There you go, Belinda. Janine'll sort out the bill. With you in a mo, Mrs Laithwaite.'

Olivia sniffed and turned a page. Amy grinned at her mother. 'Can you do me a cut and colour, Mum?'

'When?'

'Soonish?'

'Of course, deary. Want to come round mine at the weekend?'

'That'd be great.'

'Not changing the colour or nothing, are you?'

'Same old, same old. Anyway, I like being blond.'

Janine rang up Belinda's bill and the till pinged open.

Mags reached over and took out a couple of twenties. 'I know things are a bit tight for you and Ashley.'

'Mum!'

Mags pressed the notes into Amy's hand. 'Go on, take it. Don't want to see you two going short.'

'Thanks, Mum. Best I get going...' She popped the money in her handbag and zipped it up. 'Off to do for Heather.'

'Tell her hello from me. I'll see her at the WI.'

Olivia coughed loudly and impatiently and Amy, standing with her back to her, winked at her mum.

'Bye then. Bye, Mrs L. See you later in the week.'

'Indeed.'

Amy grinned to herself as she left the shop. Bloody hell, waiting a couple of minutes wasn't going to kill her, was it? She walked along the high street and past The Beeches. The sound of children laughing made her look over the gate. Thank gawd for that, she thought, someone had finally moved in. Months and months it had been since the previous owners had moved out; months and months of her not being required to clean it. The old owners had employed her twice a week and the hole in her income, when they'd sold up and gone, had made quite a difference to her. That was one of the reasons she and her son were finding it a bit of a struggle to keep body and soul together – as her mum liked to put it.

She'd tried to get other cleaning jobs but the people who might want a cleaner already had one, and the people who couldn't afford one, or who preferred to clean their own places, were hardly likely to change their minds and employ her out of charity. She sometimes managed to pick up the odd extra shift behind the post office counter – another of her part-time jobs – but it didn't always make up the difference. Amy made up her mind to speak to the new people, once they'd had a chance to settle in, to see if they wanted some domestic help. Surely, if they were loaded enough to afford a place that size, they could afford to have a cleaner too.

She watched the two boys playing for a couple more seconds then a foreign-looking girl came round the corner of the house, shot a frightened look at Amy, and swished them away. It was, thought Amy, as if she was scared of something. Although, what there was to be scared of in a place like this was beyond her.

Heather Simmonds was tidying up the vicarage prior to Amy's arrival. Her long pepper-and-salt hair was tied up and stuffed into a messy bun held with a clip. Heather wasn't one for vanity and as long as she looked clean and tidy she never bothered much about her appearance – anyway, she didn't have the spare cash for luxuries like make-up. Besides, she'd been blessed with good bones, and although she was still in her mid-fifties she knew she looked quite youthful. And she'd kept her figure too – although that was possibly due to the fact that, with cash always being a bit tight, she and Brian could rarely indulge in anything other than a pretty basic diet. No cream cakes or bottles of wine except on special occasions. Being as poor as the proverbial church mouse, she mused, had some benefits as she could fit into clothes she'd had for years. She had skirts older than most of the choir.

She turned her attention back to the tidying. It was, she thought, a Herculean task, given her husband's utter inability to put anything back in the place in which he'd found it. She knew people thought her mad for cleaning for the cleaner but she paid Amy to dust and hoover, and if Amy had to spend the first hour of her time shifting Brian's books, correspondence, half-finished sermons and other muddles, most of the house wouldn't get dealt with.

She shuffled a bunch of papers into a tidyish pile and carted them through to Brian's study.

'Tea?' she offered as she put everything on a corner of his desk.

'What, love?' He looked up from his computer screen, his glasses halfway down his aquiline nose, toast crumbs from breakfast down the front of his sweater, his brown eyes looking into the distance rather than at her, and his silver hair was spiky because he had a tendency to run his fingers through it when he was thinking. When brushed, his fringe flopped over his high forehead but that generally only lasted until he sat at the breakfast table and began to read the paper; the first headline was usually enough for him to push his hair off his face and give him an untidy Mohican. Consequently, when he was at home, and not expecting visitors, he looked like an unmade bed. The trouble was, being a vicar, visitors arrived whether they were expected or not. Still, thought Heather, he was paid to minister to his flock and not to be a poster-boy for his vocation, and anyway, his parishioners didn't seem to mind. Although, sometimes, she wished he didn't look quite so ramshackle. It made her look like a bad wife, as if she didn't look after him properly, which was grossly unfair.

'I'm offering tea. Would you like a cup?'

'If you're making one.'

Heather smiled inwardly. No, she wasn't making one for herself, she was offering to make Brian one... never mind.

She pottered into the kitchen, with its hideous lime-green tiles and chipped enamel sink, filled the kettle and plugged it in then looked out of the window. Across the garden she could see the old vicarage – a beautiful Regency house, with sash windows, a pretty wrought-iron porch and a walled garden. Very *Pride and*

Prejudice, she always thought, with the symmetrical arrangement of a window on either side of the front door, three windows above and then two dormers set into the old stone tiles on the roof. So much nicer to look at than her sixties box, the new vicarage, which was what the Church had built for the incumbent when they'd sold off the old one. Heather tried to console herself with the knowledge that the old vicarage probably cost a fortune to heat and had antique plumbing and, because it was grade II listed, any sort of repairs or alterations were nigh-on impossible, but it was small compensation for the sheer ugliness of her current home.

The doorbell rang and was followed by the click of a key in the lock.

'Coo-ee,' chirped Amy's voice.

'Morning, Amy,' said Heather. She liked Amy, who didn't have an easy life being a single mum, but she was invariably cheerful and she was a hard worker. 'The kettle's on.'

'Wouldn't say no, Mrs S. Parched, I am.' She came into the kitchen, shrugging off her mac as she walked, revealing a low-cut blouse, a fair bit of cleavage and a minuscule skirt. Given her curves there seemed to be more of Amy unclothed than clothed and, not for the first time, Heather thought she looked like a young Barbara Windsor. She hung her coat over the back of one of the kitchen chairs and grabbed her pinny off the hook behind the door. 'Someone is moving into The Beeches.'

'Really?'

'Taken a while, hasn't it? Mind you,' said Amy as she tied the apron strings behind her back, 'they wanted nearly two mill for it.' She sighed. Heather thought it sounded a little wistful. 'Fancy having that sort of cash to spend.'

'Indeed. Although money doesn't make you happy.'

'Really?' said Amy with raised eyebrows. 'Trust me, not having any isn't much of a giggle either.'

'No.' Heather knew that; vicars certainly did their job for love, not money.

The kettle on the counter crescendoed to a boil and clicked off. Heather took two mugs off the shelf and made the tea.

'Could you take that through to Brian?' she asked Amy, handing her a mug.

'You not having one?'

'No, I've got to go and see Olivia Laithwaite about the church flowers. The ones we did for Easter have gone over and I really must sort new ones out for the weekend.' She sighed. 'I shouldn't have to do it but... well, I've been let down.'

'You'll be out of luck with Mrs L,' said Amy. 'I saw her in Mum's salon. And I'm sure she's got some meeting tonight... I might be wrong but I doubt if she'll have time today – you know what she's like.'

Heather did. She sighed. 'Dash it.' She looked at Amy. 'I don't suppose you'd...'

'What? You want me to do the flowers? Sorry, Mrs S, no can do. For one I wouldn't know how and two, when have I got time? Some of us have to work for a living.' Amy left the kitchen to take Brian his tea while Heather wondered about telling Amy that being a vicar's wife was not all coffee mornings and flower arranging.

'I mean,' said Amy as she returned to the kitchen, 'I know you work at the comp part-time and all, but you get lots of holidays, don't you – like now, and all those weeks in the summer.'

'Oh yes, holidays.' Those weeks when Heather caught up with everything that had slipped through the cracks because of her part-time job; all those other tasks that came with the post of being a vicar's wife. And obviously she employed a cleaner because she had money to burn, not because there just weren't enough hours in the day to get everything done and keep the house decent. Heather looked at Amy and thought about telling her that she worked at the comp as a teaching assistant as it helped make sure she and Brian could afford to eat *and* keep the lights on because, sometimes, they came very close to having to choose. Heather took a breath before she said, 'Maybe I'll ask Joan.'

'Joan Makepiece?'

Heather nodded. 'She's a good sort. She may help. And Bert's always got lots of lovely flowers on his allotment even at this time of year. I'll go and ask her.' Heather gave Amy instructions as to that week's cleaning priorities before she took her coat off the peg in the hall, picked up her battered handbag, and let herself out of the house.

As soon as the front door had shut, Amy opened a kitchen cupboard. Keeping one eye on the study door she stretched up, revealing a great deal of plump thigh, took out the biscuit tin and opened it. Inside was a supply of upmarket biscuits that the Simmonds kept for the meetings and Bible groups that met at the house. Amy helped herself to several before putting the lid back on and shoving the tin back where it lived.

Brian heard the front door slam shut, threw his pen down, leaned out of his desk chair and pushed the door to the study firmly shut. If his door was shut, Amy knew not to disturb him, and what Brian wanted more than anything was space to think.

He put his elbows on his desk and rested his chin in his hands as he gazed, unseeing, across the front lawn. What was the matter with him? Where had the doubts come from? All his certainties about his faith seemed to be trickling away like water out of a breached dam. And why? He felt like asking God *why*? But what was the point – not now he wasn't sure there *was* a God? And as for *life eternal...* What if there wasn't? What if the humanists were right and everyone ended up as nothing more than worm food? And the worst thing was, he couldn't confide in Heather; she didn't need the burden of his doubt, not on top of trying to make ends meet on his stipend, not on top of what she put up with for his vocation – the endless stream of parishioners wanting to talk, wanting comfort, wanting advice, to say nothing of the crappy vicarages they had to put up with, the constant rounds of meetings, the fundraising, the turning-the-other-cheek, the expectations that they both had to be nice to everyone – even the people they couldn't stand... everything. He *wanted* to confide in Heather but he didn't dare. Supposing she had similar doubts? Supposing she was fed up with making ends meet, with living in houses that were inadequate and dreary? Supposing she had had enough of being at the beck and call of the parish twenty-four-seven? Supposing she said, *Great, let's throw in the towel and get a proper job*? Then what?

Brian felt himself sagging with despair and weariness. What if his life so far had been an utter, total waste of time and energy? What then?

Heather walked up the road, under the ancient oaks and yews, across the brook and past the cemetery, the old, rather higgledy-piggledy gravestones basking in the ever-strengthening April sunshine. Above her the rooks cawed incessantly as they wheeled over the rookery in the trees behind the Norman church, with its weathered grey stone walls and squat tower, and the only other noise was the distant hum of the ring road, the other side of the cricket pitch. The peace of the scene was deeply calming. Sometimes, in the summer, when there was a cricket match on and the bell-ringers were practising, she felt it was the kind of place that John Betjeman could have immortalised in a poem; leather on willow, an occasional spattering of applause, cries of 'howzat' and the slightly arrhythmic bing-bong-ding-dong of a peal of bells. Utter cliché but utter English bliss.

She strolled on knowing that she could have phoned Joan to ask about the flowers but she always liked an excuse to take this walk, and besides, she was mindful that neither Joan nor her husband Bert had been in the best of health since the winter – Joan had had a nasty virus and was only recently on the mend – and they might appreciate a visit. Plus, there was every possibility that Bert would offer some of his own flowers from his allotment for the church, and every little helped. Bert's allotment didn't just yield a cornucopia of vegetables every year, but dahlias, hellebores, foxgloves, hollyhocks and a dozen other types of flowers that Heather would accept gratefully for the church arrangement whilst having only the vaguest of idea as to what they were called. And, even if it was a bit early for the best of Bert's flowers, he would certainly have foliage which, in itself, was very useful.

Towards the top of the road, the quiet was dissipated by the bustle of the high street but Heather didn't mind. She loved the town's wide main street with its wiggly roof line, its big market square and pretty Georgian town hall. It mightn't be the sort of place you moved to for the shopping – Bluewater it wasn't – but the boutiques and delis, the cafés and the pub and the hanging baskets full of winter pansies and the tubs of daffs and tulips more than made up for the lack of major retailers. And today was market day so there was the extra bustle and activity that that always brought. It was a proper small market town, she always thought. Perfect – well, perfect as long as you didn't scratch too deep. Like everywhere they had problems with poverty, drugs and the occasional crime but there were worse places to live in the country. Far worse. She knew that – Brian had been a vicar in one or two.

She was looking in the window of the cake shop and wondering about treating herself and Brian to a custard tart each when she heard her name being called. She turned and saw the pub's landlady. As always, Belinda had a smile on her face. She was a life-enhancer, thought Heather. Brian might deal with the town's moral well-being but Belinda provided an equally important service on the mental health side of things by listening to their woes, being unfailingly cheerful and totally non-judgemental. Her sunny outlook radiated out of her and sparkled out of her blue eyes.

'Belinda, hello. You well?'

'Yes, thank you. You?'

Heather nodded.

'I've just been to the hairdresser,' said Belinda. 'That always makes me feel better. Good for morale, don't you think?'

Heather gazed at Belinda's beautifully cut bob that framed her smiling face and wished she knew. She couldn't remember the last time she'd had a professional hair-do. She washed her own hair and pinned it up to keep it out of the way. Not smart or fashionable but suitable for a vicar's wife. Cheap to maintain, and when it got too long, she hacked bits off with the kitchen scissors.

'It must be,' she said, smiling and quenching the tiny pang of envy she felt. 'By the way, Amy says someone is moving into The Beeches.'

'Well, if Amy says so it *must* be true. Anyway, I'd better get on; not long till opening time and I mustn't keep the punters waiting. Will you be coming to the next book club?'

'I will. I can't say I was thrilled by the last choice but it was an interesting read.'

'Good. Well... Good you found it interesting, at any rate. If everyone did, it'll be the basis for a lively discussion.'

'Will you be there?'

'Should be if the new girl shows up. We've had so much trouble with our part-timers recently. Don't the young want to earn extra money? And don't they realise that letting an employer down is more than just bad manners...' Belinda stopped. 'Sorry, I was about to go into rant mode.'

'Rant away. I do it all the time – although, generally speaking, I have to do it in my head. If I said what I really think to some of Brian's parishioners, Brian would have been defrocked years ago.'

Belinda laughed. 'Must get on. Much as I love chatting to you, this isn't getting the pub open.'

Heather strolled on, through the main square, past all the market stalls, towards the little bungalows where the Makepieces lived; close to the station and behind the main recreation ground in the town. She cut through the park, smiling at the mothers whose little ones were toddling around on the grass or being pushed on swings in the play area. Older kids, enjoying the Easter break, were thrashing their BMXs and skateboards over the concrete of the skatepark or hanging round in groups, chatting, taking selfies and a couple were puffing on illicit fags, trying to look as if they were enjoying it. Behind the ramps and half-pipes she could see the cane wigwams for runner beans in the allotments standing proud above the chain-link fence that surrounded the park. Not that you could see the mesh of the fence for the convolvulus that trailed over it. Heather always thought that it was a shame it was such a terrible weed – the huge white trumpet-shaped flowers were so beautiful – but Bert left her in no doubt as to what a bane it was where his veg patch was concerned. She ambled along to the far end of the park and turned into the Makepieces's road and then up their garden path.

Joan Makepiece was sitting in her armchair near the window and waved as she saw the vicar's wife approach.

'Come in, m'dear,' she said, opening the door before Heather could ring the bell. 'What brings you round here?'

Heather stepped over the threshold. 'I came to see you, of course.' She smiled at the elderly woman and was rewarded with a twinkling smile back. She was the epitome of a little old lady – the sort you'd find in the pages of a child's picture book with her snow-white hair set in soft curls, piercing blue eyes and peaches-and-cream skin creased with wrinkles.

Joan nodded. 'And...?'

'Beg a cup of tea?'

'And...?'

'There's no flies on you, are there, Joan.'

'You don't get to my age through being stupid.' Joan led the way into the kitchen.

Heather didn't retort that she knew plenty who had. Instead she said, 'I need help with the flowers.' She put her bag on the counter.

'When?'

'Today, for preference.'

'And flowers?'

'Well...'

'Let's have a cuppa, then we can go and see Bert – he's up on the allotment now – and I'm sure he'll let you have what you need. He's got some lovely daffs and his hellebores are a treat. I expect there'll be some snowdrops too. Then he can run us back to yours. Now, what's this I hear about The Beeches having a new family in it? The postie told me.'

Goodness, thought Heather, news really did travel fast in this town.

2

Olivia looked at the reflection of the back of her head in the second mirror that Mags was holding up behind her. Most satisfactory. Her short bob was neatly cut and, thanks to Mags's expert highlighting, all the grey was covered and her hair was back to the correct shade of honey. Her eyes shifted from her hair to her face. She could still pass for forty, she reckoned. She peered at her eyes – almost no crow's feet and no bags. Good skin care was the secret; the Queen knew that and look how well she had aged.

'Thank you,' she said to Mags.

She reached for her purse and extracted a fiver which she passed over. 'A bit extra for doing such a good job.'

'No problem,' said Mags, stuffing the note into her trouser pocket. 'And thanks.'

'And what do I owe?'

'Janine'll sort that out for you, and make you another appointment if you'd like. See you, Mrs L.' Mags disappeared out to the back of the salon and Olivia went to pay. She was glad the weather was still decent. The forecasted rain for later hadn't materialised and she wanted to check out the state of the nature reserve. She'd heard rumours about children hanging around in it, getting up to no good. There'd been complaints and she wanted to see for herself how bad it was. Maybe the council needed to take action. The blue-haired receptionist rang up the bill on the till. Sixty pounds – good grief! Not that the price had gone up, but the amount always managed to shock her. She handed over her card and tapped in her PIN. She wouldn't be admitting to Nigel what it cost to get her hair sorted. He'd been bloody funny about money recently and he'd go off on one – as her son Zac would say – if he knew what it cost to stay looking presentable. Half the time she was sure he didn't notice. Sometimes she thought that he wouldn't notice if she wore a bin bag or got a tattoo – OK, she conceded mentally, he'd notice a tattoo. But he wouldn't notice if she left her hair unwashed for a month. Men.

With her head held high, proud of her newly styled hair, Olivia left the salon and headed down the high street to the turning that led to the nature reserve. Once she was off the main road the hum of traffic was soon replaced by the cawing of rooks and the alarm call of a blackbird startled by her presence on this quiet side street. She walked past the walled back gardens of the premises that fronted onto the high street, and then into open country. The lane was now flanked by an avenue of chestnut trees until it petered out at the entrance to the large meadow that formed the town's nature reserve. The sticky buds on the ancient chestnuts were still shut fast against the sudden chills and bad weather that might still happen even though it was almost springtime but the lack of foliage made the trees starkly beautiful. The land ahead was bisected by the river Catte. The locals might call it a river but at this stage of its journey it was little more than a brook that babbled over a bed of chalk, shallow enough for kids to paddle in safely in the summer and where dogs splashed all year round. There was a stand of pines on this side, and a little network of paths that led walkers through the reserve, over the bridge that crossed the stream and took visitors through a copse, past the nest boxes nailed to the trunks of the willows that flanked the banks and the signs telling them what to look out for in the way of flora and fauna. The reserve wasn't big but it was popular and even at this time there were a number of mums with their toddlers in pushchairs, and even more dog walkers. As it was the school holidays a few teenagers were hanging around one of the benches by the main path but they didn't seem to be up to anything too antisocial.

Olivia cast a critical eye over the open space. On the face of it, it didn't look too bad. Yes, the rubbish bin nearest her needed emptying, the lid wouldn't shut properly, but at least it meant visitors were using it. She headed along the path that led to the bridge and then the copse. She stopped on the bridge and looked into the water. A small fish was visible – its tail waving lazily to hold it steady in the current. Olivia wondered what it might be. A minnow? A trout? She had no idea but she was pleased to see it. It meant the water quality was high. So far so good. She strolled on to the tiny wood and looked at the thicket of bushes that made up the understorey. There was a visible path, beaten through the light scrub. Olivia pushed her way along it. In the middle of the trees she stopped and stared at the ground in horror.

Empty bottles, discarded cans, pizza boxes, polystyrene cartons from the burger van, newspaper, plastic bags... the place was a tip. It was disgusting, disgraceful. Olivia shook her head. No wonder people had been complaining. She looked more closely at the bottles – mostly alcohol; no surprise there. She checked the labels; cider, vodka, Malbec... She did a double take. Malbec?! What the hell were the local yobs doing drinking Malbec? It was Nigel's favourite tipple, quite apart from anything else, and far too sophisticated for the kind of youths who were likely to hang out in a spot like this. They probably nicked it from the supermarket in Cattebury and had no idea what they'd pinched and didn't care either, just as long as it was booze.

Olivia sniffed. She'd tell the town clerk and get him to organise the town's refuse team to sort it. But how they could they stop it from happening again? She knew for a fact the police wouldn't be interested. It might be ugly and antisocial but it was hardly the crime of the century and even Olivia could see that littering would be the lowest of low priorities.

She turned to go and barked her ankle on a sharp object. She looked to see what it was. A primus stove. Then she saw the tinfoil, the spoons, the tiny plastic bags, and a series of connections were triggered in her brain. She knew just enough about drugs to realise the significance. Dear God, supposing there were used needles here? Worse and worse. And yet, the police would have to take an interest in the misuse of illegal substances. Where there were drugs there would be dealers. Olivia shook her head, aghast at the implications for Little Woodford. Maybe if the police patrolled the reserve for a while the druggies would all move on elsewhere. Frankly, she thought, if there were children who wanted to ruin their lives by snorting banned substances she didn't really care. If they wanted to grow up to be deadbeats that was their problem. Just as long as they didn't do it in this town and spoil the place for everyone else or pass their noxious habits onto children like her Zac. Not that he'd ever do drugs; she and Nigel had brought him up properly.

Olivia shook her head and pushed her way back along the overgrown path through the thicket and out into the sunshine and the meadow. She stopped as she rejoined the main path; left would take her to the top end of town where she lived or she could retrace her steps and head for the town hall to report this matter. She was longing for a cup of coffee but her civic duty took precedence. She turned to the right and headed back to the town centre.

Belinda patted her newly cut page-boy bob and glanced at the mirror behind the shelves of glasses to admire it. Like Olivia, she reckoned she didn't look too bad for her age but peered closer and checked out the start of a few crow's feet by her grey eyes. Hmmm – she might have to increase the old night-cream regime if she wanted to keep them under control. It was all very well to call them laughter lines but everyone knew that was a euphemism for old and wrinkly. She focused her eyes from her face to the bar behind her. The three old boys who were lunchtime regulars were sitting at their usual table by the window and had enough in their glasses to keep them going for a few minutes. Good, she had a job she wanted to do. She put her head round the kitchen door.

'Just popping upstairs,' she told Miles, her partner. 'I shouldn't be long but if you could just keep an eye on the bar till I get back – in case we get another customer. Everyone else is all right for a mo.'

Miles nodded and carried on slicing carrots.

'It's the Stitch and Bitch ladies tomorrow – I want to get the room ready while I think about it and while it's quiet,' Belinda explained.

Miles nodded again. 'Want to prop the door open till you get back?'

Belinda pushed a wooden wedge under the door with her foot. 'Call me if there's a sudden rush.'

She went back into the bar, grabbed a damp cloth and ran up the stairs to the room that snuggled under the eaves. They called it the function room but it was more of a meeting room – it was hard to fit more than a couple of dozen people in at any one time but it was a perfect space for the craft group to meet, and a whole host of other clubs and committees that kept the townsfolk of Little Woodford entertained or busy or both. And Belinda was more than happy for these little groups to use the room free of charge. More often than not she was asked to supply refreshments so it was good for business.

Swiftly, she rearranged the chairs there into a circle and placed some low tables in the middle. Then she wiped them down before she had a good look at the carpet. Did it need the hoover running over it? The light wasn't terrific so she went over to the dormer and pulled the blind up fully. As she did a movement in the big house next door caught her eye; there was a blonde –

youngish... mid-thirties? – at one of the upstairs windows. Duh – she remembered the news about the new people moving in.

Belinda's eyes met those of the woman next-door. She smiled and waved and got a broad grin back. She wondered what the new neighbours were going to be like – rather nice if first impressions were anything to go by.

Bex Millar was wondering about the wisdom of moving in next to a pub as she stared out of the window and across the wall. The estate agent had assured her that it was really well run and the previous owners of her house had had no complaints on that score. But they would say that, wouldn't they? She reckoned the walled garden, the shrubbery and the trees would act as a bit of a barrier against any noise and besides, however noisy it might be it was going to be a darn sight more tranquil here than where they'd lived in London. There they'd been on a route to a major hospital and under the approach to Heathrow. Planes flying over every waking moment and blues and twos twenty-four-seven. She didn't think a few rowdy locals were going to impinge on her family's sleep – not given what they could already sleep through. She noticed that there was a woman looking out of the dormer in the roof opposite. The landlady? She smiled and waved and looked really friendly so Bex couldn't stop herself from smiling back. She felt quite bizarrely happy that this total stranger seemed to be welcoming her. Maybe moving here was exactly what the doctor ordered.

'Mum, Mum, can Alfie and I go and play in the garden?'

Bex turned away from the window to look at her eldest son, eight-year-old Lewis. 'Have you explored the whole house?' she asked him as he ran across the floor towards her followed by his little brother Alfie who stumbled along on his chubby legs. She brushed Lewis's floppy blonde fringe off his earnest face then stroked his cheek.

'Everywhere, Mummy.'

'Evware,' lisped four-year-old Alfie in solemn agreement. He gazed at his brother – his hero-worship plain in his grey eyes.

'OK, go outside but you must stay at the back of the house and if you hear the furniture van arrive you must both come in and tell me.' The last thing Bex wanted was for the boys to get under the feet of the removal men. 'Understand?'

Both boys nodded before racing down the main stairs to the ground floor. It might have been two small boys running through the house but Bex reckoned they made as much racket as a herd of stampeding horses. Silence fell a moment after the sound of the front door slamming behind them reverberated throughout the house.

In the ensuing quiet Bex wondered about her stepdaughter Megan. The move was going to affect her the most and not only because she was fifteen and hormonal and painfully shy. She'd also had a lot of shit happen in her life – they all had – and although the move was to help them make a fresh start, a change of school at this time of year and in the year before she did her GCSEs was a gamble. It was no wonder, given all the circumstances, she wasn't always calm; a fact not helped by the fact that her birth mother had been a Spaniard.

Bex often thought about Megan's mother because, other than her nationality and the fact that she'd abandoned Megan when she had only been three, she knew next to nothing about her. Apparently Imelda, Megan's mother, had upped and returned to Spain one morning and had ignored all pleas and exhortations from Megan's father, Richard, to come home again. For a few weeks Richard had managed to rely on the goodwill of family, friends and neighbours for emergency childcare but, when none of his texts and emails to his wife had been returned and his phone calls went unanswered, he'd had to hire a nanny – Bex. Obviously, as the hired help, it wasn't up to her to question the family's circumstances and, when she'd wound up falling in love with her boss and then marrying him, all he was willing to say on the subject of his first wife was that she had been 'a bit temperamental'. Bex suspected that the hurt Imelda had inflicted had been a terrible wound and she wasn't going to pick at the scab – it wasn't hers to pick. On the positive side, Megan had no memories of Imelda, although the fact she'd been deserted by her mother had to have on-going repercussions. To be 'not wanted' by a parent had to be a terrible concept for any child to grasp and Bex had spent the previous twelve years doing her level best to prove to Megan that she was wanted – very much. But then... then the accident had happened.

Bex decided to see how Megan was faring. She went across the landing to the precipitous, narrow stairs that led up into the attic.

'Only me,' she called at the bottom before she climbed the steep flight.

Megan was sitting on the floor of the bare room tapping the screen of her phone with her thumbs, her glorious black hair tumbled over her face.

'Hello,' she said to Bex without looking up.

'I wanted to see how you are getting on,' said Bex, brightly. 'Have you worked out where you want your stuff to go?'

Megan shrugged.

'You OK?' said Bex.

'Kind of.' She looked at her stepmother with her dark brown eyes. Had she been crying – again?

'It'll be better here, promise. New school, new start, new friends...'

Megan shrugged.

Bex hunkered down on the floor beside her stepdaughter. 'The thing is, no one here knows what happened back in London. We'll probably have to tell them about Daddy but all they need know is that he died in a traffic accident. Everything else is no one's business but ours.'

'I suppose.' Megan sounded far from convinced.

'Now then, why don't you go down to the garden too and keep an eye on the boys while I finish making sure everything is ready for when our van gets here. There's a football in the boot of the car. Have a kick around with them.'

Megan trailed out of the room and down the stairs, watched by Bex whose heart broke again that her stepdaughter had had to endure so much sadness and awfulness over the previous months, and on top of what her mother had done to her. Bex sighed and hoped against hope that this move would push it all away and allow the family to move on. It was going to be hard without Richard but they'd manage somehow. They'd have to. And they were going to have to do this by themselves, what with her parents living in Cumbria and rarely making the trip south and her in-laws living in Cyprus and rarely making the trip back. Phone calls and emails meant they kept in touch but 'keeping in touch' wasn't the same as having them around and that wasn't going to happen much – not now. Her dad was losing his sight and her mum would only drive short distances so a journey down the M6 was right out of the question, and Richard's parents had been badly hit by the fall in the exchange rate and, while their pensions kept them afloat, it didn't really allow for the expense of flights from the Med.

She'd thought about moving to be nearer her relatives, of course she had, but had decided it wasn't really fair on the kids. Where her parents lived in the Lake District there was breathtaking scenery but precious little for them to do – not for children brought up with easy access to shops, cinemas and all sorts of urban amenities. Yes, the boys would have probably adjusted in time but Megan? And as for taking them out to Cyprus... Well, quite apart from the issue of their schooling Bex really didn't think it was fair to uproot them completely from all that was familiar.

Come the summer, thought Bex, she'd take the kids to visit their grandparents but until then they'd have to go it alone.

3

Joan, having finished the church flowers, declined Heather's offer of a bite of lunch because she was due at Mags's salon for her fortnightly shampoo and set. As she trudged from the church to the town centre she wondered about the wisdom of having agreed to do the flower arranging, knowing she would be having her hair done later. Too late to worry about that now, but no two ways about it, she thought, she was knackered. That bug she'd had over the winter had knocked her for six and no mistake. Still, on the positive side, she'd get to sit down for the next hour or so and, anyway, having her hair done always made her feel more chipper. Wearily she pushed open the door to Cutz and Curlz and was assaulted by a gust of warm steamy air and the scent of a dozen different hairdressing products. She crossed the small lobby to the reception desk. The receptionist's hair was a startling shade of blue. She could have sworn the last time she'd been in it had been pink... or had it been green?

'Hi, Joan.' said the girl, barely looking up.

'Afternoon, Janine.'

'I'll tell her you're here. Wanna give me your coat?'

Joan shrugged her mac off and handed it over.

'Take a seat,' said Janine as she bunged the mac on a hanger and shoved it on the rail. Joan resisted the temptation to remove it, put it on the hanger properly, with the top button done up, and the creases shaken out.

Janine gestured laconically to the tiny sofa and then slouched off to the door that led to the staff restroom. She returned seconds later, followed by Mags.

'Hello, Joan,' said Mags proffering a gown for Joan to slip on. 'The usual? Or can I tempt you to a few highlights, or a nice asymmetric cut, or maybe a bit of colour?' She nodded in Janine's direction, as she tucked a towel around Joan's neck. 'All the rage.'

'No, ta. Just my usual shampoo and set, thanks.'

'Come on through then and we'll get you started.'

Joan sat on the seat, tipped her head back towards the basin and shut her eyes while Mags got the water the right temperature and then started work with her deft fingers and the shampoo.

'Amy had some news earlier.'

'Oh, yes?' said Joan.

'A family has moved into The Beeches. Just arrived, she said.'

'I know, I heard first thing this morning from the postman.'

'Oh.' Mags sounded rather put out. 'Anyway, Amy says it's a young family. Three kids.'

'That's nice.' Joan wasn't really interested. She was luxuriating in having her scalp massaged.

'Amy's hoping she can get her old cleaning job back.'

'Hmmm.' She felt totally relaxed and didn't want to spoil the feeling with chit-chat.

'It'll be nice having more kids around in the town. Nothing personal, Joan, but there's precious few young families here these days, not with house prices the way they are. Amy said she'd heard the primary school is worried about numbers.'

'Hmmm.'

'On the other hand, those new houses they're building round the back of the station might help though I doubt many of the young families around here'll be able to find enough to buy one. Apparently there's some built for the housing association and a whole bunch that's supposed to be affordable but I heard even

the smallest of the other ones start at half a mill. Half a *mill*?'
Mags voice rose to a shrill crescendo. 'I ask you.'

'Indeed.'

Mags began to rinse out the first application of shampoo.
'Water all right?'

'Lovely.'

'Amy said one of the kids moving in looked a bit of a basket
case; looked like she was scared to death of her own shadow.
I mean, what's to be scared of in a place like this? 'Tisn't like she's
moving to some place with guns and drugs like you hear about
on the news. You take what you hear about the big cities...'

But Joan had stopped listening and was drifting into a doze
as Mags's magic fingers washed and rinsed and conditioned her
hair and she yakked on about the state of the country, the young
of today and what she thought the police should do about it all.

As Mags installed Joan under a drier, the removal van arrived at
The Beeches. Bex made the guys mugs of tea all round and then
went to the foot of the stairs. She could hear the boys playing with
some game or other on their iPads in one of the bedrooms but she
had no idea where Megan had got to – probably back upstairs in
her room; she seemed to love it up there at the top of the house.

'Megan? Megan, can you come down for a minute, please?'
she bellowed up the stairwell.

Big houses were all very well, she thought, but there were a
lot of stairs. If she had to run up and down to get hold of Megan
every time she needed her she was going to get incredibly fit.

A few seconds ticked by before Megan appeared on the upstairs
landing. She leaned over the banister.

'Yeah?'

'Can you take the boys out for a little bit, while the men get
the furniture in? I really don't want them to get underfoot and
I'm going to be busy directing where things are to go.'

Megan's sigh was audible down in the hall. 'If I must.'

'It's a lovely day, you could take them for a walk.'

'Where?'

'Into town.'

'And do what?'

'I don't know. Maybe there's a play park somewhere. See if you can find one.'

'I suppose.'

Megan disappeared from view and Bex heard her telling the boys to get their coats. They clattered down the stairs just as two burly removal men appeared, hauling the sofa.

Megan grabbed both the boys' arms and tugged them out of the way as the men struggled to wrestle it through the sitting room door. Bex thrust a ten-pound note in Megan's hand. 'Buy an ice cream or something while you're out. I'd like the boys out of the way while the men get the worst of the job done – the heavy stuff.'

'Cheers.' She stuffed the note in her jeans' pocket. Then, 'Come on, boys,' she said as she led them out through the front door.

The van filled the gravel drive and the three children had to squeeze past it. Alfie was mesmerised with the huge cavernous space filled with their possessions.

'Horsey!' he shouted, catching sight of the rocking horse. 'Want Horsey.'

'Horsey will be in your room when we get back,' promised Megan. 'Come on, we'll go and explore the town.'

Grasping Alfie's hand firmly and ignoring his protests she led the two boys down the drive and out onto the main street.

It was busy with shoppers and kids. Megan looked at the faces of the children she passed and wondered if any were in her new class. What would the kids be like? Would they be nice to her? She knew that the girl who'd joined her class late, at her old school, hadn't had the best time to start with. She felt guilty about that now because she should have been nicer and it would serve her right if she had a bit of a struggle to fit in herself. She wished she'd behaved differently but it was too late to put things right now. It seemed to Megan that she spent a lot of time these days wishing 'if only...'

She and the boys continued walking through the town. Megan thought about stopping a passer-by and asking for directions or even if there *was* a play park in the town. The kids seemed happy to keep walking though and Alfie, who had apparently forgotten about Horsey, was skipping along by her side. They passed a sign to the station.

'Let's go and see if we can see some trains,' suggested Megan. But when they got there, the display board made it fairly obvious that the trains to Little Woodford at this time of day were few and far between, or few and far between compared to the lines that ran close to their house in London, and the next one wasn't due for another thirty minutes. On the other hand there was a building site on the far side of the tracks and Alfie spent a happy few minutes watching the diggers scooping up the soil and dumping it into the backs of tipper trucks.

'Where's my digger?' asked Alfie. He'd been given a huge Tonka bulldozer the previous Christmas and he'd loved playing with it in their sandpit back at their old house.

'Somewhere on that big lorry at home,' answered Megan.

'Can I have it when we get back?'

'I'll try and find it for you. Now, talking about finding things, let's see if we can find a play park.'

The three trailed back to the high street and continued their walk through town. Just as Megan was thinking of abandoning her quest she came to a big pair of wrought iron gates, behind which were acres of grass, a swing park in the far corner and skateboard ramps opposite it. Bingo. She let go of the boys' hands and they tore off across the grass like a pair of greyhounds out of the traps. Megan followed on and by the time she reached them they were balanced on a see-saw, their feet dangling inches above the ground, neither able to push off and give them the impetus to get going.

'Push us, Megs,' exhorted Lewis.

Obligingly, Megan stood at the pivot and pushed down one side then the other. The two boys shrieked in delight as they bounced up and down. After a few minutes they got bored with the see-saw and charged off to the swings. Lewis was big enough to reach the ground and to propel himself higher and higher but Alfie dangled rather pathetically. Again Megan came to the rescue and soon Alfie was swooping up and down nearly as high as his brother. And then they had a go on the roundabout for quite a while until the slide caught their attention. Then it was back to the swings and Megan was called on to help, once again. When Alfie didn't need her Megan sat on a bench with her phone and kept an eye on her half-brothers and another on Facebook and Snapchat. Across the park she was aware of older children – mostly around her age, she thought – on their BMX bikes and skateboards performing tricks and stunts on the ramps. It was all very pleasant and relaxing as the minutes ticked past and Megan, warmed by the sun, lost track of time. Suddenly she saw one of the kids grab his skateboard and head off across the grass. He tore off at such a rate he looked as if he was worried about being late for something.

Late! Megan checked the time. Shit, they'd been out for ages – Bex would be getting worried.

'Boys, boys! Time to go.'

The pair were reluctant to leave the park and Alfie was close to tears.

'No,' he wailed. 'Want to stay.'

'Mummy'll want us home.'

'Don't care.' Alfie turned to run back to the swings but Megan caught his arm.

'Time to go,' she said firmly, starting to drag him towards the gate.

Alfie's sobs grew louder. 'No, no, no.'

Megan remembered the tenner in her pocket.

'I'll buy you an ice cream.'

'Don't want one.'

'How about a big chocolate one?'

'With sprinkles on.'

'Hundreds and thousands of sprinkles. As many as you want.'

'And me?' said Lewis.

'Of course you too.'

Meltdown averted, Alfie allowed himself to be led towards the road. As they passed the ramps the boys lingered to watch the stunts for a second or two. One of the boys performed a trick whereby he turned through a half circle in mid-air and landed halfway down one of the ramps. Megan was impressed. She was also impressed by his looks; blond curly hair and nice eyes. Lush, she thought.

The lad saw her staring and grinned, revealing very white and even teeth. She wondered if he went to her school. He looked nice as well as fit, she thought, and hoped he did.

4

'Hello, Mrs Laithwaite,' called Amy as she let herself in to the big barn conversion where she was working the next morning. Olivia Laithwaite liked things to be on a formal footing – no chumminess between employer and employee. She listened for a response. Olivia was on more committees than most of the residents of Little Woodford knew even existed and, consequently, was rarely home – or, at least, rarely for someone who didn't have a nine-to-five job.

There was a muffled thump from upstairs. 'Coo-ee.' Olivia Laithwaite's voice floated over the banisters of the humungous house. Amy gazed up to the vast beamed ceiling thirty feet above her head.

'What do you want done today, Mrs Laithwaite?'

'Hang on...'

Amy took her coat off and waited patiently. If Olivia kept her waiting, it was time she'd get paid for while not having to graft. No skin off her nose. A couple of minutes later Olivia Laithwaite appeared at the top of the stairs. She was wearing what Amy always thought of as Olivia's councillor-kit: a tartan skirt, smart blouse and jacket. Give her her due, she always looked smart, although never fashionable, and she was always well-groomed. Amy thought she'd rather die than go out without lippy on. She reckoned her boss had been quite pretty in her youth because she was what people called 'handsome' now – which Amy translated as *quite attractive in a run-of-the-mill kind of way* – or she would be if she cracked a smile. Given that she was married to a guy who made a mint of money she ought to be a blooming sight happier than she was; she always seemed to have something she was bitching about. Mind you, thought Amy, having Zac for a son was enough to spoil anyone's day because, in her opinion, he was spoilt, sulky and obnoxious; going to a public school had turned him into an arrogant snob. Not that she'd ever say that to Olivia. The kid hadn't been too bad while he'd been at primary school and Amy had seen quite a lot of Zac back then because her own son, Ashley, and he had been great mates. They still were mates but they were drifting apart and it was probably only a shared interest in skateboards that provided sufficient glue to keep the friendship tottering on.

'Off out? Council meeting?' she said.

'At this time of day? No, I've got a meeting about the church fête, then a council meeting tonight. Busy, busy, busy.'

Busy*body*, more like, thought Amy. 'Where do you want me to start, Mrs Laithwaite?'

'Just the usual. Next time you come though I'd like you to clean the windows – well, the ones you can reach.'

Amy looked at the vast window that stretched floor to ceiling and filled about a third of the long wall that looked over the back garden. It was a spectacular feature but there was no way anyone could clean the upper section without a cherry-picker at the very least. Not for the first time Amy wondered how the hell the top panes got cleaned. Still, not her problem.

While Olivia fussed around finding a notebook and her handbag, Amy went into the kitchen and got out her box of cleaning materials and set to work. Sometimes, she thought, as she started moving items off the counter tops so she could clean them down, she almost felt sorry for Olivia; *almost*... but not quite. She did so much round the town but from what she could see, Nigel – her husband – was a bit of a bastard and her son was awful.

If Ash ever talked to her like Zac did to his mother she'd give him a clip round his ear.

Amy supposed Olivia had friends but she never seemed to be with other people unless it was at some committee meeting or other. Certainly, some of Amy's pals, the people who lived on the same estate as her and her mum, thought Olivia Laithwaite was a bit of a laughing stock. But, if having a finger in every pie in town made Olivia happy – because in Amy's opinion not much else could – then it was nobody's business but her own.

'Your money is on the coffee table, Amy,' said Olivia a couple of minutes later as she took her keys off the hook in the kitchen. 'Don't forget to lock up when you go.'

'No, Mrs Laithwaite.'

'Good. Goodbye then, Amy.' Olivia swept out, slamming the front door behind her. She noticed as she went that the grass needed cutting. She'd have to get Nigel to cut it soon. She just hoped it didn't cause a row like last time. Maybe she ought to bite the bullet and buy a cheap hover mower that she could manage, unlike that brute of a petrol mower. Doing that, however, was just as likely to anger him as asking him to cut it. Damned either way. And yes, she appreciated he had a tough commute to work each day, that he worked long hours, and that he liked a pint at the pub at the weekend, but was it too much to ask that he got the mower out once a week? After all, she did the rest of the garden.

She got out her bike from the garage, put her bag in the basket and rode down the hill to the main street. Olivia felt very strongly that she should set an example to other residents regarding car use. There was nowhere in Little Woodford that wasn't within easy walking or biking distance and given that parking was a perennial problem she refused to take her car into town unless it was absolutely unavoidable. It saddened her, though, that despite her example precious few of the town's residents followed her lead.

As she pedalled she passed The Beeches. She really ought to call in at some stage and welcome the new family to the area. She turned down the road that led to the cricket pitch and the community centre. Heather Simmonds had called a meeting about the church fête which was due to be held later in the year and Olivia liked to think she and her ideas were essential to the smooth running of the annual fund-raiser.

The community centre was, in essence, a glorified shed set on land to the side of the cricket ground. It was quite large and reasonably attractive as sheds go but it was still a building made of clapboard with a pitched roof covered in tarred felt. In the summer it could be unbearably hot – even with all the windows open wide – and in the winter, the heating struggled to keep the interior temperature vaguely comfortable. Olivia let herself in and unbuttoned her coat.

'Hello, Jack, Miriam,' she said to the couple who had arrived before her.

'Hello, Olivia,' chorused the Browns. They did everything together, always looking at each other for confirmation before they did the least thing. They even walked through the town holding hands, which Olivia found faintly ridiculous. At their age. And no Heather, she noticed. As the chair of the committee she really ought to be amongst the first to arrive.

'Who are we waiting for,' she asked, 'apart from Heather?' although she had a pretty good idea.

Miriam reeled off a list of names. Olivia checked her watch. In another five minutes they'd be late. Actually, as far as she was concerned they were already late – by the time they all got here, got their coats off, sat down, got settled and had generally faffed about, the meeting would be late starting. There was a flurry as more of the committee members came in and the hubbub of chit-chat filled the echoey space.

Olivia cleared her throat. 'Ahem,' she added loudly when she realised that she'd been ignored. 'Don't you think we ought to make a start?'

'Heather isn't here yet,' said Miriam, nervously.

'She's late,' replied Olivia. 'We'll start and she'll have to catch up with anything she's missed afterwards. And, until she gets here, I'll take the chair. Anyone got a problem with that?'

Miriam looked at Jack for reassurance. 'No...' chorused the group.

'Right.' Olivia took her seat at the head of the long table that had been set up in the middle of the room. She shuffled her papers and then put her glasses on. 'Welcome, everyone. Glad you could all make it. Now, we've not had any apologies... we'll see if Heather turns up. So, I trust you've all read the minutes of the last meeting.'

She was interrupted from proceeding further by the door to the community centre slamming open and Heather scooting in at full tilt.

'Sorry, sorry I'm late. I got held up.'

'Obviously,' snapped Olivia. 'We've started, so if you'd like...'

'I got held up by Ted Burrows. He was telling me something fascinating.' Olivia held her hand up to silence Heather, but she was completely ignored. 'He was telling me that old man McGregor – you know, he's got the ramshackle farm next door to Ted's? – well, Ted said that McGregor has had men in high-vis jackets and with all sorts of equipment all over that tatty old meadow by the ring road; you know, the one by the bridge...?' Heather looked at her small audience to gauge if they were following her, which they were to judge by their nods of understanding. 'Ted reckons he's selling it for housing.'

'Housing?' Olivia was shocked. 'He can't.'

'It's his land,' said Heather, not unreasonably. 'And it's not a site of special scientific interest and the area of outstanding natural beauty finishes ten miles from here. And – and this is what Ted said – McGregor used to have a load of farm buildings on the piece that was being surveyed so it might make it brown field land not green belt.'

Olivia was horrified. 'But the last thing this town needs is another housing estate. The council gave the go-ahead to the one on the old railway yard because we had to – the county council gave us no choice – but enough is enough. Besides, it'd be outside the town envelope. Little Woodford mustn't be allowed to sprawl.'

Heather looked taken aback. 'I don't think a few houses on a scruffy old bit of land constitutes urban sprawl.'

'It's the thin end of the wedge,' countered Olivia.

'But, surely, more houses must be a good thing, especially if they're not ridiculously large executive houses.' Olivia ignored the rather pointed reference to her own home. 'Can't the council,' Heather looked at Olivia with a raised eyebrow, 'make sure this development includes proper social housing? The sort of houses that are actually needed, not ones out to maximise the developers' profit margins.'

'But another council estate?' Olivia was aghast. 'Have I told you what I found up at the nature reserve yesterday? A drug den, that's what.'

Heather looked bemused. 'What's that got to do with the council estate?'

'Come off it, Heather, who else is likely to be snorting coke or swigging White Lightning?'

Heather glared at Olivia. 'So you think that anyone who lives on the council estate has to be a bad lot, is that it?'

'Not everyone, I admit, but yes, some of them.'

Heather sniffed. 'Then we'll have to agree to disagree, won't we. Just because some people in this town don't have pots of money doesn't automatically make their children delinquents.'

'Huh.' Olivia glared at Heather.

Heather stared back at Olivia until she lowered her eyes.

'This discussion isn't getting the fête organised,' muttered Olivia.

'No,' said Heather.

'So, the minutes…' said Olivia picking up the papers.

Heather smiled at her. 'Actually, as chairman, shall I read

them?' and she reached across the table and filched them from Olivia's grasp.

Nigel Laithwaite, Olivia's husband, was sitting at his desk in his office, facing a bank of computer screens, dressed in a pair of pinstriped trousers, a pink shirt and a black and pink tie. He looked every inch the stockbroker he was, right down to the slight paunch, the thinning hair and the rather red nose. Years of sedentary employment and over-indulgence had taken its toll. He was looking at the barrage of information about international markets and working out if it was going to be worth selling gold and buying oil instead. There was also a TV showing the BBC's twenty-four-hour news service but with the sound muted. A red banner trailed across the bottom of the screen with the news headlines. As a fund manager he needed to know what was going on in the world; a coup here, an election result there, could trigger a whole series of events and send the markets haywire. *England collapse* read the scrolling headline. Nigel went white. How could they? They were set to win. This was impossible. *England all out for 152.*

Nigel stood up so suddenly he knocked his chair over and crushed the Savile Row suit jacket hanging on the back. Heads turned as it crashed.

'You all right, Nige?' asked a co-worker.

Nigel couldn't form words. Besides, the cricket wasn't something he should have had his eye on. He felt bile rising in his throat. He clamped his hanky to his mouth and legged it towards the Gents.

'Nige?'

Ten minutes later he was back at his desk. Someone had righted his chair.

'What's up, Nige?'

Nigel slapped on a smile. 'Dunno. Just felt bloody awful for a mo. All right now though. Nothing to worry about.' He grinned around the office, as if to prove how well he was.

'Good,' said his nearest neighbour. 'Me and Jack were thinking of going to the Ship at close of play – a quick snifter before home time. Fancy joining us?'

'No, better get home. Things to do...'

'Hey,' said someone from the other side of the office. 'Bloody England have collapsed. I'd have put good money on them winning the match and the series.'

'So would I,' said Nigel, under his breath. 'So would I.'

Amy finished the hoovering and put the vacuum cleaner back in the big cupboard in the utility room. While she didn't envy Olivia's big house – lots of rooms equalled lots of carpet to clean, in her opinion – she did envy Olivia's kitchen; all those lovely appliances, all that space. She had a tiny utility room; not much bigger than the storage cupboard she'd put the Dyson in. Hers was more of a *futility* room, really. Still, at least she had a roof and, even if the money was a bit tight, she reckoned she and Ash were pretty happy. A bloody sight happier than the Laithwaites were, if she was any kind of judge. She glanced at the kitchen clock. She'd finished, with fifteen minutes to spare. That deserved a reward.

She put on her posh voice and said, 'Fancy a snifter, Miss Pullen?'

'Don't mind if I do, ta very much,' she replied to herself in her ordinary voice.

Amy went over to the sideboard, took out a glass then poured herself a large gin from one of the bottles that sat on the counter in the kitchen. She topped it up with tonic before getting the ice and lemon out of the fridge. Her drink made, she sat on the sofa, eased her shoes off, put her feet up on the cushions and switched on the TV.

'Cheers, Mrs L,' she said as she took a swig.

5

Amy, having finished at Olivia's, did the shopping on her way home with the cash she'd been given, had a go at her own house and then, finally, did her laundry. Having put her feet up for a well-deserved rest for an hour or so she was now in her kitchen cooking supper. She heard the front door slam. 'Is that you, Ashley?' she called.

'Hi, Mum.' Ashley loped into the tiny kitchen, his skateboard tucked in under his arm. 'What's for supper? Smells good.'

Amy paused in stirring the onions frying gently in the pan and offered up her cheek to be kissed. 'Good day? And it's mince and mash.'

'Great, I'm famished.' Ash propped his board in the corner with the hoover and perched on a stool. 'Yeah, the day was all right. Called in at the salon to see Gran on my way home.'

'That was nice of you.' Amy picked up a pack of mince and began shredding it into the onions. 'How was she?'

'You know Gran, when she wasn't bitching about the neighbours she was banging on about the bin collection. Oh, and giving me the low-down about the latest goings-on.'

Amy grinned at her son. 'She does like a good gossip.'

'And she said could you go round tomorrow – she says she needs to turn her mattress. I offered but she said it was woman's work.'

Amy raised her eyebrows. 'She really doesn't get sex-equality, does she?'

Ash laughed as he shook his head. 'I said I didn't mind but…'

'No, I know you wouldn't. And talking of beds and bedrooms—'

'Which we weren't…'

'I want yours sorted out, please.' Amy reached for an open tin of tomatoes sitting on the counter and tipped them onto the sizzling meat.

'It's not that bad.'

Amy stared at her son as she stirred the mixture.

'OK, it's a bit of a mess,' he admitted.

'It's a total mess.'

'I'll do it tomorrow.'

'You could make a start tonight.'

'Must I?'

'No, but it's got to be done soon or I'll do it.' Amy's ultimate threat. Last time she'd thrown out what she'd thought was a bag of rubbish only to discover later that it was a collection of magazine pictures that Ash had been putting together for an art project – and of course the bin men had been round between Amy shoving the bag in the bin and Ash coming home to discover the loss. Oops. 'Go on – make a start. Supper's going to be a while; you could probably get it done before then.'

Ashley trailed up the stairs to his room and then Amy heard the sound of his footsteps pacing back and forth across the tiny floor as he picked up his possessions and began clearing up the mess. He was, thought Amy, a good lad. His father might have been a dud but Ash had turned out all right. Better than Zac Laithwaite, at any rate.

Zac – the object of Amy's thoughts – was in his room playing war games on his PlayStation. In a lull in the action he heard his mother's voice floating up the stairs.

'Zac? Zac?'

Shit, what did she want *now*? God, she was always on his case. He quickly plugged the headphone jack into the system and stuffed the earbuds in so he could pretend that he hadn't heard her. He concentrated on his game until he saw a flicker of movement out of the corner of his eye. He swung round, ripping out his headphones.

'What?' He glared at his mother.

'Hello, darling. I'm going to be doing supper soon.'

'So?'

'I know it's early but I've got to go out... council meeting. Is that OK?'

God, every night she said the same sort of dumb things. 'Yeah, whatever.'

'Good.'

He didn't respond and concentrated on his game. Would she now get the hint and leave him alone?

She hesitated by the bedroom door. 'And you'll be all right till your father gets home, won't you? I'll have to leave his supper in the fridge for him to heat up...'

Zac couldn't be arsed to answer her. Did she think he cared? Her voice petered out.

'So, that's fine then. I'll leave you to get on, shall I?'

Yes, now fuck off. 'Anything else?' he asked, pointedly.

'No, no. I'll call when supper's ready.' She left but didn't shut the door. She never fucking did. Irritated, Zac lunged off his chair and slammed it behind her.

He pulled his dressing table away from the wall, reached behind it and extracted a small plastic bag, a packet of Rizlas and a pouch of tobacco. Carefully, he made himself a spliff and then opened the windows of his room. He leaned out and sparked up. Slowly he felt calmer, his rage at his mother faded and he felt at peace. He drew in another hit and held it before slowly exhaling the smoke which drifted away from the house. Zac watched it dissipate and wondered what would happen to any birds that flew through it. The thought of the local starlings getting high made him chuckle. He finished his rollie and stubbed it out against the outside wall of the house, under the window sill. He then hitched himself onto the sill and reached up to put the fag end into the gutter above the room. No evidence remained except the reek of tobacco and pot in his room. Zac picked up a can of Lynx and sprayed it liberally. He chuckled again at the thought that his dad hated the smell of Lynx and it would piss him off no end if he caught a whiff when he came home. But not as much as it would if he knew what it was masking. He laughed out loud even more at that.

Bex slumped on a chair in her new kitchen. It was a lovely kitchen, she adored it and it had an Aga – her idea of heaven although, if she were honest, she wasn't quite sure how it worked. But it couldn't be that hard, could it, and the previous owners had left a manual... though where the hell it was was a mystery right now. And an Aga was, when all was said and done, basically an oven. She looked at her watch – seven. Too early for bed although she was tired enough to fall asleep right now but she couldn't indulge herself like that – she still had far too much to do. The day before, after the removal men had finished, she'd got all the beds made up, they'd had a takeaway from the local pizza parlour and found time to call both sets of grandparents and tell them they'd arrived safely before they'd all crashed out; Bex collapsing in her bed only a couple of hours after the boys.

Today, her first priority had been to make the sitting room habitable enough so the boys could watch TV which kept them entertained while she and Megan had got on with yet more unpacking. And now they'd all had supper and the boys were in bed, another day of running up and down stairs, shifting boxes and furniture, unpacking and putting away had caught up with her. But there was so much still to be done although she needed a moment to herself before she started again on the packing cases.

'Well, Richard,' she whispered to the shadows in the kitchen, 'we made it. Wish you had too.' She swallowed down a whoosh of self-pity and sorrow. She leaned back in the chair and blinked back tears. The silence was total. Not even a clock ticked and the space seemed big and empty. Even the pile of cartons in the corner, which had almost filled their last kitchen in London, didn't seem to take up much space here. She suddenly felt very alone. Which is ridiculous, she told herself, with three children upstairs. Maybe it was loneliness rather than being alone. She wished Richard was here to see this house, to know that his dream of moving to the country had come to fruition. How bitterly ironic that it was partly his life insurance that had made it possible. Bex could almost weep at the unfairness of life – and death.

She sighed and leaned back in the big carver chair, running her fingers over the curved ends of the arms, remembering how Richard had done that whenever he sat in it.

How she wished he was still alive. It wasn't just that she needed his strength and stability to cope with this move – Megan needed him too, and the boys did. She couldn't fill his shoes; she couldn't be the *other* parent as well. She couldn't do this on her own. And yet she had to.

Sitting here moping wasn't getting the unpacking done. Wearily she stood up again. She'd promised herself she'd get the kitchen straight tonight but first, a drink. There was a case of wine that she'd directed the removal men to cart down to the cellar. She and Richard had bought it for their tenth wedding anniversary, but he'd died before they'd reached that milestone. Not much point in saving it now. She went to the door in the corner of the kitchen that led down to the basement and flicked the switch at the top of the stairs. A smell of damp and mould and ancient dust wafted upwards and a couple of antique cobwebs, hanging from the sloping ceiling of the stairwell, moved around in the disturbed air. One day, when she had the energy, she'd sort this place out, give it a proper floor, heat it maybe – and it would make the most splendid den for the boys. But it wasn't on her list of priorities right now and, knowing how much had to be done to get the whole house straight before she could even *think* about extras like a den for Lewis and Alfie, she reckoned they might be leaving for university before she managed to get around to it. She clutched the handrail and made her way down the steep stairs into the basement. A bare light bulb illuminated the space which was, she thought, disappointingly small, given the size of the house. But there, in the middle of the beaten-earth floor, was the case of wine.

She pulled open the lid to reveal a dozen ruby-red lead foils. She picked out a bottle and carried it back upstairs, flicking the light off before she shut the door. Back in the kitchen she examined her booty. Bugger – a proper cork. Well, given the quality of the wine she shouldn't be surprised, but now she had to find the blooming corkscrew before she could enjoy a glass – and that meant more unpacking. She knew she had to get the boxes emptied but she'd really hoped to have a few minutes' relaxing before she put her back into it again. Bollocks.

She set the bottle down and pulled one of the big cardboard cartons off the stack and carried it over to the table. She opened the flaps and began to pull out, and unwrap, newspaper parcel after newspaper parcel. At her feet the drift of paper got bigger and higher and on the table the pile of mixing bowls and kitchen tools also grew. She picked out the final item from the box but she could tell instantly from the size and weight it definitely wasn't a corkscrew. She peeled the protective paper off. No – a Kilner jar.

Bums.

Bex gathered up the newsprint and checked that she'd not missed anything before she shoved it back in the box and then bunged it all under the table. Then she went back over to the stack of packing cases, grabbed another one and began the process over again.

6

As Olivia walked back from her council meeting, which had concluded its business with admirable rapidity, she noticed lights on in the upstairs windows of The Beeches. She stopped by the gate and stared at the big old house then glanced at her watch. It was only seven thirty so there was no time like the present. She turned and walked up the drive, scrunching over the gravel.

It took a few seconds for the door to open after she'd rung the bell.

'Hello?'

'Hello. I'm Olivia Laithwaite. I hope you don't think me presumptuous if I take it upon myself to welcome you to Little Woodford.'

'Er... no. And thank you.'

Olivia instantly sized up the newcomer to the town and confirmed what she'd thought when she'd caught a glimpse of her getting out of the car the day before; young, very pretty and blonde. She was reminded of someone... who...? Then she got it; Goldie Hawn in her younger days. But if she was living in a whacking great house like this, she was no dizzy blond. Mind you, she told herself, neither was Goldie Hawn, regardless of the image she presented to the world. Maybe this was a second wife, she told herself. A young couple wouldn't be able to afford a place like this – not unless they'd inherited a mint of money or won the lottery.

'I'm sure you'll be very happy here. It is a lovely town, quite unspoilt really. I was going to call in earlier but... well, the day got away from me.' She smiled.

'Sorry,' said the newcomer and stuck out her hand. 'I'm Bex, Bex Millar. Would you like to come in? It's chaos, as you can imagine. We only arrived yesterday.' She opened the door wider to allow Olivia to step in.

'Are you sure?'

'Frankly, I'd be glad of an excuse to stop. Although at the moment I'm trying to find a corkscrew so I can have a glass of wine. I had planned to get the kitchen unpacked tonight but I think I'm running out of energy.' Bex shut the door and led the way along the hall and into the kitchen. 'As I can't offer you wine, how about tea... or coffee?'

'Coffee would be lovely. Have you got decaf?'

'Not that I've managed to find.'

Olivia suppressed a sigh. The caffeine would play havoc with her sleep but she'd have to cope. 'Never mind then, full strength will just have to do.' She looked around at the chaos in the kitchen. Where was the order? Where was the plan? She wasn't quite sure what to say, so she opted for, 'You seem to have done a fair bit of unpacking already.'

Bex filled the kettle. 'Not really. Not as much as I'd have liked.' She plugged the kettle in and took a couple of clean mugs out of the cupboard. 'And then there's the children to feed and look after.'

So where was Mr Millar? Shirking, stuck in a job in another location, off the scene entirely...? After all, a man who had divorced once might be perfectly capable of doing it again. Not that Olivia felt she could pry but she was agog with curiosity. 'You sound as if you're on your own.'

Bex nodded. 'I am – sort of. There are three children upstairs but I've lost my husband. He was killed last year in a traffic accident, on his way to work.'

Olivia felt awful. That wasn't the answer she'd been expecting at all. 'Oh, my dear! I am *so* sorry.'

'Thank you,' she said.

It sounded to Olivia like she'd had to say 'thank you' an awful lot – and she supposed it was true. After all, what else *was* there to say when people offered you sympathy? 'I expect you're finding things very tough on your own. And now a house move. It's a lot to contend with, without...'

'... without Richard?' supplied Bex. 'Yes, it is, but life goes on. Or mine does at any rate.' She didn't add the obvious statement that her husband's hadn't. 'I keep expecting things to get easier but they don't,' she added, baldly.

'No, no I'm sure they don't. You're very brave to move house on your own though. I mean, wouldn't it have been easier not to?'

Bex sighed. 'Not really.' The kettle clicked off and she began to make the coffee. 'If we'd stayed in London I would have had to walk past the spot where he died on an almost daily basis, and Richard always wanted to move to the country. He'd lived in a little town like this as a kid and he always wanted his kids to grow up somewhere similar; to do the things he did...' There was a pause and Olivia wondered if Bex was going to cry but then she flashed Olivia a slightly embarrassed grin. 'So I kind of felt I didn't have much choice.'

'You poor thing,' said Olivia, glad she hadn't had to deal with an emotional scene. She decided to move away from the subject of Richard; keep things positive. No point dwelling on the unpleasant past. 'But you're here now,' she said, briskly. 'That's the main thing and in a week or two I expect you'll feel as if you've been here for ages, and the children will love growing up here. Mine have, I know.'

'Bex?' quavered a voice from the doorway.

Olivia swung round. 'And who is this?' She stared at the teenager. No way was she the daughter of Bex – not with that colouring and dramatic beauty. Bex was pretty enough in a china-doll kind of way but this girl was in another league. Not that her looks seemed to have given her any sort of self-confidence – she looked as if she'd flee or cry at the least thing.

'This is Megan – my stepdaughter. Megan, this is Mrs Laithwaite. Mrs Laithwaite has dropped by to welcome us to Little Woodford.'

'Hello,' mumbled Megan, failing to make any sort of eye contact.

Stepdaughter – so *that* explained the lack of family likeness. 'I was just telling your mother how much my children have loved it here. You must meet Zac. I think you and he must be about the same age and I'm sure you'd get on. So, are you going to St Anselm's?'

Olivia saw Megan look at her stepmother as if she didn't know the answer herself.

'Er, no,' Bex answered, passing a steaming mug to Olivia and then offering her guest the milk carton. 'Richard didn't believe in private education so Megan is going to the local comp. She'll be starting after the Easter holidays.'

'Really?' Surely not? She poured a splash of milk into her drink.

'Yes, really,' affirmed Bex. 'It seems to have a good reputation and it's what Richard would have chosen.'

'Well, yes... it gets good reports – for a comp. It's just living here...' Olivia waved her free hand to indicate the entire house, the neighbourhood, the posh end of town... 'Well, the type of people who live at this end of the town tend to send their children to St Anselm's. Let's just say none of the council estate children go there and St Anselm's does get truly outstanding results.'

'I'm sure children with ability do just as well at the comp,' said Bex firmly.

'Yes, of course.' If that's what Bex wanted to believe.

Bex turned to Megan. 'Did you want something, sweetheart?'

'I came to get a drink of milk.'

'Help yourself.'

'Where are the glasses?'

She pointed to the cupboard by the sink. 'In there.'

Megan trailed across the quarry-tiled floor and pulled open

the door, before returning to the fridge and slopping milk into the glass. Then she left again after giving Olivia another frightened look.

'Teenagers,' said Bex, lightly.

'Indeed. Like I said, I've got one about the same age and he can be a bit tricky. Hormones, I expect.'

'How many children have you got?'

'Four. But Zac was a bit of an afterthought so he's the only one at home. His brothers and sister are all off earning their own livings. Well, one is still at uni, doing an MA, but she'll be out in the big world in the summer. You?'

'Just the three. Megan has two younger brothers... half-brothers. They'll go to the local primary.'

'Good.' Olivia nodded approvingly. 'Lovely school. Very nurturing and caring. Mine thrived there.' She put her mug down on the table. 'Look, why don't I give you a hand for a bit? I feel guilty that I've held you up and I'm sure, together, we could get these boxes here unpacked tonight if we try.'

'No,' said Bex. 'That's not fair. You didn't come here to graft.'

But Olivia had already crossed the kitchen and was hauling a carton off the pile which she brought over to the table. 'I'll unpack – you put away. Only...' she paused as she opened the lid; it was the least she could do to try and help Bex to sort out the mess. 'Tell me if I'm teaching you to suck eggs but I think we might be better off if you get the stuff that's already unpacked put away before you do any more. And you ought to decide where you *really* want things to live, right from the outset. In my experience, it makes things much easier in the long run.'

'Really?'

Olivia nodded. 'Really. Now, where do you want your china to live? Maybe near where you are likely to serve food?'

'I suppose.'

'How about this cupboard by this counter?'

'Maybe.'

'Good.' Olivia picked up a pile of plates and put them on the shelf. Really, if Bex was going to get straight before the crack of doom someone had to take control.

The pair worked as a team and, with two pairs of hands, they first cleared the backlog of items on the work surfaces and then they began on the pile of full cartons, which diminished rather quickly. The corkscrew was found and their coffees were swapped for glasses of wine and it seemed to them both that the work went even faster after that. As they worked Olivia made it her business to tell Bex about all the great things that went on in the town that made it such a wonderful place to live.

'Virtually Utopia,' said Bex.

'I like to think so.'

Olivia failed to spot Bex's slight but disbelieving shake of her head.

'Now then,' said Olivia in a brief lull between boxes, 'we need to get you involved in the town. That's the best way to make friends and get integrated.'

'I'm not being funny,' said Bex, 'but to be honest, I've got a lot on my plate right now; too much to consider anything else. Getting "integrated" isn't that high on my list of priorities.'

Olivia ripped off the tape from the top of another full box. 'You can't unpack and try and get straight every minute of every day. And even if you do, you'll finish eventually and you'll need to start to join in then.'

'Really? So, what do you suggest?'

Olivia refused to be daunted by the lack of enthusiasm in Bex's voice. 'The WI is a *must*.'

'The WI?!'

'I know what you're thinking. You're thinking you're not old enough for that but believe me it's the perfect way of meeting people; people like you and me.'

'I don't know...'

'You'd love it.'

Bex shook her head. 'But I couldn't. I'd need a babysitter.'

'Couldn't Megan look after your boys?'

'Olivia, she's in a big new house, in a strange town, having recently lost her dad. I don't think abandoning her while I go off gallivanting is appropriate.'

That was no excuse in Olivia's book, but she could hardly frogmarch this new inhabitant into the function room of the pub. She sniffed. 'As you wish.'

They carried on unpacking in silence for a few minutes – Olivia lifting items out of the box, unwrapping them from their newspaper cocoons before handing them to Bex to stack or put away.

'Amy would babysit.'

'Amy?'

'My cleaner.'

'I don't know, Olivia. I know nothing about this Amy woman.'

'She's utterly reliable, I've known her for years, she works in the post office and she cleans for me, the vicar's wife and a few others in the town. Her son and mine are friends.'

'I'm sorry but that doesn't mean she's suitable. I'm not saying she might be a modern day Myra Hindley—'

'Oh really!'

'—but it doesn't give her a green light to look after other people's kids. I'm a qualified nanny and I know about the rules and regulations and, trust me, I've no intention of breaking them and certainly not where my own children are concerned.'

'Ask Heather, the vicar's wife. She'll tell you what a gem Amy is.'

'Look, I know you mean well, Olivia, but I only arrived in the town yesterday.'

'You need to strike while the iron is hot.'

'Let's leave it for a bit.'

Olivia saw that she'd met her match. 'I shall hold you to that.'

The unpacking continued in silence again while both of them simmered down.

'You said you were a nanny,' said Olivia after a few minutes. 'How lovely.'

'It was a wonderful job. I adored it.'

'And it must be wonderful for your children – just think, a real life Mary Poppins as a mother.'

'I wish. Sadly, I can't click my fingers to get things done. I still have to slog at things the hard way.' Bex looked significantly at the diminishing pile of packing cases in the corner.

Finally, the pair emptied the last box, and Olivia stripped the tape off the bottom, folded it flat and put it in the corner with the rest of the packing materials, ready to be taken to the dump.

'There,' she said. She looked at the kitchen. No, not perfect but not bad, not too bad at all. Better than it would have been without her intervention, she thought.

Bex picked up the bottle. 'Top up?'

'Love one.' Olivia pulled out a chair and plumped down on to it. 'And then, as soon as I've had this, I'll be off. You must be shattered.' She glanced at the timer on the microwave. It was almost nine thirty. Definitely time to leave her new friend in peace.

'I've had less stressful days,' agreed Bex as she poured wine into Olivia's glass and then refilled her own. She sat down too and leaned her elbows on the big kitchen table. 'And thanks for the help. I wouldn't have managed nearly so much on my own. To be honest I was on the verge of giving up for today so thank you for spurring me on to finish.' She smiled gratefully at Olivia.

'If you feel the need to get away from the unpacking you must come up to mine. Just give me a ring first, to make sure I'm home – I'm quite busy. On lots of committees, lots of voluntary work... you know, that sort of thing. Here...' Olivia got up from the table and picked her handbag up from where she'd dumped it on a window sill. She rummaged in it for a second or two before producing a business card. 'All the contact details are on that. And the house, the barn conversion, is almost bang opposite the primary school – you can't miss it.'

Bex took the card and put it on a counter. 'Let's hope I don't lose it.'

Ten minutes later Olivia had drained her glass. She said her goodbyes then walked up the hill to The Grange. As she approached the front door she could hear the row going on. Zac and her husband were at daggers drawn – again. She wondered what had caused the altercation this time? What with Nigel's touchiness and Zac's hormones the house was a powder keg of emotions, although she didn't stop to consider that none of her other children had been prone to quite such violent mood swings. With a sigh she let herself in and shut the door behind her. And as for Nigel… he'd been a nightmare to live with for some months now. Touchy as anything. She'd tried asking him if there was anything wrong but he always said things were fine. Mid-life crisis, she supposed.

She walked down to the kitchen area of the vast space that was the central living room of the barn conversion. Zac and her husband were so busy yelling at each other, they were oblivious to her reappearance until she was right beside them.

'What does it matter?' shouted Zac. 'It's what we have Amy for.'

'Amy is not paid by your mother to clean up after you.'

'Then why *do* we pay her? What is she, a charity case?'

'I won't have you speak to me like that.'

'Or what?' sneered Zac.

'Stop it, the pair of you,' said Olivia, stepping between them. She hated them rowing and, if she could, she usually tried to head Zac off before he actually locked horns. But today it was too late. 'Just stop it.'

'Keep out of this, Oli,' said Nigel. He tried to push her out of the way.

But Olivia – how she loathed Nigel calling her Oli, although now was not the moment to mention it – didn't budge. 'What's Zac done?' she demanded.

'Look,' said Nigel, pointing to the worktop on which was the detritus left from some mid-evening snack that Zac had made for himself. There was a dirty plate, crumbs everywhere, to say nothing of a couple of dollops of jam and a loaf left on the breadboard. Nigel had a point, it was a mess and Olivia knew, when she'd gone out earlier, she certainly hadn't left the kitchen in such a state, but it could be swiftly put right. She went to the sink and picked up the dishcloth and wrung it out.

'Don't you dare,' snapped Nigel. 'I've told Zac to clear it up.'

But Olivia began to use the cloth to sweep the crumbs into her hand.

'I said *stop*!'

She stopped and turned to face him. 'It's just a few crumbs, Nigel.'

'And I've told Zac to clear them up.'

'It'll only take me a second.'

Nigel reached forward and snatched the dishcloth off her, scattering crumbs onto the floor.

'Oh, Nigel,' said Olivia. She'd have to get the dustpan out now.

'This is Zac's mess, I've told him to clear it up and I will *not* have you undermining me.'

Olivia realised she'd gone too far. 'Sorry, Nigel. Zac – do as your father says.'

Zac, now he had both parents against him, realised that he had no choice. 'Oh, for fuck's sake,' he snarled as he picked up the plate, opened the dishwasher door and almost threw it in.

Nigel grabbed his son's arm. 'What did you say?'

Zac straightened up and glowered at his dad. 'Nothing,' he muttered.

'Apologise to your mother this instant. I will not have you using that sort of language in front of her.'

There was a pause and for a second Olivia wondered if the two were actually going to exchange blows. And then Zac mumbled an apology of sorts before he carried on tidying up. Olivia relaxed a fraction.

'And make sure you do it properly,' said Nigel.

'Jesus, Dad, I'm doing it, aren't I?'

Olivia was on guard again, ready for it to kick off once more, but thankfully Nigel only responded with a gruff 'good' before he left his son to it.

God Almighty, thought Olivia, feeling exhausted by the incident. She'd only been out for a few hours but, without her there to keep the peace, all hell had broken loose. Men! There were occasions when she didn't much like her family. On the other hand, at least Zac had some spirit, unlike that child of Bex's. Megan, was it? Olivia didn't give much for her chances of surviving in a melting pot like the comp – not given that she didn't seem to have any backbone and wouldn't say boo to a goose. On balance she'd rather have Zac – at least he stood up for himself.

'You've got to get a grip of Zac,' said Nigel after he'd finished tidying and thumped upstairs, making as much noise as was humanly possible.

'Me?'

'You indulge him, you make excuses. He's got to be made to take responsibility for his actions.'

'He's at that difficult age.'

'You see, you're doing it again. His brother and sisters weren't like this.'

Nigel had a point. Zac was either so laid-back he was almost catatonic or his temper was on a hair-trigger. Olivia admitted to herself that she did tend to tiptoe round him to avoid upsetting him but she had enough going on in her life without having constant rows with her son.

'Maybe if you didn't work such long hours...' She regretted it almost as soon as the words were out.

'Jesus, Oli, have you *any* idea about the size of this mortgage? What it costs to keep this place running? And that's before I get on to what it cost to educate the kids, paying off their gap-year debts, helping out with their rents in London, *your* cleaner... Shit, do you think I *like* working all the hours God sends?'

'No, I'm sorry.'

Nigel glared at her. 'And if you stopped being Lady Fucking Bountiful and got a job, I might be able to ease off.'

'Yes, dear,' she said, hoping that would placate him, because she had absolutely no plans whatsoever to go back to work.

Besides, she'd been out of the job market ever since Mike, her eldest, had been born and he was nearly thirty. Anyway, Nigel earned pots of money – more than enough to keep them in this lifestyle. She didn't know why he was making such an issue of it now. He never had in the past.

After Olivia had taken her leave Bex poured another glass of wine. Stuff it – she deserved it – and then leant back in the chair. She felt utterly exhausted. Olivia was lovely but she did seem to be quite... Bex searched for the right word. Energetic? Bossy? Opinionated? Yes, she was certainly all that. Bex sighed and sipped her wine.

Olivia had been right, of course; she did need to join in some-time soon, find things to do, find new friends, because she was under no illusions about what would happen to the friends she'd left behind in London. One or two might make the trek out to the countryside in the first year or so – especially as the children would like to see some of their old school chums, but the visits would get less frequent until they petered out entirely. Then all that would be left was an exchange of Christmas cards until that too eventually fell by the wayside.

No, she needed to make new friends here if she was going to move on and Olivia was a start – even if Bex didn't think that they were destined to become bosom buddies. Still, with two boys at primary school there would be ample opportunity to meet other mums and Bex was sure they'd soon slot in to the local community. There was also Olivia's suggestion of joining some of the local groups and societies. There was, according to Olivia, a comprehensive list on the town hall notice board. Bex resolved to go and have a look the next morning – although she was sure that Olivia must have covered pretty much everything. She finished her wine, thought about finishing the bottle but decided against it, and took the cork off the corkscrew before slapping it firmly back in the neck. She'd save the rest for tomorrow.

Despite the fact that it was only about ten, Bex went upstairs to her room, got ready for bed and then slipped under the covers. She put her hand under her pillow and dragged out an old T-shirt. She put it to her nose and inhaled the smell – the scent of her husband; the merest whiff that still remained of his aftershave and a hint of his sweat. Exhausted by the day, she was asleep before she cried – as she had almost every other night since his death.

7

Megan was woken by a strange scrabbling noise and for a while she couldn't work out what the hell was going on. Rats? Then she realised it was a bird hopping about on the skylight above her head. She could see a large feathery bum and pink feet – a wood pigeon. Then she heard it cooing and the sound was rather pleasant and comforting. Above the pigeon she could see the branches of the beeches that gave the house its name. Was she imagining it or was there a mist of green around the twigs? Was spring really springing – as her dad used to say. She sighed. Why did he have to go and get himself killed? If only that hadn't happened none of the rest of it would... if only, if only...

Megan rolled onto her side and gave in to self-pity. Things might have gone horribly wrong when they lived in London but at least she knew everybody. She didn't know a soul here and she dreaded going to the new school. She didn't want to be the new kid. She'd seen how new kids got treated at her old school – hanging around on the edges of the gangs of the popular pupils, trying to join in, being ignored, ending up with the losers... Once she'd been in the popular group – or at least she thought she had. Then it turned out that her 'friends' weren't friends at all, not really. Not when push came to shove.

Megan threw back her duvet and got out of bed. She wandered over to the window and looked down into the garden. The two boys were already up and running about again. It didn't take much to make them happy, she thought, and they probably weren't the least bit worried about a new school. Alfie certainly wouldn't be – he'd only been at his old one for a couple of terms – and Lewis was the sort of kid who took most things in his stride. Of course the death of his dad had knocked him for six. Megan remembered how awful he'd been for weeks afterwards; not sleeping, throwing tantrums, fighting in the school playground, being moody and clingy. For months he'd been a total pain in the arse. Thank God he seemed to be over it. And Alfie... he was too young to understand it all, too young to remember Daddy. Megan wasn't sure if that was a blessing or not. Maybe things were easier if you couldn't remember.

She put on her dressing gown and pattered downstairs. The rest of the house was silent; maybe Bex was showering. She got herself some bread and butter and a glass of milk and took it all back up to her bedroom. As she got to the top of the main stairs she could hear Bex humming in her room and the sound of drawers opening and shutting. More unpacking. Which reminded her – her own room needed doing. She climbed back into her attic and surveyed the pile of boxes as she chewed on her bread. *Standing looking at it isn't going to get it done*, she heard her dad say in her head.

She finished her breakfast, threw off her dressing gown and reached into the shower stall to turn on the tap. In a minute, steam was fogging the mirror over the basin and Megan stepped into the hot jet. The water washed away her anxieties. Bliss. Bigger bliss was that this was her space. She didn't have to share. She revelled in the warm water, luxuriating in knowing that no one might come hammering on the door, wanting the loo – as had happened all too often at the London house. Finally she switched off the tap and got out, wrapping herself in the towel before drifting into her room and flicking open her case containing essentials that hadn't been packed on the van. Minutes later, dry and dressed, she looked at the first of the cartons with 'Meg's room' written in thick marker pen on the side. She pulled the tape off the top and flipped open the flaps. A glance inside told her that it contained the contents of her chest of drawers. Now then, how did she want her furniture arranged? At the moment it was all pushed against one wall. Megan stood in the middle of the floor and worked out where she wanted everything to be and then dragged her chest, her dressing table and her bookcase into position. Finally she shunted her desk over the carpet and under the window. It'd be nice to be able to look out over the garden to the street when she was doing her homework.

She pulled the open box across the floor to the chest and began putting the clothes into the drawers, in the same places they had lived before. It didn't take long to empty that box and so she started on another. She found she quite enjoyed sorting her stuff out; deciding where everything should go; finding homes for her possessions on the shelves that had been left by the previous owners, putting her clothes and shoes in the built-in wardrobe. Her books took longer to arrange and she got distracted when she found an old favourite and began to reread it. In fact, she was so absorbed in her book that she forgot the time and was surprised when Bex yelled up the stairs to say she'd made sandwiches and it was lunchtime.

'Brian, darling,' said Heather, dipping her spoon into her soup. She and Brian were eating their lunch of home-made vegetable soup at one end of the dining room table – the other end being covered in the church accounts which Brian had been going through. 'Do you think it would be a good idea if I visited the new people?'

'Hmmm?' Brian didn't look up from the *Guardian*.

'The new people... should I visit them?'

'If you like.'

Heather sighed. 'But what do *you* think?'

'Hmm.'

This was hopeless. Heather banged her spoon down on her plate. 'Really, Brian. I am a parishioner too. If I was anyone else in the parish asking for advice you'd give me your full attention.'

The tone of Heather's voice made Brian look up. He took off his glasses. 'OK. This is what I think. If the new family are paid-up, card-carrying, full-on members of the Church of England they'll be at church on Sunday come hell or high water. If they're high-days and holidays Christians we may see them at Christmas and Easter, and if they're neither of those, then you'll be wasting your time and the last thing they'll want is a visit from the vicar's wife. Of course, if your reason for wanting to call is because, ever since we arrived here, you've been gagging to have an excuse to see inside that house – well, go right ahead and do it.' Brian took a spoonful of soup and returned to his paper, leaving Heather to wonder what her motives really were, although she knew, deep down, that Brian was right; the previous occupants had been in residence when Brian had been given this living and Heather, not being friends with that family, had never been able to find an excuse to call – till now.

An hour later she rang the bell of The Beeches. A young blonde, mid-thirties, guessed Heather, opened the door. She was carrying a wad of crumpled newspaper in one hand.

'Yes?'

'I'm Heather Simmonds. I thought I'd drop by and say hello.'

'Oh, well, hello then. I'm Bex Millar.'

'I live over there.' Heather waved a hand in the vague direction of the church.

'That's nice.'

'I just wanted to welcome you to Little Woodford.'

'Thank you.' Behind Bex two small boys erupted out of the sitting room and thundered past the two women and into the garden. 'No going out of the gate, remember,' Bex called after them. Whether or not the boys heard was hard to tell. 'My sons, Lewis and Alfie. Look, would you like a cuppa? I could do with one. Unpacking is thirsty business.'

'Well... only if you're having one.'

'I am.' Bex opened the door wide and then shut it behind Heather. She led the way into the kitchen.

'Oh, this is lovely,' said Heather, with genuine enthusiasm. She was quite surprised how light the kitchen was but it had been extended and had a couple of skylights in the new section which probably made all the difference. She looked around and took in the wood floor, the Belfast sink, bespoke units... so very different from her own ghastly kitchen.

'It is rather, isn't it? Nothing to do with me, it's how it was when I arrived here. And it looks tidy because the kids haven't had a chance to make it untidy yet. They will, when they've got all their possessions out of the boxes and the novelty of putting things away has completely worn off.' Bex smiled. 'Tea? Coffee?'

'Tea would be lovely. My kitchen is awful. It desperately needs updating but well...'

'It's an expensive business,' said Bex as she went about making the tea.

Heather pulled a chair out from under the kitchen table and sat on it. There was a lull in the conversation as Bex worked. Then a stunning teenager, all smouldering eyes and dark hair, wandered in. She reminded Heather of a young Sophia Loren.

'Say hello, Megan. This is my stepdaughter.'

Which explained the complete lack of similarity between her and Bex.

Megan said hello, helped herself to a glass of water and drifted out again.

'Does she take after her father?' asked Heather.

'Her birth mother was Spanish.'

'Oh.' Heather was bursting with curiosity to know more about the family but was far too polite and English to ask direct questions. 'So what brought you to Little Woodford?'

'My husband, Richard, always wanted to live in the country. So... now we do.' Bex brought two mugs of tea over to the table and sat opposite Heather.

'Lucky you – a dream come true.'

Bex put her mug on the table. 'Nope,' she said. 'Not lucky at all.' Heather assumed she was going to be told that it was all down to careful planning or networking or some other more prosaic reason the family had wound up here but that *fate* had definitely not been involved.

'No,' continued Bex. 'Our luck stopped when he was on his bike on his way to work in London and a truck ran a red light.'

'Oh, my dear...' Heather put her mug down on the table. She gazed at Bex. 'Oh, how terrible.'

'Yes, it was rather.' Bex knew she sounded matter-of-fact but she couldn't allow herself to show her true feelings – not and maintain any sort of control. 'So I decided we should come here anyway. A fresh start for us all, somewhere without a zillion painful memories.'

'Of course. And how are you coping?'

'Some days well, other days it's awful.' Bex shrugged.

'I do understand. Truly I do.'

Bex looked sceptical.

'My husband is the vicar here – bereavement is one of the things we "do".'

'Ah.' Now she looked wary.

'It's all right,' said Heather. 'I'm not going to say "It was God's will" or anything like that. If I did, I wouldn't blame you for thumping me.'

Bex gave her the ghost of a smile. 'I've heard that a fair bit and, trust me, I've been tempted.'

'And I didn't drop by to try and press-gang you into joining the congregation. Of course, if you'd like to, we'd love to see you but... Anyway, this is a genuine social call and let you know that if you want to know anything about the town, activities for your children, clubs you might like to join... the WI?' Heather saw the look on Bex's face. 'Maybe not. However, may I just say, it probably isn't a bit like you think it is. Honest.' She saw Bex raise an eyebrow. 'OK... But there's a great book club run by

the bookshop, the Woodford Players, a ladies' cricket team...'
Heather petered out. Bex's lack of enthusiasm was still apparent.
'All I'm saying is that when you're settled and have more time
there's a load of things to do and if you want any information
all you have to do is ask me.' She paused. 'I don't suppose you're
any good at flower arranging, are you?' Bex shook her head. 'Ah
well. The flower rota needs more people and I'm always on the
lookout. Right then, I'll leave you in peace.' Heather got to her
feet and gathered her things together. 'But if you want anything
– a chat, information, whatever, the vicarage is easy enough to
find. But not the lovely old Regency one. The vile sixties job a bit
further along Church Road.'

'Thanks, I'll bear that in mind. What with you and Olivia—'

'Olivia? You've met her already?'

'She dropped in last night.'

'Oh well, you don't need me then.' Heather smiled.

'She's very... well-informed.'

'"Well-informed"? Is that a euphemism?'

'Possibly.'

Heather grinned. 'She's not everyone's cup of tea but she's a
grafter and she never lets anyone down. She adores this town and
will do anything to keep it a lovely place that people, like you,
want to move to. If she says she's going to do something, she does
it. One "Olivia" is worth three of most people.'

'Yeah, I can see that. I think all towns should have an "Olivia".'

'Exactly.'

'Even I could see how much she loves this place.'

Heather said her goodbyes and made her way back home. It
was lovely to see a young family move into the town. With house
prices the way they were going, the population seemed to be
getting older and older as fewer and fewer of the next generation
were able to afford to buy and opted to live further afield in
less desirable locations. Bex and her family would definitely be
an asset.

8

The following Tuesday, the alarm next to Nigel's side of the bed went off, as it did every morning, at six. Blearily he opened an eye and groaned and, as he always did, he switched the alarm off on the radio and hit the button next to it to catch the start of the *Today* programme.

'Good morning,' said John Humphrys.

'There's nothing fucking *good* about it,' muttered Nigel.

'Did you say something, darling?' mumbled Olivia, her voice muffled by the pillow.

'No. Go back to sleep.'

In the pale morning light that filtered through the plantation blinds Nigel saw Olivia roll on to her back. He got out of bed and headed into the en suite and switched on the shower. Five minutes later he was back in the bedroom, showered, shaved and wrapped in a towel. He dressed in the clothes he'd left ready the night before and then opened his wardrobe to find a sports bag. Into it he shoved a pair of shorts, spare socks and a T-shirt.

'Ol. Oli!'

'Wha...?'

'Ol, have you seen my trainers?'

Olivia propped herself up on one elbow. 'What do you want trainers for?' She yawned.

'I told you, I've joined the company badminton club. We've a match tonight.'

Olivia shook her head. 'Badminton?'

'Get with the programme Ol, I told you. The MD's new initiative.'

'Did you?'

'Oh, for God's sake, do you *ever* listen to a word I say?'

'Of course. I remember now.'

Nigel, frankly, doubted it. 'So… my trainers?'

'Probably in your wardrobe.'

Nigel scrabbled around in his cupboard and pulled them out. He stuffed them in his bag with his other sports kit. 'Found. Right, I'll be late home tonight.'

'How late?'

'Nineish, maybe later.'

'Fine.'

Nigel switched off the radio that neither of them had listened to and left the bedroom. Olivia sank down beneath the duvet again, certain she knew nothing about the badminton club. But it was obviously her fault. Nigel was right – she couldn't have listened. She really ought to pay more attention or he'd have yet more excuses to lose his temper.

Mags was busy shampooing the doctor's wife's hair.

'Have you met the new people at The Beeches yet, Jacqui?'

'No, but I saw the van there last week. I wonder what they're like?'

'What, apart from filthy rich? Did you see what the previous owners were asking for that place?'

'Wasn't it nearly two mill?'

'Something like that. Of course it didn't mean they got it. It was on the market for an age.'

'Even so,' said Jacqui Connolly, 'it's a lot to pay for bricks and mortar. Makes you wonder what you'd get for your own place.'

'Not me,' said Mags. 'I live in a council house, remember.'
Silence fell for a few seconds. 'Amy said there were some kids
playing in the garden.'

'So it's a young family that's moved in,' said Jacqui.

'Seems like it.'

'That's nice. Reverses a trend.'

'So it seems.' Mags turned the taps on and started to rinse her
client's hair.

'You've noticed too. There seem to be fewer and fewer young
families round and about. It's the cost of housing.'

'Stands to reason.'

'Well, we've really noticed at the surgery. The numbers for the
antenatal classes are down, there are fewer inoculations each
year; honestly, the entire town is in danger of becoming one big
old-peoples' home.'

Mags frowned. 'I've heard the school is worried.'

'They've extended the catchment area. What we need,' said
Jacqui, 'is more affordable houses. If...' She stopped and drew in
a deep breath. 'If Lisa had lived, there's no way she'd have been
able to afford to buy anything here.'

Oh gawd, here we go again. She was very sorry for the doctor
and his wife – their daughter dying just after she'd gone to uni
had been a terrible tragedy – but it had been years ago now, three
at least. Mind you, thought Mags, rumour had it that Jacqui
blamed herself because Lisa had phoned home complaining of
feeling ill, and her mum had told her to stop making a fuss. Of
course, it turned out Lisa had contracted meningitis. But even
so, did Jacqui Connolly have to bang on about her daughter
at every opportunity? 'No,' said Mags, trying to keep her voice
measured. 'But buying isn't the be-all and end-all. My Amy rents
and is quite happy about it. And there's Cattebury.'

'Well, yes...' Jacqui's tone spoke reams. Cattebury wasn't for
the likes of the doctor's daughter.

Mags felt like saying that perhaps it was just as well she was
dead and didn't have to face the awfulness of being consigned

to the sinkhole that was the next town. No, that would be going too far. 'Water all right?' she asked instead.

'Lovely.'

'Going to the WI tonight?'

'As the new president I don't think I get much choice.'

'No, well...'

And the conversation moved away from the affordability of local housing.

Bex was making a start on the dining room. Now she had such a fabulous kitchen she couldn't see them using it much, but maybe if they had visitors... maybe if she made friends and had people round to supper... Or maybe not. Even so, she couldn't leave it as it was with pictures stacked against the wall and Richard's parents' dinner service, that they'd given him when they'd moved overseas, still in boxes.

'Mum, Mum,' said Alfie, racing in through the door, an expression of indignation on his face and tears in his eyes. 'Lewis hit me.'

Bex sighed. No wonder the boys were getting cranky. They'd had precious little attention paid to them recently, all things considered.

'Did he now?'

'He did, Mummy, he did.'

Bex stopped opening the boxes and went to the back door. She called Lewis over and spoke to him about being nice to his little brother.

'But he started it,' said Lewis.

'Didn't,' said Alfie.

'Did.'

'Didn't.'

'Shush. Just stop it, the pair of you.' She walked through the kitchen to the foot of the stairs.

'Megan!' she yelled.

'What?' bellowed Megan back down.

'You busy?'

'I was putting away the toys in the boys' rooms.'

'Could you do me a favour?'

'Hang on.' There was some thumping and then the sound of footsteps. Megan came to the landing. 'What?'

'Take the boys to the park. They're bored and need to let off steam.'

'OK.' Megan padded down the stairs. 'Come on,' she said to her half-brothers, 'let's go to the swings.'

Alfie stopped looking miserable and perked up and even Lewis looked less sulky.

As they got to the gate at the end of the drive, Megan grasped Alfie's hand tightly and, with an exhortation to Lewis to walk sensibly and to look where he was going, she led them through the little town. It was, she thought, really quite pretty with the honey-coloured stone that it was built from, and moss-covered roofs that were all different angles and heights. Very different from their bit of London which had consisted of almost identical roads of Victorian, red-brick, terraced houses and a shopping mall in the unexciting high street which was much like any other shopping mall in the country. Their old suburb of London might have had a slew of amenities and transport links, but it was bland. This, on the other hand, was quite chocolate-boxy.

She walked along the high street until, finally, she reached the entrance to the park and turned in. She let go of Alfie's hand and, with his recent tiff with Lewis completely forgotten, he and his brother raced off to play on the slide as all the other activities were stiff with children. While all the kids played, the parents – mostly mums – were clustered in groups, chatting. It hadn't been like that in the play park near their house in London. No one had spoken to anyone there – except their own kids.

Megan stood by the fence that delineated the boundary between the play area and the rest of the park and watched the boys. They seemed happy enough without her assistance for the time being and had now managed to insinuate themselves onto the roundabout which was being turned by a couple of slightly older kids. She leaned against the fence post and shut her eyes, basking in the spring sunshine.

'Hi.'

Megan was jerked back into sudden reality. Her eyes snapped open and for a nano-second she was unsure of her location. Then her brain kicked in; she knew where she was, it was the school holidays and she'd recently moved house. She raised her eyes to check out who had spoken to her.

It was the boy who'd done the trick on the skateboard when she'd been up to the park before, she was sure of it. And sheesh, now she saw him close up, he was fit. She tried not to stare but those grey eyes with the dark rings around the irises, the long honey-coloured eyelashes and the dirty-blond curls... God, he was gorgeous. He had a skateboard tucked under his arm and he was wearing ripped jeans. Megan thought he was the hottest thing she'd ever seen.

'Hello,' she said shyly.

He frowned at her. 'Look... I know this is going to sound like I'm a bit of a saddo but you're new around here, aren't you?'

'Might be.'

'Thought so.'

Megan pulled a brunette lock across her cheek self-consciously.

'So, you've moved into The Beeches then, have you?'

'Yeah,' said Megan, nodding. 'How did you know?'

'You're kidding me, right? You move into the biggest house in town and you don't reckon that *everyone* is going to take an interest?'

'I suppose.'

'Trust me, there's not much to talk about around here so when anything does happen... well, the likes of my mum and gran have a field day.' He gave her a wide smile.

Megan smiled back.

'So, where've you come from?'

'London.'

'Shit, you're going to find this place a bit quiet, aren't you?'

'Perhaps.'

'Seriously, you want to take a look at the local paper. The only headlines we get is stuff like "Church fête runs out of cucumber sandwiches".'

Megan laughed out loud.

'So, you going to St Anselm's?' asked Megan's new friend.

'Why does everyone ask that?'

'Posh house, posh school.'

'Well, I'm not. I'm going to the comp.'

'Seriously?'

Megan nodded.

'I go there. I'm Ashley, by the way. Ashley Pullen.'

'And I'm Megan.'

'Nice to meet you, Megan.'

'Oi,' came a yell from over by the skate ramps.

Megan and her new friend looked across the park.

'Oi,' yelled the dark boy, from the top of the highest ramp. 'You slacking, Ash? Thought you were going to try out that one-eighty ollie.'

'Sod off, Zac. Give me a couple of minutes.' The boy turned back to Megan.

'Do you board?'

Megan shook her head. 'No.'

'Want a go?'

Megan thought about it and then thought about the jeans she had on. They were new, from Next, and if she fell off she might muck them up and if she did that where was she going to buy another pair? 'Dunno. Never thought about boarding. Maybe another day.'

'Cool. Zac...' Ashley indicated the boy who'd shouted. 'Zac and I are here most days – well, in the holidays. If you'd like we could show you the basics one day.'

'OK.'

'Ash!' yelled Zac, impatiently.

'Gotta go.' Ashley flipped his skateboard up with his toe and caught it deftly. 'See you around, Megan.'

He sauntered back to the ramp and Megan watched him exchange a few words with Zac before Zac looked over in her direction. She wondered what Ashley was saying about her. God, she hoped it was all positive. She really wanted him to like her.

Ashley could barely take his eyes off Megan. There were some hot girls at his school but this new girl knocked the spots off all of them. Those sexy eyes and that mouth... She was like a real life Lara Croft and, God knew, he'd fantasised over her enough when he'd played Tomb Raider on Zac's PlayStation.

'Who's that?' asked Zac.

'Her family have moved into The Beeches.'

'A rich bitch, eh? What's she doing talking to you?'

'Maybe she fancies me.'

'Fancies you?' Zac's voice was larded with incredulity.

'Why not? Anyway, I've got more of a chance with her than you; she's going to be going to my school, not yours.'

'That means nothing, Ash. I bet you a tenner I get in her knickers before you do.'

Ashley suddenly felt disgusted by Zac. Megan was too perfect to be talked about in those terms but then Zac had a habit of pushing the boundaries, always going a bit too far. If Zac's boasting was to be believed, he even dabbled in drugs. Ashley supposed that's what came of having money to burn... literally. But part of him envied Zac – his confidence, his wealth, his sense of privilege and entitlement.

Ashley knew, in his heart, that he didn't stand a chance with a girl like Megan even if she was going to be going to the comp; she lived at the posh end of town while he lived on the council estate and was permanently skint. Life sucked.

9

After Zac had had his supper that night, he indulged in a bit of recreational drug-taking – to round things off nicely. He was taking a second deep lungful of smoke by the open window when he heard a peremptory knock at the door. Instantly he flicked his spliff out of the window onto the patio below and exhaled as fast as he could. The dog-end had barely left his fingers and he hadn't managed to draw the breath back in to say 'yes?' when the door opened.

'Mum!'

He saw his mother look around the room like she suspected something. Gawd, could she smell the pot? Her gaze came to rest on his computer screen where a game had been paused – a soldier was caught in mid-killing spree, his space-gun ready to waste an alien.

'I hope you've been getting on with the homework you were set for the holidays,' she said. 'Not spending *all* your time playing stupid games. And, good grief, Zac, what on earth are you doing with the window wide open? You'll catch your death.' She marched across the carpet and slammed it shut.

Despite the calming effect of the pot he'd just smoked, his heart rate went off the scale: what if she'd looked down onto the patio and seen the burning fag?

'Can. You. Not. Just. Barge. In. Here,' said Zac enunciating every word clearly, with a small pause between each for effect.

'I didn't barge, I knocked first.'

Zac snorted and shook his head. His mother was the fucking limit.

'I came up here to tell you I'm off to the WI. Your father is going to be late home so you'll be on your own for a while.'

'Whatever.'

'I'll be home about nine thirty.'

'OK.'

'Bye then.'

She hung around by the door. What did she want – a goodbye kiss? She left and Zac walked across the room and slammed the door shut. He waited for a couple of minutes before he cracked it open again, listening for any sign she might still be in the house, then he went across the landing to the window. There she was, pushing her bike over the gravel to the road where she mounted it carefully and pedalled down the hill.

Zac ran back to his room and grabbed his mobile, his thumbs flashing across the keyboard as he sent a text. A reply pinged in about a minute later and as soon as he'd scanned it he grabbed his hoodie, ran downstairs and across the open-plan living room to his dad's desk. He pulled the top drawer open fully and moved the pile of envelopes to one side before he picked up the two keys that lay underneath. His dad thought he was so clever with his hiding place, only he wasn't. No match for me, thought Zac as he picked them up and unlocked the small filing cabinet that sat next to the desk. He slid out the middle drawer with a metallic rumble and reached in to pull out the cash box before unlocking it. He flipped up the lid.

Bugger! It was empty. But his dad always had a wodge of twenties stashed in it. He turned it upside down and shook it as if that might make some money magically appear. But... but...? In disgust he threw it back into the filing cabinet and heaved a sigh. Shit! Now what? On autopilot Zac relocked the cash box and then put everything back where he'd found it, including the keys. Bollocks, he thought as he slammed shut the desk drawer.

He considered cancelling his meeting but he needed to score. Knowing he had no drugs left was making him anxious and jumpy and already he could feel his skin itching. His dealer would cut him some slack, surely. He was a good customer, the pusher would understand. Zac let himself out of the house and walked around the back to the patio, where he picked up the roach and chucked it into a flower bed. He hadn't even been able to finish his last joint properly, thanks to his mum. Angrily he kicked out at a plant pot which fell over and smashed. Yeah, that would serve her fucking right.

Bert Makepiece was hoeing between his early potatoes in the last of the evening light. The setting sun was warm on his weather-beaten and lined face, his skin tanned from working on his allotment in all weathers and the frill of white hair, like a monk's tonsure, caught the low rays of the sun and shone like a halo. Everyone else on the allotments had gone home for their tea and the kids that usually frequented the play area had departed too. Even the skate ramps had been abandoned. If it hadn't been for the cooing of wood pigeons and the songs of a couple of blackbirds the area would have been blessed by deep silence. Bert knew it would be dark in another half-hour but he needed to finish this job. The shadows from the trees on the far side of the park stretched across to his allotment, dappling the rich soil he was weeding, and the sky behind the trees was now changing from pale, robin's egg blue to apricot and orange, and the wisps of cloud were tinged with pink. It was a glorious evening.

Supporting himself using the handle of his hoe, Bert bent down and pulled on a long pale root that was as thick as a pencil. He felt resistance and moved his fingers along it to where it had buried itself even deeper in the ground. Carefully he teased it out of the earth and looked with satisfaction at the ten-inch length of bindweed root before he straightened up and tossed it onto the pile of weeds he was going to burn the next day. 'Bloody stuff,' he muttered. He knew he was fighting a losing battle with the bindweed that encroached on his patch but it didn't stop him from trying.

He remembered a lesson his primary school teacher had given his class years before. Must be over sixty years since, he thought. He could still recall the garish pictures she'd held up, showing the twelve labours of Hercules and the one of him hacking heads off a serpent. The trouble was, every time he lopped off one, two more grew back. Bert couldn't remember how Hercules had finally got the better of it but he knew how the Greek hero felt and frankly he could do with him right now to give a hand on his allotment with the bindweed. Maybe if he had that foreign chappy's super-human powers to help him, he might stand a chance.

Bert turned his face to the last of the sun's rays, feeling its warmth on his skin. He loved this time of year – so full of promise. And everything was coming along a treat, despite the blooming bindweed. He gazed at his neat, weed-free beds, at the rows of peas sprouting under their arch of pea-sticks, at the runner beans starting to curl around their bamboo wigwam, at his cabbages and caulis. Which reminded them, he must get the net over them soon to stop the cabbage whites from laying their eggs on them. A couple of years previously he'd been late with the netting and the little buggers had stripped a couple of complete plants. He was all for live and let live but drew the line at feeding the cater-pillars. He turned back to the sun, shielding his eyes and gazed at the ancient trees. Yes, they were definitely greening up.

Movement near their fat trunks caught his eye. There was a bloke hanging around over by the far fence. Bert peered across the grass. As he did so he saw another youth loping up the path wearing a hoodie. The other chap moved out of the shade and came to meet the lad. They both looked around. Furtive, thought Bert. That was it, they both looked furtive. Still, no business of his and why shouldn't two guys meet in a public space? Meeting a buddy wasn't against the law. But some instinct made Bert keep watching. The two were gesticulating. It looked, to all intents and purposes, like they were squaring up for a fight. There was a flash. A knife? Then one pushed the other and almost instantly put his hands up as if he was apologising. Things seemed to calm down. And then they shook hands – or maybe something changed hands – and then the guy who'd been hanging out under the tree jogged off, leaving the youth on his own.

Bert moved into the shadow of his shed. He wasn't sure what he'd just witnessed but he had a suspicion that the pair hadn't wanted an audience. Something hadn't been right. The other lad was leaving now… no, he wasn't. He came towards the skatepark, his head down, and sat on one of the ramps. Then Bert saw him roll a cigarette. He didn't blame him. Back when he'd been a smoker, back when fags had cost less than five bob a packet, he'd have probably wanted a smoke after a run-in like that. Then the lad turned and propped himself against the curve of one of the half-pipes and pushed his hood back. Zac. Did his mother know about the sort of company he kept? Or that he smoked? Bert suspected that she didn't.

Olivia was in bed and reading when Nigel came back. He dropped his sports bag on the bedroom floor and started to take off his tie.

'You're late.' She stifled a yawn.

'I told you, I played badminton.'

'I know but I didn't expect you to be quite as late as this.'

'We went for a swift half afterwards.' Nigel kicked off his shoes and lined them up under the stool on his side of the bed.

'That's nice. How did you get on?'

'Get on?'

'You said you had a match.'

'Oh – er, no, it was more of a friendly. A knock-up.'

'OK.'

Nigel switched on his bedside light and went to the en suite from where Olivia heard the buzz of the electric toothbrush. She switched off her light and rolled over under the duvet. He hadn't asked about her evening with the WI... *plus ça change*. He rarely seemed to take an interest in anything she did, she thought as she drifted off to sleep.

The next morning, after Nigel had gone to work, Olivia had a row with Zac about getting out of bed because, even though it was the Easter holidays, he had schoolwork to do and it wasn't healthy to lie about doing nothing all day. She'd won the row but now doubted if it had been worth the appalling atmosphere it had created before Zac had finally stormed off out. After he'd slammed the front door, with such force that the windows had rattled, she decided that it was time she found out the truth about the rumoured development on Coombe Farm for herself. Once again she got her bike out of the garage and headed for the town centre.

It was market day and instead of cars neatly parked in the bays on the town square the asphalt was covered with stalls selling everything from rucksacks to fish. The locals strolled between the stalls, stopping to chat with acquaintances – their conversations often interrupted by a stallholder yelling his wares. The sun was kept off the produce by candy-striped awnings and behind and beside the stands, empty fruit and veg boxes were piled high waiting for the refuse lorry to come and take them away. Olivia ignored the displays of tempting produce and chained her bike to the rack at the far end of the market, collected her handbag from the wicker basket and then strode purposefully into the town hall. She banged on the bell at the front desk to get the receptionist out of her office.

'Councillor Laithwaite,' said the receptionist. 'What can I do for you?'

'I want to see all the applications for planning consent, please, Cynthia.'

'All of them?'

Olivia blinked slowly and breathed deeply. 'No, just the most recent ones.'

'That's still a lot. Could you be more specific?'

'The one for Mr McGregor's farm – Coombe Farm.'

Cynthia looked puzzled. 'I don't think we've received anything for that. Of course it may not have come down to us from the district council yet. You do know applications go to district in the first instance?'

Olivia bit back a comment that as she'd been on the council for getting on for eight years she probably knew more about the planning process than most. 'I am aware of that but I'd like you to check, if it isn't too much trouble.'

Cynthia disappeared through a door in the corner. Olivia could hear her talking but couldn't quite overhear what was being said.

'No,' said the receptionist on her return. 'We've had nothing filed for that farm.'

'But there were surveyors seen there.'

'It doesn't mean we've been asked for planning consent.'

'Sorry to have bothered you,' said Olivia as she headed for the main door. Not that she meant it; after all, Cynthia was there to be bothered – that was her job.

She got back on her bike and headed out of the car park, down the road past the cricket pavilion, till she got to the ring road on the edge of town. It wasn't a ring road in the true sense of the word but it did provide a way of avoiding the town centre on market day when things could get very busy and there were actual traffic jams. The residents were encouraged to use it to take the strain off the town centre at peak periods, but not everyone did. Actually, in Olivia's eyes, it was the council estate residents who were the worst offenders for driving through the middle of the town to get to Cattebury and who cluttered up the high street in the rush hour. Olivia never bothered to consider that the residents at her end of town – the ones who commuted by train to the city – were just as guilty when they journeyed to the station. But obviously her neighbours were entitled to clutter up the main street, the council house occupants were not.

She rode past the cricket club, past the entrance to the church-yard and up to the roundabout where she took the left turn that led to McGregor's farm. She wanted to see the lie of the land for herself – literally. If Olivia was honest with herself she'd never really noticed the farm in any detail, beyond that it was there and that there were a number of broken down outbuildings and barns which were a total blot on the landscape and about which she'd always felt that something ought to be done. But whatever should be done should definitely *not* involve replacing them with a housing development, as Heather – if what Ted Burrows had told her was correct – thought might be going on.

Olivia pedalled a few hundred yards along the ring road and stopped opposite the farm. There was nothing to be seen that suggested the builders were about to move in but then there wouldn't be, would there, not without the approval of a planning application? A planning application which hadn't even been sub-mitted, apparently. Olivia got off her bike and crossed the road before flipping down the stand with her foot and parking it on the verge. She then leaned on a gate to the scrubby meadow and assessed the scene for herself.

It was obvious that the land wasn't much good as pasture. The grass, even to Olivia's untrained eye, looked to be of poor quality and it was thick with nettles and thistles. In one corner of the field there was a rusting pile of old farm equipment and in another were the crumbling remains of what might have been some old stables and a barn, both built from corrugated iron and breeze blocks. The whole place was an eyesore. Thank God, thought Olivia, that it was behind a thick hawthorn hedge and most passers-by, whizzing along the ring road, would be completely unaware of the lurking dereliction.

A voice behind her startled her so much she jumped.

'Oi, you. What you looking at?'

She spun round. 'Mr McGregor?'

'And who would you be, wanting to know? Peter Rabbit?' The old man, with appalling teeth, Olivia noticed, laughed at his own joke.

'I'm Councillor Olivia Laithwaite and I'm also on the committee of the Little Woodford Historical Association and the Chairman of the Friends of the Community Centre group.'

'Are 'e. And is that supposed to impress I?'

'Well no, but I've heard a rumour you might be developing this field.'

'Have 'e, now. And what business is it of yourn if I am?'

'There's regulations.'

'So?'

'Well, they're there to be obeyed.'

'An' who says I'm breaking 'em?'

'No one – not yet.'

'Then until that happens – which it won't – I suggest that you, Councillor Olivia Laithwaite, slings your hook.'

'Really!'

'Yes, really. Now git orf my land.'

'I'm on the footpath.'

'No, you ain't.' Mr McGregor took a step to the left. 'This is the footpath.'

Olivia sniffed. What an obnoxious and ill-mannered man he was. And if he thought that he was going to get away with any sort of building on this field it would be over her dead body.

'Git,' said McGregor more aggressively.

Olivia 'got'.

10

While Olivia was pedalling away from McGregor's farm, Brian Simmonds sat in his study, staring at a blank sheet of A4. He picked up a pen and doodled on it. Someone, somewhere, had said that doodling freed up the creative mind. Really? His was still as blank as the piece of paper – blanker now that the paper had a series of interlocking circles on it. With a sigh he put down the pen again and went into the kitchen to make a cup of tea.

Writing a sermon, he thought as he filled the kettle, should be a doddle at this time of year; Easter had just been and gone, spring was awash with new life, winter had been banished, life after death, hope eternal, regeneration... He shook his head; this was hopeless. He put the kettle down on the counter and a minute later he was walking down the path to the church. Maybe something would come to him there.

He let himself in through the vestry door and made his way to the choir stalls. He knelt and bowed his head but even as he did he felt awkward. He wanted to believe in God, he wanted to connect to Him through prayer, but he felt that, even by doing something as habitual as reciting the Lord's Prayer which was as much a part of his life as breathing was, he was a fake, a fraud, a hypocrite. Before, he'd always felt as if there was a presence with him, like he always knew when Heather was in the house, even if they were in separate rooms. But now... nothing. A void, a silence. It was like he was being shunned. Blanked. Did that mean that God was testing his faith, or – and this was almost unthinkable and yet he thought it all the same – or, did this mean this was the new reality? That there was no God? He kept telling himself everyone had doubts occasionally. But the more he tried to battle onwards the harder it was becoming.

There was a clatter from the vestry which startled him. He hauled himself to his feet. He saw Joan coming into the body of the church pushing a vacuum cleaner.

'Hello, Reverend.'

'Hello, Joan.'

'Thought I'd give the carpet by the altar a going over. I thought it needed doing when I was down here doing the flowers last week.'

'Thank you.'

'But if you'd rather I didn't disturb you...'

'No, no, you go ahead.' Brian smiled at her and began to make his way back to the vestry. As he turned he heard Joan gasp. He swung back. She was clutching the altar rail as a spasm of pain crossed her face.

'Joan, what on earth is it? Are you all right?'

Joan screwed up her eyes and nodded. After a few seconds she managed to gasp, 'I'm fine. Don't worry about me.'

'You don't look fine.'

'Just a touch of heartburn. Honest.'

'Here.' Brian went over to her, took her arm and led her to one of the choir stalls and sat her down. Her top lip had a sheen of sweat on it and her mouth was set in a tight line.

'I'll be right as ninepence in a minute.'

'If you say so.' Brian sat down beside her. 'I'll get the car and run you home.'

She shook her head. 'You'll do nothing of the sort, Reverend. Just give me a minute to catch my breath.'

The pair sat in silence for a minute or two then Joan sighed. 'Phew,' she said. 'Glad that's over.'

'Heartburn?' said Brian, his disbelief obvious.

'Yes,' said Joan, firmly. 'And I don't want you mentioning this to Bert.' She skewered him with a hard stare.

'If that's what you want.'

'I do.'

'Is that fair on Bert?'

'What the eye don't see…'

'I suppose.' Brian thought about what he was keeping from Heather. 'I suppose we all sometimes keep quiet, keep things from our loved ones, to protect them from stuff that might worry them.'

'Heartburn ain't nothing to worry about.'

'No, *heartburn* isn't…' Brian left the implication to hang in the air. 'Have you seen Dr Connolly?'

'Not worth going to bother him with it.'

'Really?'

Joan stood up. 'Yes, really.' She took the flex off the hook on the back of the hoover and began to uncoil it. 'Anyway, what are you keeping from Heather?'

Brian glanced up. He'd forgotten how sharp she was, despite her advanced years. 'Oh, nothing. No, I didn't mean me.'

'Really?'

The pair exchanged a look, neither believing the other.

'Whatever you say, Reverend. But if you want someone to talk about it to…'

'And the same goes for you,' said Brian.

'Yeah, well.' Joan walked over to a socket hidden behind one of the pillars and plugged in the vacuum. 'I'll think about it.' She switched on the machine.

Later that day, Bex was busy unpacking, folding, putting away, hanging up, sorting, arranging and tidying and generally getting the house straight.

'Mum, Mum, have you found Dougie the Digger yet?' Alfie tugged on Bex's cardigan to make sure she paid him attention.

'Not yet, sweetie.'

'But you promised.' Alfie's lip trembled.

Bex put down the stack of books she'd heaved out of a box and knelt on the floor beside her son.

'I promised I'd find it, and I will.'

'Then why haven't you?'

Bex gestured to the stacks of boxes that still had to be tackled. 'If I knew which box it was in I'd get it for you straight away, but I don't.'

'But I want to play with it *now*.'

Bex began to feel her patience waning. 'You'll have to play with something else. You've lots of toys in your room.'

'I don't want to play with anything else. I want Dougie.' Alfie stamped his foot.

Bex sighed and went to the door of the sitting room. 'Megan. *Megan!*'

Her voice echoed down the stairs from the landing. 'What? I'm sorting out the airing cupboard.'

'I know, love, but...'

'Hang on...' Megan looked down over the banisters.

Bex lowered her voice by a decibel or two. 'I know but I just wondered if you've any idea where Alfie's digger is?'

'You're kidding me, right?'

Bex shook her head. 'Alfie so wants to play with it.'

'God, Bex, he's got a room full of toys.'

'I know but...'

Alfie wandered out of the sitting room, tears rolling down his face.

'How about if I take him to see the real diggers up at the building site behind the station.'

'Yeah!' said Alfie. 'Diggers.'

'Do you mind?'

'No, besides I'm totally fed up with sorting out sheets and pillow cases.'

'Do you mind taking Lewis as well?'

'Not really. We might go on to the play park.'

'Why don't you. The weather's not too bad although the forecast was for rain later. You might as well make the most of it.'

Once the children had gone out the house went very quiet. Bex carried on emptying boxes, finding places to put things, until she suddenly ran out of energy. She went into the kitchen to make a cup of tea and have a biscuit or two – she felt in desperate need of a sugar rush. Bugger – the tin was empty. So the choice was simple; go without or pop up the road to the little Co-op and buy a packet or two. But even as she looked at her options she knew what she ought to do because the boys wouldn't be best pleased if they came back from the play park tired and hungry and there wasn't anything to nibble on.

She threw a jacket on, grabbed her handbag and a carrier bag and walked the two hundred yards to the shop. The automatic doors swished open as she stepped up to them and she gazed around at the little supermarket, wondering where the biscuits might be kept.

'Hello. It's Bex, isn't it?'

She turned. The vicar's wife. 'Hiya,' she said cheerily.

'Lovely to run into you. How's it going?'

'Still chaos.'

'I'm going to have to try and persuade you to give the WI a try, you know.'

Bex raised her eyebrows.

'Seriously, last night's talk was a hoot. It was all about Victorian underwear. God, the things women had to put up with in those days in the name of fashion, it makes me so glad I live in the here and now. The "good old days"? Tosh!'

'It sounds as if it was interesting.'

'Absolutely fascinating. Maybe next time.'

'Maybe. Olivia's promised to fix me up with a babysitter – someone called Amy – but, however much Olivia recommends her, I can't possibly leave my kids with a stranger.'

'I can see that. But I can assure you that Amy is lovely. She cleans for me.'

'I'm sure she's great, but you must see it from my perspective.'

'I do, totally. I'll have to arrange for you to meet her sometime; that is, if you'd like a babysitter.'

'I think once we've settled here I could probably trust Megan to do it for me, but while everything is new and strange...'

'Yes, of course.'

'Anyway, I must get on. We've run out of biscuits and I need to have some for when Megan and the boys get back from their walk.'

'Just one thing...' Heather put her hand on Bex's arm. 'Don't dismiss joining in with things here just because Olivia might have been a bit heavy-handed.' She smiled. 'I know *exactly* what she can be like. But maybe, in a week or two, you might like to give the book club a whirl? That meets in the pub too – so handy for you to pop home if you felt you needed to.'

'Maybe. I'll think about it.'

Amy was walking through town when she saw the blonde woman turn into The Beeches. The new occupant; the woman she'd seen get out of the car earlier in the Easter holidays. She dithered with the idea of running after her and asking for her old job back but that smacked of being a bit desperate. Best leave it a bit longer, she told herself, although, by heck, she could do with the extra cash.

'Ames!'

She spun round. She saw a lanky, thirty-something in grubby jeans and a T-shirt, no jacket despite the brisk breeze, and carefully slicked-back hair strolling towards her. 'Billy. What you doing here? Shouldn't you be at work?' Billy Rogers worked as a mechanic for the local car dealership. Amy always reckoned that if she could ever afford a car he'd not only be able to lay his hands on a good one for her but he'd probably get it for her cheap *and* he'd know how to look after it for her. It was worth putting up with his filthy fingernails for that.

Billy stuck his hands in his jeans pockets. He bent down and dropped a kiss on her neck. 'Nah, day off.'

'Jammy bugger,' said Amy. 'Can't remember the last time I had a day off.'

'What you doing this evening?'

'Dunno. Watching the telly with my Ash, more than likely.'

'Fancy going out for a drink?'

Amy shook her head. 'Course I fancy doing that – trouble is, going out costs and I'm skint. Staying in is much cheaper.'

'My treat.' Billy pulled a roll of twenties out of his jeans pocket.

'Bloody hell, Bill. Where'd you get that from?'

'Bit of freelance work.' Billy tapped the side of his nose.

'Doesn't your boss mind?'

Billy leaned closer to Amy. 'My boss doesn't know. More to the point, neither does the tax man. And it's going to stay that way.' He gave Amy a knowing nod. 'Savvy? No blabbing it around town that I make extra cash on the side.'

'As if I would,' said Amy, pained. Besides, other than the post office job, which didn't give her the option, she was a cash-in-hand worker too. No point in giving away your earnings to the government if you didn't have to, was how she looked at it.

'Good. So, meet me in the Talbot at eight?'

'It's a date.'

Joan leaned against the counter in her kitchen as she felt the pain in her chest start to blossom. Not again, she thought. Her desire for a nice cuppa swept away by the stabbing, burning sensation, she staggered back into the sitting room and flopped onto the sofa, thankful that Bert was out at his allotment. She kept telling herself, like she had told the vicar, that it was heartburn, but what if it wasn't? What if it was something more serious? She hadn't been quite right since the winter when she'd had that horrible bug. And yet she was terrified of going to see Dr Connolly in case her worst fears were confirmed. And what if he sent her to hospital? Who would look after Bert? He barely knew how to make a cup of tea, let alone feed himself properly. He'd gone straight from living with his mum, to National Service where he'd met her in the NAAFI canteen in the barracks. As far as Joan knew, Bert had never cooked a meal for himself in his life. The rising feeling of panic didn't help matters and she found herself getting short of breath. Joan shut her eyes and concentrated on drawing air, as steadily as she could, into her lungs. In... out... in... out...

She began to feel better. The clammy sweat, brought on by the pain, dissipated and she pulled a hanky from her sleeve and mopped her brow.

She heard the click of Bert's key in the lock.

'Just getting me boots off,' he called through from the porch.

Galvanised, Joan hauled herself off the sofa and shot across the hall and shut herself in the loo. She wanted another couple of minutes to get herself properly under control before she faced him. The last thing she wanted was for him to worry about her. And anyway, it was probably nothing; nothing that time wouldn't sort.

'I'm off out, Ash, love,' Amy called up the stairs.

'Where are you going?' he shouted back.

'Just the pub. I'm meeting Billy.'

'OK, have a nice time.'

Amy did up her mac as she headed out the front door and snapped up her umbrella before she got to the pavement. It was nice to be going out for a change. She tramped along the wet pavements, cars swishing past, splashing her occasionally, while she, once again, wished she could afford one. Then she switched her thoughts to Billy – was he a keeper? She began to add up the things she liked about him; he always had money, which was a real plus. He got on all right with Ash – or, at least, they didn't hate each other. He had a steady job. And he was OK in bed. Oh, and he took an interest in her; he was always asking her about her day, about her ladies, getting her to tell him about the swanky houses she looked after. And the negatives…? He ought to do something about his fingernails but then he was a mechanic so she supposed all his workmates were the same. But if he didn't worry about his nails he was bonkers about his hair. He was always whipping out a comb and faffing with it, like he was the Fonz. But neither of those two things were deal-breakers. No, so… if he popped the question one day, she wouldn't say no. Mulling over the possible shape of her future and the bloke she wouldn't mind sharing it with got her to the door of the pub. She collapsed her umbrella and shook the worst of the rain off it before she opened the door to the smell of beer and the sound of people chatting.

'Wotcha,' said Billy from a table near the door. 'Got you a white wine in.'

As Amy slipped her wet coat off she bent forward to kiss him.

'Oi, you're getting me wet.'

'Sorry, babes.' She hung it on a hook nearby then sat down and picked up her glass. 'Cheers.'

'Tell me about your day.'

'I cleaned for the doctor's wife today.'

'Her with the dead kid.'

'That's right. Won't let me touch her room. There's something not right there, if you ask me…'

'Go on.'

So Amy did, once again telling Billy everything she knew about what it was like behind the front doors of the posh houses in the town.

It was almost closing time when the pair left the pub.

'I'll walk you home, Ames,' said Billy. He put his hand under her elbow as she swayed rather alarmingly on the edge of the kerb.

'I'm fine,' she protested. 'Jusht a bit tipshy, thatsh all.' She giggled.

'Pissed as a fart, more like,' muttered Billy. He led the way along the high street and Amy stumbled, tripped and cannoned off street furniture till they got to her house.

'Where's your keys, love?' said Billy as he propped her against the wall.

'In my bag,' she slurred. She started to rummage. 'Here they are.' She handed over a bunch to Billy.

'So which one is it?'

Amy squinted at the keys, trying to get her eyes to focus. 'Oopsh, not those. Those are the keys to my ladies' houses. Silly me.' She hiccupped. She had another look in her bag and produced a second bunch with a flourish. 'Here we are.' She picked out a brass Yale key and tried to get it in the lock but each thrust at the keyhole was wide of the mark.

'What are you like,' said Billy with a sigh. He took the key and had the door open in a second.

Amy stumbled in over the doorstep and Billy assessed the stairs and Amy's condition. He put one arm around her waist and put her right arm over his shoulder and half-dragging, half-carrying her he got her up to her room where he laid her on her bed.

'You going to be all right?'

But Amy was already out for the count.

Olivia was sitting at the kitchen table making a shopping list when the doorbell went. She put down her pencil and went to answer the door. Amy was standing on the doorstep wearing a pair of dark glasses.

'Amy? Where are your keys?'

'Dunno, Mrs L. They'll be at home somewhere. I didn't realise I didn't have them till I got here.' Amy stepped over the threshold and took her sunglasses off.

Olivia peered more closely at her cleaner. 'Are you all right?'

'Not really. Woke up this morning with a banging headache. Can't think why.'

'I'm sorry to hear that. I hope you're not going down with something.'

'You and me both. Think it might have been something I ate.'

'Do want to leave it for today then?'

Any shook her head and then winced. 'Not really. I can't afford the hit, money-wise.'

'No, no, I quite understand. Well, don't overdo it.'

'I'll be fine. I'll just take it slowly. I could murder a cuppa though.'

'Of course.'

'With some sugar in it?' Amy added, hopefully.

'OK.' Olivia led the way to the kitchen and reckoned that, if she was any sort of judge, Amy's headache hadn't been brought on by something she'd eaten but something she'd drunk – and quite a lot of that *something* if Amy's bloodshot eyes were anything to go by. Well, why shouldn't she? It wasn't as if it was the norm and she was a hard worker and why shouldn't she let her hair down now and again?

11

The next week brought the end of the school holidays. On the first day of the summer term, Megan awoke with her alarm and stared up at the skylight, watching the rain pattering onto the glass. Grey, lowering clouds scudded past and the beech trees that gave the house its name were thrashing about like the Hogwarts' Whomping Willow. School, she thought, and a feeling of dread swamped her. Would she fit in? Would she make friends? Would she be accepted? She threw back her duvet, swung her legs out of bed and made her way into the shower. Even a long soak failed to allay her anxieties or lift her spirits. She wandered back into her bedroom and opened her wardrobe door. Megan picked out her new uniform; bottle green sweatshirt, grey skirt – although she could wear trousers if she preferred – and a pastel green shirt. It was, she thought, completely repulsive – especially the shirt. Whoever thought that particular shade of pale green was attractive needed shooting. Her old school uniform had been nothing to write home about but no one could get upset about navy and white. Megan took the pistachio-coloured shirt out of the wardrobe and held it under her chin. Even with her strikingly dark hair and eyes and her faintly olive skin, she looked washed out. God only knew what it would do to kids who had a naturally pale complexion to start with. She threw it on, brushed her hair and ran downstairs to grab some breakfast.

'Morning, sweetie,' said Bex, who was loading the boys' break-fast plates into the dishwasher. 'All ready for school?'

'Kind of,' mumbled Megan into her cereal bowl.

'It'll be fine,' said Bex. 'And it's all local kids. You'll have a whole bunch of new friends in no time.'

'Maybe.'

'What about your old ones? Heard much from them?'

Megan looked at Bex. Did she tell the truth – that she'd posted on Facebook and Instagram about the new house and her new town and she hadn't had a single 'like'? Not one. It was like she was diseased or didn't exist. She decided to tell a half-truth.

'Not a lot. They were probably all busy – you know, holidays and stuff.' She hoped she sounded like she didn't care, that it was normal.

Bex stopped stacking the machine and stood up. She laid a hand on Megan's arm. 'Away for the holidays – and with no Wi-Fi? At all? Any of them? If they're going to be like that, you're better off without them. Fair-weather friends are no friends at all.'

Megan wasn't convinced but she smiled at Bex anyway. 'Maybe.'

'Trust me, this is for the best. A fresh start where no one knows about…'

'About all the shit that happened back in London? No, I won't be telling anyone about that.'

'Exactly. And I'm really sorry I can't come with you for your first day.'

'Bex, we've been through this. My school's at one end of town and the boys' is at the other. I'm fifteen, I can get there on my own.'

'I know…'

'Anyway, it'll look lame if I have to have a grown-up to hold my hand.'

Bex laughed. 'Yes, it would – but even so…'

'I'll be fine,' said Megan with completely faked confidence.

'Have you got everything?'

Megan nodded and pushed back her fringe. 'Yes.' She glanced up at the kitchen clock. 'I'm off. I'll see you later.'

'Good luck.'

'Yeah, whatevs.' In a display of bravado that she didn't feel, Megan swung her backpack over her shoulder and sauntered out of the kitchen. Inside she was bricking it but it would be so uncool to show it. She grabbed her school blazer off the peg on the wall before opening the front door – God, it was still pissing down. She got herself sorted out with her jacket and rucksack, then slammed the door shut before running down the drive to the gate. She put her brolly up before she stepped out to cross the road. The imperious *dring-dring* of a bike bell made her skid to a halt.

'Careful,' yelled a woman as she swerved to avoid hitting Megan. The cyclist stopped. It was that posh woman who had visited. Megan couldn't remember her name.

'Sorry,' said Megan.

'You must be more careful. You nearly caused an accident.'

'Yes... sorry...'

'It's Megan, isn't it?'

Megan nodded.

'Off to school?'

Megan was tempted to respond that she was going sunbathing but thought better of it. 'Yes.'

'Have a good day, then. I hope you enjoy it.' The woman pedalled off.

'I won't,' she muttered. Checking more carefully for traffic and waiting till the road was clear, Megan ran across.

She walked up the high street. Ahead of her she could see small groups of schoolchildren going in the same direction as her. Like migrating animals, she thought. Or lemmings heading for their doom. Everyone seemed to be walking in a group or a pair. She was, as far as she could see, the only loner. She tried not to care but her sense of isolation and vulnerability increased. She went past the coffee shop, past the town hall, past the station, the play park and, as she did, more and more kids poured out of side roads and turnings to join the tide heading for the comp.

'Hiya.'

Megan jumped and turned. 'Ash!' Her heart raced.

'Thought it was you,' he said cheerfully. 'Looking forward to it? First day and all that.'

Megan shrugged. 'Kind of.'

'So, whose tutor group are you in, do you know?'

'The school wrote and said I'd be in Mrs Blake's.'

'Mrs Blake's? But that's great. So am I.'

Megan felt her face flushing with happiness. She looked at the pavement, hoping Ashley didn't guess how she felt. 'What's she like?' She moved her umbrella sideways so it sheltered Ashley too.

'Could be worse. Actually, she's all right – she teaches humanities. She has her favourites but then which teacher doesn't? She's better than old man Johnson who teaches maths. He's a proper bastard.'

Megan's heart sank. She was OK at maths but that was all. 'He sounds great,' she said with heavy sarcasm.

'He's got a temper on him. Hands out detentions for the least thing, gets really grumpy about almost anything and has zero sense of humour. I'm lucky – I don't have a problem with maths so he and I get on but for some of the others...' Ashley grimaced.

Megan swallowed. Oh whoopee. Besides, if she was honest, she didn't see the point of maths, not when her phone had a calculator.

'Nearly there,' said Ashley cheerfully as they turned off the main road. Ahead was the sign that advertised the entrance to the comp. 'You all right?'

She was terrified. 'I'm fine.'

'Do you want me to show you the way?'

'Yeah.' She swallowed. 'Yeah, that'd be good.'

'You don't want to look like a numpty on your first day.' Ashley wasn't wrong there.

She swallowed and gave him a weak smile. 'No. Not if I can help it. I only need to get to reception. I've been told Mrs Blake'll meet me there.'

They headed through the main gate and along the drive. On one side was the staff car park and on the other, a sports pitch. Megan tried to control her breathing but she was feeling increasingly panicky. She wondered if she looked as scared as she felt. Ashley squeezed her arm. Startled, she glanced at him.

'You'll be fine. Promise. I'll stay with you till Mrs Blake arrives.'

Under normal circumstances Megan might have protested that she could manage but today was far from normal.

'Thank you,' she whispered, feeling suddenly teary.

'This way,' he said.

Megan trotted along at his side as he strode confidently along the footpath that led beside a modern steel and concrete block towards an older building. It was comforting to have Ashley alongside her; especially as he seemed one of the popular kids at school to judge by the number of pupils they passed who greeted him. Being associated with one of the cool kids couldn't do any harm, thought Megan. She began to relax slightly.

They reached the main school door and Ashley, in an old-fashioned gesture of chivalry, opened it for Megan.

'Ladies first,' he said with a grin.

She stopped on the doormat, shut her brolly and shook the worst of the drips off it.

Once again, under more normal circumstances, Megan might have made a pithy come-back but not today.

She entered the airy, tiled space of the school reception area with its harsh lighting, honour boards around the walls naming head prefects, the group photos and the noticeboards detailing achievements by various extra-curricular groups, like the school sports teams. It was, thought Megan, much like her old school. Probably much like any school. It was just a case of fitting in.

'Megan?' A voice of authority brought her back to the present.

'Yes.' Her voice came out in a squeak.

'Thank you, Ashley. I'll look after Megan now.'

'Gotta go,' said Ashley and with a cursory wave he disappeared down a corridor.

Megan felt suddenly abandoned but she hid it with a smile to her new tutor. 'Good morning, Mrs Blake.'

There was no welcoming smile in return. 'Morning, Megan. Lovely to meet you. You had a nice Easter holiday, I trust.'

'We moved house…' She shrugged. 'Bex, my stepmum, was a bit busy.'

'Ah yes.' Mrs Blake looked a bit discomfited. Megan reckoned she'd just remembered about her dad being dead. 'Yes, of course.' There was a pause of a couple of seconds and then she continued. 'But this is a new start for you, a clean break, a time to move forward. It's not good to dwell on the past.'

'I suppose.' Megan stared at her new tutor. Was she telling Megan to forget about her dad? She took an instant dislike to her but knew that she'd have to mask it. Now was not the time to make an enemy and certainly not with her new tutor.

'Now then…' Mrs Blake produced a file and handed it over to Megan. 'This contains your timetable and a map of the school but I have assigned one of the girls in the tutor group to look after you till you find your feet. Of course, you can always come to me for anything and I'm sure you'll be settled in before we can say "Jack Robinson".' Mrs Blake smiled at her, except it was lacking in warmth. Megan was reminded of a dog baring its teeth.

She forced a smile back.

'Now then, shall we go to our tutor room?'

Megan wondered what would happen if she said that she'd rather not. She followed Mrs Blake down a corridor, up a flight of stairs and into a light, airy classroom with walls covered in maps and handmade posters and artwork about food resources – cocoa, coffee, bananas and the like. In the classroom there were also around thirty pupils dressed identically to herself, all talking, laughing, sitting on desks and chairs and all, with the exception of Ashley, strangers to Megan.

Mrs Blake stood in the doorway and clapped her hands. 'Everyone, this is Megan. Megan has joined us from London and is completely new to the area.'

'Bully for her,' muttered a girl's voice from the back of the class.

'I know you'll all make her feel welcome.' Mrs Blake looked around the classroom. 'Lily?' A hand went up at the back of the class – from the spot where the snide aside had come from. 'Ah, Lily. Come and say hello to Megan.'

Lily stood up – all endless legs and wavy brown hair. Megan noticed, with a deep stab of envy, that she was a natural beauty, with hazel eyes and long, long lashes; Bambi in human form. She even made the dire school uniform look elegant.

'Hi,' she drawled as she approached Megan and looked down her neat retroussé nose at her. 'I'm supposed to make you feel at home.'

Behind her, her friends tittered and Lily turned towards them, swapping her sneer for a smile, revealing a dimple.

Megan didn't like the use of the word 'supposed'.

'There's no "supposed" about it,' said Mrs Blake, briskly. 'I'm sure you'll do a lovely job, Lily.'

But Megan really wasn't so sure. She glanced at Ashley for support but he was in the middle of a group of lads who seemed to be enthralled by something on an iPhone.

Mrs Blake followed Megan's look.

'Phones away, boys. You know the rules.'

There was a shuffling and scuffling in the boys' corner as they obeyed but still Ashley didn't make eye contact. Megan tried not to care. Maybe, even out here in the sticks, it wasn't cool to own up to knowing the new kid.

Mrs Blake told everyone to sit down and Megan found an empty seat – one right at the front that no one else wanted – the register was taken and then the bell went for first period. Chairs were scraped back, the pupils grabbed their bags, the noise level took off again and Megan felt another churn of panic as she didn't know what she was supposed to be doing or where she was supposed to go. She looked around for Lily but Lily was already on her way out of the classroom and Ashley hadn't waited for her either. Megan grabbed her bag, coat and file and legged it after her. As she scooted along, she tried to read the timetable in the file – maths, J4, it said. Megan didn't have a clue what that meant. Finally, the surge of pupils stopped and lined up outside another classroom. Over the door it said J4. At least she was in the right place at the right time, she thought with relief.

A teacher appeared and the queue fell silent. He unlocked the door and the class filed in. Once again Megan found herself forced to the front.

'A new girl,' said the teacher looking directly at her.

'Yes, sir.'

'Name?'

'Megan Millar.'

She heard soft laughter behind her. Then some wag whispered, 'I bet she's *windy*.' Louder laughter followed. Megan felt her face flush.

'Silence!' It worked. 'Right, let's get on. Good morning, class.'

'Good morning, Mr Johnson,' chorused the pupils.

Oh, gawd, thought Megan. The teacher with the short temper and the intolerance for maths dunces. Just perfect. Just sodding perfect.

'Oi! Oi, Ames.'

Amy, hurrying on her way to the post office to work her morning shift there, stopped in the street and turned. Oh, Billy. 'Hiya, stranger. Thought you might be blanking me – you know, after last week…'

'Gawd, Amy, you didn't half put it away.'

'I didn't have that much. I'm not used to it, that's all.'

'Not like the doctor's wife, eh? What did you say… four bottles of vodka a week in her recycling?'

'Shhh. I didn't tell you that, did I?'

'Shit-a-brick, Ames, it was more a case of what you *didn't* tell me.'

Amy felt her face flare. 'You're not to go repeating any of it.' Even as she said it she knew it was a massive case of pots and kettles.

'How were you the next day?' asked Billy.

'Not too clever. I was sick twice before I got out the front door.'

'You never went to work, not after that?'

'No choice, Bill. Ash and I aren't flush like you.'

'No, well. Anyway, I got something for you.'

'What.'

Billy put his hand in his pocket and pulled out a bunch of keys.

'My keys! Where did you find them? I've searched high and low for them. I even asked at the pub in case I'd dropped them there.'

'You gave them to me to hold when you were trying to get in the other evening. I must have stuffed them in a pocket when I dragged you upstairs.'

'You did that?'

'Ames, there was no way you'd have got up them stairs on your own. Don't you remember?'

But Amy had already realised there was quite a chunk of her evening out which was a total blank. 'Not really, no.'

'Anyway, when I came across them, I realised they were yours, so... here they are.' Billy handed them over with a flourish.

Amy stood on tiptoe and gave Billy a fat kiss on his cheek. 'You're a lifesaver.' She gave him a wink. 'Big treats for you, Billy-boy, next time my Ash is out for the evening.'

'I'll hold you to that, doll.' Billy rubbed his crotch before he sauntered off with an even bigger swagger than usual.

12

Although she'd only been back working at the school for a week, Heather was already feeling as though there weren't enough hours in the day. She'd almost got on top of everything over the Easter holidays but now things seemed to be sliding out of control once again. She was finishing washing up the breakfast things when the doorbell rang. She chucked the dishcloth back into the sink and dried her hands on a tea towel. She glanced at the kitchen clock and sincerely hoped this was someone for Brian and not her because she had a mass of stuff to do before she headed up to the school where she was due to work that afternoon.

'Oh… Bex,' she said as she opened the door.

'Sorry to bother you. Is this a good time?'

'Of course,' lied Heather, thinking of the yet-to-be-made beds upstairs, and the minutes of the church restoration fund meeting that had to be typed up, to say nothing of proofreading the parish newsletter. 'Come in.' She opened the door wide. 'Tea? Coffee?'

'Well, if you're sure… tea would be lovely. I've got the day to myself now the kids have gone back and I thought I needed to stop sorting out the house and start sorting out other stuff.'

'Good plan.' Heather led the way into the kitchen. 'As you can see, a far cry from your lovely house.'

'Nice view, though.' Bex stood by the window and looked down the garden to the stunning house at the other end of it.

'That's the old vicarage.'

'Oh. It's probably a nightmare to heat.'

Heather laughed wryly. 'That's what I tell myself.' She filled the kettle with water and plugged it in. 'So, what can I do for you?'

'Amy.'

'Amy?'

'You said she cleans for you.'

'Yup, that's right.'

'Do you think she'd be able to take me on too?'

'She's pretty busy but she used to clean for the previous owners of your house and when they moved I don't think she got another job to fill the gap. Assuming that I'm right, I think she'd jump at the chance.'

'Really?'

'Mind you, if you've got any skeletons in the cupboard—' Heather put her hand over her mouth. 'Oh, damn – I didn't mean...'

Bex shook her head. 'I know what you mean and it's fine. Truly.'

'Even so.' Heather shook her head in disbelief at what she'd said.

'You were saying...' prompted Bex.

'Oh yes... Amy isn't the discreetest of souls. Actually, that's far too much of an understatement. Amy is the town radio – she broadcasts everything. She's an ace cleaner but never, *ever* tell her anything in confidence because it'll be round Little Woodford in a heartbeat.'

'Thanks for the tip.'

The kettle clicked off and Heather made the tea by mashing the tea bags in a couple of mugs.

'And what's the best way to get hold of her?' asked Bex.

'As it's Tuesday she'll be doing a morning shift in the post office so you could catch her there.' Heather looked vaguely around the kitchen. 'I've got her mobile number somewhere but...'

'Why don't I go to the post office – it'll save you having to hunt around.'

'OK.' Heather got the milk out and sloshed some in before passing Bex her drink. 'How are you settling in?'

'Getting there. I felt quite teary when I left little Alfie in the playground last week. It's his first term of going all day. They grow up so fast.'

Heather nodded. 'They do indeed. I can hardly believe that my two are almost thirty. I've no idea where the years went.'

'Exactly, but I have to admit that, much as I love the holidays and having them around, it is going to be easier to finish getting straight without two small boys underfoot.'

'I can imagine.'

Bex sipped her tea. 'With all this free time on my hands I'm thinking about finding a job. I can't sit at home all day, I'll go spare.'

'What did you do before?'

'I was a nanny.'

'How lovely. Well, I am sure there's a call for a properly quali-fied childminder around here. All the young mums seem to have to go back to work these days so they can afford the mortgage. Mind you, given the price of houses in the area we have fewer and fewer young families around here – you might find you'll have to travel over to Cattebury to get regular work.'

'To be honest, I only want something part-time, something to fill a few hours while the kids are at school. Maybe shop work or something. I haven't really thought, I just know I need to do *something*. Something that'll get me out of the house, something that won't be stressful, something that'll mean I meet people, talk to people. I can't type and I can't do accounts or anything like that, so I'm quite limited.'

'But surely you don't need a job.' Heather thought about what Bex's house had cost.

'No.' Bex looked a tiny bit embarrassed. 'No, I don't, but I think it would set a good example to the kids if they see me go to work every day. Although I worry that I might be taking a job from someone who might need it more.'

'I think,' said Heather, 'the people around here who want to work have got jobs, and the ones who are happy to live on benefits won't be persuaded otherwise.'

'I don't want people to think I'm being greedy or anything.'

'I very much doubt that.'

'Good.'

'Then I suggest that, when you're talking to Amy, you ought to ask her if anyone needs staff. There's very little that goes on in Little Woodford that she doesn't know about.'

'I'll do that, thank you.'

Fifteen minutes later Bex bade farewell from Heather Simmonds and headed up the road, past the cricket club and into the town. She hurried along the high street, head down against the bitter, damp spring wind that battered the hanging baskets and made the daffs in the tubs thrash around miserably. For the tail-end of April it was rotten weather and if it wasn't for the spring flowers that brightened up the high street it could almost be January. It was with relief she pushed open the door into the warmth of the post office. She joined the end of the queue that snaked away from the counter. There was only one position open and it seemed to Bex that everyone in Little Woodford was either collecting their pension, or, if too young for that, sending a zillions things back to mail-order companies – all of which needed proof of posting. She waited patiently for her turn as a young blonde woman with a round face and a dimply smile dispensed cash, stamps and chit-chat. Less chit-chat, thought Bex, would make the queue move a lot faster but nobody else seemed to mind so she waited patiently and tried not to lose the will to live. Finally it was her turn. She approached the counter.

'Yes?' the blonde said.

'Would you be Amy?'

'Might be. Why?'

'Heather Simmonds says you might be available to do a spot of cleaning.'

'Mrs S said that, did she?'

Bex nodded. She could sense the queue behind her getting impatient. Chit-chat was obviously OK if one was actually doing a transaction at the counter – and she wasn't. She could almost hear the tutting.

'Look, this isn't the best place to talk and you're busy. Could you come to The Beeches sometime?'

'Of course. I finish here at twelve thirty. Will you be in then?'

Bex nodded.

'See you then. Next!'

Bex left the post office rather wishing that everything in life could be as simple and as satisfactory as her morning had just been.

Lily sat at a table at the edge of the school canteen with her best friend, Summer. The two girls were like chalk and cheese: Lily, tall, elegant, beautiful and gazelle-like; and Summer, blonde, overweight and pasty-faced. On the plus-side, Summer's dad was minted and she had a pony and her house boasted a swimming pool. Lily stared moodily across the room to where Megan sat with a group of other girls.

'I don't see why they're all sucking up to her,' she said as she picked some of the crust off her chicken salad baguette and nibbled it.

'It's cos she's new.'

Lily stared at Summer and sighed. 'No shit, Sherlock.'

'Don't take it out on me – just because you're jealous.'

'Me? Jealous? I'm not jealous – let's face it, I'm form captain.' Lily's voice went up half an octave. 'Besides, you only have to look at her to know she's some sort of foreign freak. I'm surprised she can even speak English. I wonder where she comes from.'

'London,' said Summer.

Lily rolled her eyes. 'I mean, *really* comes from, you moron.' She ate some more of her baguette. 'And why's she changed schools at Easter, that's what I want to know? Don't kids normally move in the summer?'

Summer shrugged. 'I dunno. Maybe her dad changed jobs or they've moved here to be nearer relations or... I dunno, Lily. Does it matter?'

Lily put her baguette down on her plate. 'Of course it matters. She's swanked into *our* school and she's taking *my* friends and I'm not having it.'

'What you going to do, Lil?'

'Not sure yet.' Lily tossed her long brown hair over her shoulder. 'But I'll think of something.'

Amy felt pretty chipper when she handed over her shift at the post office and set off for The Beeches, hoping against hope that nothing would go wrong with this interview. Getting her old job back would help her finances out a fair bit. Besides, she hated taking handouts from her mum.

The short walk along the high street only took her a couple of minutes and it wasn't long before she was ringing the bell. She hoped this wouldn't take too long as she needed to be at Mrs Laithwaite's place later. She'd sent a text through to warn her she might be a few minutes late but she didn't want to push her luck.

'Hello,' she said as the door opened.

'Amy. How nice. Come in, come in. I've just put the kettle on. Would you like a cuppa?'

Amy glanced at her watch. 'A quick one would be lovely. Got to be somewhere else in thirty minutes.'

Her new boss led her into the kitchen. Amy looked at the new arrangement of furniture, the unfamiliar china and glasses in the glass-fronted units.

'This is nice. And you're almost straight.'

'Well, we've been here almost three weeks now. It's those last bits that seem to be the hardest to sort out. But we're getting there. I'm Bex, Bex Millar.'

Bex stuck out her hand and Amy shook it. 'Nice to meet you.' Bex took two mugs out of the cupboard. 'Is builders' tea OK?'

'Lovely. And just milk, thanks. So, best we get the business done first; I can do Monday afternoon or Friday morning. Three hours at a time. I'll get here about nine for a morning or one if it's an afternoon.'

'That sounds perfect and could you do both?' The kettle clicked off and Bex sloshed the water into the mugs.

'Don't see why not, if that's what you want.'

'And ten pounds an hour is acceptable?'

'It's what the others pay. And I don't do ironing – just saying. I hate doing my own so I won't do other people's.'

'No, no, that's fine.' Bex fished the tea bags out and poured in the milk before she handed Amy a mug. 'Take a pew.'

The two women sat at the big kitchen table, facing each other.

'Where did you move from?'

'London.'

'This place must be a bit of a culture shock then. I love Little Woodford, lived here all my life, but don't people want to move *to* London, not away from it?'

'My husband always wanted the family to live in the country.' Bex stopped and looked over the rim of her mug at Amy. 'He was killed in a traffic accident.'

'Oh.' Shit, what did you say to a statement like that? She made a stab at an appropriate response. 'I'm really sorry, Bex. That's a bummer.' Bummer?! What a crass thing to say. It wasn't a 'bummer' it was *devastating*. She slurped her tea to cover her embarrassment.

Bex smiled at her. 'It was certainly that. Still, I'm not the only one-parent family in the world and I'm not the only widow so I just have to make the best of the situation.'

'My Ashley – my son – he doesn't have a dad. Not that he's dead, he just buggered off when he found out I was in the family way. It's not easy, is it – being both parents?'

Bex shook her head. 'No, it isn't.' She sighed.

'Yeah, OK. So… about references – do you want ones from my other ladies?'

'I don't think you'd have a job at the post office if you weren't honest. *And* you were recommended to me by Heather. I should think that's enough, isn't it?'

'If you say so. Just let me know if you change your mind. So, how you settling in?'

'OK, I think. I've still got a bit to do and apart from you, Heather and Olivia—

'You know Mrs L?'

Bex nodded.

'I do for her too.'

Bex laughed. 'So she told me. Would it be easier to list who you don't clean for?'

'Maybe.'

'Anyway, beyond those two and you, I haven't really met anyone yet.'

'Well, you don't want to rush into these things, do you? There's some people in town who are proper bonkers – and I should know cos I work for a few of them. Take Mrs Rivers – Sylvia. I'm sure her husband beats her or something. She's potty about cleaning her house. Now, I'm not saying I don't like a tidy place but seriously – cleaning skirting boards with a toothbrush? Why would you do that?'

Bex frowned. 'It doesn't mean her husband is a wife-beater though, does it?'

'No, but she always seems scared of something. She has that look – know what I mean?'

Bex shrugged.

'And then there's the doctor's wife. She lost her daughter some years back and the kid's room is like some sort of shrine. I mean, it was all very tragic and everything but she goes and sits in it every day. And then there's the drink. You should see the number of bottles in their recycling bin. Not that I'd ever say anything to anyone—'

Bex's tea must have gone down the wrong way because she had a coughing fit. Amy paused till she got over it.

'—but she's obviously got a problem.'

'Grief takes people different ways.' Bex sounded a bit chilly and then Amy remembered what Bex had just told her about her husband croaking. Shit. Her and her big mouth.

There was a lull in the conversation and both women sipped their tea. 'One other thing, Amy.'

'Yes?'

'I'm thinking of going back to work part-time. Heather said to ask you if you knew of anyone who needs someone to do a few hours a week; shop assistant, receptionist, that sort of thing.'

Amy screwed up her face as she thought. 'Not off hand, but I'll keep my ears open.' She glanced at her watch. 'I should be going, soon. Due at Mrs L's in a bit.' Amy gulped the last of her tea and stood up. 'Thanks for the tea and I'll see you Friday?'

'Perfect.' Blimey, thought Bex, Heather hadn't been wrong about Amy and gossip.

13

Joan pinged open the door to Mags's salon in time for her fortnightly shampoo and set. This week, she noticed, Janine's hair was pink. What was wrong with blond... or even brunette?

'Hiya, Joan,' said Janine. 'Here for your usual?'

'Yes, ta.' Joan took a seat and waited for Mags to finish with her previous customer. After about five minutes Mags finished and Janine offered Joan a gown to put over her clothes.

'How have you been keeping?' asked Mags as she settled Joan in front of the sink and got her to lean her head back.

'Oh... you know, OK-ish.'

'Haven't you been well?' Mags squirted on some shampoo.

'Mustn't grumble. Getting old, that's my problem. Still better than the alternative, I always say.'

It took Mags a second or two to understand Joan's meaning. 'I suppose.'

'There was a break-in round our way yesterday.'

'Get away.'

Joan nodded as Mags's fingers lathered up the suds.

'There was one down our road too,' chimed in Janine from by the reception desk. 'Couple of days ago. The burglar got in through a vent that had been left open. Gives you the creeps, don't it, to think of a stranger in your house when you're asleep.'

'It certainly does,' said Mags. 'Did your neighbours lose much, Joan?'

'Don't rightly know.'

'My mum,' said Janine, 'says our neighbours lost a laptop, jewellery and cash. They said it could've been worse.'

'Sounds bad enough to me,' said Joan.

'I suppose they could've been murdered in their beds,' said Janine. 'I mean, I watch *Midsomer Murders* and there's always a stack of bodies in that. Nothing exciting ever happens here.'

'And let's hope it stays that way,' said Joan with a shudder. 'You be careful what you wish for, young lady.'

Later that afternoon, Olivia Laithwaite made her way up the hill to her house on her bike. At the top of her drive she got off and wheeled it over the gravel then let herself in.

'Zac. *Zac?* I'm home.' Silence. He was late, where was he? She shrugged her jacket off and hung it on the coat rack when she heard the clatter of the letter box and the thump of something landing on the mat. She went to get whatever had been delivered – the local paper, as it turned out. She took it back to her open-plan kitchen, hitched herself onto a stool by the breakfast bar and scanned the front page. There was nothing of import – a woman was going to do a run to raise money for a cancer charity and the local MP had reopened a café in the town centre after a major refurbishment. And why hadn't she been invited to that last event? she wondered. As a member of the local council it would have been a courtesy at the very least. She sniffed. Of course, she wouldn't have gone – she had far too many things in her diary as it stood without adding anything as trivial as that. Although, on second thoughts, she might have made an exception... after all, the MP had been there and it never hurt to press the flesh of those more influential than oneself. Still, water under the bridge.

She turned the page to the letters column – the usual mix of complaints about dog mess and potholes and locals moaning about empty wine and beer bottles up at the park. Well, she'd done her best by reporting it to the police – there was little else she could do, short of taking a bin bag up there herself and litter-picking and she wasn't going to do *that*. Lord alone knew what she might find. She shuddered. No, now it was up to the police.

Her eye moved down the page to the planning applications: *Application for residential development for up to 60 new dwellings at Coombe Farm, Rowan Road, Little Woodford.* Coombe Farm was McGregor's place. Sixty? Olivia boggled. Sixty! That was a huge development. And why hadn't Cynthia at the town hall rung her to let her know? It wasn't as if she hadn't made it plain that she was interested. She scanned the application for further details. She noticed who the developer was – a local company who'd done some other projects in the surrounding villages. They had a reputation for building high-spec, well-crafted, well-designed and well-finished buildings. If it wasn't for the size and position of the development Olivia might almost be tempted to back it but no... Too big and in the wrong place. She scanned down the rest of the details... *vehicular access off Rowan Road, blah, blah, blah, landscaping, blah, blah, children's play area, forty per cent affordable and social housing.* Hah! That last was a sop to try and sweeten the pill for the trendy-lefty-do-gooders. In Olivia's opinion, the last thing Little Woodford needed was another load of council homes – even if they were nicely built ones. The ones at the other end of town caused quite enough trouble. No, no, that was the tin lid. She was definitely going to fight it all the way.

'No!' she said out loud, and slammed her hand down on the counter. 'Over my dead body,' she added as she reread the notice in the paper.

The front door banged open and Zac slouched in.

'Hi, Zac,' she called. 'Nice day at school? Tea?'

Zac glared at her. 'It was school, Mum. Of course it wasn't *nice*. And I'm still getting the piss ripped out of me because I'm the only kid in my year who didn't go away at Easter.'

'I'm sure that's not true,' said Olivia.

'Ha. Everyone else went skiing or somewhere hot and had proper holidays and what did we do? Fuck all.'

'Don't swear, dear. You know your father doesn't approve.'

'I look like a real loser.'

'Does it matter? Your father was busy at work and couldn't take the time off.'

'He never takes time off – and d'you know why? Because he hates spending time with us.'

'Don't be ridiculous,' said Olivia, mildly. Really, where did Zac get his ideas from? Yes, Nigel could be tricky, but that was because he worked so hard. Of course he didn't hate his family. Although she would prefer it if he got home earlier in the evening, and now he'd taken up this badminton club nonsense... Which reminded her, he'd be late back tonight because of it.

'Anyway, you're late home. Did you go into town?'

'Jeez, Mum, I'm fifteen, what's it to you if I did?'

'I was only asking,' said Olivia, nettled.

'Well, don't.' And with that Zac stormed off to his room.

It's his hormones, Olivia told herself. Except she couldn't remember her other three being quite so volatile.

Nigel picked up his sports bag as he stood up, pushed his swivel chair back under his desk and hit the button on his computer to put the terminal to sleep.

'Bye, guys,' he said to no one in particular as he left the office. He was one of the first to leave but he'd worked through his lunch hour so it wasn't as if he hadn't put in the hours.

'See ya, Nige,' someone called after him as he made his way through the ranks of desks.

Out on the street he swung his bag over one shoulder and clutched his briefcase in his free hand as he headed for the Tube and then the mainline station. The streets were thick with people making their way home and the Underground was smelly and fetid and hot. As a rule Nigel travelled home later than this and he loathed the awfulness of the rush hour but it couldn't be avoided as he had something he wanted to do.

He was lucky to get a seat on the train back to Little Woodford and, with his sports bag between his feet, he put his briefcase on his lap and hauled out some papers, a bunch of bank statements and a calculator. He was so engrossed in his work that he almost missed his stop and he had to make a mad dash to get his papers put away and get off before the train pulled away again. Panting, he sorted out his possessions on the platform while all the other commuters streamed to the car park. Unlike his fellow travellers, Nigel turned left and went over the bridge across the railway to the new development and the show house in its manicured garden beside a huge advertising hoarding telling anyone who was interested that COMING SOON *stunning 3- and 4-bedroomed executive houses from as little as £475,000.*

It was late when Nigel got back home.

'How was your badminton club?' asked Olivia as he threw his sports bag down on the stairs and then headed to the kitchen to pour himself a drink.

'OK.' He got out the gin bottle and looked at the level. 'Have you been hitting this, Oli?'

'Me? No, I had a glass or two of wine.'

Nigel shook his head like he didn't believe her as he made his drink.

'So what is it? A league, a ladder...?'

'What?' Nigel took a swig of G & T.

'Your badminton club.'

'Oh... it's a ladder.'

'So how are you doing?'

'God, Ol, I've just got in. What's with the Spanish Inquisition?'

'I thought you'd like me to take an interest.' Olivia got off the sofa and went to join her husband in the kitchen. 'Zac and I had lasagne for supper. There's plenty left for you. It won't take me a mo to heat it in the microwave.'

'Sure, yeah, whatever.'

Olivia pinged her husband's supper and took it to him where he was now sitting on the sofa, plipping through the channels on the TV, then she put the dirty gratin dish into soak in the sink.

Nigel found an episode of *Family Guy* and settled down to watch it.

Olivia loathed the show. She grabbed his sports bag and took it upstairs where she took out his trainers then tipped the rest of the contents into the laundry basket before going through the laundry bag to find enough other whites to make up a load. She returned downstairs to shove the washing on. The forecast for the next day was for dry weather so she could peg it all out first thing.

'I think I might have a nice long soak before I hit the sack,' she told Nigel.

Nigel shovelled in some of his supper and mumbled something unintelligible before he wound the volume up another notch on the TV.

Olivia went upstairs, grabbed her book and then went into their en suite and turned both taps on.

It was only when she was stepping into the hot scented water and sinking down with a contented sigh that she realised that Nigel's badminton kit had looked remarkably uncrumpled when she'd stuffed it into the washing machine.

14

The next morning, as Heather went towards the stairs to make the bed and have a general tidy up before the arrival of Amy, she glanced through the study door at the back view of her husband. He'd barely talked over breakfast, which wasn't especially unusual, but he'd hardly talked to her the day before either, or the day before that. She didn't expect a running commentary, far from it, but this silence wasn't contemplative but morose. She was sure something was bothering Brian. Again, that wasn't unusual. He was often burdened by the problems of his parishioners, who seemed to expect him to be able to provide some sort of magic solution to their troubles, an expectation which weighed heavily on Brian when he couldn't. Heather paused at the foot of the stairs, her hand on the newel post, as she thought about her husband's silence, and then she turned and went to the study door.

'Brian, darling, is something the matter?'

He spun round in his office chair. 'Whatever gives you that idea?'

'You've been very quiet… thoughtful.'

'I'm not the comedy turn,' he said. 'I'm sorry I've not been more entertaining.'

'That's not what I meant. Is it money? I could always ask for more work at the school.'

Brian shook his head. 'It's not money. Honest.'

'The bishop?'

'Nor the bishop. Really, Heather, if I was worried about either of those I'd tell you.' He stared at her over the top of his glasses. 'Now then, you must let me get on. I've got to go and talk to the primary school year sixes this morning and I need to read through my notes before I do.'

Heather left him shuffling through the papers on his desk and pattered upstairs. She made the bed, tidied the bathroom, folded the towels and picked up the washing to take back down with her. Laden with laundry she returned downstairs slowly, her slippers making almost no noise on the carpet. When she got to the landing a pair of socks fell off her armful and she stopped to pick them up. The house was silent – apart from the sound of a muffled sob. Brian?

Heather tiptoed down the remainder of the flight.

'Brian?'

His chair remained turned away from the door for a second. She saw his hand move to his face – to dash the tears away? – and then he turned.

'Heather. You startled me. I didn't hear you come back down.'

Obviously, she thought. She dropped the washing and went into the study. 'What is it, Brian? Don't deny it, I'm not stupid, please tell me what the matter is.'

'I can't. It's confidential.'

'One of your parishioners?'

Brian nodded but he didn't meet her eye.

'Is there nothing I can do to help?'

Brian shook his head. 'A lost cause, I fear.'

'Oh, darling. I am so sorry this is upsetting you. If circumstances change, and there *is* something for me to do, you must let me know.'

'In that unlikely event, yes, I'll tell you.' Brian fished a crumpled hanky out of his trouser pocket and blew his nose. 'Now, I really must get on.'

Heather returned to the hall where she gathered up the laundry and took it to the kitchen. As she pushed it into the washing machine she cast her thoughts over the regulars in the congregation, the ones she and Brian knew best, the ones he'd care about the most, and tried to work out which of them it might be who was causing her husband such distress.

Belinda walked to the bank clutching her handbag tight against her side, aware that she had an awful lot of cash in it. After years of running a pub she knew she ought to be used to banking the takings but she always worried that someone might mug her. And recently there had been talk of break-ins in the town and neighbouring villages; nothing too serious, nothing violent, no one had been attacked, but it was slightly unsettling all the same. According to the gossip in the pub it had mostly involved the theft of small items of jewellery, cash, laptops – items of value that could be easily fenced, thought Belinda. The word was that it was druggies from Cattebury hitting on soft targets like Little Woodford because, like lots of small country towns, the police station had been closed long ago and bobbies on the beat were as rare as rocking-horse balls. They had Leanne Knowles, the local police community support officer, but there was only so much one woman could do.

Belinda felt a familiar slight whoosh of relief when she got to the bank and stepped in through the door. There were only two people queuing ahead of her and she was soon at the counter.

'Hi, Belinda,' said the teller.

Belinda opened her bag and took out the bags of coins and bundles of notes which the bank clerk put on the scales or through the automatic counting machine. As the money was counted she ticked off the sums on the deposit slip. 'That's fine,' she said, finally, as the last of the money was put in the drawer under the counter. 'Business is looking good.'

'Yes, but I wish I could get decent staff. There must be someone in town who wants a part-time job. I like to think that Miles and I are good employers so I don't understand why we don't seem to be able to keep people, although, to be fair, my last part-timer has got a new baby as an excuse for leaving. Anyway, I think I'm going to have to put yet another ad in the post office window – but if we get anyone reliable it'll be a triumph of hope over experience.'

'Good luck.'

Feeling more relaxed now she'd off-loaded the takings at the bank, Belinda wandered back along the road towards the pub. Ahead of her she could see Amy gazing into a shop window and an idea suddenly struck her. She ran to catch up with her.

'Hi, Amy.'

Amy spun round. 'Oh, hello, Belinda.'

'Listen, I was wondering if you could help me.'

'If I can I will, but it's got to be quick – I'm almost late for Heather's.'

'I just wondered if you know of anyone who needs a job – part-time, at the pub.'

'That new woman who's moved into The Beeches – she told me she was after a part-time job.'

'But she won't want to work in a bar, will she?'

'Dunno. When she spoke to me she didn't sound as if she was picky. I think she wants something to get her out of the house and take her mind off the fact her old man got killed not long back.

'Killed?'

'Traffic accident, so she said. Mind you, she'll probably only want to do daytime shifts, what with having young kids and being on her own and everything.'

'Even so...'

'Ask her. She can always tell you to get lost.'

'True. Maybe I'll pop round there later and have a word. Anyway, it'll be nice to meet the new neighbour.'

★

Later that morning, Brian walked to the ancient church and unlocked the vestry door. He remembered his wedding vows and all those promises about sticking with your spouse through thick and thin. Would Heather want to stick with him if she knew what was going on? It was one thing coping with sickness and the bad patches but how would she feel if she discovered that she was married to an out-and-out hypocrite? For weeks now he'd been lying to her, lying to his congregation, pretending he was a Christian, a believer, when the reality was he was a sham, a charlatan, someone no better than a snake-oil salesman, peddling something he had no faith in whatsoever, and now he was about to do the same to a group of primary school children. As a man who ought to be able to inspire them to be good, truthful and honest, he was about to let them down.

He went through to the cool vastness of the nave. Sunlight shining though the stained glass dappled colour onto old stone flags, worn smooth by thousands upon thousands of footsteps. The footsteps of people who had believed and still *did* believe, without question, that there was a God, there was life ever after, that prayer had the power to cure the sick and calm the troubled... So, why couldn't he any more? He knelt down in front of the altar and gazed at the cross above. Nothing. He shut his eyes and listened to the silence. Nothing. No comforting feeling that he was not alone, no reassuring presence. Wearily, he got to his feet again and headed back out of the church wondering how long he could carry on living a lie.

Bex was trying to decide if she liked the way the sitting room furniture was arranged when the doorbell went. She opened the door to a stranger.

'Hello.'

'Hi, I'm your next-door neighbour. I run the pub. I'm Belinda.' The woman stuck out her hand. 'Nice to meet you.'

Bex took the hand and shook it. 'Hi, I'm Bex. I think we waved at each other some while back when I had, literally, just moved in.'

'We did.'

Bex opened the door wide. 'Come in. And lovely to meet you too.'

'Actually,' said Belinda, 'I'm here for a reason. This is a bit cheeky, but Amy told me that you're looking for a job.'

'Amy?'

Belinda smiled and nodded. 'Are you? I mean, Amy often gets the wrong end of the stick – that doesn't stop her from talking, but her information isn't always completely reliable.'

'Fake news?'

Belinda grinned and nodded.

'This time she's right, I am. But only part-time.'

'Well, Miles – he's my partner – Miles and I are run off our feet at the pub, my last part-timer went off to have a baby and we're really keen to try and recruit people to do some of the shifts.'

Bex frowned as she thought about the idea. 'Bar work?'

'Look, I'm sorry, it was a long shot…'

'No, no, I'm not offended that you asked me but I've never done anything like that before.'

'It's not tricky, honest. The till's dead easy to work and I'm sure you can pour a drink.'

'I suppose.' Bex had been in pubs and she'd seen how busy they could get. Would she be able to remember a long list of drinks, tot up the total, clear the tables, load and unload the glass washer without pissing off the customers by keeping them waiting or getting it horribly wrong? In theory it shouldn't be difficult but in practice…?

'To be honest, if you did the lunchtime shifts it'd be pretty quiet. Market day can be busier but I wouldn't let you cope on your own – or not till you really knew what you were doing.'

'I can't say I'm not flattered at being headhunted—'

'There's a "but" coming, isn't there?'

Bex nodded. 'I suppose it's because...' She paused. 'I don't know.' Then she said, 'It's just a bit sudden, that's all.'

'Look, think about it, you want a job, I want staff...'

'Put like that... Maybe if I had a look at the pub.'

'Now?'

'Why not? I mean, if it's OK with you.'

Belinda nodded.

'I just need to lock up and grab my bag.'

'Sure.'

Two minutes later Belinda unlocked the front door of the pub and led Bex inside. The ceiling was beamed and there was a fire crackling in the grate of the big inglenook that stretched across one of the walls. Above it was a long shelf, crammed with books. The brass handles of the beer pumps gleamed on the polished wood of the bar, there were pictures of local scenes on the walls, and a pile of newspapers and magazines on the sill of the bay window, and the place smelt of beer and wood smoke. Everything was as it should be in an English country pub.

'This is lovely.'

Belinda laughed. 'Don't sound so surprised!'

'I'm not, but I've come from London and the pubs around us were more...' she searched for the word, 'more functional. This is a bit like being in someone's house.' She looked about. 'Coo, that makes a change – no fruit machine.'

'No fruit machines, no jukebox, no TV, no piped music... Peaceful, isn't it?'

Bex nodded. 'It's lovely. Perfect.'

'Thank you. So, this is the bar, obviously. We don't have a saloon and public bar, only this.' Belinda opened up the flap on the bar and led the way through. 'The kitchen is through here.' She rested her hand on a swing door.

'Kitchen? There's food to cope with as well?'

'Nothing too fancy: sandwiches, pasties, salads, egg and chips, that sort of thing. Bar snacks really.'

Belinda pushed the door fully open and Bex saw a small but

highly functional kitchen filled with stainless steel appliances. 'And this is my partner, Miles.'

A man busy slicing tomatoes with lightning dexterity stopped chopping and looked up. The first thing that Bex notice were his incredibly blue and smiley eyes. Lucky Belinda, she thought. Good-looking and a cook! She gazed at him and realised that this was the first time since Richard's death that she'd felt any sort of attraction to a member of the opposite sex. It had been nearly a year since he'd died – maybe she was starting to get over it. People had said that she would and she'd tried to believe them, but for months and months she'd felt sad and desolate. Being busy, finding things to do and, more recently, moving house had helped keep the worst at bay but it was always there in the background. But suddenly, here she was, staring at a strange man and thinking how attractive he was.

'Hiya,' he said. He smiled at her and she smiled back before he began chopping again, reducing the last whole tomato to half a dozen slices in a couple of seconds.

'This is Bex,' said Belinda.

Miles reached for a stainless steel bowl and swept all the neatly sliced tomatoes into it.

'Hiya, Bex.' He wiped his hands on a damp cloth and held his right one out. 'And to what do I owe this pleasure?'

Bex shook his hand. 'Belinda is trying to persuade me to come and work for you.'

'Is she now?' He dropped his voice to a stage whisper. 'Take my advice, don't. She's a slave driver.'

'Oh, shut up, Miles. That's not helpful.' But she was laughing. 'Right, we'll leave you in peace.'

Belinda led the way back to the bar and unlocked a door next to the Ladies. She flicked on a light switch and Bex saw stairs leading downwards. 'And this, pretty obviously, is the cellar.'

She led the way down the steep wooden stairs where a row of eight barrels were lined up against the wall. There were also piles of cases of wine and trays of soft drinks and mixers covered in shrink wrap. In a far corner were huge boxes of crisps. A draught came through the metal trapdoor that presumably allowed the delivery men direct access to the cellar from the street. But other than that, the cellar was spotlessly clean and dry. No smell of damp, no mustiness, no beaten earth floor like her own one under the kitchen.

'So, what do you think?'

'It's a lovely pub but I'm still not sure I'm the right person for the job. I really won't be able to work weekends and I couldn't manage evenings either – not with the kids. And then there's the school holidays... I'd better come clean, I'm a single mum... well, a widow if I'm honest.'

'I know, Amy said.'

'Ah... Amy.'

Belinda gave her a rueful smile. 'I didn't like to say anything in case Amy had got it wrong.'

Bex sighed. 'Not this time, sadly.'

'I'm sorry.'

'Yeah... well...'

'But not being able to work late or in the holidays won't be a problem. The thing about running a pub is that it's not only about pulling pints and chatting to customers over the bar – there's the VAT returns, stock control, ordering, the accounts... it all takes time and that's what I don't have at the moment, not since my last barmaid went off to have a baby. It's all I can do to keep the place clean and tidy.' Belinda smiled at Bex. 'If you do a shift at lunchtime I can get on with the admin, instead of having to do it before we open or when we shut in the afternoon. Trust me, working from nine in the morning till closing time is quite knackering.' She smiled. 'That's an understatement, by the way.'

Bex grinned back.

'I pay the living wage – in case you wanted to know.'

Bex felt a bit of a fool; for many people the hourly rate would have been a key question and she hadn't even thought about the wages.

'Please think about it. It's a great way to meet people, honest,' said Belinda.

'OK, I will. I'll let you know later. Promise.'

'That'd be great. And just think, it's a doddle of a commute.'

Bex laughed. 'You're not wrong there.'

15

Megan picked up her bag from where she'd slung it on her chair and put it on her desk so she could sit down for afternoon registration. Life at the school was definitely getting easier. She'd made some friends in the class and she knew her way around but, on the downside, Lily was still sniping and sniggering and giving her knowing looks, whispering stuff to her sidekick, Summer. Sure, with the exception of Lily and her little gang of acolytes, the others were all right but most of the kids had been pals since primary school and, even though they were nice enough to her, she couldn't call anyone a 'best friend'. Everyone already had their bessies and they didn't need her tagging along like a gooseberry. And, moreover, most of the kids lived at the other end of the town, on the housing estate near the school. As Ashley had told her, the people in the posh houses, on her side of the town, went to St Anselm's in Cattebury so there was no one near her to hang out with after school. Ashley was nice, he always waited on the corner of his road to walk the last bit to school with her but, as it wasn't the done thing for the boys to be seen with girls in school hours, they barely spoke to each other once they got through the gates. And she hadn't gone to the play park for ages because the weather had been too shit to bother so, if she was honest, their friendship was pretty embryonic. And she certainly didn't yet have a close girlfriend in Little Woodford who she could have a giggle with, confide in about boys she fancied, listen to One Direction with, or shop with. Bex kept telling her it was early days yet, but it didn't stop her from feeling lonely.

She pulled her timetable from her bag and checked what was on the menu next; food tech, then maths. Great. She put the timetable back and got out a comb and a handbag mirror and checked her hair.

'Yeah, like that's going to make you look better,' hissed Lily in her ear.

Megan swivelled round in her chair to face her. 'Piss off, Lily.'

'Oo-oo-oh, hark at her.' Lily's group sniggered as Lily sauntered forwards a couple of steps and parked her bum on Megan's desk. 'You want to watch it, you do. My dad's a governor of this school and he could get you expelled. Just like you were from your last place.'

Megan reeled. She hadn't been expelled. That wasn't why she'd left. 'I wasn't.'

Lily looked over to her friends. 'She would say that, wouldn't she?'

'But...but...' Megan was so bowled over by the enormity of Lily's accusation she was unable to react. She glanced across the room to see if she could catch Ashley's eye but he wasn't there. He must have left the room for some reason – gone to fetch something from the cloakroom perhaps – but his absence made Megan feel totally vulnerable. She always felt that when he was around, because he was a friend, if Lily really kicked off he might be her knight in shining armour.

'There, you see – she doesn't deny it. How could she when it's true.' Lily laughed. 'So... gypsy's warning, as my old gran would say – you'd better be nice to me and my friends or you won't have a happy time here.'

Megan felt Lily, more than likely, could deliver that threat. She stared back at her tormentor. 'Really,' she said with a bravado that was entirely false.

Lily nodded. 'Yeah, really.' She put her hand on Megan's unzipped backpack and flipped it off the desk. As it fell it turned upside down so that everything tumbled out onto the floor, including the ingredients that Megan had brought in for food tech. The container containing the flour hit the top of the pile and the lid came off, sending flour everywhere.

'Oops,' said Lily before she sauntered back to her group. 'Clumsy old me.'

A second later, as Megan was staring at the mess at her feet, Mrs Blake walked in.

'For heaven's sake, Megan, what a mess. Pick up your things at once and then get a brush. What were you thinking about?'

Behind her, Megan heard the other girls snort and splutter.

I will not cry, Megan told herself. I won't.

On the school bus that took the kids who lived in the villages surrounding Little Woodford home, Lily was sitting next to Summer and toying with her phone.

'Is it true, then?' said Summer.

'About Megan getting expelled from her last school?' Summer nodded. 'Well, my dad said there had been "an incident".'

'What kind of incident?'

'Dunno, I overheard Dad talking to Mum about her but then he shut the door so I didn't hear all of it – but something deffo went on there, that's why she had to leave. It stands to reason it had to be something serious if they had to move, and I intend to find out.'

'How?' Summer swivelled round in her seat. 'Hey, do you suppose Ash knows? I've seen him and Megan walking to school together.'

'He does *what*?'

'He walks with Megan.'

Lily frowned. 'Has she got her nasty little foreign hooks into him?'

Summer shrugged. 'They only walk together.'

Lily chewed on a fingernail. She wanted Ashley to be interested in *her*, not Megan. All the boys fancied her so why didn't he? And, if Ash fancied Megan instead, he'd totally overstepped the mark. Megan must have been giving him the eye, encouraging him, otherwise why would Ash like that jumped up little incomer instead of herself? Lily acknowledged that Megan was pretty but only if you liked that sort of thing. She wasn't *English*. Well, that was it, Megan had gone too far. Lily decided it was time to put her in her place once and for all. She opened her Facebook account and tapped a few icons.

'Hey,' she said to Summer. 'I've just asked Windy to be a friend on Facebook.'

'You what?'

'You heard.'

'Why did you do that?'

'Because, if she accepts we can *friend* her other friends – if she's got any.'

Summer sniggered. Then she frowned. 'Why d'ya want to do that?'

Lily rolled her eyes. 'Because, thicko, there's stuff Windy isn't telling us and I want to find out. Maybe she wasn't expelled but something happened at her old school. Bet there's kids at her old school who know and if we get pally with them on Facebook...'

Summer's jaw slackened. 'Fucking hell, Lil,' she said, her eyes wide with admiration.

Lily smiled smugly.

'Megan? Megan!' Bex hollered up the stairs. Much as she loved this house, having three floors could be a serious pain, especially as Megan seemed to spend a lot of her time, when she was home, up in her eyrie. Bex waited for a reply, wondering if she'd have to yell again.

'Yeah?' came Megan's voice, floating down the stairwell.

'I'm popping out. Can you look after the boys?'

'What?'

Oh, God, she couldn't keep yelling like this; it set a bad example to the boys. The last thing she wanted was for the entire family to shout from one room – or one floor – to another instead of talking in normal tones, face-to-face. Bex began to climb the stairs. As she got to the first landing Megan appeared at the bottom of the attic stairs.

'Sorry?' she said.

Bex stared at her. Her long eyelashes were spiky and stuck together. Had she been crying? 'Are you all right?'

'Fine,' said Megan.

'You look like you've been crying.'

Megan shook her head. 'Of course not.'

Did she pry – demand the truth? 'OK. I've got to go out. Can you keep an eye on the boys? They've done their homework and I'll be back in plenty of time to cook supper. I'm only going to be a short while.'

'No problem.'

Bex went back downstairs and told Lewis and Alfie, who were watching cartoons, that if they needed anything they were to ask their big sister, before she let herself out and walked the few yards to the pub.

She pushed open the door and saw that there were a number of people enjoying a swift post-work drink. The occupants looked at her with curiosity – a stranger? In their pub?

She saw Belinda behind the bar, hanging up a new display of bags of pork scratchings.

'Hello, Belinda.'

'Bex! Good to see you. So… what's the decision?'

'Yes, yes I'd like to take the offer.'

'That's brilliant. Hey, guys.' A dozen pairs of eyes swivelled towards the bar and conversations stilled. 'This is Bex – the new barmaid.'

There was a friendly chorus of greetings and Bex felt oddly

pleased and embarrassed at the attention. She waved shyly at the locals.

'I won't bother introducing them to you at this stage but you'll get to know each other over the next few weeks or so. When can you start?'

'When do you want me?'

'Honestly? Right now! But I understand about you only being available at lunchtimes. Tomorrow?'

Bex took a deep breath. Crikey, this was all happening fast. But she thought about it; seriously, why not? The kids would all be at school, most of the unpacking had been done, what else did she have to do? She'd set herself two goals of making friends and getting a job – wasn't this the ideal way to go about it?

'Yes.' Although she'd have to make some sort of arrangement with Amy as she wouldn't be there to let her in on the next Monday afternoon. She'd talk to her cleaner when she came to 'do' for her on Friday.

'We open at twelve so get here for eleven and I'll show you the ropes. And don't worry, I won't let you manage on your own to start with.'

'You break her in gentle-like,' heckled a voice from by the window. 'I know what a tough cookie you can be, Belinda.'

'We all do,' said another customer. 'Likes the whip hand, so I've heard.'

A bellow of laughter greeted that comment.

'And you mind your own business, Bert Makepiece,' chided Belinda. 'It's hard enough getting good staff without you scuppering things.'

'How do you know I'm good?' said Bex quietly.

'I don't, but I'll take a chance on you if you'll take a chance on me and Miles. Deal?'

'Deal.'

16

'Let's try that again,' said Belinda, patiently.

Bex took a deep breath and stared at the touch screen of the till. 'I enter my ID number... then I press *wine*, then I press *Merlot*, then I press *large*, then I press *return*, then I press *beer*, then I press *pint*—'

'No! Then you press *Guinness.*'

Bex sighed. 'Maybe you'd be better off with someone else.'

'Honestly, you'll be fine. It takes everyone a little while to learn how to operate the till.'

'But we haven't even started on spirits and mixers and I dread to think what I'll be like when we get onto food.'

'And I won't leave you on your own behind the bar until you get the hang of it.'

'Then you'll be holding my hand till I draw my pension.'

Belinda heard the pub clock chime. 'Never mind that now. Opening time.'

Bex felt her heart-rate increase. Stage fright, she thought. Supposing she got everything wrong? Supposing she really pissed off Belinda's customers? As if her employer guessed her feelings, Belinda put her hand on Bex's and gave it a reassuring squeeze before she went to the front door and unbolted it. And... nothing. If Bex had expected people to be waiting, gasping for refreshment on the doorstep, she was disappointed. She looked questioningly at her boss.

'Give it a few minutes,' said Belinda. 'The regulars don't like to look too keen – smacks of being the town drunks.'

Bex carried on with trying to ring up practice rounds of drinks for another five minutes or so before the first customer opened the door.

'Afternoon, Harry,' said Belinda.

'Morning, Belinda.'

'It's gone midday,' corrected Belinda.

'I ain't had my lunch yet, so that makes it morning. And a pint of the usual, please.'

'And Harry, meet Bex. She's going to be working here.'

'Morning, Bex. A pint of London Pride, please.'

Bex reached for a pint glass and carefully pulled the pump forward a couple of times till the amber liquid reached the mark on the glass. She passed the drink to Harry, carefully avoiding the beer pumps, then she painstaking entered Harry's drink into the computerised till.

'Three pounds sixty, please, Harry,' she said.

Harry handed over a fiver and Bex took a deep breath before she began tapping on the screen of the till. 'Forty-six pounds and forty pence change?!' she squawked.

'At least you recognised it as the wrong amount,' said Belinda. 'I've had bar staff who've cheerfully handed over that sort of money. You got the decimal point in the wrong place. Cancel the transaction and try again.'

Bex pressed the cancel button. 'One pound forty – that's better.' The till drawer pinged open, Bex put in the fiver and took out the change.

'There, that wasn't so difficult, was it?' said Belinda.

Bex knew she was supposed to agree cheerfully that it had been a doddle but actually she felt more like reaching for the gin bottle that was on the shelf right beside her. Instead she handed Harry his money.

'Want to know what I just saw?' said Harry.

'What's that?'

'Leanne Knowles going into old Doc Connolly's place. Seems they got burgled last night.'

'No!' said Belinda. 'Not another break-in. I've heard there have been a few round and about.'

''Tis terrible. A proper crime-wave,' agreed Harry.

'And I thought this town was as safe as houses after London,' said Bex.

Belinda shook her head. 'Sadly, I don't think anywhere is truly safe any more. Just make sure you keep everything nice and secure, is all I can say. Especially given that you live in the big house.'

Bex stared at Belinda, horrified. It was a very unsettling thought that she might be a target because of where she lived. She'd have to start double locking the doors at night.

By the time the pub had a dozen regulars enjoying a lunchtime drink, Bex was starting to get the hang of the till, and where all the various drinks, mixers and snacks were kept. She was still painfully slow but the customers were a patient, pleasant lot and cut her the slack she needed. Belinda cleared the tables and dealt with the food and, when things were quiet, she got on with a stock-check ready for an order she wanted to place with their suppliers later that day.

'There, you see,' said Belinda. 'I couldn't be doing that if I were running this place single-handed. You've already saved me a big job I'd have had to have done this afternoon after we've closed.'

That comment chuffed Bex quite a lot as, until then, she'd felt she'd been more of a hindrance than a help.

In the occasional lulls between customers Bex listened to the conversations going on. With no music it was easy to eavesdrop – not that she had done so deliberately to start with, but it was difficult not to take an interest in what was being said.

She leaned on the bar and focused her hearing on a group of four men in the corner.

'It's them druggie layabouts from Cattebury doing all the thieving,' said one.

'How do you know that, George?' said the one Bex remembered as being Harry.

'Stands to reason, don't it. There ain't no drugs here in Little Woodford.'

'I wouldn't be so sure about that. I heard that Mrs Laithwaite told the town clerk there was a whole bunch of druggie goings-on up at the nature reserve.'

'Get away.'

''Tis true.'

There was a pause while the foursome assimilated the information.

Bex felt sad. She'd hoped that this outwardly perfect little market town was just that – perfect. But apparently not. It seemed like everywhere, the surface veneer of flawlessness was an illusion. Chip it away and it was like everywhere else. All she had to hope was that it wasn't quite as bad as some bits of the rest of the country – like London, for example.

Amy was feeling a bit tired after spending the morning cleaning for Olivia, and wasn't looking forward to her afternoon stint at Jacqui Connolly's, but she perked up no end when, as she turned into the Connolly's drive, she saw a police car there.

'What the…?' she said out loud. Whatever it was, the presence of a cop car never meant good news. Gawd, she hoped they hadn't had another tragedy because that might send Jacqui completely over the top. Not, thought Amy, that Jacqui could put away much more than she already did to judge by what she saw when she emptied the bins – and looked in the cupboards to see where Jacqui hid it. She was quite inventive; behind the cleaning products in the kitchen, in the loo cistern, in her knitting bag… And she hid her drinking pretty well too. Amy reckoned that if she had to do anything – go out, go to the book club or the

WI – she had to be very careful about how much she had to drink during the day because no one else had ever mentioned to her that Jacqui liked the sauce. But Amy was sure that on the days when she stayed at home, she knocked back the vodka like there was no tomorrow. There'd been a couple of occasions when Amy'd come round to clean and she'd been poorly. Huh, hungover more like. The first couple of times it had happened Amy hadn't twigged but then she'd started to notice the number of bottles in the recycling and so it was only human nature to dig a bit deeper... Anyone would, wouldn't they? And then there was the business that she and her husband, David, had separate bedrooms. That always meant a marriage was in trouble, didn't it? Amy reckoned he couldn't approve of the amount she drank; not with him being a doctor and everything.

Amy got to the front door and rang the bell. Normally she'd have opened the door with her key and bowled in but, today, some instinct told her that it might be better if she didn't. It was opened after a few seconds by the local police community support officer, Leanne Knowles.

'It's Amy, isn't it?' said Leanne.

Amy nodded. 'Hi, Leanne.' Everyone in the town knew Leanne's name. She'd been helping police the town for over a decade and was often on patrol on the streets. 'I've come to clean for Mrs Connolly.'

'Not sure it's convenient right now.'

Amy wasn't going to be done out of her earnings if she could help it. Besides, she was gagging to know what was going on. 'I can keep out of your way – do the upstairs if you're downstairs.'

'Who is it?' called Jacqui's voice from somewhere inside.

Leanne called back over her shoulder, 'It's Amy.'

'Let her in.'

Amy gave Leanne a triumphant look as she shouldered past.

'Hey, Jacqui,' she said as she got into the sitting room. 'What's with the cops?'

'We got burgled last night.'

'No!' Amy was genuinely shocked. She'd heard there'd been some burglaries in the town but she wasn't expecting anyone she knew to get done over.

Jacqui nodded sadly.

'Did they take much?'

'Some cash, my laptop, David's camera, some other bits and pieces. Some jewellery,' she added.

'Not too bad then.'

Jacqui rounded on Amy. 'What do you mean, "not too bad"? We had strangers in our house, while we were asleep. We might have been murdered in our beds, they might have ransacked Lisa's room...' A tear trickled down her face.

'But that's what I meant,' said Amy. 'That other stuff *might* have happened and the things that's been nicked... well, it's just things. You can replace them. Anyway, the insurance will cover the cost.'

'I suppose,' said Jacqui. She didn't sound convinced. 'But I still feel scared and violated and... Oh, it's just horrible to think that some scumbag was creeping around *my* house at the dead of night.' She shuddered. 'I feel like I want to have the whole place deep cleaned.'

'Good job I'm here then, ain't it,' said Amy, cheerfully. 'Where do you want me to start?'

'Nowhere,' said Leanne. 'Not till the fingerprint people have been round.'

Amy rolled her eyes. 'Aw, come on, Leanne, I've got a living to make.'

'And I've got a string of crimes on my patch.'

The two women glared at each other.

'Amy,' said Jacqui, 'if you want to come another time, I'll happily pay you for those hours. I will seriously want some help when the police have finished.'

Amy sniffed. 'I suppose. Not sure when I can manage it but I'll do what I can. Rushed off my feet, I am, so I'll have to squeeze you in. Maybe after I've finished some of my other jobs.'

'Thank you, Amy. Thank you. Just let me know.'

'I'm sure you can see yourself out,' said Leanne.

Gawd, thought Amy as she headed for the front door. Give a woman a uniform and she turns into a mini dictator. Then she cheered herself up with the thought that she had time off and a really juicy story to tell her mum.

17

Later that afternoon Amy was sitting in the coffee shop in the centre of town, enjoying a latte and a slice of cake, when her mobile buzzed. She checked out the caller ID.

'Hiya, Billy,' she said cheerfully as she answered it.

'You all right to talk?'

'Yeah, course. I've got the afternoon off.'

'How come?'

'Jacqui Connolly's house got done over last night and the cops are there. They told me to bugger off. Proper *CSI* scene it was and all.'

'Get away! Mrs Connolly's gaff? That's awful.'

'They didn't get much, she says.'

'Really? I'm surprised they didn't wake up if there was someone creeping round their house.'

Amy snorted. 'Mrs Connolly? Wake up? With the amount she puts away every night?'

'True,' said Billy. 'But the doctor's not an alkie, is he?'

'Don't think so. Who knows?'

'Anyway, I'm glad you're free. I've got something to show you.'

'And what might that be?'

'A new set of wheels.'

'Give over. How can you afford that?'

'I can – never you mind how.'

Probably because of those other jobs he'd done, on the sly, for cash, thought Amy. Jammy bugger – extra money, tax free on top of his proper wage. Amy wished she could earn money like that. She worked her arse off for about half what Billy earned – if that.

'Where are you?' asked Billy. 'At home?'

'At the coffee shop.'

'I'll come into town. Give me ten minutes. I'll meet you in the market place.'

Amy finished her drink and made her way there. Billy was already there with a little red roadster.

'Nice,' said Amy approvingly as she caressed the sleek bonnet.

'Fancy a run out in it?' offered Billy.

'Can't, got to get back to cook Ash his tea.'

'Another time then.'

'When?'

'Saturday. We could go out. I'll buy you dinner.'

'Really?' Amy's voice was shrill with excitement.

'You deserve a treat,' said Billy.

'A new car and dinner out. What you been doing, Billy-boy? Robbing banks?'

Billy laughed. 'Yeah, of course. I'm a regular Clyde and you can be my Bonnie if you like.'

'Not sure about that. Didn't they wind up dead?'

'But we won't. I'm too clever.'

Amy couldn't dispute that – not if he had enough for a car and to treat her to a slap-up meal out.

Olivia looked at her emails, wanting something to take her mind off the fact that her son was over an hour late home from school. The first one to catch her eye was a notification from the town hall about the next full council meeting. It would, it said, include a meeting with the police about the spate of local burglaries. Olivia had heard the odd rumour about a break-in or two but *a spate*? This sounded serious. It would give Little Woodford a bad reputation. It would scare the likes of the Makepieces who didn't need to feel vulnerable and threatened at their age. What was more, it might affect house prices and she wasn't having that. She read the email in detail. Twenty break-ins in as many days. Twenty! The email was right, it was a crime wave. Maybe she ought to put her jewellery somewhere safer.

Olivia shut her laptop, climbed the stairs and headed for her bedroom. She sat at her dressing table, pulled open the middle drawer and took out her jewellery box. She also had a few smaller boxes that contained her pearls, an emerald brooch, her mother's eternity ring and some other bits and pieces. Some of her stuff was quite valuable and even if she wore jewellery only rarely she certainly didn't want to lose any of it. She carried it all downstairs and found Nigel's keys to his filing cabinet. She popped the boxes in one of the drawers under a file of bank statements and relocked it. Not ideal but it might hide them from a thief unless he or she was really determined.

She'd just hidden the keys again when Zac banged into the house, slamming the front door behind him, dropping his school bag noisily on the wood floor and then kicking off his shoes and leaving them in the middle of the room.

'Zac,' Olivia remonstrated. Her relief fuelling her irritation at his behaviour.

'What?' he snarled.

'Shoes, bag,' she said, as mildly as she could.

'For fuck's sake, Mum. I've only just got in.'

Olivia took a deep breath and stopped herself from pointing out that it was just as easy to put things away tidily as it was to chuck them all over the place.

She glanced pointedly at her watch. 'You're late. Was there a problem with the bus?'

Zac stared at his mother. 'No. I went to see a mate. I'm allowed to do that, aren't I? Jeez, Mum, I'm fifteen.'

'I know. But I'm your mother and I sometimes worry. It's what mothers do.'

Zac gave her a withering look and headed for the stairs. 'Whatever. I've got homework to do.'

'Then you can take your shoes up with you.' It wasn't an unreasonable request.

Zac spun round. 'Why should I? They're not doing any harm where they are. If you want them moved, you do it. What *is* your problem?'

Olivia lost it. 'My problem is having a nasty, stroppy little ingrate for a son who doesn't appreciate anything and who thinks he can treat me like dirt. Well, you can't.'

'Really?' Zac sneered.

'Really. And I'd like an apology.'

'Fuck off.'

'Don't you *dare* talk to me like that.'

'Why? What are you going to do?'

Olivia stared at him coldly. 'I'm going to stop your allowance, that's what I'm going to do.' That worked, thought Olivia. Zac went pale.

'You can't.'

'Try me.'

'But... but... I need that money.'

'Tough.'

'You can't do this to me, Mum. Please.'

He sounded so worried, so distraught, that for a second Olivia was almost inclined to relent. Almost. 'I'm sorry, Zac, but you need to learn a lesson. I will *not* be spoken to like that.'

'Fuck you then, Mum,' he screamed at her before he ran upstairs to his room and slammed the door with such force Olivia wouldn't have been surprised if it had come off its hinges.

She stared at it, feeling rather shaky. She'd never seen him that angry and he'd thrown quite a few strops in his time. But, enough was enough. And after that last display of outrageous temper she wasn't going to back down. She'd never been so determined to carry out a threat in her life. Besides, going short for a month wasn't going to do him any harm, was it?

*

Zac leaned against his bedroom door and felt sick with fear. What was he going to do now? He'd promised his dealer that he'd repay all the money he owed on the first of May. And now… Shit. Zac slid down the door till he was hunkered against it in a foetal position. He'd never been so scared in all his life. Even when Ash had dared him to grind down a rail and all he could think about was how much it would hurt if he came off – which he did and it had. But this was worse than that. Dan had a knife and he'd told Zac he'd cut his face *wide open* if he didn't come across with the money when it was due.

Zac crawled to his feet and went to look in the mirror. He traced a line down his cheek and imagined what it might feel like to be cut. He screwed his eyes up at the awfulness of the thought. He had to get the money. He had to.

He needed space, he needed to think, he needed to be out of the house. He opened his door and sped back down the stairs.

'Where are you going, Zac?' called his mother as he ran across the living room to the front door, grabbing his shoes off the floor as he went.

'Out.'

'But your supper…'

Zac dropped his shoes onto the floor by the front door and stuffed his feet into them, not caring if he was breaking down the backs. 'Shove it.'

He slammed the door behind him.

He hopped down the drive as he put his shoes on properly before he loped down to the skatepark. He wanted to think about what he could do, who he could go to, but all his thoughts were dominated by visions of Dan brandishing his knife the last time he'd scored some drugs and hadn't been able to pay.

'You do know what'll happen if you don't pay me, Zaccy-boy, don't you?'

He'd waved the craft knife right by Zac's eyes and Zac had instinctively shoved him away out of sheer fear.

'Don't you push me.' Dan's voice had been full of menace.

Zac had put his hands up. 'Sorry, I didn't mean to.'

'Good. We understand each other. So, I want my money on the first or your face mightn't look so pretty, hey?'

Zac had three days to come up with the cash. Ash was no good, and if he asked his mates at school he'd look poor and a loser; they might have loads of dosh but it would be humiliating to ask them for handouts, like a poor relation. He already sensed he was an object of pity because his family hadn't been on an exotic long-haul holiday recently, like everyone else. But maybe it would be better to be pitied than to be disfigured. No, he decided, he had to get the money and his parents could provide it.

He slunk home before it got dark and found the driveway still empty of his father's car. That was something to be grateful for. At least he wouldn't have his father on his back – well, not yet anyway.

'Your supper is in the fridge,' said his mother, coldly. She was sitting on the sofa, watching some nature programme on the TV. She didn't even bother to look at him and she didn't ask him where he'd been. It was like she didn't care.

Maybe she didn't, he thought. Maybe he'd really gone too far this time. Part of Zac wanted to confess about what was going on; tell her the situation, plead for forgiveness – and a handout. Ask her to pay off his dealer. Save him from the threat. But he couldn't face it. It wasn't just the row, it was the knowledge that she would be so gutted, so disappointed in him. That she'd never, ever trust him again. And shit – what if she told Dad?

'Thanks,' he mumbled. He suddenly felt ashamed of how he'd spoken to her earlier. 'Sorry about earlier,' he added.

His mother turned round. 'Too little and too late,' was all she said before she turned back to the television.

Ashamed, scared and close to tears, Zac took the plate of food and pinged it in the microwave for a couple of minutes before he grabbed a fork out of the drawer and took his meal up to his room to eat. Not that he was hungry but he sat on his bed and shovelled in an occasional mouthful out of habit.

He felt completely bowed down by his situation and try as he might he could only think of one way out of it; he'd have to stay awake and creep downstairs when both his parents were asleep and see what cash he could nick. His mum often left her handbag lying around, although he didn't think his dad took his wallet out of his jacket pocket and he always hung that up in his wardrobe. Zac contemplated the prospect of sneaking into the master bedroom to rifle that, but that was too risky. Maybe his dad had refilled the cash box... God, he had to hope. He bunged his plate on the floor by his bed and began to play a computer game – anything to kill the time till he could act.

18

The next morning, Olivia was hanging up some freshly ironed shirts for Nigel in his wardrobe when she found his sports bag stuffed in the bottom on top of his shoes. Really! she thought. And exactly how did he think his kit was going to get washed if he didn't leave it where she'd find it? She opened his bag and hauled out his shirt and shorts. As she did so the smell of fabric conditioner wafted out. Olivia stopped and stared into space. Maybe she hadn't been imagining things when she'd thought his badminton kit looked unworn the last time she'd washed it. Clutching his sports kit, she dropped the bag onto the bed and sank onto the duvet, beside it. So... if he wasn't playing badminton, what the hell was he doing? She examined his clothes more closely and couldn't make up her mind as to whether they'd been worn or not. They had been unfolded and then scrunched up in the bag but, and there was no two ways about it, they didn't smell sweaty. Whatever else he'd done with this stuff, he hadn't put it on and run around. Maybe he'd put them on but not played. Or maybe he'd played but not energetically enough to perspire. The only thing she was sure about was that the clothes didn't need washing. Slowly she folded them up and replaced everything in his bag.

Something didn't add up. His moods, the way he seemed to bang on about money and now this. 'What's going on?' she whispered to herself. Realistically, she knew the only way to find an answer was to confront him but there was a bit of her that shrank from the idea. Supposing she got an answer that she didn't like? If she ignored it, it might go away.

Olivia picked up the bag and put it back into the wardrobe then shut the door.

In the afternoon, Megan hung around by the school gate, waiting for Ashley. A couple of buses rolled past, belching diesel, stuffed with kids, then a third one stopped – waiting for a gap in the traffic so it could pull out onto the main road. Megan glanced up and saw Lily staring coldly down at her from one of the windows.

It was completely apparent to Megan that she and Lily were never going to be friends and she did her best to stay out of Lily's way. And, while Megan was pretty sure Lily still made the occasional snide comment behind her back, it seemed that, as long as she didn't cross Lily's path, then the pair pretty much ignored each other. It wasn't particularly comfortable but it was as good as it was going to get.

The bus was still waiting to pull out when Ashley ran up to Megan.

'Sorry I was so long,' he said.

Involuntarily, Megan looked up at Lily again and saw her eyes narrowed. Ashley followed her gaze.

'What's up with her?' he said as the bus revved its engine and moved off. Ashley and Megan followed it down the main road.

'How should I know?' said Megan – although she could guess. She'd seen the way Lily looked at Ashley in school and it was obvious to anyone with half an eye she fancied him despite the fact that Ashley didn't seem to notice. So, no way was she going to be happy with the fact that she and Ash walked to and from school together.

'Lily likes to think she's the class queen,' said Ashley.

'And?' said Megan. 'If she wants to be that, I'm not fighting her for it. And let's face it, she is form captain. Some people must like her.'

'Yeah, but you're here now.'

'What's that got to do with it?'

'Maybe she's just fallen down the popularity stakes.'

'I don't follow you.'

'You're nicer than she is – and prettier,' Ashley mumbled.

'Me? Don't be stupid.'

'It's true.'

'Now you've really lost the plot.'

'I haven't. All the boys fancy you.'

Megan stopped in the middle of the pavement. 'No, they don't.'

'Trust me, they do.' Ashley was blushing furiously.

'Really?'

Ashley nodded. 'The thing is, a few have dated Lily and she can be quite a bitch. "Treat 'em mean keep 'em keen" is her motto only she hasn't figured it out that it doesn't work like that.'

Why am I not surprised that Lily is considered to be quite a bitch? thought Megan. Instead she said in a non-committal way, 'No... well...'

Ashley nodded. 'I don't think you're a bitch,' he said shyly.

'Oh, I don't know,' said Megan, lightly. 'I expect I could be if I wanted to.'

Ashley grinned. 'Think we all can be.'

They walked on down the road in silence for a few paces. 'Thought I might go to the skatepark after I've had my tea,' said Ashley. 'Do you fancy coming down?'

'I don't know. I might, I'll see. But thanks for the invite.' They walked a few more yards in silence then Megan said, 'I need some advice.'

'What about?'

'Lily. She's sent me a friend request on Facebook. I mean, given that she obviously doesn't like me, I can't think why. But will I make things worse if I don't accept? Is it a test to see if I blank her? Or does she really want to be friends and what goes on in school is an act? It kind of doesn't make sense and I can't work it out. I don't know whether to accept it or not. You hear about people who bully other kids online... do you think she'd do that?'

'You're asking me how Lily's mind works.'

Megan looked at him. 'You've known her longer than I have.'

Ashley sighed. 'Who knows what goes on in her head? But, I suppose, why not? You can always unfriend her again if she turns out to be a pain in the arse. Let's face it, if you are friends with her online at least you can see what she's getting up to.'

'I suppose.'

They reached Ashley's road. 'See you,' he said as he rounded the corner.

'Yeah, bye.'

Megan went home feeling happier than she had since she'd started her new school, hugging to herself the news that the boys fancied her. And that Ashley thought she was nicer and prettier than Lily. She liked Ash – that meant a lot. And maybe Lily's Facebook request was a bit of an olive branch – maybe it might be a good thing to accept it. She'd do just that, she decided, when she got home. After all, it couldn't do any harm.

Bert had popped down to his allotment after his tea. The evenings were getting quite light and although it was gone seven thirty the sun still hadn't set and he had plenty of time to get his spuds hoed. His back twinged and he stopped and leaned on his hoe for a minute or two. Time was, when he'd been in the army, he'd been as fit as a butcher's dog, but old age was starting to get the better of him. His neighbour on the plot, a nice woman called Marjorie, was also working her patch, kneeling on an old bit of carpet and grubbing around in the soil with her hands. She looked over to Bert.

'Hard work, ain't it, keeping on top of it all.'

'You're not wrong there,' said Bert. 'Turn your back for a minute, at this time of year, and nature turns it back to a wilderness.'

Marjorie staggered to her feet and eased her back. 'That's enough for me for today. My old joints won't cope with no more.' She picked up her kneeling pad and gathered the weeds she'd pulled and chucked them on the pile she planned to burn later.

'I'm off home, Bert. See you again soon.'

Marjorie locked up her shed and left Bert still taking a break, leaning on his hoe and staring at the goings-on in the park.

He was watching the older kids on skateboards who were rumbling up and down the ramps, shrieking and wheeling and just missing each other, while overhead the swifts did exactly the same thing but with no bad language and more grace and style. Bert rolled his shoulders and watched the birds for a few seconds with a feeling of quiet contentment. Swifts – a sure sign that summer was right around the corner.

Across from the ramps he saw the furtive bloke hanging around by the big trees again. Joan had told him that Olivia had found a load of druggie goings-on up at the nature reserve. Well, by what he'd seen here recently, the nature reserve wasn't the only place the junkies hung out. Except Bert wasn't sure it all added up. A lad like Zac wouldn't be doing drugs, would he? He'd been brought up proper. But what if he was? Bloody hell, Olivia Laithwaite would have a conniption fit. Bert chuckled softly at the thought. It was almost worth wanting it to be true just to see her reaction.

As he was mulling over the possible expression on Olivia's face he saw a lad in a hoodie jog across the grass towards the trees. Young Master Zac, maybe? He was too far away for Bert to be sure. Again there was an exchange and the lad ran back the way he'd come. Well, whatever it was it weren't none of his business.

Marjorie pottered back through the allotments, the sound of the playing children growing ever fainter, towards the bungalows where she and the Makepieces were neighbours. It was a lovely evening and most of the little houses had their windows open wide and quite a few of the occupants were in their gardens doing a spot of tidying up. She saw Joan in her garden, dead-heading the daffs and tying up the leaves with twine to allow them to die back properly.

'How do, Joan. Your old man's working hard on his plot.'

Joan straightened up. 'Glad to hear it. Mind, I never know what he finds to do with all the time he spends up there. Still, keeps him out from under my feet.'

She bent down to pick up the twine and gave out an agonising cry.

'Joan?'

Joan stayed doubled over.

Marjorie pushed open the gate and ran over to her friend. 'Joan? Are you all right?'

'Give me a mo, I'll be fine,' she gasped.

'You don't look fine. Here,' she said. She hooked one of Joan's arms over her shoulder and led her over to the house. She pushed open the front door and took Joan inside where she managed to get her into the sitting room. She plonked her patient down on the sofa then went and fetched a glass of water. 'Here,' she said, thrusting it into Joan's hand.

'It's nothing,' said Joan. 'Don't fuss, I'm fine.'

Marjorie stood in front of her. 'It don't look like nothing from where I am.'

'Just a touch of lumbago, I'll be bound. Maybe heartburn.'

'Really? Does it happen often?'

Joan nodded and winced. 'A bit.'

'I know it's none of my business—'

'Which it ain't.'

'—but I think you ought to see Doc Connolly.'

'I'm fine.'

'Does Bert know?'

'No, and don't you go telling him.' She gave Marjorie a long stare. 'Understand?' Marjorie nodded. 'I've just been overdoing it, that's all.'

Marjorie looked unconvinced. 'I still say you should get checked over. If it's nothing, no harm done, and if it's something then the doc can make it better. What have you got to lose?'

'It'll be a waste of the doc's time,' grumbled Joan. 'Anyway, I think you'd better get off before Bert comes home and wants to know what's going on.' She hauled herself to her feet, and began to shepherd Marjorie towards the door.

'You think about what I said, Joan Makepiece,' said Marjorie as she stepped over the threshold and began to walk down the path. 'Better safe than sorry,' she added, over her shoulder.

But Joan ignored her and shut the door. Still wincing, she leaned against it.

19

Bex stood in the playground watching Alfie and Lewis hare around with their friends in the May sunshine and waiting for the bell to go, which was the signal for the kids to line up and the parents to leave. She exchanged the occasional smile and nod with the other mothers, as she'd done for quite a few weeks now, and wondered how long it was going to take for her to be on first-name terms with them. Most of them stood around in little groups, chatting, their friendships having been forged when the kids joined the school aged five – or even before that in a little place like this; at the mother and toddler groups or possibly even at antenatal classes. Bex knew it would take time to become integrated and accepted and, as far as she knew, there was no quick fix. The boys were making friends with their classmates but as yet there'd been no invitations for birthday parties or play-dates. It'll come, Bex told herself, and, when it did, that would be when she got to know the parents. It was a shame, she thought, that Lewis's birthday always fell in the summer holidays and Alfie's birthday wasn't until Christmas. Maybe, she mused, she ought to have an un-birthday tea-party – invite a bunch of small boys around to play in the garden. Or would that smack of showing off that she lived in a big house?

She could not force people to be friends with her but working in the pub was helping – although, as yet, she'd not met anyone she recognised from the school playground. The people who popped in for a lunchtime drink and a snack were mostly old men, like Harry and his friends, or people who worked in the town centre. Not shop staff but men in suits – like estate agents and solicitors. Very few women, Bex had noticed. They were probably too busy racing round, getting shopping or multitasking in the way that working women generally had to. So much for the equality of the sexes.

The bell rang and Bex waited till the boys had been led into their classrooms by their teachers before she turned to go.

'Excuse me?'

Bex turned. 'Yes?' she said, brightly.

'I'm Jo Singleton. I'm the chair of the PTA.'

'Oh, yes.' Bex fixed a smile on her face because she knew what was coming next. In her experience the people who ran PTAs approached other mums in the playground when they wanted something.

'I expect you've heard,' began Jo, 'but it's the school summer fair coming up in a few weeks.'

Bex nodded. Her instincts had been right.

'I was wondering if you'd like to help out.'

'In what way?'

'Run a stall for me?'

'Possibly. It rather depends what it entails.'

'Oh, the committee do most of the donkey work. All we will need you to do on the day is turn up and take money or sell tickets or whatever. And, of course, before that, if you could bring any donations for the other stalls in to the school we'd be ever so grateful; cakes, bric-a-brac, prizes for the tombola...' Jo smiled at Bex.

'Yes, of course.'

'That's brilliant.' Jo whipped out a notebook. 'So, if I could have your name and contact number.'

Bex reeled them off. 'I love baking. I'll do you some cakes, shall I? A dozen or so?'

'A dozen?'

'More?'

'Whatever you feel happy to produce. The cake stall always sells out.'

'I know.'

'That's wonderful.' Jo made another note. 'So – are you the family who have moved into The Beeches?'

Bex nodded.

'And you have two boys here, is that right?'

'Yes, Lewis and Alfie – in years four and one.'

'Lovely.'

'And my stepdaughter goes to the comp.'

'Not St Anselm's?'

'My late husband wasn't a fan of private education.'

'Late? Oh... I am so sorry.'

'Yeah... well...'

An awkward silence fell. 'Anyway,' said Jo, 'thanks for volunteering, I mustn't keep you.'

'No.' And as Bex was about to say goodbye, Jo raced off. Bex sighed. Death isn't contagious, she wanted to shout after her. Or maybe she was busy, late for an appointment. Maybe. On the other hand, being involved in the school fête was probably another good way of meeting people, as long as they could cope with the fact she had a dead husband.

Later that morning she trotted next door to her shift at the pub. Belinda let her in with a cheery 'hello' and then asked Bex to help her with the bottling up.

'I might have to leave you on your own today for a bit,' she said as she picked up a crate of mixers to lug up the cellar stairs.

'Really?' Bex knew she had come on in leaps and bounds in terms of competence since she'd started work there but she still had glitches. She grabbed a crate of bitter lemon and prepared to follow Belinda.

'I've got to take the car over to Cattebury for its MOT. Miles'll help if you have a problem,' said Belinda over her shoulder. 'Not that you will of course.'

'I suppose.'

'You'll be fine. It's got to happen one day.' She put the heavy crate down on the bar with an 'oof'.

'I suppose.' Bex put her crate down on the floor.

'But I'd better warn you, he's in a mood because we had a late booking for the function room tonight and they want a finger buffet for fifteen. He's not a happy chappy – in fact he's in a foul mood.'

Great, thought Bex. She hoped she wouldn't do anything to make it worse.

Belinda smiled. 'But this isn't getting the bottling up done. While I put this lot on the shelves can you bring up a crate of Coronas, please?'

The pair worked until the shelves were full.

'Right,' said Belinda. 'I'm off out, so I'll leave you to open up,' she glanced at the pub clock, 'in about five minutes. Good luck.'

'I am hoping I'm going to rely on skill and training rather than luck,' responded Bex.

'Indeed.'

Five minutes after the door was unbolted Harry and Alf came in for their daily pint – or two – of beer. Bex poured their drinks, operated the till and handed over their change all without a hitch. And then a party of around ten men barrelled in, none of whom she recognised. The noise level in the pub went through the roof and Harry and Alf looked grumpy at this invasion of strangers into *their* pub.

Bex battled as best she could making gin and tonics, pouring pints and glasses of wine and then the Guinness ran out. Flustered, she ran into the kitchen and saw that Miles seemed to be up to his proverbial ears in pastry, mixing bowls and saucepans.

'Hi, Miles, I need a hand to change a barrel.'

'Which one?' he said, as he hauled a tray of vol-au-vent cases out of the oven.

'The Guinness.'

'Haven't you learned how yet?' He sounded exasperated as he put the hot tray down on the counter and picked up another of uncooked sausage rolls. He checked the oven temperature, adjusted it and slammed them in.

'No, not yet.'

Bex stood back to allow him out of the door and returned to her customers. As he lifted the bar flap she thought she heard him mutter, 'For God's sake,' as he went.

She felt a bit aggrieved. It was hardly her fault that that was a skill she had yet to be taught, nor that Belinda had left her on her own when Miles was so obviously stretched. She took the money then promised to bring the two missing pints of Guinness over in a minute.

'It's sorted,' said Miles appearing at the top of the cellar stairs.

'Thanks.' She was starting to feel out of her depth again as a couple more customers came in and waited for their turn to be served. As she was about to deal with the missing drinks from the original order, another group of people came in.

She stuck her head around the kitchen door.

'Miles? I need a hand.'

'Again?' he snapped.

Bex almost had a go at him back but she decided that it might be better not to antagonise him further. Besides, she was too busy, even with him helping out, to waste breath on sticking up for herself. In a few minutes things began to get under control and the queue was dealt with.

'Can I order some food?' said one of the men from the big group.

'Of course.'

'Best I get back to the kitchen,' said Miles. 'And let's hope the food for tonight's not ruined.'

Bex, ignoring the inference that, if it was, it would be down to her, grabbed her pad and the businessman began to rattle off the order.

'Hang on,' she said as she struggled to write the order down as fast as it was being given. 'So that's three tuna on brown, one with no cucumber, two pizzas, one toasted BLT—'

'Two toasted BLTs,' she was corrected.

'—two BLTs.'

'One on brown.'

'One on brown, a soup of the day and a pasty.'

'Yes.' The guy sounded slightly shirty. 'And if you could make it snappy – we've got to be somewhere else in about thirty minutes.'

'We'll do our best.'

'Good.'

She began to enter the food order into the till but made a mistake and had to start again. The guy on the other side of the bar sighed heavily. Finally she got the entries all correct. 'That's fifty-three pounds and forty eight pence.'

The man handed over a credit card and Bex tapped the buttons. While she waited for the machine to connect to the bank she popped the order into the kitchen.

'The group says they're in a hurry.'

'Then they should have gone to a McDonald's,' said Miles pulling a chopping board towards him and getting some bacon on the griddle.

Bex zipped back to the bar where the man was drumming his fingers on the bar.

She got him to enter his PIN, finished the transaction, and then handed him the receipt.

'The chef says he'll be as quick as he can.' She thought that was more diplomatic than repeating what Miles had actually said.

The number of customers in the pub continued to grow but, with Miles busy cooking, Bex had to rely on her own skills, which she soon discovered weren't that good when she was under pressure. Pouring drinks, ferrying food, clearing tables and taking money seemed so much harder to combine now she was pushed and the more flustered she got the worse it became.

She dashed into the kitchen in response to the little light that flashed by the till which was Miles's signal that another food order was ready.

'Two pizzas,' he said.

She picked up the plates and turned round and one of the pizzas flew off the plate like a frisbee and landed, right-way up, on the floor.

'Shit,' groaned Bex.

'Oh, for fuck's sake!'

Bex felt ridiculously close to tears.

'At least you didn't do it in front of the punters,' said Miles. He dashed over and swished it up, brushed off the underside and dumped it on the plate.

'Miles!'

'They'll never know,' he said. 'Go on – before it gets cold.'

Bex walked back into the bar and hoped she didn't look guilty. She'd *dropped* the pizza and she was about to serve it to a total stranger. Supposing he got ill?

She pushed the thought from her brain and put the plates on the tables. 'I hope you enjoy it.'

'And the quiche?' said shirty-man.

'What quiche?'

'We ordered a quiche.'

They hadn't. She could swear blind they hadn't.

'I'll check with the kitchen.'

She dashed back to see Miles. 'They want a quiche. They didn't order it. I know they didn't.'

'Really?' said Miles, his disbelief obvious. In about a minute he'd arranged a slice of quiche on a plate with a dollop of potato salad and a small pile of green leaves. 'Go,' he said.

Things had quietened down considerably when Belinda returned.

'How did you get on?' she asked, as she took off her jacket and set about clearing some of the tables that Bex hadn't found the time to deal with herself.

'I had to get Miles to help a couple of times.'

'I bet he wasn't happy about that.'

Bex wasn't sure whether to be loyal or lie. 'Well, you know... I need to learn to change a barrel.'

'Is that all? We'll do that first thing tomorrow. It's not hard, honest. Now, you get off, I can deal with the rest of the shift. You deserve to go home and put your feet up before you have to go and get the kids.'

'You sure?'

Belinda nodded. 'It's hardly busy, is it? Not now.' Which was true. There were only a handful of customers left. 'Go!'

Bex said goodbye and made her way to the door while Belinda headed for the kitchen. It was only as Bex was about to turn into her drive that she remembered she'd left her mac hanging on the peg in the pub. She returned and let herself in.

The door to the kitchen was open and she could hear Miles's voice.

'Bloody hell, Belinda, I thought you said she'd be all right.'

'You having to change a barrel is hardly the end of the world,' replied Belinda.

'But I had more than enough to do without nursemaiding her.'

'You coped.'

'That's not the point. I know you like her but it doesn't make up for the fact she's verging on incompetent.'

'That's the thing, Miles, I *do* like her and she'll learn. And you're exaggerating.'

'Huh.'

'You're in a foul mood because of a late order for tonight and you're taking it out on Bex.'

'Rubbish.'

'It isn't,' said Belinda standing her ground.

'I don't like being put under that sort of pressure, that's all. If you'd been behind the bar I could have got on with the buffet and the lunch service not had to keep abandoning them both to prop up Bex. If she doesn't shape up, I suggest you make her ship out.'

Bex grabbed her coat and slipped out. At least she knew where she stood with Miles – on rocky ground.

20

L ater that week, Olivia left the town hall after the council meeting and went to find her bike at the rack. As she pedalled due west, up the high street towards her house, she shielded her eyes with one hand against the blinding light of the low sun and thought about what had been said by Leanne Knowles and the local police sergeant in their report to the councillors about the crime situation which was, as the council had acknowledged, all very unsettling.

'And it's not just the break-ins and the burglaries and the thefts – what about the kids doing drugs in the nature reserve?' Olivia had asked when questions had been invited after the police had made their report.

'I patrol it on a regular basis,' said Leanne. 'The trouble is they see me coming and run off.'

Olivia sniffed. It didn't seem much of an excuse for not nabbing the little delinquents.

'They shouldn't be there in the first place.'

'It's a big public open space,' said Leanne. 'I can't prevent people from using it.'

'Even if they're off their heads on drink or skunk or whatever they do?' asked Olivia.

'I can move them on and tell them not to come back if I think they may be committing antisocial behaviour – but, as I said, I have to catch them.'

'I imagine you know who frequents this open-air drug-den,' said Olivia. 'The usual suspects, no doubt.'

'A few probably are, yes.'

'And, no doubt, they're responsible for all the break-ins.'

'We have no evidence as such,' said the police sergeant, butting in.

'But it stands to reason,' said Olivia. 'Everyone knows that drug addicts have to thieve to support their habits.'

'Not all of them,' said Leanne. 'I've met a load of addicts who come from perfectly nice, middle-class families, much like your own. They're the kids with the money and so they're able to afford the drugs in the first place.'

As if, thought Olivia, as she pedalled up the hill. Her son and his fellow pupils at St Anselm's had been brought up with decent values. Besides, St Anselm's had a zero-tolerance policy to drugs and the kids wouldn't risk losing their places for a puff on a spliff, she was absolutely sure about that.

As she neared the house the security system tripped and flooded the garden with light. That should put off any burglars, thought Olivia. She opened the garage door, pushed her bike inside and then locked it up, checking carefully that it really was secure before she let herself into the house.

'Zac? Zac, I'm home.'

Silence. She wasn't surprised as he'd only grunted at her since she'd stopped his allowance. Let him sulk, she thought.

She went into the kitchen and got a bottle of wine out of the rack. A nice Malbec was what the doctor ordered. She poured herself a glass and went to sit on the sofa before she picked up the remote and flicked through the channels. Nothing. Zilch. As she sipped her wine she heard the key in the lock. Instinctively she glanced at the clock – getting on for eight. As Nigel came into the house, Olivia picked up her wine and made her way into the kitchen.

'Evening, darling. Have you had a good day at work?'

'It was work.'

'Drink?' Olivia held up the bottle.

Nigel nodded. He came over to the counter as Olivia got out a glass, poured his wine and handed it to him.

'Cheers,' she said, clinking her glass against his.

'The thing is, Ol, I've been thinking.'

Why, thought Olivia, did that sound ominous? But she said, 'Really, darling,' in what she hoped sounded was a bright and positive way.

Nigel went over to the sofa, put his drink onto the coffee table, and flopped down. He stared at his glass.

Olivia leaned against a worktop in the kitchen and resisted the temptation to tell him to spit it out.

'The thing is, there's a lot of financial uncertainty at the moment.'

Olivia narrowed her eyes. What was he beating up to? 'And?'

'And the markets are jittery.'

'Yes, but...'

'Things are unstable.'

'But we're all right.' She said it as a statement of fact not as a question.

'I don't think anyone can be sure of that at the moment.'

'What are you trying to tell me?'

'I think we ought to release the equity in this house. I think we ought to downsize.'

Olivia had taken a sip of her drink and instead of swallowing it, she inhaled it. She coughed until her eyes watered. She finally got her breath.

'Downsize,' she gasped as she wiped the tears off her cheeks.

'Yes. The other evening I had a look at those houses up behind the station on my way home. Well, I had a look at the show home; nothing else much is finished yet.'

'But they're crap. They're being thrown up, they're not solid and built to last like this place. I should know, I was at the planning meeting when they were approved.'

'They're not that bad.'

'Huh.' Olivia took a gulp of wine. 'But why? Why the hell do you want to move – and to *there*?'

'Face it, Ol, we don't need a place as big as this. The kids have left home and Zac will be off to uni soon. We rattle around in this place and it costs a fortune to run.'

'But it's our home,' she protested.

'It's a house.'

'But what about Christmas – when everyone comes home for the holidays?'

'So you're telling me we keep this place going for a couple of days a year when the kids may or may not come and stay.'

'Yes. And why not?'

'Because it's a waste of money.'

'So? We can afford it.'

'Yes, but if we both die then the kids get stuck with a vast inheritance tax bill.'

'For God's sake, Nigel, we've years ahead of us yet.' Olivia stopped and stared at Nigel. 'You're not... you aren't...?'

'No. No, of course not.'

Olivia didn't think there was any 'of course' about it; his short-ness of temper, his erratic behaviour, and now this. 'Really?'

'Yes, *really*.'

She didn't have much choice but to believe him. But if he *was* lying she could hardly call his bluff, march him down to Dr Connolly and demand an examination then and there. Besides, she was as fit as a fiddle and they *both* had to die before the kids got stung by a tax bill.

'Then in that case I can see no reason at all for what you suggest.'

'But, Ol—'

'No, Nigel. This is my home. I love this house and that's that.'

'But think of the equity we'd release.'

Olivia drained her drink. 'Which bit of "no" don't you under-stand?'

'And which bit of "this place is too big" don't *you* understand?'

She stamped back into the kitchen to pour herself another glass of wine and cook dinner for herself and Nigel. Not that he deserved a decent meal after that, in her opinion.

*

Olivia lay on her back in bed, wide-eyed, staring into the dark. What the hell was going on? What exactly did Nigel mean about things being unstable and uncertain? Was he about to be shown the door? Had he already been shown the door? No, that didn't make sense and anyway, he'd tell her, wouldn't he? Yes, she'd read in the papers that house prices might fall but, given they'd bought this house for around two hundred grand when they'd first moved here and it was now worth well over a million, that wasn't ever going to affect them. And yes, it was big and it wasn't cheap to run but they could easily afford to on Nigel's income. And it was the family home. However Olivia looked at Nigel's desire to downsize, it didn't add up. The only way any of it made sense was if he needed the money for something else.

Olivia turned her head on her pillow and looked at her sleeping husband. There was only one reason she could think why he might need a sum of money like they'd get from selling the house – and that was if he needed to buy another one, for himself... Two small houses rather than one big one. And there was only one reason why he'd want to do that that she could think of. She turned her head back to stare at the ceiling again.

Was that what he did on a Tuesday? Was that why his sports kit tended to look unworn? Was there a third person in the marriage? Silent tears slid down Olivia's temples and onto the bed.

'Good morning, Olivia,' said Heather. She peered at her visitor. 'Are you all right?'

'No, no, I don't think I am.'

Heather flung the door wide and tried not to think about everything she had had planned for the morning. Olivia looked awful and obviously needed a shoulder to cry on – that was if she had any tears left, because, by the look of her, she'd already cried a river.

'Come in. Tea?'

'I'd rather have a coffee.'

'I've only got instant, will that do?'

Olivia nodded as Heather turned and led the way into the kitchen. Olivia took a seat at the kitchen table as Heather bustled around getting out mugs and the milk and putting the kettle on and wondered what on earth might have upset Olivia so badly.

Olivia stared at her wedding ring as she twisted it. 'Heather, I'm worried.'

'What about?'

'Nigel.'

Heather wanted to tell Olivia that she was worried about her own husband and she really didn't need someone else's problems on top. But that wouldn't have been Christian so she said, 'Why, what's he done?'

Olivia looked at Heather. 'That's it, I don't know.'

Heather sat down opposite Olivia. 'So...?'

'He wants us to downsize.'

Heather shrugged. 'Well, it is an awfully big house for just the three of you.'

'I know, but he was talking about releasing the equity. Why?'

Heather felt that Olivia was talking to the wrong person if she wanted financial advice. She shrugged. 'Is that so bad?'

'But why? It isn't as if we need the cash.'

'He must have a reason.'

'That's the thing.' Olivia's eyes glistened with unshed tears. 'If Nigel needs such a huge amount of money, I can only come to one conclusion.'

The kettle clicked off but Heather ignored it. 'And?'

'That he wants to buy another house.'

'I'm not with you.'

'For himself... if we sold The Grange we could afford two smaller houses.'

'Oh. You mean...? You think...?'

Olivia nodded. 'There's something else.'

'What?'

'He says he plays badminton on a Tuesday night.'

'You've lost me,' murmured Heather. She turned round and made the tea and coffee.

'Only I don't think he does. He takes sports kit to work with him but it comes home pretty much as clean as it went.' Olivia raised her eyes to meet Heather's as Heather put the steaming mugs on the table. 'So just what *is* he doing after work?'

'You've got to talk to him.'

'I'm so frightened of what the answer might be. Heather, we've been married for over thirty years and I know he's not the easiest bloke on the planet, but he's *my* bloke. I can't bear the thought of being abandoned by him.'

Heather reached across the table and took Olivia's hands in hers.

'And supposing,' continued Olivia, 'he's not having an affair. If I confront him about what he's getting up to, it shows I've lost faith in him, that I don't trust him, and what would that do to our relationship?'

'I can see that.' Heather thought for a moment. 'You need to find out about the badminton for certain – one way or the other.'

'But how?'

'Ring his office?'

'And say what? What possible excuse might I have to ask, without making it obvious that I think he's lying to me?'

'Good point.' Silence fell as both women considered the problem.

'I suppose,' said Heather, 'you could do something like take his trainers out of his sports bag, or take one out. If he really is playing and his kit got sabotaged then he'd be pretty mad and be sure to mention it.'

Olivia nodded. 'And if he doesn't, it means he isn't. Bloody hell, Heather, you really are quite Machiavellian, aren't you?'

Heather preened. 'Thank you.'

21

On Sunday, Olivia was in two minds as to whether to go to church or not. She liked church, she liked the calm that it brought to her busy life – the enforced rest that sitting in a pew, not being able to *organise*, or *do*, or *achieve*, gave her. She liked the peace, the predictability of the order of service, the space it gave her to think... And that was the trouble. She wasn't entirely sure she did want to *think* right now because if she did she knew what would dominate her thoughts. *Nigel!* And worse... if he was doing what she reckoned he was doing where did that leave her? She really didn't want to think about what her future might be because, while he might be impossible to live with right now, she couldn't imagine *not* living with him.

Olivia sat on her dressing table stool in her undies and stared at her reflection. She wasn't bad-looking for her age but supposing Nigel had found someone a lot younger? Someone who didn't have small folds of slightly crepey skin at her neck, a couple of crow's feet by her eyes, a wrinkle between her brows, and tits which were, frankly, heading south. How could she compete with youth? And middle-aged men did this sort of thing; trade in the old girl for a newer model. She read about it in the glossy gossip mags all the time; seen pictures of ageing film stars and their new, young, beautiful trophy wives. She sighed and came to a decision; she couldn't watch Nigel every second so she might as well go to church – pray for Nigel to see sense, pray she would find a way to deal with it, pray for the composure to stop her from killing him if she was proved right. She'd definitely be better off in the company of God.

Swiftly she applied a lick of make-up and then put on her skirt and blouse. She grabbed her coat from the wardrobe and went downstairs. Nigel was still at the kitchen table, in his pyjamas and dressing gown and reading the Sunday paper.

'Off to church?' he said, barely looking up.

She nodded. How can you be so calm when you are destroying my life? she wanted to yell. Instead, she said, 'Back in a couple of hours. If you could make the time to cut the grass...?'

Nigel glanced up. 'God, must I? I've had a tough week, I'm knackered.'

And if you spent less time screwing your mistress you might have more energy. 'Yes.'

'Can't Zac do it?'

Olivia looked at him for a beat. 'I don't ask you to do much to look after the house and garden so I don't think I'm being unreasonable.'

'And I don't think I am either – not in saying Zac could pull *his* finger out once in a while.'

'I don't have time for a row now. I'll be late.' She turned and swept out of the house. She unlocked the garage and got her bike out, now feeling angry on top being unsettled and scared. A few weeks ago she'd felt quite smug about her future – lovely house, husband with a good job and a decent pension, four kids doing all right... How things could turn on a sixpence. She certainly didn't feel smug now.

Heather hauled herself off her knees and slid her bottom back onto the pew. She looked over her shoulder and saw that the church was almost empty – thirty, maybe forty in the congregation, out of a town of almost six thousand. The slight surge that Easter had produced had fallen away again.

'Can I sit next to you?' came a low voice beside her. Heather turned back towards the aisle and looked up to see Olivia.

'Of course.' Heather budged up to give her space to sit down.

Olivia put her handbag down at her feet, opened her prayer book at the page for matins and then found the first hymn they were due to sing in her hymn book. Having got herself organised she leaned forwards and prayed for a couple of minutes then straightened up.

'How's Nigel? Has he said any more about downsizing?' asked Heather.

'No,' admitted Olivia. 'And I haven't mentioned it either. I'm hoping that I'm imagining it. Except I'll know, one way or the other, after Tuesday and badminton.'

Heather gave her a long stare then said, 'I truly hope you're completely wrong.'

Olivia nodded.

The organ struck up, everyone stood as Brian and the choir processed down the aisle and took their seats near the altar and Heather squeezed Olivia's arm and whispered, 'I'll pray for you.'

'Thanks,' whispered back Olivia. 'I need as much help as I can get.'

And I would like to ask Olivia to pray for me, thought Heather, because maybe God knew what was causing Brian so much angst; she certainly didn't, and she felt she ought to. Otherwise, how on earth could she help him?

The service progressed and Heather participated on autopilot, making the responses, singing the hymns while her mind tussled with other issues, like what was the matter with Brian and what the hell was Nigel up to? Not that Olivia and Nigel's affairs were anyone's business but their own but Olivia was Heather's friend and she couldn't help but be concerned.

She watched her husband leave his seat and climb the few stairs into the pulpit.

'May the words of my mouth and the meditations of our hearts be acceptable in thy sight, O Lord, our rock and redeemer,' she heard her husband say.

The congregation chorused 'amen' and sat down.

'I was thinking about spring this week, and the change in the seasons,' began Brian, but Heather let her mind wander as she looked at the flowers on the altar and wondered if they'd last till the following Sunday.

The foliage might, she thought, if she changed the water. Maybe, after the service and while everyone was hanging around having tea and coffee at the back of the church, she'd get that done. And she ought to get round to checking the kneelers. Brian said that someone had told him that a number of them needed their seams repairing. Heather looked at the one she'd been using. It looked all right. She pushed it through a hundred and eighty degrees with her toes to check the other side. No, it was fine.

She suddenly realised that silence reigned in the church.

She glanced up at Brian. He was standing there, his mouth open, but he was saying nothing. How odd. He seemed to be staring at the back of the church so Heather swivelled in her pew to see what the distraction was but there was nothing. The silence continued. The congregation began to shuffle. Something was obviously going horribly wrong. Olivia looked at Heather.

'Is Brian all right?' she murmured.

'No, no I don't think so,' said Heather. Feeling desperately self-conscious and worried that she might be doing completely the wrong thing, she stood up and pushed past Olivia to reach the aisle then walked to the pulpit. She stood at the bottom of the stairs.

'Brian? Brian, are you OK?' she hissed.

Nothing, no response, no acknowledgement…

The congregation was getting quite restless and the hubbub of speculation increased in volume.

'Brian?' Heather put her hand on the rail and her foot on the bottom step. '*Brian!*'

He didn't even turn his head. Heather made a decision and mounted the stairs. She grasped his arm firmly. 'Brian, come with me.' She tugged on his elbow.

Sightlessly and wordlessly he turned.

'Come on, darling. Careful on the stairs.' She backed down the steps, pulling him with her and he followed, but like someone sleepwalking. She led him into the vestry while behind her the muted whispers erupted into full-on talking.

She shut the door to block out the noise and led Brian to a chair.

'Sit down, honey,' she said, kneeling in front of him. 'Brian, Brian, what's the matter? What happened?' She shook him. 'Brian!'

He turned his face to her. 'Heather?'

'Brian, what happened?'

He passed his hand over his face. 'Happened?'

'You were delivering your sermon and you just... you just stopped.'

Worry clouded Brian's face as he looked about him, at the sink and the clutter in the vestry. 'I stopped?'

Heather nodded. 'What's the matter?'

Brian's face cleared slightly. 'I felt ill. Yes, I felt ill. Dizzy.'

'Do you want me to get Dr Connolly?'

'No. No, I'm fine now.'

'Are you?'

Brian sagged. 'Well... not really. I don't think I can finish the service.'

From the other side of the door came the sound of the organ striking up the final hymn.

'I think Bert Makepiece has got things in hand,' said Heather. She tried to sound cheerful. 'This is probably the most excitement he's ever had since he's been a churchwarden.'

Brian shook his head. He looked close to tears.

'Come on, I'm going to take you home.' Heather got to her feet. Her knees cracked as she straightened.

Brian gazed up at her. 'I can go out there. I can't face them.'

'We can go out through this door.' She nodded at the vestry entrance. Heather pulled her husband to his feet and then opened the door. 'Let's get you home and then you can tell me what's really going on.'

'I told you,' said Brian, stubbornly, 'I felt ill.'

Amy had almost finished cleaning Bex's house the following afternoon when her employer came back from the pub.

'Hi, Amy,' called Bex as she let herself in. 'I'm going to put the kettle on, would you like one?'

'Love one,' Amy shouted back down over the banisters.

Bex was hoiking the teabags out of a couple of mugs when Amy clattered down the stairs a minute or so later.

'Good weekend?' she asked Amy.

'Great, thank you. My Billy took me to the Old Mill on Saturday.'

'The Old Mill?'

'It's a right posh resto. All the toffs from round here go there.'

'That was some treat.'

'It certainly was. Must have cost him a mint but it was so lush.' Amy looked dreamy at the memory.

'Lucky you.'

'So...' said Amy as she got the milk out and sloshed it into the mugs, 'how are you getting on at the pub?'

'I thought I was doing fine. Then I had to cope on my own for a bit. God, Amy, it was so tricky.'

Amy laughed. 'You'll get the hang of it.'

'I hope so. I don't want Belinda to have to sack me. Actually, I think Belinda is OK about my lack of experience – I'm not so sure about Miles. But hey...'

'You'll get there. Everyone has to start at the bottom.' Amy sipped her tea. 'Anyway, this ain't getting your house finished off, is it?' She turned to go back upstairs. 'Ooh, want to know something else I heard?'

'Go on.'

'The vicar had a meltdown in church yesterday. Lost it completely while he was giving the sermon.'

'What? Had a go at someone?'

'No, nothing like that. I heard he kind of dried up; just stood there – lights on but no one home. His missus had to take him back to the vicarage and old Bert Makepiece, seeing as how he's a churchwarden, had to take over.'

'That's sad. Maybe he was poorly.'

'That's what Heather is saying.'

'Then I expect he was,' said Bex, briskly.

'Maybe.' Amy looked sceptical. 'But you hear about people losing their marbles, forgetting where they are, what they're doing...'

'Even so, I don't think it's for us to speculate about what was going on. Especially as neither of us was there.'

Amy shrugged. It seemed to Bex that her words had fallen on very deaf ears.

Olivia rang the bell of the vicarage and waited in the shelter of the porch, warmed by the May sunshine, until Heather opened it.

'Oh, hello,' said Heather. 'How lovely to see you. Have you time for a coffee?'

'Not really. I came round to see how Brian is and to ask if you're going to the book club tonight.'

'Oh... Brian says he's fine. A dizzy spell apparently.'

'Nothing serious then.'

'No.'

Olivia didn't push the issue but she felt that Heather was lying, possibly to herself. 'And the book club?'

Yes, I'm looking forward to it; I loved that book.'

'Hadn't you read it before?'

'No, it must have passed me by, although I adored *Rebecca*.'

'And that didn't spur you on to read her others?'

'No, I suppose life got in the way. Anyway, isn't that the whole reason for book clubs,' said Heather, 'to make you read things, like *Frenchman's Creek*, that you would have otherwise missed?'

'Yes, I suppose so. I thought I'd ask Bex if she'd like to come along.'

'That's a nice idea. Apart from an initial visit I've hardly seen her since. And maybe now she's had a chance to settle in she might like the idea.'

'Yes. I really feel she ought to integrate more. I know she works lunchtimes at the pub, but... well...'

'She'll meet a better class of person at something like the book club?'

Olivia completely failed to catch the joking tone of Heather's voice. 'Precisely,' she said. 'Right, well, I'll see you this evening. I'll drop in on Bex and see if I can persuade her to come along.'

'You do that.'

Olivia said goodbye and walked up the road, past the cricket pitch where a groundsman was driving the heavy roller over the wicket, and continued up to the high street. She hoped Bex was in as she rang the bell. The car was on the drive but, living where she did, Bex was unlikely to take her car to go shopping, not unless she was doing a big weekly one at the supermarket in Cattebury.

She heard footsteps on the other side of the front door. Good. 'Hello, Bex. I'm here on a mission.'

A flicker of anxiety flashed across Bex's face.

'Oh, it's all right. I'm not nobbling you for anything.'

'Good. I got spammed to run a stall at the school fête last week.'

'Ah, Jo Singleton cornered you, did she?'

'She did indeed. So...?'

'Fancy coming to the book club tonight? It's upstairs at the pub.'

'Not much point, really.'

'Why?'

'I won't have read the book.'

Olivia couldn't fault the logic. 'It's not all about the books though. It's very social. If you want to get to know people it's a good place to start. And now you've settled in... you said before that Megan might babysit for you once you had been here for a bit.'

'I did.' Bex paused for a couple of seconds. 'So what book did the club read?'

'*Frenchman's Creek.*'

'Oh, I loved that book. I've even got a copy somewhere, although Lord knows where it is.'

'Well then, why don't you come along? And it doesn't matter if you can't find your copy. I'm sure you can remember the story well enough not to have to refer to the book.'

'I suppose. It's been a while since I read it.'

Olivia could see that Bex was wavering. She moved in for the proverbial kill. 'Shall I call for you on the way past?'

'Ummm.'

'You'll only be next door.'

'Oh, OK.'

'I'll be here for you at seven fifteen. We start at seven thirty but that'll give you a chance to meet everyone first.'

'Great.'

Mission accomplished, Olivia walked on through town towards the station and the new houses. Knowledge was power, she'd told herself, and the more she knew about the new houses the more ammunition she would have to hand to argue against any idea of downsizing to one of them. Besides, assuming that Nigel's stated objective about 'releasing equity' wasn't a cover for some other plan, the new estate was the last place she'd want to downsize to. Olivia pushed the thoughts out of her head. She couldn't, *wouldn't*, worry about that till she'd carried out her – or rather, Heather's – plan.

22

Zac was still angry with his mother about his allowance being stopped but at least he'd managed to nick enough off her to square away his dealer so, although he was still broke, he wasn't broke *and* scared. In fact, given what he'd pinched he was in a nice bit of credit with Dan. And stealing off her served her right for being so arsey. He imagined that one day she'd spot that a ring had gone from her jewellery collection but she rarely, if ever, wore any of it. He was curious as to why she'd moved it to his dad's filing cabinet but he could hardly ask – not without revealing that he knew where the keys were hidden and, more importantly, had used them. He supposed it might be because of the burglaries happening in and around Little Woodford so, if she did notice its loss, she might think she'd been another victim. Maybe he ought to steal more and make it look like a proper job. Of course, that plan was flawed because getting rid of it wasn't quite the doddle he'd imagined it to be. He'd taken it to the pawnbroker in Cattebury thinking that all he had to do was hand it over and pocket the cash. Easy. Only it hadn't played out like that.

'Where did you get this, then?' the old guy who ran the shop had asked, as he examined the rubies set in the ring.

'My nan left it to me,' said Zac, glibly. 'She said I should give it to my fiancée when I decide to get married. But I'd rather have the dosh.'

'Really.' The guy had sounded sceptical. 'And you're over eighteen, are you?'

'Of course,' Zac had lied again.

'So, before we do business I'm going to need proof of your ID, address and age. And it's got to be proper documents; passport, utility bill, driving licence – that sort of thing.'

'Oh.'

'That going to be a problem?'

'No, just I didn't know so I haven't got anything on me.'

'Best you come back when you have.'

'Yeah, OK.' He held out his hand for the ring. 'Can you tell me what you'd give me for it, though?'

'It might be worth about a grand. I'd give you five hundred.'

'Five hundred!' Blimey, much better than he'd hoped

'Ballpark figure. I'd have to give it a proper look when you bring it back – see how good the stones are, that sort of thing. I'm not promising five hundred, though. It might be worth less.'

Zac tucked the ring back in his pocket feeling pretty happy. Of course, having cash would be much better but if he gave the ring to Dan, Dan could flog it. Dan was over eighteen and would have those documents. He could take it to the pawnbroker.

And Dan had been cool with the plan. Dan had told him he'd only got a couple of hundred for it but Zac didn't care. He had credit with his pusher which would last until his allowance started again – and he was sure his mum would relent next month – so he was feeling pretty good as he headed for the play park shortly after his mother had gone out to her book club. As always he had arranged to meet Dan over by the stand of trees at the edge of the recreation area.

Dan was waiting for him.

'What do you want today?' said Dan.

'Got any Special K?'

'Might have. How much do you want?'

'Five grams.'

'Hand over the cash.'

Zac felt his world rock. 'But I gave you that ring. You said you'd got a couple of hundred.'

'What ring?'

Zac stared at him as dizziness swept over him. 'You're joking me.'

'What ring, Zac?'

Zac flew at him, his fists flailing, but Dan sidestepped him and pulled out his knife. 'I wouldn't want to hurt you, Zac, but I suggest you calm down.' His voice was full of menace. He waved the craft knife around. The little blade caught the sun and flashed. 'So, if you want your Kit Kat you'd better find the money.'

Zac felt his eyes pricking. 'You can't.'

'I can do what I like. I'm the one with the gear, remember. And what are you going to do? Go to the police? Tell them you stole from your mummy?' he sneered. 'I don't think so.'

Zac wished he was bigger, tougher... less scared. Dan was right, there was nothing he could do and he was desperate for a hit. 'Give me some credit, Dan. Please. I'll pay you back, you know that.'

Dan got out his knife and examined the blade. 'Just as long as you do. But, I'm telling you, Zaccy-boy, this is the last time. From here on in I want cash upfront. Understand?'

Shit – and with his allowance stopped this was going to be a problem.

The ladies of Little Woodford book club drained the last of their wine, and prepared to disperse. They stood around chatting, exchanging pleasantries and enjoying each other's company with no one wanting to be the party-pooper and break up the event.

'Did you enjoy that?' said Olivia. She picked her capacious handbag off the floor and put it on the table.

'It was fun,' said Bex.

Beside her Jacqui Connolly picked up a near empty bottle of

Merlot and poured the dregs into her glass. 'Waste not, want not,' she said as she swigged it down. Then, 'Right, I'm off.' She turned, stumbled and cannoned into the table sending Olivia's handbag flying. It was undone and the contents flew out, scattering everywhere.

'Silly me,' said Jacqui, staring at the mess rather blearily.

'No harm done,' said Olivia, her lips tight with disapproval and irritation.

Across the other side of the table, where most of Olivia's possessions had landed, the lady whom Bex now knew was called Sylvia, and Heather, scrambled to pick her stuff up.

'Beeching Rise?' queried Sylvia, holding up the glossy sales brochure.

'So?'

'Why would you want this?'

'I don't think it's any of—'

'So why do you want a brochure? Are you planning on buying there?' Sylvia's eyes widened. 'You're going to buy to let, aren't you?'

'Frankly, Sylvia, just because I have picked up a brochure doesn't mean that I'm planning on buying there.'

The two women eyeballed each other across the table like a pair of cats squaring up for a fight. Then Olivia dropped her gaze, picked up her handbag and held out her hand for the possessions that Sylvia and Heather had gathered.

After that spat the atmosphere in the function room shifted slightly and the members of the book club started making excuses, saying their goodbyes and drifting down the stairs. Finally it was only Heather, Olivia and Bex left in the room.

'Would you like a coffee at mine?' offered Bex.

'If you can bear to be seen in my company, considering that Sylvia thinks I am some sort of Judas.'

'Don't be silly, of course I don't think that. And personally,' added Bex, cheerfully, 'I love a good nose around a show house. Who doesn't?'

The three women headed down the stairs and made their way through the bar. Bex said goodbye to Belinda who was busy working. 'See you tomorrow.'

'You'll have to tell me how you got on with the book club,' was the response.

They left the pub and were at Bex's front door a few moments later.

'I'm back,' called Bex, up the stairs.

Bex took her friends' coats and led the way into the kitchen. As she put the kettle on she heard footsteps thundering down the wooden staircase.

'Did you have a nice time?' said Megan, as she skidded into the kitchen. 'Oh, hello,' she added, seeing the visitors. 'Hello, Mrs Simmonds.'

'You know Heather?' asked Bex.

Megan nodded.

'I work at the school – teaching assistant. Part-time,' explained Heather.

'And we've met too, haven't we,' said Olivia.

'Have we?' asked Megan.

'The day you moved in. I told you about my son, Zac.'

'Oh yeah, I think I've met him – he's a friend of Ashley's.'

'Yes, that's him. How lovely. I sure you two have so much in common. You ought to get to know him better. Maybe you'd like to come to have tea at ours.'

'Maybe.'

Bex suppressed a smile. Megan sounded utterly indifferent. 'Were the boys okay?'

'They were fine, they haven't stirred.'

'Great.'

Megan said a shy goodbye and slid out of the kitchen.

Bex turned to Heather. 'How's she settling into school? Naturally, I've asked her how she is getting on, but you know what kids are like; their parents are the last to be told anything.'

'To be honest I don't have much to do with her. I generally

have to deal with the kids who are more challenging – the ones with special needs, either mental or physical.'

'Yes of course. It's just...'

'Yes?' prompted Heather.

'She wasn't happy at her last school. It was another reason why I decided to move.'

'Was she bullied?' asked Olivia. 'Of course, St Anselm's has a very strict policy regarding bullies.' The implication that the comp didn't came across loud and clear.

'I am sure the local school is equally strict; every school is these days. It doesn't stop it, though, does it? Kids will be kids,' countered Bex.

Heather intervened. 'If you'd like, I can make a few discreet enquiries in the staffroom. I'm sure Mrs Blake would tell me if Megan was failing to settle in. I find that, because I am a vicar's wife, people will tell me things they mightn't tell others.' She smiled. 'It can be a bit of a double-edged sword.'

'I bet it is. It's bad enough coping with one's own problems, let alone coping with other people's,' said Bex.

'But you'd listen to a friend with troubles, surely?' said Olivia to Bex.

'Probably. But I bet poor old Heather gets all sorts crying on her shoulders.'

Heather shrugged. 'I can't complain. It isn't as if I didn't know what Brian did for a living when I married him.'

The kettle boiled. 'Tea, coffee?' asked Bex.

'Coffee,' said her guests in unison.

'Decaff?' added Olivia, hopefully.

While Bex was making their drinks, Olivia said, 'I ought to confess, now it's just us.'

'What about?' said Heather.

'About Beeching Rise. Nigel thinks we should move there. Heather already knows but I think it's only fair to put you in the picture, too, Bex.'

'Move there? But why?'

Olivia shrugged and shook her head. 'I wish I knew. But I suspect I will in a day or so.' She looked at Heather.

Bex longed to ask questions, to find out more, but it all seemed rather too nosy. She had to content herself with the thought that, if Olivia wanted her to know at some point in the future, she'd be told.

The next morning, at break time, Heather Simmonds walked to the table at the back of the staffroom, collected a mug, spooned in some coffee granules and then joined the queue for the urn of boiling water, the milk and the biscuits. As she waited for her turn she checked out who else was in. As usual most of the staff were grouped by their departments, the exception being the IT teachers, who never seemed to want to associate with each other or the other staff but, instead, were glued to their smart phones or their iPads. Heather spotted the humanities staff gathered in one of the corners. Once she'd got her coffee, she wandered over.

'Hello, Irene,' she said to Mrs Blake.

'Heather? What can I do for you?'

'I was just wondering how things are?'

'Longing for half-term, if I'm honest. I really need to recharge my batteries. I can't imagine how knackered I'll be when we get to the summer holidays.'

'I know what you mean. Of course, with Brian being a vicar, the summer break is the only one we get when both of us can kick back.'

'Oh, yes, of course. I'd never thought of it like that.' Irene Blake looked suitably abashed.

'I ran into the people who moved into The Beeches the other day.' Heather hoped God would forgive the barefaced lie, considering she'd actively sought the first meeting by ringing the doorbell. 'Well, I ran into *her* – the poor woman being a widow and everything. I think her daughter is in your tutor group.'

'Megan, yes.'

'Can't be easy for a kid to move house and move schools all on top of losing one's dad.'

'She's a funny kid. A bit stand-offish if you ask me. She doesn't seem to want to be friends with Lily Breckenridge and you know how popular she is. In fact, I asked Lily to take her under her wing especially and it seems to me that Megan goes out of her way to rebuff all Lily's efforts. I did my best; I think it's up to Megan now to sort herself out.'

'Kids, eh?'

Irene Blake nodded.

Heather wandered off. Lily Breckenridge? Popular? Well, that was one view of the child. Personally, she had little time for her. As far as she had observed the way Lily behaved at school, either the other pupils kowtowed to her or she made life as miserable as possible for them. Frankly, she didn't blame Megan for shrugging off that particular hand of friendship. Heather thought that it was probably a wise move. But, did she tell Bex that Mrs Blake might have made a bit of an error with Megan's pastoral care?

23

'Got the cow,' crowed Lily to Summer as they ate their lunch together in the school canteen.

'I'm not with you, Lil.'

Lily rolled her eyes. 'Oh, do try and keep up. You know I friended Windy on Facebook?'

'Yeah.'

'Well, I've been getting to know some of her old pals – not that she had many.'

'What's the point in that? They live in London.'

Lily sighed. 'Yes, but they went to Windy's old school.'

'OK?'

'And now I know why Windy had to change schools.'

'Oh yeah?' Summer shovelled a forkful of macaroni cheese into her mouth. 'So?'

'So, it's dynamite.'

Summer stopped chewing. 'Tell me.'

'No. I want it to be a surprise.'

Summer lost interest and ate some more of her lunch.

'Aren't you going to ask me when I'm going to spring this surprise?' said Lily, annoyed that Summer wasn't more curious, wasn't more desperate to try and prise the information out of her.

'No, because the chances are you won't tell me that either

and, even if you did, it wouldn't be a surprise then, would it.' She chewed some more.

Lily shook her head and wondered why she bothered with Summer except she was the only other kid from her class who lived in her village, her dad was pretty loaded and she had a pony which she allowed Lily to ride. She had her uses.

'This surprise,' said Summer. 'Are you going to spring it soon?'

'Dunno. Got to make sure I can do it without getting caught.'

Summer lowered her fork onto her plate. 'Doesn't sound like it's something Mr Smithson's going to like.'

'Of course he won't. But once the cat is out of the bag there's no way anyone – even Smithy – will be able to stuff it back in again.'

'Why would Smithy want to stuff a cat in a bag?'

Lily stared at Summer in slack-jawed disbelief. How thick could you get? Well, if Summer was anything to go by, the answer was – unbelievably.

All through Tuesday, Olivia tried to keep herself busy, trying to do anything that would stop her thinking about Nigel and his badminton club and the fact that, when he'd had his shower before he left for work, she'd crept out of bed and taken one of his trainers out of his sports bag. She'd thought about taking both out but had decided it would have left the bag feeling too light and he might have noticed. And now she was trying to act as normally as possible while waiting for her husband to get back in. Finally, while she was watching the late evening news, she saw the lights of his car sweep up the drive and the click of his key in the lock. He came in, dropped his sports bag by the front door and headed for the kitchen.

'Evening, darling,' Olivia forced herself to say despite her hammering heart. 'There's supper for you in the fridge if you'd like it.'

'I need a drink first,' said Nigel picking up the wine bottle on the counter and pouring himself a glass.

'Sure,' said Olivia. 'And how was badminton?'

'Oh, just fine. Won my match.'

Did you now, she thought, as she willed her heart not to break.

Olivia was trying to carry on as normal the next morning, and failing miserably, when the doorbell rang. It was Heather.

'Come in,' said Olivia.

'And dare I ask? asked Heather as she stepped over the threshold.

Olivia led the way into the kitchen and picked up the sports bag which she put on the work surface and began to unpack. She held up the pair to the single trainer she'd removed.

'I asked Nigel how his badminton was last night. He said he won his match.' Then she held his T-shirt against her nose and sniffed. 'And this still smells of fabric conditioner, not sweat.'

'Oh.'

'So, what's he up to? What is he doing on a Tuesday night that gives him a reason to stay up in town for a few extra hours and which doesn't involve badminton?'

Heather sighed and shrugged.

'I'm not imagining it and I can only think of one thing. I mean, can you think of anything else?'

Heather stared at Olivia, not wishing to supply the obvious answer.

Olivia shook her head. 'What do I do, Heather? Do I pretend everything is OK and that I know nothing, or do I confront him? Have it out?'

'Maybe there is something going on but Nigel wanting to downsize doesn't mean he's planning to leave you. Maybe he's not playing badminton but maybe he needs money for his pension or he wants to set up a trust fund for the kids…'

'Or maybe Nigel's having an affair and is getting his other' – Olivia made double quotation marks in the air with her fingers – '"*affairs*" in order before he gets rid of me.'

'Then you have to talk to him.' She reached out and gave Olivia a hug. For Olivia this simple act of kindness was the last straw and she broke down in sobs.

Later that day the papers for the next day's council meeting appeared in the Dropbox on Olivia's iPad. They were, she thought, a welcome distraction – something to think about other than what might be happening to her marriage. She began to read through the applications for planning consent. Coombe Farm was one of the issues to be discussed.

Olivia stared at the screen of her tablet as she read the detailed application from the developers. In her head she knew she ought to oppose these houses, but her heart told her that it was, despite the proximity to some social housing, altogether a nicer, classier estate than the jerry-built one that was going up behind the station. If her life was about to go belly-up, she thought she'd rather wind up at Coombe Farm than Beeching Rise. She carried on reading the council papers and decided that there was only one course of action she could take. She knew it would make her unpopular but, given the mess her life seemed to be in, a bit of unpopularity would be a small price to pay if she could make her future less bleak.

Joan got the big key out of her mac pocket and opened the vestry door, stepping into the cool room that, as always, smelt faintly musty. She slipped off her mac and put on her pinny which she kept hanging up in the next cupboard to the one the vicar kept his vestments in. Then she picked up a tin of polish and a couple of yellow dusters and made her way into the body of the church. Pews and pulpit today, she decided as she began to work. She headed to the back of the church. She had a method; first she'd work from the back forwards, down the pews on the left of the main aisle then the ones on the right, till she got to the ones nearest the main church door. That way nothing got missed. And while she was at it she'd have a look at the kneelers.

Joan slid into the pew the furthest from the altar and began polishing and dusting the shelf for the prayer books, shuffling along every few seconds to reach the next section. As she went she picked the kneelers off their hooks and gave each one a once-over. Those that needed some repairs she left on the seat. She worked quickly and efficiently and in silence. She was about halfway along when she heard someone else enter the church.

She glanced towards the vestry door from behind a pillar. It was the vicar. As she watched she saw him go to the choir stalls and take a seat. Then he bowed his head. Joan carried on cleaning, being as quiet as possible, not wanting to disturb his prayers.

As she finished the pew she was working on she stood up to tiptoe into the next one and was stopped in her tracks by a noise. A sob.

This ain't right, she thought. She stood stock-still and listened. Another muffled wail. What on earth was up with the Reverend? Something wasn't right if he was here, on his own, having a cry. Joan leaned on the end of the pew. Should she go to him? Should she pretend she wasn't around? But what if he spotted her? She made up her mind. She dropped her can of spray polish on the old stone flags. It made a resounding and satisfactory clatter.

'Darn it,' she said loudly as she made a show of scuffling around on the floor to retrieve it.

'Is that you, Joan?' she heard the vicar call.

'Oh, Reverend! Good heavens, you gave me quite a start! I didn't hear you come in.' She squeezed her way through to the main aisle. 'I just popped in to give the pews a once-over. I hope I'm not in your way.'

'No, no, you carry on. I came in to have a bit of a think but you needn't mind me.'

'Whatever you say, Reverend.' Joan turned to go back to where she'd left off when an agonising stab of pain hit her. She gasped, involuntarily. Brian jumped out of his seat and ran towards her.

'Are you all right?'

'Not really,' said Joan, lowering herself into a pew. She shut her

eyes as she waited for the spasm to pass. Brian crouched beside
her and patted her hand.

'Don't tell me this is heartburn,' he said.

'Yes, it is,' Joan insisted through clenched teeth.

Brian stared at her. 'Look, Joan, call me a fusspot but this is
twice I've seen you in pain. I think I ought to tell Bert you're not
well.'

Joan opened her eyes and stared at him. 'You breathe a word
to Bert and I'll tell Heather you were in here crying.'

'I wasn't.'

Joan pursed her lips and shook her head. 'Lying, and in God's
house.' She tutted.

Brian stared back at her, defiantly, but couldn't hold her gaze.
'Deal,' he said. 'But I want you to promise me you'll see the doc.'

'I'll promise to do that, if you'll tell me what's bothering you.'
Wincing, Joan budged up along the pew and patted the space
she'd left. 'Come on, Reverend, what's so terrible you can't tell
your missus?'

'You really want to know?'

Joan nodded.

'I... I think I've lost my faith.'

Joan almost said 'Is that all?' before she realised that, for the
vicar, it was a very big deal indeed. 'Is that what caused you
to have that turn when you were giving your sermon the other
Sunday?'

Brian nodded. 'I felt I was on a cliff-edge – that there was
nothing underneath me. It was terrifying and it was all I could
think about. I lost the plot. I suddenly felt that my whole life had
been a completely futile waste of time.'

'Don't say that, Reverend. Not with all that you've done for
people over the years.'

Brian shook his head. 'But for what?'

'Does it matter if you've brought them comfort? It can't have
been wrong to do good.'

'Maybe.' He didn't sound convinced.

She nodded, gravely. 'So, what's brought on this business with your faith?'

Brian sighed and shrugged. 'That's the point; I don't know. It just went.' He paused then said, 'One day I felt like I was praying into a great big empty space, a void... nothing.'

'So,' said Joan, 'there's nothing to say it mayn't come back then.'

'I suppose.'

'I mean, it might only be temporary.'

'It might not be.'

'But you don't know. Like whatever it is that's not right with me.' Brian looked perplexed. 'It may be the same with you – only the other way round, so to speak, cos you had something you wanted and it's gone but you'd like it back. On the other hand I've got summat I don't want and but I'm expecting it to go away and never return.'

'Maybe.' The vicar sounded supremely doubtful. 'And in the meantime I'm being a complete hypocrite.'

'The congregation don't know that,' said Joan. The spasm had passed and she spoke with more energy.

'But *I* do.'

'So?'

'But it's wrong. You said yourself it was wrong to lie in church.'

'There's *lying* and there's *not sharing everything with everyone*.' She saw Brian suppress a smile. 'And, if you ask me, them what come to church believe, and they don't need to know you're having a bit of a moment with your faith. As long as you do everything you're paid to do they'll be happy. You having a crisis won't help them and if your faith comes back no one need be any the wiser.'

'And if it doesn't?'

'Don't meet trouble halfway, I say.'

Brian stared at her. He was sure there was a deep theological argument that he should use to tell Joan that her reasoning was hopelessly flawed and yet... and yet what she said made sense in a perverse way.

'What you got to lose, Reverend?' Joan hauled herself to her feet. 'And this ain't getting the church clean,' she said.

'You promise me you'll see the doc?'

'I said I would, didn't I?'

'Good.' Brian stayed in the pew looking at the altar as Joan huffed and puffed her way over to the side pews and carried on with her cleaning.

24

The following morning Amy let herself into Olivia's house and called out a greeting.

In reply she heard, 'I'm upstairs, Amy. Could you come up here, please?'

Amy sighed and went up to the first floor. 'Where are you?'

'In Zac's room.'

Amy walked along the corridor to the open door. She peered in. If Ashley let his room get into this state she'd give him a clip round his ear. And, oh God, what was that smell?

'I know, it's awful, isn't it?' said Olivia, reading Amy's mind. 'And I've had the windows wide open for about half an hour.' She sighed. 'I know I've always said you don't have to deal with Zac's room but it's got beyond a joke. I asked him at the weekend to tidy it... Well, as he didn't then it's going to be tidied for him.'

Amy was tempted to ask for extra money to deal with this shithole.

'I'll do my best.'

'That's all I can ask.'

'I won't get nothing else done today.'

'I realise that. But if that's what it takes to sort this out, then so be it.'

Amy gazed at the mess and decided that she wasn't going to touch anything without rubber gloves on. She suppressed a shudder. 'Whatever you say, Mrs L.'

'Do the best you can.'

Amy shook her head slowly. 'I can't promise I'll get it sorted in three hours. Besides, won't your Zac have a view about me messing with his stuff?'

'Huh! Given the way he's behaved recently I don't very much care if he does.'

Oo-er. The apple of Mrs L's eye must have pissed her off. Mind you, thought Amy, if he'd been her son she'd have told him he'd crossed the line a few years back. He'd got right out of hand, if half of what her Ash said was true. Cocky little bastard.

'OK, then, Mrs L. Whatever you say.'

'I've got to go out. I'll leave your money in the kitchen as always. I'll see you next time.'

Amy surveyed the room as Olivia went off and worked out what she'd need to do a proper job before she went back downstairs and collected a whole bunch of cleaning fluids and cloths from the kitchen cupboards, plus some rubber gloves and the hoover and lugged everything upstairs. Then she went to the airing cupboard and got out a set of clean bedding. No point in spoiling the ship for the proverbial ha'porth.

Amy eyed the bed. With a finger and thumb she pinched a corner of the duvet and pulled it back. Gross. When had the sheets on that last been changed? Maybe that was a question best left unanswered. She squared her shoulders and braced herself for the task ahead as she pulled on her rubber gloves and set about stripping the bed. Half an hour later the bed had fresh sheets, the windows were shining, the waste-paper basket was empty and all Zac's dirty linen and discarded clothes were in the laundry basket behind the door in the bathroom and order was starting to emerge. Amy decided that the room smelt fresh enough now to shut the windows and make a start on clearing up the rest of the muddles that were strewn around; the half-empty mugs of tea and coffee, the dirty plates, the piles of books, the DVDs out of their boxes…

She stacked the crockery and carried it downstairs and put it in the dishwasher. The washer, she noticed, was almost full so she found a detergent tablet and bunged it in the drawer. If the cycle finished before she was done for the morning she'd empty it for Mrs L before she left.

She returned to Zac's bedroom and began to stack books and papers with a ruthless efficiency. She finished with the books and began on the DVDs and PlayStation games. She swept up all the discs and their boxes and piled them on the bed where she sat beside them, snapping the shiny discs into their right containers and then tossing them gently onto the dressing table ready to be slotted into the rack when she'd sorted them all out. She pitched a case with less care than she intended and it slid across the polished surface and tipped between the piece of furniture and the wall.

'Bollocks,' she swore. She tried to get her hand down the back of the dressing table but the gap was far too narrow. She braced herself, got a bit of leverage and dragged it away from the wall. She knelt beside it and squeezed her arm into the gap at skirting board level and felt around for the case.

'Don't know why I'm bothering,' she told herself. 'Zac won't know it's missing in amongst that lot.' She eyed the large collection of films and games in his possession, piled up in front of her. Spoilt little sod. She touched something soft and squashy and jumped, a little squeak of disgust escaping from her. Then she realised it was a plastic bag and not something sinister. She pulled it out and examined it. She knew pot when she saw it. She pulled the furniture even further away from the wall and found another bag, and a whole bunch of other stuff. That was quite a habit he had going there. The thing was, what was she going to do about it? Should she tell Mrs L or not? While it might be quite satisfactory to get Zac into some very hot water, it wasn't really any of her business. And anyway, Mrs L mightn't take kindly to being told her Zac wasn't the blue-eyed boy she liked to think he was – and she certainly wouldn't like to hear it from her cleaner. She pushed it back where she'd found it and decided to think about what she ought to do later.

Zac stared at his room in disbelief. What the fuck? Then he spun round and thundered towards the stairs before he skidded to a halt on the polished wood of the landing. He shot back to his room and levered his dressing table away from the wall. There, on the carpet, was his stash. He sagged with relief. Thank fuck that hadn't been found. He could just imagine the row from his parents if they knew he was on drugs, quite apart from the fact that it would have cost him to replace it and Zac didn't think that Dan would back down over his decision about not offering him any more credit. And he'd need more soon – what he had hidden wasn't going to last much longer. As things stood it would be tricky to make it stretch till he was due his next allowance, assuming he got it, he thought as he pushed his dressing table back where it belonged.

'You had no right,' he yelled, confronting his mother in the kitchen. She stopped chopping vegetables and turned around.

She looked up at him and narrowed her eyes. 'If you're talking about your room then I had every right. It was a disgrace. I asked you to tidy it at the weekend and you did nothing about it. I told you that if you didn't do it, I'd get Amy to sort it. Well... you ignored me and I decided it was time you learned a lesson.'

What was the matter with her? First his allowance and now this. For fuck's sake, why couldn't she leave him alone – let him get on with his own life?

'But why? It's my room. I like it like that.'

'It smelt.'

'So?'

His mother rolled her eyes. 'Because this is my house and I won't have you treating it like a squat. I've had enough of you ignoring me, of never doing anything I ask. Your father is right – your brother and sisters were never like this and it's time you stopped behaving like a total waste of space.'

'I'm not.'

His mother eyed him. 'Then don't behave like you are.'

'Amy had no business to go through my things.'

'She didn't "go through" your things. She tidied up. It took her three hours and frankly, *if* I decide to let you have next month's allowance, I am sorely tempted to take the money I paid her, out of it.'

'That's not fair.'

Olivia took a step closer to him and leaned towards him, the knife she was holding pointing at his nose. 'I don't care.'

Zac backed away, suddenly intimidated. 'No need to get arsey,' he said.

'Arsey? Look who's talking. Anyway, I haven't time to argue. If you don't want a repeat of this incident then I suggest you keep your room tidy in future. I bet Megan Millar doesn't behave like this.'

'How would you know?'

'Because I've met her and her stepmother and she's a nice kid. Unlike you these days.'

'Well, maybe her mother isn't a total cow like you,' Zac shouted at her as he stormed out of the house.

25

'Megan, Megan,' came Bex's voice from the bottom of the stairs.

Megan dropped her pen and went down to the landing where she leaned over the banisters.

'Yes?'

Bex stood in the hall, her hand on the newel post.

'Are you busy?'

'Got a bunch of French vocab to learn.'

'Oh.'

'Why?'

'Alfie wants to go and see the diggers and when I said I was too busy to take him he had a full-on meltdown. I'd do it, but I've got spammed for making cakes for the school fair as well as running a stall and I was hoping to get a couple of batches of fairy cakes baked before supper.'

Megan sighed. She supposed she could always do her homework after supper. 'Look, tell Alfie I'll take him in about fifteen minutes. Let me learn my French and then I can do the rest when we get back.'

'Megan, you're a star.'

'And I can take Lewis as well, if he doesn't mind watching JCBs for a while, and then we can go to the swings after.'

'That'd be wonderful. Perfect. And I'll save you some buns. You'll have earned them.'

Getting Alfie to the diggers was a doddle but tearing him away was a whole other issue. Obviously, in his mind, because the battle had been so hard fought he wasn't going to give up his victory lightly. Lewis, normally a placid child, began to get cross and whiny and resentful because every second spent watching earth-moving equipment meant a second less at the play park.

'Come *on*, Alf. I'm bored.' Lewis kicked at the security fencing surrounding the site, then he grabbed it with both hands and shook it in frustration. The fencing sections were secured by the metal vertical posts being driven into hollow breeze-blocks. As Lewis shook the fencing the breeze block split and the section of fence sagged rather alarmingly.

'Stop it, Lewis,' said Megan aghast. 'Look what you've done!'

Lewis looked shocked. 'Sorry, I didn't mean to.'

'Mean to or not, we need to go before someone sees the damage you've done and wants to have a word with us.' Megan grabbed Alfie's hand and dragged him away. Alfie must have picked up on the tension because this time he didn't protest.

'Play park,' said Megan. 'Twenty minutes on the swings for being patient and good.'

'I wasn't,' mumbled Lewis. 'I broke the fence.'

'You didn't mean to, I know that, really. It was an accident.'

'Accidump,' repeated Alfie.

'Yeah, an accidump,' said Megan.

When they got to the park, Megan had a quick scan of the skate ramps to see if she could spot Ashley and felt a pang of disappointment that he wasn't there. Then her heart sank further; Zac was. She quickly turned back to the slide to pretend she hadn't seen him and concentrated on looking after the boys – not that Lewis needed her but Alfie always wanted a helping hand or a push or someone to 'watch me!'

'Hiya, Megan. Thought it was you.'

Bugger. She turned. 'Oh, hello, Zac.' She hoped she sounded surprised.

'Poor you.'

'Why?'

'Getting stuck with your kid brothers. That's a bummer.'

'Actually, I really like my kid brothers.'

Zac gave her a look like he didn't believe her for a second. 'Whatever,' he said.

'Look, just because you don't seem to like your family very much—'

'*Very much?* Ha. I hate them.'

'If you're going to be like that, I'm off,' said Megan.

'Don't.'

'Then stop being horrible about your mum and dad.'

'But you've met my mum.'

'So?'

'So you've seen what a cow she is.'

Megan turned around. 'Alfie, Lewis, we're going home.' The boys, queuing for the stairs to climb to the top of the slide, looked over towards her.

'No!' said Lewis.

'Come on,' said Megan, walking towards them.

'Stop,' said Zac. He grabbed her arm.

Megan stared at his hand and frowned. Zac let her go.

'I'm sorry, don't go. I need... I need someone to talk to.'

He sounded so miserable that Megan relented. 'OK, boys. Ten more minutes.' She turned back to Zac. 'What about?'

'I'm in deep shit.'

'What have you done?'

'I can't tell you but... it's bad.'

'If I don't know what it is, I don't think I can help.'

'Have you got any money?'

'Not a lot. Why?'

'I owe someone some money. I need to pay it back.'

'What?'

'Never mind.'

There was silence for a few seconds as Megan and Zac watched Alfie zoom down the polished aluminium of the slide. Megan thought about her savings. She hadn't been lying when she told Zac she didn't have much cash but she did have a building society account – her grandparents had put in a hundred pounds each birthday so she'd have a nest egg when she got to eighteen. She knew where the book was – in the desk drawer in the study.

'If I did get some money, when would you be able to pay me back?'

'I thought you said you didn't have any,' Zac groused.

'"Thank you" and a straight answer might be nice.'

'Sorry. Yes, thank you and I'll pay you back out of next month's allowance.'

'How much do you need?'

'Fifty.'

'How much?' Megan was flabbergasted; she'd thought he say a tenner at the most. 'How much is your allowance?'

'Two hundred.'

'A *month*?'

'So?'

And yet he couldn't manage his finances despite being given so much. 'What the hell do you spent it on?'

'Stuff – games, music, phone. I don't know, it just goes. If you can't manage fifty, forty would help. Anything...' He sounded desperate.

'And you'll promise me you'll pay it back.'

'I said so, didn't I?'

'It might take me a few days to get it. I'll have to go to Cattebury to draw the money out. It can't be before Saturday.'

Zac sagged with relief. 'Thanks, Megan. I'll make it up to you. Promise.'

★

Later that evening, Olivia took her place at the semicircular table in the council chamber and poured herself a glass of water before she switched on her iPad. She'd had a shit day, what with the row with her son, and now the planning committee meeting was due to discuss the new development and she was going to have to show her hand. And when she did... She just knew she'd be the subject of speculation and gossip. People would pry. She shuddered.

The other councillors drifted in and took their seats round the table, nodded greetings to each other, checked their iPads, and engaged in chit-chat. Olivia made an assessment on how they were each likely to vote on the new estate. She was pretty certain the promise of 40 per cent affordable housing would mean a block vote from the Labour councillors but there were precious few of them. She had a feeling a couple of the independents would go along with them too. Which left the Greens and the Tories... and herself. The developers had made a point about sustainable living with solar water panels to be installed on each roof, triple-glazed windows and high-spec insulation so the Greens might vote in favour too. On the other hand, it was *another* housing development, more farmland lost, so they might not. Olivia added up the votes. It was going to be tight.

Her calculations were interrupted when the chairman of the committee took his place at the head of the table and switched on his microphone whilst bashing his gavel on the wooden block.

'I declare the meeting open,' he said.

The first couple of items on the agenda were dispensed with and then came the moment when statements from the public were called for.

Len McGregor approached the microphone and rustled his papers. The town clerk started the stop watch for his allotted five minutes and Mr McGregor put his case as to why the land was ripe for development. As the five minutes neared the end he said, 'And it's no good for grazing,' he said. 'And it's my under-standing it's a brownfield site.'

The chairman held his hand up to stop him as the clock ticked to zero. 'Thank you, Mr McGregor.'

Len McGregor wandered back to his seat in the main body of the chamber and the chairman looked around the councillors.

'Any comments?' The mayor stared at Olivia. Everyone on the council knew what a Rottweiler Olivia was when it came to protecting Little Woodford from unwelcome developments. Surely she'd have a really strong view over this one.

Olivia looked at her hands. She was itching to point out the proposal for sixty houses would mean overdevelopment of the space, that the traffic during construction would be detrimental to the town, that, when the houses were occupied, parking in the town centre – already tricky – would become impossible, that the doctor's surgery would be stretched... God, so many things to be said that justified refusing planning permission. Olivia took a deep breath and raised her hand. She might as well make her position plain now rather than at the vote.

'Councillor Laithwaite?' said the mayor.

'I propose that the council recommends that planning permission is approved.'

The other councillors stared at her open-mouthed. Even Len McGregor looked gob-smacked.

Megan waited until Bex was upstairs reading Lewis a bedtime story before she tiptoed into the study and headed for the desk under the window. She stopped and listened before she opened the top drawer, hearing only the occasional creak of the old house and the very soft murmur of Bex's voice. Slowly and carefully she pulled open the drawer while still keeping her ears strained for any change in the ambient sounds. She was confronted with a stack of papers which had obviously been chucked in there. Carefully, she pulled them out in a thick wodge and there underneath was her bank book.

And the memory book.

She stared at it, tears welling up as the book did what it was designed to do – bring back memories. The trouble was, the memories it was supposed to bring back were ones about her father, not ones that had been caused by the memory book itself. The book, a large, beautifully bound notebook, had been filled with mementoes, photos, pieces written and drawn by Megan, Lewis and Alfie and was designed to help them come to terms with their dad's death. But then Megan had taken it to her old school – 'bring your favourite book to school for World Book Day,' her previous form teacher had instructed. So Megan had and the consequences of such an innocent action had had completely unforeseen repercussions; repercussions more ghastly than anyone could have imagined.

Shocked, Megan grabbed her bank book, threw the papers back in the drawer and pushed it shut, before she hurled herself up the stairs and into the sanctuary of her attic eyrie.

Olivia's decision seemed to be the talk of the town by the next morning. Amy was full of it when she came to clean for Bex.

'How do you know?' Bex was certain that the last place anyone would find Amy on a Thursday night was in the town hall, attending a council meeting.

'I heard it off of a mate whose husband is a chum of the chairman of the planning committee.'

Almost first-hand then, thought Bex. 'But surely it can't be such a big deal how Olivia voted?' she queried. 'Everyone knows there's a massive housing shortage.'

'You don't know Olivia like I do,' said Amy. Which was indisputably true. 'She never does nothing for no reason.'

It took Bex a second or two to pick the sense out of what Amy had said from the storm of double negatives.

'You mark my words,' said Amy, 'she's voted for those houses because there's something in it for her.'

'Really? I'd say that Olivia is the one person I've met so far

– with the possible exception of Heather – who would put the interests of this place way ahead of her own.' Not, thought Bex, that she'd met that many people, but Olivia's obvious commitment to Little Woodford was rock solid. 'And,' she added, 'I'd be a bit careful who you say things like that to.'

Amy sniffed. 'Whatever.'

When Bex got into work the conversation at the pub was much the same, with the lunchtime regulars speculating about the council's decision. In some respects Bex found it slightly comforting that this little town had little better to worry about than how a councillor had voted. Frankly, she thought, if a few new houses was the worst thing that the townsfolk had happen to their town then they should think themselves blooming lucky.

26

Megan knew there was something wrong when she got to the door of her tutor room after lunch, ready for afternoon registration. The few classmates who had preceded her were unusually silent and were staring alternately at the whiteboard and then at each other with looks of consternation. Megan looked around to see what the cause of such anxiety was. In massive red letters, written across the width of the board was:

MEGAN MILLAR
IS A KILLER

For a second, Megan was as dumbfounded as they were but then the awfulness of the accusation hit her and she turned and ran, barging through the other pupils crowding to get into the room.

'Megan,' yelled Ashley who had just seen the words. Behind him, Lily and Summer gave each other a high five.

But Megan was oblivious to everything. Shocked, horrified and scared she wanted out of the classroom, out of the school, out of everything. She raced past teachers in the corridors, she almost bowled over Mrs Simmonds who was standing in reception, before she cannoned through the front door and ran till she was out of breath.

The stitch in her side was so intense she bent double to ease it and then, when she straightened, she took in where she was; by the gates to the park. She knew she was already in trouble for leaving school without permission so she didn't think it was going to make much difference if she was absent for only five minutes or for the rest of the afternoon.

The play park was almost empty so she wandered over the grass and sat on one of the swings, her feet scuffing on the rubberised matting beneath it as she swayed to and fro.

She thought she'd be safe here in Little Woodford. Bex had promised no one would know. How on earth had anyone found out? Tears welled up and plopped onto her lap as terrible events, events that she'd thought she had left safely behind in London, began to crowd into her mind again.

It was the memory book. The memory book was to blame for everything. It was like it was cursed. She hadn't even looked at it since they'd arrive in Little Woodford, she'd almost forgotten all about it in the chaos of the move and the business of settling into a new school. But she'd touched it last night and now look what had happened. And it had been the memory book that had sparked everything in the first place.

Why was life so unfair? Why her? But there didn't seem to be an answer.

'Megan?'

Megan looked up. 'Mrs Simmonds.'

'Do you mind if I join you?'

Megan wiped her nose on the back of her hand and used both palms to wipe away her tears.

'If you want.' She knew she sounded less than gracious but was past caring.

'Do want to tell me what happened?'

Megan shook her head.

Mrs Simmonds pushed herself backwards a few inches with her

feet and let the swing arc forwards. 'I can't remember the last time I sat on a swing. I was probably about your age. So... centuries ago.'

Megan gave her a wan smile.

'I like this park,' said Mrs Simmonds. 'I love the way everyone uses it. The old folks who live in the bungalows over there use it as a short cut, the mums bring the little ones here for picnics and the older kids all hang out here – well, apart from the ones on the alcopops down at the nature reserve.'

'I wouldn't know,' mumbled Megan.

'I should hope not,' said Mrs Simmonds. She pushed backwards again, this time more vigorously, and the swing zipped forwards so that Megan's hair was ruffled by the breeze it created. She let the momentum run its course. When the swing finally stilled again, Heather said, 'Have you texted your mum to tell her that someone upset you?'

Megan shook her head. 'Who said someone upset me?'

Heather stared at her. 'So what was it? A B minus for your science homework? I don't think so. You left school like the hounds of hell were after you and I knew that something really serious had happened – something at afternoon registration. I'm not stupid, Megan. Someone in your tutor group has said, or done, something really mean, haven't they?'

'Maybe.'

'So... have you told your mum?'

'I don't want to worry her.'

'Don't you think, when the school tells her that you took an unauthorised leave of absence...' Heather smiled at her. 'That's the official jargon for bunking off, by the way – that your mother will want to know what's at the bottom of it?'

'Maybe.'

'I don't think there's any sort of "maybe" about it.' The pair sat on the swings in silence for a few seconds, using their feet to rock backwards and forwards a few inches while Megan considered her options.

'When will the school tell her?'

'I think it'll be quite soon. You missed afternoon registration.'

Silence fell again and the pair swung gently to and fro.

'Do you want to tell me what happened?' said Heather. 'I'm a good listener.'

'I...' Megan sagged. 'It's all to do with my old school. Bex said that no one here would know.'

'And now someone *has* found out, found out about whatever it was you didn't want anyone to know. Is that it?'

Megan nodded. 'And told the rest of the class.'

'That was mean.'

'They wrote it on the board.'

'What did they write?'

Megan turned sideways and looked Heather Simmonds straight in the eyes. '"Megan Millar is a killer."'

'They wrote *what*?'

Megan nodded and repeated the phrase.

'Is it... is it true?' The incredulity in Heather's voice rang out. A tear ran down Megan's face. 'Kind of.'

'Kind of?'

'A girl... Stella... died. Some of the kids blamed me.'

'But that's awful. I take it you weren't at fault.'

Another tear plopped onto Megan's school skirt. Heather pulled out a wad of tissues from her sleeve and handed one to Megan. 'It's clean,' she promised.

Megan wiped her face and blew her nose. 'Thanks.' She scrunched the tissue in her hand.

'Do you want to tell me about it? I'd like to hear your side of the story then, if I hear anything else, I'll know what the truth is. I might even be able to persuade people not to listen to ugly rumours.'

'I suppose.' Megan stared at her hands in her lap as she pulled at the tissue, tearing little bits off which drifted away like snowflakes. 'When Dad died, Bex suggested we should make a memory book – some counsellor told her it would be a good idea. So we bought this lush notebook and began to fill it full of things about Dad – a piece of his favourite sweater, a CD he really liked, pictures, photos... just stuff, really.'

'Lovely idea,' murmured Heather.

Megan nodded. 'Anyway, it was World Book Day and we had to take our favourite book into school.'

'And you took the memory book.'

Megan nodded again. 'I didn't tell Bex. She said the book wasn't to leave the house, she said it was too precious.'

'Oh.'

'I know.' Megan sniffed. 'Anyway, we had to tell the class about our book and why we liked it – so I did. But afterwards, Stella told me she thought my book was lame and that I ought to get over my dad and that no one was interested or cared and then she snatched it out of my hand and ran off with it.'

There was a long pause. 'Go on,' prompted Heather, gently.

'So, I chased her.' Megan turned to look at Heather. 'I had to get the book back. I'd disobeyed Bex and everything was going horribly wrong. I was scared Stella was going to chuck the book in the school pond or in one of the bins. Bex would have been so angry with me. It would have been awful.'

Heather nodded.

'Anyway, Stella was running away from me, and she turned to look to see if I was catching her, and she tripped... she fell... she hit her head on a low wall.' Megan paused as she recalled the awfulness of the event, then she began to cry; huge juddering sobs. 'They sw-sw-sw-switched off her life su-su-su-pport a c-c-c-couple of weeks later.'

Heather's heart broke for the teenager she barely knew. She got up from her swing, crouched in front of Megan and took her hands. 'It wasn't your fault. You aren't to blame.'

'But I wa-wa-wa-was. I chased her.'

'That doesn't mean you caused her death. It was a ghastly accident.'

Megan blew her nose again and Heather handed her another tissue. 'That's what the police said.'

'There you go then.'

'But everyone at school said it was my fault. That's why we had to move.'

'Oh, sweetie, it doesn't sound as if the others at your school were very nice. And Stella certainly wasn't. What she said and did were hateful.'

Megan nodded. Then she said, 'Other people didn't think so. She was form captain. Everyone liked her.'

'Ah – another Lily Breckenridge? She likes to think she's the most popular girl in the school too.'

'Kind of. Ashley doesn't like her, though.'

'Ashley Pullen is a fine judge of character.'

Megan smiled weakly and blew her nose again.

'So,' said Heather. 'Don't you think you ought to tell your mum what happened? Apart from anything else, if I were her, I would want to have a word with Mr Smithson about it.'

'He won't be able to do anything.'

'I wouldn't be too sure about that. And when he finds out who wrote that horrible message on the board, I wouldn't want to be in their shoes.'

'I suppose.' Megan wasn't convinced.

'How about I come back home with you?'

'She won't be there, she'll be at work.'

'At the pub?' Megan nodded. 'I'm sure she could be allowed a quick break.'

'Maybe.'

'I am totally certain Belinda will let her have a few minutes to talk to you. Come on.' Heather let go of Megan's hands and stood up, groaning as her knees cracked as she straightened.

Megan got off her swing and the pair left the park and headed through town.

'Here we are,' said Heather, pushing open the door to the bar.

'I've not been in a pub before,' muttered Megan as she followed Heather inside.

They approached the bar where Bex was busy putting clean glasses on a shelf.

'Bex,' said Heather.

She turned. 'Hel—' She stopped mid-greeting. 'Megan, what on earth are you doing here?'

The lunchtime regulars all put their drinks on the tables and swivelled to look at what was going on.

Bex lifted the flap in the bar and ushered the pair through. 'Let's go into the kitchen,' she muttered.

Her visitors followed her through and a hubbub of speculation did too until the swing door closed softly.

''Scuse us, Miles,' she said to her bemused boss.

'Sure,' he said. 'Hello, Heather – and this is…?'

'My stepdaughter, Megan.'

'Ooh-kaaay.' He looked completely at sea. 'What is this? Bring Your Child to Work Day?'

'Don't be facetious,' snapped Heather.

'Sorry.' Miles glared at her. 'Want me to make myself scarce?'

'If you don't mind,' said Heather.

'Sure thing. I'll mind the bar, shall I?' he offered sarcastically as he left.

'So what's all this about?' asked Bex.

Heather glanced at Megan who nodded.

'You tell her,' whispered Megan.

Heather began to recount the goings-on of the past hour, looking at Megan every now and again to check that she was getting her facts right as she told the tale.

Bex looked alternately as if she were on the brink of tears or furiously angry.

'So, who did it?' she demanded to know at the end.

Megan shook her head. 'I don't know.'

'You must have some idea.'

Megan looked as if she might burst into tears again. 'But I don't,' she wailed.

'Someone must know,' hissed Bex. 'And when I find out...'

'Please don't,' said Megan. 'You'll make it worse.'

'Worse?! How could it be worse? Some little toerag has made an unfounded and libellous accusation, upset you and made me spit feathers... And how did they find out, that's what I want to know?' Bex's eyes blazed with anger and upset and righteous indignation. 'No, I'm sorry, Megan, but as soon as I get home I'm going to ring Mr Smithson and demand he takes action.'

Megan looked upset.

Bex's tone softened. 'Megan, you can't let people get away with things like this.'

'I agree,' said Heather.

Miles opened the door. 'Sorry to interrupt,' he said, 'but I've got an order for a toasted BLT.' He shuffled awkwardly.

'And we're cluttering up your kitchen,' said Bex.

'Look, I'll get Belinda down from upstairs. She's only catching up with the accounts and I'm sure she can cover for you. Why don't you push off – you've obviously got more important things going on than pulling pints.'

'Well...' started Bex.

'Excellent idea,' said Heather firmly. 'Come on, you two.' She took Bex's arm and pulled her towards the door. 'Bye, Miles, and thank you.'

27

Brian sat in his church and, yet again, mulled over what Joan had said the day before. He'd barely thought about anything else now, for the best part of twenty-four hours, and he hadn't managed to come up with a better solution than the one Joan had suggested. He could only come to one conclusion – she might be right; his parishioners didn't need to be troubled with his problems. Could he continue to provide a service, go through the motions, until everything righted itself? Would they twig that it was a sham, a façade? Why would they? he decided. So, as a plan it might work. And if this was only a temporary bad patch, a glitch, and even though he was frightened and depressed by the turn of events, he had to hope and pray it would pass and until it did… well, he'd cross that bridge when he came to it. He didn't need to broadcast his own problems. One day, he had no idea when but, one day, surely, his faith would return. Until then, because the parishioners needed him, Heather was happy here, to say nothing of the more trivial reason that he liked this living… he should try to muddle through.

Given the place he now found himself in, he'd find it tricky to encourage his flock to pray when he personally doubted that prayer was going to do any good, but as long as they remained unaware and *they* believed it would help, was it going to do any harm? Hypocritical it might be but, as far as he could see, it was the only way forward without the town losing its vicar and Heather losing her home.

Brian breathed out. He needed to accept the situation as it was – maybe it was some kind of test. Maybe not quite as extreme as being thrown into a fiery furnace like Shadrach, Meshach and Abednego, or being fed to the lions like Daniel, but it was still a test and he felt acceptance, and a trust that it would end, were the key to survival. He wasn't sure he *wanted* to accept this new state. He wanted the old one back, he wanted the old certainties. Maybe he'd stay in the church a while longer and see if something approaching acceptance materialised. He shut his eyes and tried to pray.

Why, thought Joan, wasn't Bert going off out to his allotment, like he did most days? She'd made a promise to the vicar that she'd get an appointment to see the doctor and, when she went to church on Sunday, she wanted to be able to tell him she'd kept her side of the bargain. But unless Bert buggered off, and pronto, she wouldn't be able to ring the surgery until after the weekend and she couldn't do that with him hanging around like a bad smell. She didn't want him worried – not at his time of life. Her being worried was quite enough anxiety in the house to be going on with, thank you. And, if she was completely honest with herself, that last turn in the church had scared her quite a lot. The other twinges had been quite nasty but they'd passed relatively quickly and hadn't hurt half as much as that last one had. And now she'd noticed that, even when she was lying down, her chest ached. There were no two ways about it, it was getting worse and she wasn't just concerned for herself. What would happen to Bert if anything happened to her? He could barely make a cup of tea. Fine, he was great at growing stuff but when it came to what to do with it, he knew the square root of sod all.

Joan came out of the kitchen and saw Bert sitting on the sofa, reading the local paper.

'You can't sit around here all day,' she grumbled at him.

'Why not. I'm retired, ain't I?'

'I want to get the hoover out.'

'And I'm not stopping you.'

'Yes, you are. You're underfoot.'

Bert put the paper to one side and sighed. 'What's the matter with you, Joan? You've been right tetchy all day.'

'No, I ain't.'

'If you say so, dear.'

Joan glared at him. 'I do. Haven't you got summat to be doing at the allotment?'

'Not specially.'

'Thought you said your beans needed tying up.'

'They can wait.'

Joan stamped out to the kitchen. Being riled by her Bert wasn't going to help things if she were poorly. She clattered around at the sink, putting away the lunch things that had dripped dry.

'OK, have it your way,' said Bert from the door. 'I give in, I'll go and do some weeding, give you some peace and quiet, if that's what you want.'

'I don't. I just want to get on.'

'Yes, dear.'

Joan bit back a retort. Bert infuriated her when he got so conciliatory and reasonable.

Two minutes later she heard the front door slam. Thank the Lord for that. She headed back to the sitting room, picked up the phone and dialled the doctor's. First an automated voice told her to press 'one for repeat prescriptions; two for appointments...' Joan fumbled with the buttons and hit two. Then she got some violins playing. No, she didn't want that, she wanted a person.

'Please hold, a receptionist will be with you in a moment. Your call is important to us,' said another automated voice, before the violins carried on.

'Like heck it is,' said Joan to nobody. Finally, after several minutes, her call was answered. She was so pleased to hear a real person on the other end of the line she failed to hear the click of the front door as Bert, who had discovered he had forgotten his gardening twine, returned to get it.

'Yes,' she said to Dr Connolly's receptionist, 'I'd like an appointment with the doctor as soon as possible.'

'Can I ask what the matter is?'

'No, you blooming can't. That's between me and the doc but I need to see him and I won't take no for an answer.'

'I'm sorry Mrs...?'

'Mrs Makepiece.'

'Well, unless you can be a bit more specific...'

'I've had a couple of chest pains,' she admitted grudgingly.

'I see. How bad?'

'Bad enough and I'm worried.'

'Do you think you might be better going to A&E?'

'I'm not *that* worried. I just want to see the doc.'

'In that case, we can fit you in on Monday. Ten o'clock.'

'Ten, on Monday. I'll be there.'

Joan put the phone down and Bert tiptoed out of the house again.

On arrival back home, Bex had phoned the school while Megan sat on a kitchen chair and listened to Bex's half of the conversation. As the telephone call went on, Heather took charge of making tea.

'Yes, I know she left school without permission but under the circumstances I am, frankly, not surprised... And did Mrs Blake tell you the exact cause of Megan's upset? So you can see why... Indeed, she was *very* distressed... No, no she doesn't but I sincerely hope you're going to find out... I absolutely agree.'

Megan squirmed in embarrassment at being the subject of the conversation until, finally, Bex put the phone down.

'The good news is that Mr Smithson is taking it all very seriously indeed.'

Heather handed round steaming mugs of strong tea.

'And the bad news is...?'

'No one is owning up.'

Megan snorted. 'Like anyone would.'

'I'm sure they'll get to the bottom of it.'

'In the meantime everyone knows what I did and it'll be as bad as it was at my old school.'

'No, it won't,' said Heather.

Megan swivelled to look at her. 'How do you figure that out?'

'Because no one here knew Stella personally. No one here was her friend – or thought they were her friend.'

'So?'

'So, she is just a name. People lose interest very quickly in things that don't personally affect them. It'll be a seven-day wonder, mark my words.'

Megan looked unconvinced. 'It's easy for you to say, it wasn't your name on the board,' she grumbled.

Heather sat on a chair next to Megan. 'And I think that if you tell the truth about what happened—'

'No! No, I can't.'

'I think Megan would really rather put it all behind her. Telling people about what happened would be so painful,' explained Bex.

'OK, it's just a suggestion. I sincerely hope John Smithson can get to the bottom of who is behind that horrible message. And I'm sure he will.'

Heather let herself into the vicarage, shut the front door, leaned against it and let out a heavy sigh. What a week! First Olivia and her revelation that she thought Nigel was having an affair, and then poor little Megan's horror story about her part in Stella's death. Heather knew she was being quite unchristian but it sounded to her as if Stella had been a thoroughly spiteful child and, while she hadn't deserved to die, she certainly didn't deserve much sympathy either. Architect of her own downfall, thought Heather.

Wearily she made her way to her kitchen and put the kettle on. A nice cup of tea was what she needed.

'Brian? Brian, I'm home,' she called out of the kitchen door.

Silence.

'Brian.'

Still nothing. Leaving the kettle hissing and gurgling she went to her husband's study and knocked on the door. Maybe he had a visitor. She knocked again, louder. She opened the door. The study was empty. Oh well, he must have gone out.

Heather made herself a cuppa and went into the sitting room and sat on the functional but tatty sofa opposite the hideous green and cream tiled fireplace and put her tea on the table in front of her. She leant back on the cushions and wondered what she might be able to do to help Olivia and Megan. When she awoke her tea was stone cold. She rubbed her eyes and yawned and saw that the clock said it was after five. She ought to get supper on.

Taking her mug of cold tea she made her way into the kitchen. As she walked down the hall she realised that the house was utterly silent. Surely Brian wasn't still out?

Once again she called his name and listened for a response. Once again there was nothing. Where was he? Heather changed direction and headed into the study and flipped open Brian's desk diary. Maybe he had a meeting with someone that she'd forgotten about. Nope – the page for that day was blank. Maybe someone had needed him in an emergency. Yes, that was probably it. In which case, when was he going to be home?

Heather retrieved her handbag from where she'd left it on the counter and rummaged in it till she found her mobile. She pressed the buttons to find Brian's number and called him. Straight to voicemail. Damn it. Mind you, she thought, it wasn't entirely unexpected; they were as bad as each other when it came to being contactable on their mobiles.

Under normal circumstances Heather wouldn't have had the least twinge of worry but circumstances seemed to be far from normal at the moment. He'd been so distracted, so distant these past weeks, and then there had been that occasion when she'd caught him actually crying in his study. She suspected there had been other occasions – only she hadn't witnessed them. No, she told herself firmly, his absence wasn't an indication of anything more sinister than that he was out visiting a parishioner or had been called away unexpectedly on church business. To take her mind off her niggling worries she went into the kitchen, switched on the radio, and began to think about supper.

At eight o'clock she put cling film over the plate of food she'd prepared for Brian and put it in the fridge. She finished the washing up and was wiping down the kitchen surfaces when she heard the key in the lock.

'Brian!' She raced out of the kitchen and down the corridor. 'Brian, thank goodness you're home. I've been so worried.'

'Worried?' He looked bemused and confused.

'Where have you been?'

'In the church.'

'But you've been gone hours.'

'Have I?'

'Brian, it's gone eight.'

He glanced at his watch. 'Oh, I hadn't realised.'

'What were you doing all this time?'

'I'm a vicar, I was in church, what do you think I was doing?'

'I'm sorry. Yes, of course. I'll put your supper in the microwave. It'll be ready in two shakes of a lamb's tail.'

'Thank you. I take it you've eaten.'

Heather nodded. 'I didn't know how late you were going to be.'

'No, I understand. Have we got any wine?'

'There's a couple of bottles in the cupboard under the stairs.'

Brian pottered off to find them and came back, unscrewing the top of one. 'Would you like a glass?'

Heather shook her head. 'No, I think I'll stick to tea.'

'Suit yourself.' Brian reached for a glass and filled it. By the time the microwave had pinged he'd finished that one and was onto a second.

Heather looked at him; she desperately wanted to winkle out of him what it was troubling him but she knew it was hopeless. Even though her worry was tearing her apart she knew she had to bide her time.

28

Over at the pub Amy was meeting Billy for a drink.

'You flush again, Billy?' said Amy after he'd refused her offer to pay for the drinks.

'Not specially, but if a bloke can't treat his girl to a drink or two then things have come to a pretty pass.'

'Am I *your girl* then?'

'Course you are.'

'So we're dating?'

Billy handed Amy a large Chardonnay. 'What's with all the questions, babe?'

'Well, you know, if you and I are an item, maybe we ought to see a bit more of each other.'

Billy looked suddenly wary. 'How d'you mean?'

'That'll be nine pounds twenty,' interrupted Belinda as she handed Billy his pint of bitter.

Billy rummaged in his pocket and pulled out a wad of twenties. He peeled one off and handed it over.

Amy waited for him to get his change before she continued, 'My Ash likes you.' Not that she knew that for a fact but he hadn't said he didn't.

'Does he? Then he's a good kid.'

'And I like you.'

The pair made their way across the bar to a table near the window.

'And?'

'So what do you think about moving in with me?'

'You serious?'

Amy nodded and swigged her wine. 'Why not? I mean if you'd like to, that is.'

'I dunno, babe.'

Amy took another drink of her wine to hide her disappointment. She'd assumed Billy would leap at the chance – after all, did he really want to be still living with his mum at his age? 'It was just a suggestion,' she said as lightly as she could.

'Yeah, but I like to come and go a bit.'

'I wouldn't stop you.'

'But I sometimes work funny hours.'

'What? At the garage?'

'Moonlighting.'

'Oh, yes, of course. But I don't mind you being out in the evenings.'

'Sometime I work very late.'

Amy began to lose patience. 'Look, Billy, if you don't want to move in, why don't you just say so?'

'But that's it, babe, I do, it's just...'

'Just what?'

'My mum doesn't ask no questions.'

'I wouldn't either, not if you don't want me to.'

Billy looked at her over the rim of his glass. 'And she doesn't gossip.'

'I...' Amy reddened. 'I know how to hold my tongue.'

Billy raised his eyebrows.

'Anyway, why would I gossip about you? You've not got no secrets or nothing.'

Billy supped his beer and stayed shtum.

'Well, have you?'

'That'd be telling.'

'So?'

'Amy, if I told you any of my secrets they'd be all over Little Woodford in a heartbeat.'

'That's not...'

'Fair?' offered Billy.

Amy sipped her drink. 'So... you don't want to move in.' She sounded petulant.

'I didn't say that.'

'As good as.'

'Look, Amy, maybe we could do it on a kind of half-and-half basis.'

'Not with you.'

'Suppose I lived with you some days and my mum others.'

Amy brightened. 'I'd like that. Which days?'

'The weekends?'

'Yeah, that'd work.' She smiled at Billy. 'When are you going to come on over?'

'I could bring some things over tonight.'

'Oh.'

'You suggested this.'

'Yeah, but I haven't mentioned it to Ashley yet.'

'What difference is that going to make?'

'It's his home too.'

'So? I'm going to be sleeping in your room not his.' Billy laughed. 'At least, I'm assuming that's the plan.'

'Yeah, but even so, I think I should ask him first.'

Billy's laughter disappeared and his face hardened. 'Do you or don't you want me round yours?'

'Yeah, course I do it's just—'

Billy leaned across the table. 'It's *just* nothing, Ames. I'm not answering to a fifteen-year old. Understand?'

'Yeah, yeah, of course.'

'Good. Glad that's settled.' Billy was back to his affable self but Amy was rattled by the side she'd witnessed. 'Right then, drink up and let's go and get my kit.'

Obediently, not wishing to rile Billy again, Amy knocked back her drink.

Bex sat in the sitting room with a glass of wine and rubbish on the TV. She had some mending to do and the ironing pile wasn't getting any smaller but she felt shattered after the trauma of Megan's revelation about school that day. Sightless, she looked at the pictures on the screen as her mind turned over ideas how she could best support her stepdaughter. If only Richard was here to talk to. But, if he were still here, they wouldn't have made the memory book, Stella wouldn't have nicked it and they wouldn't have had to move.

Maybe moving hadn't been the solution. Maybe they should have stayed put, ridden out the storm. Bex sighed and took another sip of her drink.

The imperious *dring* of the doorbell made her jump and she spilled wine down her top.

'Bollocks,' she muttered as she wiped the drops off with her hand before she put the glass back on the table. And who the hell would call at this time? On the other hand, it might be Heather, coming to offer more support.

She got to the door and put the chain on before she answered it. She knew, as she did it, that it was probably an overreaction in a sleepy market town but years of living in London had made her wary.

She cracked open the door.

'Miles! Hang on.' She shut the door, released the chain and opened it wide and as she did she wondered what she'd done that he felt he had to come and talk to her about it now, away from the pub. Was he cross that she'd buggered off early from her shift? Was he annoyed that her daughter had appeared in the pub? 'Sorry about that,' she said, feeling she had to apologise for the faff with the chain. 'And sorry I look such a mess,' she said pointing to the mark on her top. 'I wasn't expecting visitors.'

'It's me who should be apologising for disturbing you.'

'No, you're not. What can I do for you?'

'I just popped round to see how you are.'

Really? Maybe he wanted to make sure that her domestic crisis wasn't going to affect her work. 'Come in, come in.' She led the way into the sitting room. 'And, yes... well, Megan had a bit of an upset at school today but the head is on the case.'

'Good, I'm glad to hear it. Belinda and I were worried.'

Hmm – she believed Belinda might be... She saw Miles clock the bottle of wine on the table. 'Look, as you can see, I've got a bottle of wine open; can I tempt you to a glass?'

'I'd love one.'

Bex killed the TV with the remote before she went to fetch a glass.

'I *am* disturbing you,' said Miles on her return.

Bex shook her head. 'I was watching rubbish. I'm *glad* you disturbed me.' She poured Miles a glass of the Rioja she was drinking. 'But doesn't Belinda mind – you coming here?'

'Mind? *Mind*? Why on earth would she?'

'Being abandoned to run the pub on her own.'

'I do the kitchen, she does the bar, and anyway, she said I should pop over to see how you are now the dinner service is over. She said she thought you might need someone to cheer you up.'

She imagined Belinda telling Miles that she'd go if she could but that, as she was far too busy with Friday night customers, he'd have to. And she imagined Miles huffing and puffing and Belinda insisting...

'Cheers,' she said, taking the seat opposite him. They clinked glasses and sipped.

Miles put his glass on the table and twiddled the stem. 'So, apart from poor Megan's problems at school, how is it all going?'

'Oh, you know, mostly OK.'

'Curate's egg?'

Bex nodded. 'Don't get me wrong, I love my job' – she slid a look at him – 'even if I'm not very experienced.'

'Yeah, well, you'll learn.'

At least he hadn't wholeheartedly agreed with her. Maybe now she'd learnt to change a barrel and hadn't dropped any more food she was considered to be less useless than previously. 'And I love this house, the boys seem to be settling down well, but I'm still worried that I made the wrong decision in leaving London.'

'These things take time.'

'I know. Even with kids at the local school so I have to stand in the playground twice a day, it's tough making new friends. Everyone has their own circle and it's difficult breaking in.'

'You'll get there. Although, that said, there's people who've lived here for thirty years and more and they're still treated as incomers.'

Bex, who was sipping her drink, almost choked as a giggle escaped. 'I thought you came here to cheer me up!'

'As soon as those houses get built there'll be a big influx of newbies. It'll make you seem like the oldest inhabitant in comparison.' Miles's hand flew to his mouth. 'I didn't mean it like that! I mean not the *oldest*... Shit, I mean...' He saw the look on Bex's face and laughed with her.

'I should hope not,' said Bex with mock indignation. 'I may look ancient and raddled but I'm nowhere near my pension.' She grinned at him.

'You don't look ancient or raddled – well, not yet.'

Not yet? Oh well.

'Mum, Mum,' yelled a small boy's voice from upstairs. 'I feel sick.'

Oh gawd. 'Coming,' she said out loud.

'I'll go,' said Miles. He drained his drink. 'I didn't mean to interrupt your evening, anyway – just a neighbourly call.'

As he got to the front door the sound of retching reverberated down the stairwell followed by a wail. Miles fled.

*

When Heather woke up on Saturday morning, Brian was already up and dressed. Or she assumed he was, as his side of the bed was empty. Heather yawned and stretched and checked the time on the clock radio beside the bed. Nine o'clock! How on earth had she slept so late? But maybe it wasn't so surprising given that half the night her head had seemed to be filled with worries about her own husband and Olivia's. Galvanised, she scrambled out of bed, threw on her dressing gown and ran down the stairs.

'Brian! Brian?' Silence. Oh, dear Lord, now where was he? This was getting ridiculous. She would normally have made herself a cup of tea but Brian's recent absences were becoming far from normal so, instead, she went back upstairs, had a quick shower before she dressed and went out. He'd spend a large part of yesterday at the church; maybe that was where he was again.

Outside, the May morning was sunny but chilly and the grass in the shadows was still damp with dew. It promised to be a glorious day but Heather wasn't in a mood to appreciate the weather. She walked swiftly across the garden to the lane that led to the church and then almost ran through the lytchgate and to the front door of the church.

She turned the heavy ring that formed the outside handle. The deep, cool quiet of the church was disturbed by the grating of the latch being raised. Heather pushed open the door and went in, her footsteps muffled by the massive coir mat by the entrance.

'Hello, Heather,' said Brian from a seat in the choir stalls.

'Brian. What on earth are you doing here?' she said as she made her way down the aisle, through pools of coloured light that the morning sun was spilling across the ancient flags.

'Praying.'

Heather went up the two steps by the pulpit and then perched next to him. 'You've been doing that a lot recently.'

'It's the day job.'

'How's the parishioner you were worried about?'

'Much the same, maybe a touch better.'

'That's good then – I mean, as against the alternative of things getting worse?'

Brian gave her a wan smile. 'I suppose.'

'Oh.' Heather looked at her hands and then at the motes of dust floating in the blue and red and green beams of sunshine. 'Have you had breakfast?'

'Not yet.'

'Then why don't you come home with me and I'll make us both scrambled eggs.'

'I know you mean well, Heather, but don't fuss.' He sounded irritated. 'This is something I need to deal with myself. And I am. It's going to be OK, I promise.'

'How can you be so sure?'

'Because I am. We… everything… the situation will work out.'

We? thought Heather. 'Are you sure this is something you can't tell me about?'

'Yes.' Brian said the single word with total finality.

'Fine.' Hurt, Heather stood up. She wasn't wanted; Brian was shutting her out. She could take a hint. 'I may have to go into town later – just so you know.' She left him to it. As she walked back down the aisle she remembered when she'd walked down a different aisle, over thirty years ago, the organ blaring out Pachebel's Canon, family members smiling or dabbing happy tears. For better, for worse… With a heavy heart, Heather thought that things couldn't be much worse than they seemed at the moment. She trailed home.

29

Olivia put down her empty coffee cup and went over to the sofa where Nigel was reading the Saturday papers.

'We need to talk.'

Nigel lowered the paper. 'Can't it wait?'

'No.' Olivia sat down next to him. 'I'm not stupid, Nigel.'

'Have I ever said you are?' He folded the paper up and chucked it on the coffee table.

'What's going on?'

'I'm not with you.' But he looked shifty.

'The badminton.'

'I told you, it's the MD's idea.'

'You did. But that doesn't explain why you aren't playing.'

'What the hell are you on about, Ol? I do. Every Tuesday.'

'You do something every Tuesday but it isn't playing badminton. Who is it, Nigel? Who are you seeing?'

'Don't be ridiculous.'

Olivia got up and went to the cupboard in the corner of the kitchen. She got out the sports bag she'd repacked after Heather's visit, put it on the table and tipped out the contents.

'So? My sports kit.'

Olivia held up the single shoe. 'The pair to this is in the airing cupboard – where I hid it.' She stared down at him. 'That match you told me you won... how, with only one shoe?' Nigel went brick red as Olivia chucked the shoe into Nigel's lap. 'So... I'd like the truth.'

Nigel looked at the shoe then up at Olivia. 'I can explain.'

'Go on – and this had better be good.'

'I haven't been exactly straight with you, Ol.'

Olivia sighed and crossed her arms. No shit, Sherlock, as Zac would have said. But she felt frightened – scared of what his revelation was going to be.

'You think I'm having an affair.'

'Aren't you?'

Nigel gave a mirthless snort of laughter. 'Shit, Oli, if only it were that simple.'

'Then what? Is it work?' She sat down again on the sofa. Nigel was finding this conversation hard enough without her making things worse by towering over him like some sort of interrogator.

Nigel shook his head. 'No.' He sighed heavily. 'No, work's fine.'

Olivia waited.

'I'm going to Gamblers Anonymous. They meet on a Tuesday evening, in Cattebury.'

'Don't be stupid, Nigel, of course you're not. Why would you do that? You don't gamble.'

'I do. I have done for years.'

'But... but I'd know if you did.'

'How?'

Olivia couldn't answer that.

'It's not like drinking, Ol. I don't come home drunk or reeking of betting shops.'

'No, but...'

'And I'm going to GA because we're broke.'

'Broke? We can't be.'

'Olivia, we are.'

'But... but... how?'

'I've blown it. It's all gone. Every last penny.'

Olivia shook her head. 'OK, Nigel, you've had your fun, now tell me what's really going on.'

Nigel's hand slamming on to the table made Olivia jump. 'For fuck's sake, Olivia, I am not joking.'

Olivia felt sick. No! Not them, not broke. It was just not possible. 'But, I don't understand. You couldn't have lost it all just by gambling. I mean... how?'

'Because it got out of hand. I've been putting money on the gee-gees, dogs, fruit machines, footie, cricket, the stock market... you name it, I took a punt on it.'

'But... why?' Olivia still wasn't sure she believed him. Surely he was exaggerating.

'Because I enjoyed it. Because there was no feeling like it when I won.'

'But if you won, how come we're broke?'

'I lost more than I won. Way more.' Nigel didn't look her in the eye as he said that.

'How much have you lost?' Olivia whispered, not sure she wanted to know.

'I can't give you an exact figure.'

'Hell's teeth, Nigel, how much?' Olivia took a deep breath. 'Ballpark figure.'

'Half a million – give or take.'

If Olivia hadn't been sitting down she'd have fallen down. 'Half a million,' she gasped.

Nigel nodded.

'But why... how?'

'I just couldn't stop myself.'

'You couldn't stop yourself?!' Olivia's initial shock was giving way to anger. 'You couldn't *stop* yourself?' she shouted. 'Didn't you think of your family – of me? The children?'

Nigel nodded miserably. 'But I kept thinking that one really big win would put it all right.'

'And that obviously worked as a plan,' she sneered.

'I'm sorry, Oli.'

'Don't! Don't call me Oli. I loathe it.'

Nigel looked shocked. 'Sorry,' he mumbled.

'For what? Not using my proper name or ruining everything?'

'Oli... Olivia, please...'

Olivia stood up and paced over to the window. She couldn't bear to look at Nigel any more and she had to put some distance between them or she wasn't sure she was going to be able to retain control. Without turning round she said, 'So how bad is it?'

'How do you mean?'

'I mean,' she turned and faced him, 'where do we stand? I'm assuming our savings have gone.' Nigel nodded in confirmation. 'Investments?' Another nod. 'What about the house?'

Nigel stared at her.

'The house is safe?'

He shook his head. 'We're going to have to sell. It's the only way I can pay off the debts.'

Olivia took in the bleak news. 'Sell? But can't we remortgage, or something?'

Nigel shook his head. 'Not with my credit record. That's why I went to look at those new houses. Living somewhere like that – somewhere much, much cheaper than here – is our only option. And we can't afford to get caught up in a chain; we've got to sell and sell fast. My creditors... my creditors are getting nasty. If I don't pay them soon it'll be the bailiffs or bankruptcy.'

Bankruptcy? They were threatened by bankruptcy. Them? Olivia felt sick at the prospect. She got up and walked out of the front door, slamming it hard behind her.

Brian got off his knees and looked about him. It was, as he was already very well aware, a beautiful church. The people who'd built it had had much more to contend with – plague, pestilence, famine and Lord alone knew what else – and they'd trusted in God and got on with it, created this wonderful place of worship when they could expect either themselves or their families to get struck down at any time. Some had laboured with no prospect of seeing it completed, some had probably died working on it, but they'd done it for the community, for future generations. Compared to his predecessors in this ancient town he had it easy. OK, so his life wasn't exactly cushy, but it wasn't bad. He was healthy, he had a wonderful wife, he had a roof over his head, he had enough food on the table, he had heat and light at the flick of a switch... He needed to get a grip and count his blessings.

Brian squared his shoulders. He could do this. He *would* do this. He was going to muddle through somehow because he had a duty to every one of his congregation.

Duty.

That was the key. It was his *duty*. He'd had a calling, he'd answered it, and now he had to see it through. End of. And, as he thought that, as he accepted his lot, he could almost feel the weight lifting.

Megan drifted downstairs and found the kitchen empty apart from the breakfast detritus left by two small boys. She picked up the empty cereal plates, mugs and used cutlery and put them in the dishwasher, then mopped down the table. Order restored after a fashion, she opened the fridge and contemplated what she could have. Orange juice for a start, she thought as she took out the carton. She'd poured herself a glass and was about to put the carton back in the fridge when the back door opened and in came Bex with an empty laundry basket.

'It's such a lovely morning I thought I'd get the washing out early because the forecast says it won't last. Sleep well?'

Megan nodded. 'You should have woken me up; it's late.'

'It's only nine. Besides, I think, after yesterday, a good night's sleep was exactly what the doctor ordered. And you feel all right – not sick or anything?'

'No, I'm fine. Why?'

'Alfie was sick yesterday evening.'

'Poor kid.'

'He's as right as rain now, though. I just thought you ought to know – in case you feel a bit off colour.'

'Is Lewis OK too?'

'Fine.'

'Maybe it was something he ate.'

'Got to hope. The last thing I want is for us all to go down with some sort of sick bug.'

Megan shuddered.

'And what are your plans for today?' said Bex, putting the laundry basket on the table.

'I thought I'd get the bus to Cattebury.'

'On your own?'

Megan shrugged. 'It's only the next town. I won't talk to strange men or anything. There's a couple of things I'd like to do.'

'Such as?'

'This and that – a bit of shopping.' The last thing Megan wanted to do was to go into detail, tell Bex she was getting money to lend to Zac.

'Oh, yes?'

'There's a top in Next that I saw online.' She hoped to God there *was* a Next in Cattebury. She'd checked out there was a branch of the building society but nothing else.

'Will you be home for lunch?'

Megan nodded.

'Right,' said Bex. 'This isn't getting the rest of the laundry done – having to do a full set of bedding on top of everything else is going to stretch the resources a bit today. Let's hope I can get it washed and dried before the rain sets in.' She went back upstairs leaving Megan fingering her bank book in her jean's pocket.

Why, she wondered, was she doing this? She wasn't sure she even *liked* Zac, but she felt sorry for him. He was in a bad place and she knew what that was like. She knew how much it meant to feel you had a friend – moreover, she knew how awful it felt if you didn't.

Taking her orange juice with her she returned to her room and picked her phone off her bedside table.

going 2 town 2 get the money she texted Zac. where shall i meet u when i get back

She was cleaning her teeth when her phone jangled.

I'll get the bus with u

Did he want to make sure she actually got the money? OK

meet me at the stop by the primary school 10.30

OK. She glanced at the time on her phone – plenty of time. Now... what to wear? Bex said it was going to rain later so maybe jeans? And did she put on make-up? She wasn't sure if she wanted Zac to be attracted to her or not. His arrogance was unsettling. On the other hand he was very good-looking. She began to rummage through her wardrobe.

30

Olivia stormed down the hill and along the main street, then took the side turn that led to the nature reserve. She wanted peace and quiet and space to think.

How could he? How could he have done that to the family? Why hadn't she spotted the signs? How could she have been so stupid? The questions, without answers, rolled round and round in her brain and with each circuit she felt more despairing. She walked deep into the reserve, unaware of her surroundings, stamping along the footpaths, not caring where she went, fighting back tears of anger, disappointment and fear until she arrived at a bench by the stream. She sat on it and stared blindly at the sparkling water.

Dear God, how she hated her husband right now. How *could* he? The waste, the deception, the betrayal, the lies... And she didn't even feel she could talk to anyone about it because the shame and humiliation were almost too much to bear. And the signs had been there; his worries about what she spent, his bad temper, the complete lack of holidays – presumably because there was no money to be able to afford them... How had she missed all of that? Because, she thought, she wouldn't have dreamed, not even in her worst nightmares, that her husband was squandering everything they possessed on a stupid addiction. Mid-life crisis was what she'd thought, maybe a mid-life crisis which had involved another woman. Well, it was a crisis all right, and looking at the situation now, had he been having an affair it might have been easier to cope with.

She contemplated leaving him. It would serve him right if she walked out on him. But then a cold sliver of logic thrust its way through the heat of her anger. Where would she go? What would she live on? Realistically she knew she would be so much worse off if she moved out. Sure, if she divorced him she might be entitled to half of everything – the harsh truth was, there was *nothing* for her to have half of. Olivia stood up and walked along the path, back through the avenue of chestnuts to the main street and then turned to head towards Beeching Rise. Dear God, Beeching Rise – her idea of hell on earth. But, if Nigel was right and the estate was the only place in Little Woodford they could realistically afford and which would allow them to buy without getting involved in a chain she needed to have another look. She supposed she could tell people that they were downsizing for environmental reasons – a smaller place to heat and light... but what if the truth came out. Jeez, the shame would be ghastly. Her, Olivia Laithwaite, one step away from penury.

No, the stark truth was, ridiculous or not, one of those tacky houses was going to be the future family home. And, much as she might have wanted to wait for the development at Coombe Farm to be built, even that luxury was going to be denied her.

Zac showered and dressed and ran down the stairs to find his father sitting on the sofa with his head in his hands.

'You all right?' he asked, although he didn't really care.

'Yeah,' came the reply.

'Mum about?'

'She's gone out.'

'Tell her I'm getting the bus to Cattebury. I may not be back for lunch.'

'Sure.'

Zac let himself out of the front door and crunched over the gravel to the main road. On the other side he saw Megan standing at the bus stop. He waved at her before he checked for traffic and ran across.

'Got the bank book?' he asked.

'"Hello, Megan, nice to see you. Thank you for giving up your Saturday morning to sort out my finances."'

'Yeah, of course. Hi, Megan.'

Megan shook her head. 'I don't know why I'm doing this.'

'Because you like me?' Zac bestowed a goofy grin on her.

Megan couldn't help herself from smiling back. 'Sometimes,' she conceded. 'By the way, what's with your mum? I saw her walking past our house and she looked well upset.'

Zac shrugged. 'Mum, upset? No idea. I haven't seen her this morning.' He thought for a second. 'Mind you, I saw Dad before I left – he looked pretty miserable. Maybe they've had a row.'

'Do they row much?'

'I dunno. I mean they do sometimes – don't all parents?'

'Mine didn't. Well, Bex and Dad didn't. I don't know about Dad and my real mum.'

The sound of a diesel engine grinding up the hill halted their conversation.

'I'll get the fare,' said Zac. The bus hissed to a halt beside them and the door swished open. He offered the driver a twenty pound note.

'I thought you were broke,' said Megan.

'I am,' said Zac. 'Mum gave me the money.' Which was kind of true, he told himself. He led the way to the back of the bus. 'I do appreciate this,' he told Megan.

She stared at him. ''S all right. Don't mind helping someone out. Just as long as I get the cash back.'

'I promised, didn't I?'

'Yeah, but you're borrowing off me to pay back someone else you've borrowed off. Just saying.'

'Don't you trust me?'

The beat before Megan answered 'yes', told the real truth.

Zac turned away from her and looked out the window. He was tempted to snipe at her but even he knew that would be unwise. After a bit his annoyance waned and he had to acknowledge that her lack of trust wasn't entirely unreasonable, given that he hadn't been straight with her about who he owed and what for.

'Sorry,' he said.

'What for?'

'Being an arse.'

'Yeah, well, you were.'

There was silence for a couple of stops as the bus bounced along the winding road.

'So, who've you borrowed off?'

'No one.'

Megan eyeballed Zac. 'Don't give me that.'

'You don't want to know.'

'I think I do. And if you want the money you'd better tell me.'

There was a pause of several seconds. 'I smoke the odd joint. I owe my dealer.'

'Bloody hell, Zac. How much?'

'Forty. I wouldn't ask to get bailed out but he's been getting nasty.'

'You do drugs? You're a twat.'

'I know. I'm going to try and stop.'

'If I'm going to lend you money you've got to do more than *try*.'

'You don't understand, it's not that easy.'

Megan stared at him then she shook her head. 'You know, maybe I shouldn't lend you the dosh.'

Zac went white. 'Please, Megan, please. He's got a knife.'

'For fuck's sake, Zac.'

'Please.' It was almost a whimper.

'OK, but only this once. Never again. And you have to promise to sort yourself out.' She gave him another stare. 'Promise. I mean it.'

Zac nodded as the bus bounced over a speed bump as it

ground its way through the suburbs of Cattebury. 'Almost there,' he said, keen to change the subject.

Megan pulled out her bank book. 'I hope you know where the building society is.'

'Yeah. Stick with me. And I'll stand you a coffee after if you like.'

'Lucky me.'

Olivia made her way into the sales office and collected another brochure. She'd chucked the previous one away after that unfortunate incident at the book club.

'Hello,' said the receptionist cheerily. 'Back for another look?'

'Well... er...'

'If you're keen you ought to get your name down shortly. An awful lot of the first phase have been sold and we're now selling the second phase off-plan.'

'Yes, well... I'll think about it.'

'Don't take too long. I can give you the forms and all the financial information now, if you're interested.'

'Well, um...' She backed towards the door. 'Anyway, I'll just take another look at the show house. Please don't bother on my account.'

Feeling flustered, Olivia fell out of the office and down the path to the show house. She opened the door and gazed inside. Nope, still tacky, still poky, she thought, despondently. No, she told herself, she must not be so judgemental. She had to look at it in a more positive light and work out how she, Nigel and Zac could possibly fit in.

She began to leaf through her replacement brochure, checking out the specifications of the other houses on the development. It seemed that this wasn't the largest house that was being built, but the price-hike for the seriously big ones probably made them unaffordable, given their new circumstances. Actually, as Olivia looked at the price list for the various plots, she wasn't sure that they'd be able to afford one like this either. She wondered what they might be reduced to – a two-bed terrace? She shut her eyes at the thought of the come-down.

'Hello, Mrs L?'

Olivia's eyes snapped open. 'Mags. How nice.' It was anything but.

'Fancy seeing you here.'

'Yes... well...'

'You thinking of buying one of these? Jacqui told me that she thought you were interested. Nice, aren't they?'

Olivia laughed, lightly. 'No, just being nosy. I love a good poke around a show house, don't you?'

'All a bit modern for me. What's wrong with a bit of chintz or some woodchip wallpaper?' Mags look disparagingly at the bold statement paper on the wall behind the mock fireplace. 'I mean, silver and black... whatever next.'

'No, not everyone's cup of tea but very on-trend.'

Mags snorted.

'Who's minding the shop?' asked Olivia. 'I'd have thought Saturday would be one of your busiest days.'

'Oh, the girls'll cope. I told my regulars I couldn't take appointments this weekend – or next week – I've given myself a week's holiday.'

'That's nice.'

'Yeah, I'm thinking of selling up. I'm not getting no younger and it's knackering being on your feet all day and I spoke to the housing association. They said with the money I'll get for the salon, and given my circumstances, I could probably buy one of their places; just a two-bed, nothing grand. But it'll mean I won't have to worry about rent no more.'

Olivia's heart sank. The last straw – living here and with Mags as a neighbour. Hoo-bloody-ray.

'Well, don't let me keep you,' said Olivia, heading for the sitting room door.

'Oh, I'm in no hurry. So... Jacqui got it wrong, did she?'

Olivia turned. 'I'm sorry?'

'Jacqui. Jacqui said you had a brochure. She told me when she had her hair done last. I mean, we all know you were dead against this estate but it's all over the town you voted for the other one – and here you are, having a good butcher's.'

'No, just taking an interest – you know, as a councillor.'

'So, not thinking of buying to let or nothing like that?'

'Of course not.' Dear God, a cock would be crowing three times in a moment, thought Olivia.

'Only I don't hold with that.'

'What?' Olivia tried not to snap but thought she might have failed.

'Buying to let.'

'No, neither do I.' She escaped out of the room and headed for the stairs.

She checked out the bedrooms again. She supposed they could use the third bedroom as a walk-in wardrobe or maybe Zac would agree to it being his room. Or maybe not. She was mulling over Zac's likely reaction to losing his beautiful big room at The Grange for this poky box room when she heard someone puffing heavily up the stairs. Mags.

Olivia shot into the family bathroom and hid behind the door. She peeked through the crack at the hinge end and saw Mags disappear into the master bedroom. Olivia tiptoed out of her hiding place and headed for the stairs.

'Glad I caught you.'

She jumped. It was the sales girl.

'I brought you that paperwork I promised. Just in case.'

'I... I didn't...'

'And remember what I said about not leaving it too long; these houses are going like the proverbial hot cakes.' The woman thrust the papers into Olivia's hands and out of the corner of her eye she saw Mags peering around the bedroom door, a knowing smile on her face and obviously adding up two and two.

Bugger. Olivia knew full well the result Mags would come to and then, so would half the town.

31

The violent anger and fear that Olivia had first felt had largely evaporated as she walked home through the town. She was still livid, she still wondered how she was going to be able to talk to Nigel without giving in to the urge to hit him, but, at least, she was now able to think straight. No matter how difficult and painful it was going to be, she had to know exactly where they stood financially, how big the debts were, how much had to be paid off each month and how much that would leave them to live on. One of the first things she had to know was, would Zac be able to continue at St Anselm's? Much as she didn't think she even wanted to be in the same *room* as Nigel right now, she and he were going to have to have a conversation.

She was about to walk past the coffee shop in town when she decided that treating herself to a large cappuccino wasn't going to make the family finances any more precarious and it would also delay going home for a few more minutes. She felt she deserved that little indulgence, given the morning she'd just had.

She went in, went to the counter and placed her order.

'Two sixty,' said the barista.

Olivia opened her wallet purse and looked for a bank note. She could have sworn she had a twenty. Just as well she had enough in change. When her coffee was ready, she took her drink to a corner table. She sipped her coffee then extracted the Beeching Rise sales brochure from her bag and flipped it open.

'Can I join you?'

Olivia's coffee slopped onto the page she was looking at. 'Heather! You made me jump.'

'So I see. I'll go and get a coffee. Back in a tick.'

Olivia mopped the shiny page with a tissue and then slid the bumph into her handbag.

A couple of minutes later Heather returned with her latte and a large slice of cake and two forks. 'You look like you could do with cheering up and I *certainly* could.' She handed a fork to Olivia. 'Tuck in.'

'I spoke to Nigel.'

Heather put her fork down. 'Oh... And?'

'And he's not having an affair.'

'Oh, Olivia, I am so relieved for you. Thank goodness.' She went to attack the chocolate gateau again.

Olivia rolled her eyes. 'It's good news and bad news.'

Again the fork went back on the plate. 'Oh goodness. He's not ill, is he?'

Olivia shook her head. 'In a way.' She sighed. 'I don't know how to tell you this...'

Heather pushed the gateau towards Olivia who dug her fork in. Heather followed suit.

'I'm listening.'

Olivia took a mouthful, chewed it and swallowed. She took a deep breath. 'Nigel has gambled all our money away.'

Heather choked, crumbs spraying over the table. 'What?'

Olivia nodded. 'All of it.'

'Bloody hell,' whispered Heather. 'Well, that puts my problems in perspective.' She snarfed another lump of chocolate goo.

'Oh, Heather, I'm sorry. Me, me, me. I should have asked why you felt like you needed cheering up,' said Olivia.

Heather reached across the table and patted Olivia's hand. 'No, you shouldn't. And not with what you've got going on.

Goodness, if I had a bombshell like that to contend with I don't think I'd even be functioning, let alone taking an interest in other people. No, the last thing you need right now is anyone else's problems. Honest.' She ate another forkful of cake.

Olivia gazed at her. 'Brian still a worry?'

Heather sighed. 'Not like Nigel. Or at least I don't think he is. He won't talk to me and I want him to, because something's really worrying him. He says it's a parishioner but...' She shrugged. 'Anyway, it's not important.' She smiled. 'Some wives might be delighted to have such a taciturn husband.'

'No... not talking isn't good. I know that.'

Both women ate some more cake.

'Poor Brian, poor you.'

'Poor *you*,' said Heather. 'What are you going to do?'

'I don't know. Not till I know how bad things are. After I've had this I'm going to head home and have a talk to Nigel – a proper talk. After he told me... well, I lost the plot a bit and had to go for a walk to calm down.'

'I'm not surprised.'

'He says we've got to sell the house. He seems to have an idea that if we sell ours and move into a place like Beeching Rise we might be OK.' Olivia tapped the brochure. So that's where I've just been. And I ran into Mags Pullen while I was there so the whole town will know by now.'

'You can't keep secrets in a small place like this.'

'No. Only she thinks I am about to join the ranks of bloated plutocrats and we're buying to let. I don't know which is worse – the shame of being threatened by bankruptcy or Mags telling the world I'm the local Rachman.'

'Who?'

'Oh, he was a slum landlord in the fifties, the original buy-to-let guy. Had a shocking reputation.'

Heather smiled.

'OK, I am exaggerating but if... *when* we move out of The Grange, rumours are going to be rife and I don't know if I can bear it – especially if the truth gets out. As you said, you can't keep secrets in a place like this. The easiest thing would be to move away, but Little Woodford is my home. I love this town.'

'I know. And you're a real asset to the place. You do so much.'

'Thank you.' She pushed the plate back towards her friend. 'You finish this, I need to get back to Nigel. And thanks for the cake and the chat.' She stood up.

'You know you can come and talk to me at any time,' said Heather.

'I know, and the same goes for you too. Husbands, eh?'

'Indeed.'

As Olivia left and headed for the cash machine to fill up her wallet the first spots of rain began to fall.

Heather let herself back into the house, unable to shift out of her mind the awful news that Olivia had told her. She was surprised to hear the sound of humming as she hung her damp jacket up on the newel post.

'Brian?'

'Yes, dear.'

She followed the sound of his voice. He was in the kitchen, making tea and toast.

'How was town?' he asked.

'Much the same as it always is. I had coffee with Olivia.'

'Oh yes, how's she?'

'She's had a bit of a shock.'

'Oh, glory. Poor Olivia. What's happened?'

Heather relayed the gist of Olivia's predicament.

Brian looked stunned. 'Nigel? I find that hard to believe. To be honest I've always had him down as the kind of dull stick who wouldn't do anything risky.'

'And gambling is certainly that.'

The toaster popped. 'Do you want some?' offered Brian.

'I had cake in town.'

'How nice.'

'I wanted cheering up.'

Brian began to butter his toast. 'Why on earth?'

'Because I've been worried sick about you.'

Brian put his knife down. 'I know, I'm sorry. I've been a bit preoccupied lately.'

'A *bit*! You've been a nightmare. You've been moping around, as miserable as sin, and every time I tried to reach out to you I got batted away.'

'I'm sorry. I've hurt you.'

Heather nodded. 'Yes, you have. I felt shut out. Brian, we've been married for nearly thirty years and if you can't confide in me, lean on me, then what use am I as a wife?' She stared at him. 'I'm your *wife*, Brian, not the live-in housekeeper.'

'I know. Anyway, the problem has been resolved.'

'Good, and I'm glad and, I must say, you seem much happier.'

'I am.'

'So, are you going to tell me what the matter was?'

'One day, maybe.'

Heather shook her head. 'I suppose I'd better be grateful that you're feeling more chipper. Let's hope it lasts.'

Brian went back to buttering his toast. 'I think it will.'

'Good.'

32

Olivia approached her house, hurrying to get out of the shower. Nigel, she noticed, had mown the lawn. Obviously he was trying to curry favour – like cutting the grass was going to make things better. She stamped up the drive to the front door and let herself back in. Nigel was still sitting on the sofa, the paper lying on the table in front of him. If it hadn't been for the mown lawn she'd have thought he hadn't moved.

'You're back,' he said.

'Why? Were you expecting me to leave? Tempting though it is, I don't think it'd help matters.'

'No,' he agreed.

'We need to talk.'

'What about?'

Olivia stared at her husband in utter disbelief. She took a couple of deep breaths to calm herself. 'For starters, can Zac stay at his school, how much will we have left when we've sold this house and paid off your debts, just exactly how bad is the situation…?' She wrapped her arms around herself, whether to try and comfort herself or to ward off the awfulness of the situation she didn't know. 'And you need to tell Zac. He has a right to know what's going on, seeing as how it's going to affect him too.'

'Zac?'

'Yes, you know, your son. Even if we can afford to keep him

at St Anselm's, he will have to leave this house, the place where he grew up, and he's going to be affected. He has a right to find out the facts first. We can tell the other children as and when – they're pretty much self-sufficient anyway so they'll be the least affected. We can't wait till we get everyone together to break the glad tidings en masse. It wouldn't be fair on Zac. We can ask him not to tell the others.'

'But what if he does?'

Olivia looked at Nigel coldly. 'I'd have thought you'd prefer that – saves you the bother of having to own up to what you've done.'

'That's a low blow.'

'Do you know something? I don't care. So... where do we stand? I want to know everything, Nigel. Every detail.'

Nigel got up and went to the filing cabinet by his desk in the corner of the living area and pulled out a file from the back of one of the drawers. He spread the papers on the desk and Olivia came over and joined him.

'I saw a debt specialist. He gave me some options.'

'Which were?'

'The easiest thing is to file for bankruptcy.'

'As you mentioned. Us... bankrupt.' She looked utterly defeated. Nigel nodded.

'And the other options?'

'Consolidate the debt, pay a chunk off every month. It'd leave us with very little to play with but it might be better in the long run.'

'Bankruptcy or penury,' said Olivia. 'Oh, dear God.'

'My bonus will help. It might even cover Zac's fees next year.'

'And if it doesn't?'

Nigel shrugged.

Olivia gave Nigel a long, cold stare. 'Do you know, if I thought I'd be in a better place if I walked out right now, I'd be sorely tempted.'

'Don't leave me, Oli... Olivia. Please.'

'Shut up, Nigel. You've got absolutely nothing to bargain with. Right, time to break the news to Zac.'

'He's out.'

'Where?'

Nigel shrugged. 'He said he was going to Cattebury on the bus and he mightn't be home for lunch.'

Olivia checked the wall clock. 'In which case, I'm going to have a look at our finances, in detail.' She sat down at the desk and pulled the pile of documents towards her. To start with she found it almost impossible to concentrate; all she could think about now was how quickly her feelings for her husband had changed. Now she knew what the situation was, how much he owed, she realised that she actually felt loathing for him. After the best part of thirty years of marriage she hated him: she hated him for what he'd done to the family, their future, their security... and as for his selfishness in using *their* money to indulge his addiction... Olivia stopped. He had an addiction. He was ill. He wasn't entirely to blame. But he *was* to blame for not telling her, for not seeking help earlier. A *lot* earlier. But, she told herself, this wasn't helping her get to grips with their new situation. She forced herself to start looking at the figures properly.

It was gone two when Zac came in and loped up the stairs. Olivia, not entirely trusting the debt adviser, was still going through all the figures and trying different combinations and permutations to work out a strategy that would enable them to pay off the debt as quickly as possible whilst not being left completely penniless. She was concentrating so hard that she didn't notice his reappearance until the sound of his music began to thump down the stairs from the mezzanine. She tried to zone out the irritating beat but after a while she gave up, threw down her pencil and climbed the stairs to Zac's bedroom. She knocked on the door. No reply. Up here, on the landing, the techno-thump from his sound system was even louder. It seemed to her as if the actual wood of his door was vibrating. Dear God, did he have to play it so loud? No wonder he hadn't heard her knock. She banged even louder.

'Yeah, what?' said Zac as he opened the door and stood slumped against the door jamb.

'Stand up straight, darling,' said Olivia, automatically.

A fug of Lynx wafted out of the room, carried into the rest of the house by the breeze from his wide-open windows. Olivia wasn't surprised he had to have the windows open given the ratio of body spray to breathable air in the room. She could almost feel her eyes stinging.

'What?' repeated Zac.

'Your father wants to have a word.'

Zac stared at her, his eyes heavy-lidded as if he hadn't slept in several days. 'Why?'

Olivia lost it. 'Jesus, Zac, for once in your life just do as you are bloody well told!' He shook his head, apparently startled by the vehemence of her tone but without looking any more inclined to obey her. If he hadn't been several inches taller than her, Olivia might have been tempted to slap him. 'Now!'

Zac ambled out of his room, slamming the door as he went.

Olivia reached past him and opened it again. 'And turn that racket off.'

Zac gave her a withering look, but returned to his room and a couple of seconds later silence replaced the awful bass beat and electronic wailing. Olivia had no idea what it was that Zac listened to but she wasn't going to dignify it by calling it 'music'.

Olivia returned downstairs with Zac trailing after her. He threw himself on the sofa opposite his father so he was lying full length with his feet on the cushions.

'So?' he said.

'Get your feet off the furniture,' snapped Olivia.

Sulkily Zac swivelled round and put his feet on the floor.

'Zac...' said Nigel.

Zac crossed his arms and eyeballed his dad. Olivia thought he looked quite shifty, guilty even. She wondered what he had on his conscience.

'Zac, I'd rather this wasn't repeated outside these four walls but we've had a bit of bad luck.' Olivia nearly choked and Nigel glanced in her direction before he amended his statement to, 'That's not entirely true. I've made a massive mistake and it's cost us money.'

'How much?'

'A lot.'

Zac shook his head and flicked a glance from one parent to the other. 'So it's nothing I've done?'

'Why did you think that?' asked Olivia.

Zac shrugged. 'I get the blame for everything.'

Well, he did get blamed for quite a lot by his father but usually because neither Zac nor his father were prepared to see each other's point of view; the alpha male thing. But this time he definitely looked as if he had a guilty conscience.

'No, it's nothing you've done,' said Nigel.

Unlike your father, Olivia was tempted to add.

'So, why you telling me?' asked Zac.

'Because there are some serious implications.'

Zac looked more engaged. 'Like?'

Nigel took a deep breath. 'For a start, there's a chance you may have to leave St Anselm's after this term. You may have to start at the comp in the autumn.'

'You're kidding me. I am *not* going to that dump.'

'There may not be a choice.'

Zac got to his feet. 'I'm not going.'

'Sit down!' roared Nigel. 'Sit down,' he repeated in a more conciliatory tone.

Zac sank back on the sofa.

'You may not get a choice. At sixteen you can go to a sixth form college or leave or do whatever the hell you like but, until then, you have to go to school.'

'Lots of your friends from primary school go there,' said Olivia, trying to soften the news.

Zac shot her a look. 'They're not my friends any more.'

'Ashley is.'

Zac ignored her. 'It'll be rank.'

'And, maybe more importantly,' said Nigel, 'we've got to sell the house.'

Zac flopped backwards. 'Move?'

Nigel nodded.

'Where?'

Nigel shrugged. 'Somewhere smaller, cheaper to run.' He sighed. 'So, given the size of this place, what the heating bills are, almost anywhere in town.' It was a poor joke.

'Let's face it,' said Olivia, almost as much to convince herself than her son, 'we don't need five bedrooms, not now you're the only one actually living here full-time.'

'But what about when the others come home?'

'Your brother and sisters have their own places, pretty much. Tamsin'll be finishing her master's this year and with any luck she'll walk into a job and be self-sufficient just like Jade and Mike.'

'And if she doesn't?'

'Let's not meet trouble halfway.'

Zac slumped. 'So let me get this right, Dad makes a massive mistake and no one shouts at him. I fail to put my plate in the dishwasher and you all get on my back.'

'Don't be childish,' snapped Olivia.

'It isn't just the house,' said Nigel. 'We're going to have to tighten our belts all round; no more foreign holidays, no more expensive TV packages, we'll probably have to get rid of one of the cars, your allowance will have to be cut.'

'My...' Zac went white. 'You can't.'

'I'm afraid we're going to have to.'

Zac looked close to tears. 'So what did Dad do?'

There was silence. It wasn't for Olivia to answer this one. The ball was in Nigel's court.

Zac looked at him. 'Well? I think I've got a right to know – given that your crappy mistake means I'm going to be skint all the time and you may have cost me my place at school.' There was a catch in his voice and Olivia was surprised. She didn't know his school meant so much to him.

Olivia half-expected Nigel to yell at Zac for his cheek but he remained silent.

'Come on, Dad.'

'I lost the money gambling,' Nigel muttered.

Zac sat bolt upright. 'You did what?'

'You heard.'

'Fucking hell,' breathed Zac. He clenched and unclenched his fists.

'Language,' said Olivia.

Zac looked from one parent to the other and snorted. 'I don't think either of you have got the right to lecture me about anything any more.' He stood up. 'What a pair of losers you two have turned out to be.' And with that he slammed out of the house.

'That went well,' said Olivia as she stared at the front door and tried not to cry.

Ashley sat on the swings at the park and swung, morosely, to and fro as he mulled over the arrival of Billy into his home. Even though there was the threat of another rain shower he didn't care. He didn't feel like he wanted to be in the house with Billy – no way. He supposed he'd always known that his mum might hook up with someone and maybe it wouldn't be such a bad thing to have someone to help with the bills. And Billy had a car... but... but he didn't like the man. He didn't actively dislike him but he felt wary of him. If he'd wanted a father-figure and he had to pick from a line-up, Billy would be amongst the last on his list. Frankly, he thought, Homer Simpson had better parenting skills than Billy probably did. He knew he was being unfair; Billy wasn't ever going to be his parent but, selfishly, if his mum had to hitch up with someone, he'd have liked her partner to be someone who might want to have a kick-around with him or who would take him to a match. He couldn't see Billy wanting to do anything like that – he'd be too worried about messing up his designer kit or scuffing his Nike Air Max trainers.

And he didn't like the way Billy had taken over in the house from the instant he'd arrived. He'd taken charge of the remote, he sat in the chair that had been his, he hogged the bathroom and he'd even ticked Ashley off for leaving his shoes in the hall. What right, thought Ashley crossly, had he to say anything about how he and his mum behaved in *their* house? He was the guest and yet he acted as if he owned the place – and worst of all, his mum either didn't notice or she didn't care. Well, he did. Ashley kicked at a stone and sent it skidding over the wet rubberised play surface.

Movement next to him caught his eye and he stopped staring at his shoes and glanced up.

'Hiya, Zac.'

'Hi.'

Ashley looked at Zac and saw he looked thoroughly miserable. 'You all right?'

Zac shook his head.

So, what is it? Your dealer getting heavy?'

Zac shook his head again.

'Want to talk about it?'

Ashley could see Zac was struggling with an answer.

'No, well… if you change your mind.' Ashley pushed back and let the swing rock forward before he jumped off. 'I suppose I ought to be getting home. Mum's expecting me back.'

'No… wait.'

Ashley sat back down on the swing.

'It's my dad.'

'He's found out about your habit, has he?'

Zac shook his head. 'No. No, he's…'

'He's what? Ill?'

'Ha. If only.' He twisted the swing round on its chains so it was facing Ashley. 'He and Mum have just told me he's gambled all our money away.'

Ashley could feel his jaw slackening and his eyes widening. 'No. He couldn't have done. All of it?'

Zac snorted. 'It's not the sort of thing you joke about, is it?'

'But *all* of it?'

'It's what he and Mum said.'

'Blimey,' whispered Ashley under his breath. It put his irritation with Billy in perspective.

'They said we're going to have to move – somewhere smaller.'

'Hey, living in a small house ain't the end of the world. Just saying.'

Zac looked at Ashley. 'Yeah, I know. Sorry.'

'Welcome to my world.'

'It's all such a mess. And they're going to cut my allowance.'

'Ahh, that was probably the thing that worried Zac the most, thought Ashley. Without that, how was he going to fund his habit? Maybe he'd have to quit, although everything Ash had ever heard about drugs seemed to indicate that coming off them was no picnic. Ash wanted to feel sorry for his friend but it was hard. It seemed to Ash that all Zac's problems were entirely avoidable and it was hard to feel sympathy for people who couldn't resist the self-destruct button – like father, like son.

'I wish I could help you, Zac,' he said. 'Maybe you could get a job to earn some cash? Do a paper round or something?'

Or maybe not, thought Ashley, when he saw the look of disgust pass over his pal's face. His feelings of sympathy waned further.

33

'Coo-ee,' said Mags as she opened Amy's front door and shook droplets off her umbrella.

'And who the hell are you?' said a thirty-something man, standing in Amy's kitchen.

'I think I'm the one who should be asking that,' said Mags, drawing herself up to her full five foot one and pushing her sleeves up her arms.

'I'm Billy. I've moved in with Ames.'

'So you're Billy.' Mags eyed him up and down. 'Well, I'm Amy's mum. Glad to meet you – at last.'

Mags turned at the sound of footsteps running down the stairs.

'Hiya, Mum. This is Billy.'

'I know,' said Mags. 'Or I do now.' She turned back to Billy. 'Is that your car outside?'

Billy nodded.

'Nice. Must have cost a bundle.'

'Mum!'

'Just asking,' said Mags, unfazed.

'Since you ask, yeah. And?' countered Billy.

'Not sure I'd want to leave a smart set of wheels like that parked around here. There's been a lot of burglaries in the town lately.'

CATHERINE JONES

'It's all been houses, though,' said Amy.

'So far,' muttered Mags. 'There was another break-in I heard about last week.'

'Another?' said Amy.

'Yeah, one of those houses over behind the cricket club.'

Amy shook her head. 'I never thought I'd say it but there's advantages to living this end of town. Whoever is doing the break-ins knows that us lot, down here at the cheap end, don't have nothing worth stealing. Ain't that right, Billy?'

'I dunno,' said Billy. He pointed at the TV in the sitting room. 'That'd be worth a bit if you knew the right person.'

'Don't say that, Billy. I'll be having sleepless nights.'

Billy winked and patted Amy's bottom. 'I thought that was the whole reason for me moving in here.'

Mags frowned and shuddered. She decided to ignore Billy. 'Do you know what I saw yesterday?' Amy shook her head. 'Your Mrs L—'

'Olivia?'

'Her. Anyway, you know I've been thinking about giving up the business.'

'Yes.'

'Well, when I sell up I'll have a bit of spare cash and I've been thinking I might buy myself somewhere to live. The housing association says I might be eligible.'

'Really? Get you!'

'Anyway, I was up at the show house, and there was Mrs L. And she said she wasn't thinking of buying but then she got given all the paperwork. So why, when she's got that huge great barn of a place, would she want another house?'

'Search me,' said Amy. 'I suppose when you're loaded like them you have to spend it on something. I can't imagine having that much dosh.'

'I can,' said Billy.

Mags looked at him. 'I can tell – what with that flash car and all.' She turned back to Amy. 'And I also came round to ask if you wanted to come round mine for roast lunch tomorrow but I can see you've probably got other plans for the weekend.' She sniffed.

'Nah, you're all right,' said Billy. 'I'm going to treat Ames and Ash to a meal at the pub.'

'Fine,' said Mags. It obviously wasn't. 'I'll see you around, Amy.'

'Yeah, bye, Mum.'

Mags let herself out again and shut the door with a smidge more force than was entirely necessary.

'You know,' said Amy, after she'd gone, 'it would have been nice if you'd invited Mum to the pub too.'

'She wouldn't want to play gooseberry though, would she?'

'Ash is coming.'

'Yeah, but he's a kid. He'll ignore us and spend all his time on his phone. Your mum would have wanted to talk to us.'

'So?'

'So, I can tell she can't half rabbit and maybe I'd rather talk to you than her. Besides, if I'm paying I think I get to say who gets invited – not you. Savvy?'

The next morning Heather was relieved and pleased to see that Brian's mood from the day before was still upbeat. He hummed 'Rock of Ages' as he shaved, which, she thought, was a good sign. She dressed ready for church and then pottered downstairs, collecting the Sunday paper from the letter box as she passed the front door, and went into the kitchen. She plugged in the kettle before she opened the fridge and got out the eggs, tomatoes and bacon. She scanned a couple of the headline stories on the front page. Gloom, doom and misery, she thought, while she grilled the bacon and fried the eggs and tomatoes. At least the worst that this little town had to cope with was a few burglaries and some under-age drinking. OK, maybe there was worse going on than that behind people's front doors but, on the whole, Little Woodford had to be one of the safer places in the world.

She flicked on the radio and the sound of some theological discussion on the Sunday morning religious programme got half-drowned by the sizzling of the tomatoes in the pan. No, too dreary. It wasn't in tune with her mood and she wanted something happier than the highs and lows of life for Coptic Christians. She opened her laptop and found a music station on the internet and replaced voices with jolly sixties pop. She jiggled in time to the music as she cooked.

'The smell of bacon and a happy wife,' said Brian. He dropped a kiss on the top of her head. 'God's in his heaven, all's right with the world.'

Heather smiled. Her world was all right. She wasn't sure about Olivia's, and Jacqui's could be a bit rocky but, after the trials and tribulations of recent weeks she felt she could indulge in a few minutes of unadulterated selfishness and ignore other people's problems.

'Put the toast on and make the tea, there's a love,' she said to Brian.

The pair worked as a team for a few minutes until their breakfast was ready and they sat at the table. How different the atmosphere was, thought Heather as she tucked in, from the past couple of weeks. She longed to know what the initial problem had been and what had caused this total turn-around but years of being a vicar's wife had taught her to be patient and to know that if Brian wanted her to know something, she would eventually find out and that if he didn't, she never would. It didn't stop from her being curious but she'd learned to curb it sufficiently that her inquisitiveness didn't drive her potty.

Brian read the main bit of the paper while Heather flicked through the Sunday supplement, looking at glossy pictures of fashion accessories for people with more money than sense and recipes that seemed to need ridiculous amounts of preparation. What's wrong with a good old shepherd's pie, she thought as she looked at a concoction which needed... she totted them up...

twenty-four separate ingredients. She flicked the magazine shut and looked at the clock.

'Nearly time to go,' she said. She stacked their plates in the sink and then ran upstairs to put a comb through her hair and slap on a bit of lippy. She glanced out of the window. It might be May but she'd need a coat. Besides, the heating in the church had been switched off at the start of April and it was going to be blooming cold in there, as it was most of the year.

'I'll head off,' she heard Brian shout up the stairs.

'OK, sweetheart,' she called back down. 'I'll be over in a few minutes. Knock 'em dead.'

The front door banged shut and the house was silent apart from the distant noise of the pop music jingling from her laptop in the kitchen.

Heather pattered downstairs again, switched off her computer and then went into the sitting room to find her handbag. She then checked the doors were locked before she followed Brian out of the front door and to the church.

As usual she was caught at the door by parishioners who wanted to chat. Quite a few of the congregation were older members of the parish and their weekly trip to a service was, pretty much, their only social interaction. Heather understood their need to talk, to gossip, to catch up and she was happy to provide a sympathetic and listening ear. It was, she always told herself, what was expected of her in her role as 'vicar's wife'.

'Is the vicar better?' asked one.

'Yes, thank you. It was just a dizzy spell.'

'And what's that I've heard about another huge housing estate?' said another.

'I don't think it's huge and we need the houses. Our children and grandchildren will all need homes and there's already a lot of homelessness.'

'I don't hold with it. Let them all go and live somewhere else. Little Woodford doesn't need any more houses. And where will they all park when they come into town, that what I want to know?'

Heather moved away before she got riled. 'And how are you, Joan?'

'Can't complain. Not happy about them there burglaries, though. Where will it all end?'

Heather shook her head and, out of the corner of her eye, saw Olivia come in. 'Excuse me.' She dashed off, trying to damp down her feeling of relief that she'd escaped from the old ladies. She drew Olivia to one side.

'How are you?'

Olivia seemed to sag. 'Nigel is sunk into gloom, Zac isn't speaking to me and I'm thinking I ought to apply for a job but who is going to want a fifty-something woman who hasn't been in employment for the best part of thirty years?'

Heather put her hand on Olivia's arm. 'This is so tough for you. It's a real trial.'

Olivia blinked rapidly. 'Don't be kind to me, Heather, or I'll cry.' She dabbed at her nose. 'One moment I was feeling pretty content with my lot, and the next...' She dabbed her nose again. 'What's that Chinese curse? "May you live in interesting times"? Well, they couldn't get any more interesting round at our place. The only positive thing is that the house is worth a mint so we should be able to clear most of the debts when we've sold it. I spent yesterday afternoon doing sums to see where we stand. It's pretty horrific but it's not quite as bad as I feared when Nigel first told me the situation.'

'That's something.' Heather glance around the church. 'I think we ought to find a pew.'

They walked towards the front and slid into an empty one.

After they'd both said their prayers, Olivia sat back up on the hard bench and said, 'And Brian?'

'I got home from having coffee with you to find a changed man.'

'That's wonderful.'

Heather nodded. 'Let's hope it's not like what you get with hurricane – you know, the eye bit, where the weather clears but then it becomes terrible again.'

'I'm sure not. I reckon whatever was causing him to be so upset and worried has been resolved.'

The organ struck up the introit and the two women stood. Olivia glanced behind her to watch Brian process down the aisle. He certainly looked OK, quite cheerful, in fact. She was glad that someone seemed to be happy with their lot because she certainly wasn't. As Brian approached the front of the church Olivia's gaze slid off him to Bert, standing next to Joan. He was looking at his wife with undisguised concern, a worried frown creasing his leathery skin. Was there anyone, wondered Olivia, who was having an easy time of things at the moment?

Amy was changing the sheets on the beds, a job she did every Sunday, when she heard the front door slam.

'Billy? Ash?'

'It's me,' called Billy's voice.

Amy gathered up the dirty sheets from where she'd dumped them on the landing and hefted them down the stairs.

'Hiya. Where've you been?'

'What's it to you?'

Amy felt slightly snubbed. 'Well... nothing. I just wondered, that's all.'

'Then don't.'

Amy walked past him into the kitchen and began to stuff the linen into the washing machine. She dosed it with laundry liquid before she slammed the door shut.

Billy was standing over her as she stood up again. 'I said on Friday, I don't want people to ask no questions. My mum doesn't but you do. Now... do you want me to stay here or not? Because if you do, no more questions.'

'I only asked where you'd been, Billy.'

'I've been out.'

'But...' Amy shut up. If Billy wanted to be so mysterious, let him. It was no skin off her nose.

'Now, then, you ready to come down the pub?'

'Yeah. Ash is going to meet us on the way; he's popped down to the skatepark to see his mates.'

'Get your coat then.'

Heather left Brian chatting to his flock at the end of the service and made her way back to the vicarage. She'd done her duty and now she wanted to get lunch on. It was only a chicken but if she didn't get it in the oven soon they'd be having it for afternoon tea, not lunch.

She walked into the kitchen and put her bag on the side, switched on the radio, filled the kettle and got the meat and some vegetables out of the fridge. It was only when she'd got the roast into the oven, had a cup of tea beside her and she was starting to peel the spuds that she realised her laptop wasn't on the counter.

Heather put the knife down. Maybe Brian had moved it. But he'd gone over to the church first. She distinctly remembered switching it off before she'd left. She stared at the space where the laptop had been, then she walked into the sitting room. The DVD player was missing, and her mother's little silver clock that sat on the mantelpiece. Heather sank down onto the sofa.

Bastards.

34

Bex was in the kitchen cooking a Sunday roast for the family. 'Mum, Mum,' wailed Alfie, plaintively as he stamped into the kitchen, dragging his Tonka digger along on a piece of string. Since it had eventually been found, Alfie had barely been parted from it.

'What, is it darling?' Bex took a pan of parboiled spuds off the hob and drained them into a colander.

'Megan won't take me to see the diggers.'

'Darling, you can't expect her to do it every time you want to go.'

'But it's not fair.'

'I expect she's busy.'

'But I want to go. You take me.'

'Alfie, I'm cooking lunch. Maybe later.'

Alfie's face crumpled. 'But I want to go now.'

'Don't you want yummy roast chicken?'

'No. No, I don't. Roast chicken is pooey.'

Bex turned away from him to hide her smile. 'We'll go after lunch – promise.'

'Want to go now.' Alfie stamped his feet and then kicked his digger but the toy was made of metal and he yelped with pain then burst into tears.

Bex crouched down and gave him a hug. 'We'll go after lunch, promise. OK?'

Alfie clung to her and sobbed onto her shoulder. 'I s'pose,' he said.

'Now, as it's not raining, why don't you go and play in the garden? Take Dougie the Digger out with you and see if you can make a big pile of earth.'

Alfie's sobs subsided and he wiped his nose on the back of his hand. Bex got to her feet, reached for the kitchen towel and tore off a square.

'Blow,' she instructed Alfie. He did and then she dried his tears with a clean corner and chucked the paper in the bin. 'Lunch will be in a while. I'll call you in when it's ready.'

Alfie trailed out of the back door and Bex turned her attention back to her cooking.

A short while later, as she was basting the chicken, Lewis walked in.

'I'm bored,' he complained.

Bex sighed. 'Go and play with Alfie.' She put the foil over the chicken and shoved it back into the oven. 'He's in the garden with his digger, but he might want to play football. Why don't you ask him? I told him I'll take him to see the diggers after lunch but he won't want to stay long because they won't be working on a Sunday. And if it doesn't rain, I thought maybe we can go to the park too. Would you like that?'

'Park? Yeah.'

'Now, I'm busy so you go and play outside till lunch.'

Lewis trotted off but was back in under a minute. 'I thought you said Alfie was outside.'

'Isn't he?' Bex took the saucepan lid off the carrots and turned the gas down a fraction to stop them boiling over.

'No.'

'Well, maybe he's in his room. Go and see.'

Off went Lewis again, shouting his brother's name. Bex went to the back door. She was sure Alfie hadn't come back in. It wasn't completely outside the bounds of possibility that he had snuck in while she'd been busy but... a little twinge of anxiety went through her. She yelled Alfie's name. She called and called.

Nothing.

'He's not in the house, Mum.'

Bex's niggle of anxiety became a bit stronger. She walked round to the front of the house. There was his digger in a flower bed and... Dear Lord, the gate was open.

Bex ran out of the garden on to the pavement and looked left and right. There was no sign of him. Would he have gone out of the garden? And if so how long had he been gone? She glanced at her watch. Not more than a few minutes, surely? Lewis ran up beside her.

'Darling, go and get Megan. Ask her to really check the house.' Bex patted her jeans' pocket. Good, she had her phone on her. 'If you find him, call me. I'm going to see if he's gone to the building site or the park on his own. Understand?'

'You will find him, won't you, Mummy?'

'Of course,' said Bex with a certainty she didn't feel.

She ran along the pavement, heading towards the station and the new houses. A couple of times she stopped passers-by and asked if they'd seen a small boy but all she got were shakes of heads. She was on the brink of ringing the police when she saw, ahead, a woman crouching down – obviously talking to someone. A child. Then the woman stood up and looked about her as if she was looking for someone as she held the child tightly by the hand.

Alfie, and he was with Jacqui – thank goodness.

Bex sprinted towards her.

'Alfie! Thank goodness. Thank you, thank you, Jacqui,' she said. She bent down to scoop up her son.

'How could you let your little boy wander off like this, all on his own? You're not fit to be a mother. I don't know. He could have been killed or kidnapped or anything.'

'But... but I didn't...' Bex's gratitude was swamped by a feeling of shame and embarrassment as the tirade continued. Other pedestrians stared, curious as to what this row was about. 'I didn't,' she protested. 'He ran off.'

'Not properly supervised. Huh. I've a good mind to report you.'

Bex picked up Alfie and swung him onto her hip.

'No, you don't understand… Alfie, what have I said about not going out of the gate?'

Jacqui carried on with her rant. 'Mothers like you don't deserve kids.'

'Yes, you're probably right,' she said. 'And it's a good job there's people like you around. And thank you. I'm very grateful. Truly. And I'll give my son a good talking-to when we get home.' She turned and walked back towards her house as Jacqui continued to question her parenting skills, raising her voice to be sure Bex could hear her despite the increasing distance between them.

'You are very, very naughty,' she told Alfie. 'You know you're not to leave the garden.'

'But I wanted to see the diggers.'

'And I said I'd take you after lunch. I'm not sure we'll go now, not now you've been so disobedient. And look at the trouble you got me into. That lady was really cross with me.'

'Sorry, Mummy,' said Alfie, clinging onto her neck.

Bex hugged him tighter to her, still shaken by the shock of his disappearance and the public dressing-down she'd just received.

As they approached their house she could see Megan standing at the gate, peering down the road. Bex waved and Megan came hurtling towards them.

'You found him!'

'Yes, safe and well and almost at the town hall.'

'Alfie!'

Alfie began to cry. 'But I wanted to see the diggers.'

'Naughty, naughty, boy,' said Megan as she ruffled his hair.

Alfie sobbed louder.

'Anyway, all's well that ends well,' said Bex, 'although I might have to think about putting a bolt on the gate.'

'Surely he won't do it again?'

'I thought he wouldn't do it a first time.'

'True.'

They walked back through the gate and Megan shut it carefully. 'And you're not to go out on your own again, Alfie, understand? You were naughty. Mummy's very cross. And I am too,' she added. 'You gave us a fright.'

Alfie buried his face in Bex's shoulder.

'Let's go in,' said Bex.

As she opened the door a bitter smell assailed her and there was a haze of smoke drifting out of the kitchen.

'The carrots!'

She dropped Alfie onto the floor and ran into the kitchen to switch off the gas. The she lifted the lid of the pan. Through the smoke she could see the carrots now resembled black sticks of charcoal. Bex carried it over to the sink and filled the pan with cold water. The smoke turned to steam as the water hit the hot metal and a resounding hiss filled the air.

'Sorry,' she said to Megan. 'I think carrots are off the menu.'

She looked at the ruined pan and felt tears well up. She knew it wasn't that making her cry but the awfulness of what might have been. Dear God, she thought, hadn't the family had enough to cope with? But it *hadn't* happened. Everything was OK. But still the tears fell.

'It could have been worse,' said Brian. On the counter behind him were the leftovers from their lunch. Neither of them had had much of an appetite and then, before they'd finished eating, the police had arrived to have a look at the crime scene, take statements and get a list of the missing items.

'Yes,' agreed Heather. 'It's just *stuff*. Things.' She took a deep breath and sighed. 'And whoever did this knew we'd be out. Perfect timing, I suppose.' She stared at the dirty dishes and knew she ought to make a start on clearing up but she couldn't be bothered.

'And it can all be replaced.'

'Mum's silver clock can't.'

Brian put his arms around his wife. 'No. No it can't. On the bright side we'll save on silver polish.'

Heather cracked a smile although she'd never felt less cheery in her life. They were sitting in the kitchen as the police worked in the sitting room, dusting for fingerprints.

'I was thinking of going over to see the Millars this afternoon. I'm not sure I feel up to it now,' said Heather. She rubbed the handle of the mug in front of her with her finger.

Brian reached across the table and put his hand over hers. 'Don't you think it might be an idea to go anyway? There's not much you can do here. The police have got your statement and if they need to speak to you again, you'll not have gone far.'

'I suppose,' said Heather.

'What do you need to see them for?'

'There was an incident at the school. I need to persuade Megan to go along with my idea. The trouble is, I'm not sure I'm in the right frame of mind to want to help other people.'

'Don't you think that if you do this it'll make you feel better? It'll be doing something positive and it might take your mind off what's happened?'

'Maybe.' She was far from convinced.

Leanne Knowles put her head around the kitchen door. 'We've just about finished.'

'Good,' said Brian.

'And you're sure you locked up properly before you went out?'

'I'm pretty sure,' said Heather. 'I mean, I'm almost certain I checked the doors were locked but...' She got up and went to the back door. 'We haven't been out again since we discovered the break-in and this is still locked and I know I slammed the front door shut.'

'You didn't double lock it?'

Heather shook her head. 'No.'

'Yale locks aren't that secure.'

'Yes, we know that – now.'

'Only, like with some of the other recent burglaries there hasn't been a sign of a forced entry,' said Leanne.

'Oh.'

'Does anyone else have a key?'

'Only our kids… and Amy, of course.'

'Amy Pullen?'

'Yes, she cleans for me.'

'She cleans for Jacqui Connolly too.'

Heather stared at Leanne. 'No, not Amy. She's cleaned for me for years and I'd trust her through and through. She's completely honest.'

Leanne didn't look convinced.

'Besides,' said Heather, 'lots of houses where Amy doesn't clean have had burglaries.'

'Maybe.'

Another police officer came into the kitchen. 'We're all done now. You've got a crime number for your insurance?'

Brian nodded.

'I doubt if we'll manage to recover anything but, if we do, we'll let you know.'

'Thank you.'

'And I advise you to double lock your house in future,' said Leanne.

'Yes, you said. A bit like the proverbial stable door, though, now,' said Heather.

'We'll be off then.'

Brian stood up and accompanied the two police officers to the front door and shut it behind them. When he got back to the kitchen Heather was running hot water into the sink and putting the meat into the fridge while the washing-up bowl filled.

'You don't suppose Amy *has* got anything to do with this?' asked Brian.

Heather shook her head. 'I'd bet my life on it. Not a chance.'

35

Amy was on her third glass of wine while Billy was enjoying a slice of sticky toffee pudding. Across the table Ashley sighed and played with his mobile.

'Do you want to go home, love?' said his mum. 'You don't mind, do you, Billy?'

Billy, his mouth full, scowled but shook his head.

'Say thank you to Billy, for your lunch,' Amy reminded him.

'Thanks, Billy,' mumbled Ashley. He pushed his chair back and stood up.

'It's OK,' said Billy after he'd swallowed.

'Think I might go to the skatepark first.'

'Whatever. See you later,' said his mum.

Billy scraped his plate and then licked his spoon. 'That was well nice,' he said.

'Thanks,' said Amy. 'I dunno, dinner at the Old Mill and now this. You're spoiling me.'

'What's the point of earning a decent wedge and not treating yourself, eh?'

'I wouldn't know,' said Amy. 'Ash and I are pushed to make ends meet some weeks.'

'You ought to make him get a job.'

'I don't want to mess with his schoolwork.'

'Pah,' said Billy. 'What good's learning stuff? Never did me no good and I'm doing all right.'

'The school said Ash is university material.' The pride in her voice was palpable.

Billy stared at her. 'Well, you want to get that idea out of his head. Waste of money and three years, if you ask me. Nah, your Ash wants to get himself a proper job, a trade.'

'But the school says—'

'"The school says",' mimicked Billy. 'What do they know?'

'They say kids with degrees earn loads more than kids without.'

'Doing what? Arty-farty jobs in poncy offices. Like I said, your Ash should get a proper trade with proper skills.'

Amy felt deflated. And maybe Billy had a point. People were always talking about how difficult it was to find a decent plumber or electrician. He'd never be out of work if he did something like that.

'And,' said Billy, jabbing a finger in her direction, 'uni costs shed-loads, don't it. Who's going to foot that bill? Nah, mark my words he'll come out with some stupid degree and a ton of debt when he could have been working and earning some dough instead.' To prove his point Billy pulled a wad of notes out of his pocket.

Amy boggled. 'Bloody hell, Billy. How much is there?'

'Five hundred, give or take.'

Amy didn't think she'd ever seen so much cash in one go. 'You oughtn't flash it about like that. Not with all those break-ins going on.'

'Yeah, well, they're not going to have a go at a house like yours, are they? Or my mum's come to that.' Billy stuffed the notes back in his pocket. 'Stands to reason that neither you or my mum won't have much worth nicking.'

'You said they might want my telly.'

'Yeah well, that's about it, isn't it?'

'They might think different if word gets around how loaded you are.'

'And who's going to open their big mouth and talk? It better hadn't be you, Amy.' His voice was hard and once again he made Amy feel slightly uncomfortable.

'Course it won't be me.'

'Good. Glad we understand each other.' Billy stood up. 'I'll get the bill, shall I?'

He walked over to the bar and Amy gathered up her coat and bag.

'Thanks, Billy,' she said when he returned. 'Like I said, that was a real treat.'

The pair left the pub and walked out into the warm May sunshine. 'Right, I got to go and see a man about a dog,' said Billy.

'What? Now? But it's Sunday.'

'Business is business.'

'When'll you be back?'

'There you go again. Always questions, questions, questions. You just don't learn, do you?' His voice was cold and angry.

'Sorry.'

'I'll be back when I am.'

Amy wanted to know if he was going to want tea when he got in but didn't dare ask. And was wanting to know when he was going to be home so unreasonable? Apparently it was.

Billy loped off past The Beeches and Amy trailed towards her end of town wondering why Billy was so against her asking the least thing. She didn't like secrets and she was sure Billy was keeping something from her and it made her worried.

Megan was helping Bex stack the dishwasher after lunch while the boys were in the sitting room watching a DVD.

'Bex, I don't want to go to school tomorrow.'

Bex finished putting the dinner plates in the rack and straightened up. 'No, I don't imagine you do. But you're going to have to sooner or later. Mr Smithson is on the case and I'm sure he'll sort it all out.'

'But what if he doesn't?'

Bex sat down on a chair and rested her hands on the table. 'I think you ought to tell everyone what really happened.' Megan shook her head. 'And what if they don't believe me? What if they think that I really *did* trip Stella up? That's what her friends said back in London.'

'Sweetie, we've been over this. Stella fell. No one was to blame for what happened, least of all you.'

Megan shook her head. 'But I took the memory book in. If I hadn't done that...'

'Stella took it off you. She *stole* it. She ran away with it. She tripped. The accident was all her fault.' As Bex finished speaking the doorbell rang. 'Go and answer that, will you, while I finish up here.' She got up and began to drop knives and forks into the cutlery basket as Megan went into the hall.

Bex heard voices as Megan greeted their visitor.

'It's Mrs Simmonds,' said Megan when she returned.

'Heather, how lovely. How are you?'

Heather sighed. 'Well, apart from still feeling a bit shocked that someone broke into the vicarage while we were at church, I'm fine.'

'Broke in? But that's awful.'

'It's not great. But, as Brian says, it's just *things* and they can be replaced – or most of them can, at any rate.'

'Bloody hell, I don't think I'd be as calm as you are. I think I'd be spitting feathers.'

'It wouldn't achieve anything, though.'

'It'd make me feel better to have a bloody good rant.'

Heather smiled. 'Anyway, I didn't come here to talk about that. I came to see Megan because I've had an idea.'

Megan looked up.

'There's an assembly on Monday afternoon. I think we ought tell everyone a cautionary tale about believing rumours and spreading lies. I know I suggested on Friday that you say what actually happened, and you didn't want to, but I've been thinking about it since and I totally think it's the best way.'

Megan looked unconvinced while Bex said, 'I agree!'

'Fake news,' said Heather. 'There's a lot of it about so it's quite topical.'

'It won't do any good,' muttered Megan.

'It will, if you tell your side. Or if someone does.'

Megan shook her head.

'That's exactly what I said,' agreed Bex.

'I could do it for you if you'd like,' said Heather. 'I'm a vicar's wife and I have no reason to lie. They'd believe me.'

'You think?'

'I do. Trust me, there's not many perks to being married to the local God-botherer but being trusted and believed are a couple of belters.' Heather smiled at Megan. 'So, what do you say?'

'I don't know.'

'What's the worst that can happen?'

Megan shrugged.

'At the moment there's a completely false rumour doing the rounds. Unless we get the truth out, that's all people have to go on. If they don't believe the truth, you're no worse off, and if they do believe it... well, job done.'

'Exactly,' said Bex.

Megan looked from her stepmother to Heather and back again. 'I suppose.'

'Good,' said Heather. 'I'll speak to Mr Smithson first thing and arrange it.' She put her arm round Megan and gave her a hug. 'Then all we have to do is find out who wrote that awful thing on the board and make sure they never do such a horrible thing again.'

'Thank you,' said Bex.

'Not a problem. And once everything is out in the open I think you'll find that everyone will be on your side and not the bully's.'

'You think?' said Megan.

'I do. I know you wanted to make a fresh start here and put that awful incident behind you. What you witnessed was dreadful and I understand your reasons for not wanting anyone to know about it, but keeping things secret isn't always the solution.'

'Maybe,' said Megan.

'Anyway, that's why I called round and now I need to get off home and clean up all the fingerprint dust the police have covered the house in.'

'I can't believe,' said Bex, 'that anyone would sink so low as to break into a vicarage!'

'I'm not sure burglars really care about their victims' careers or vocations.'

'No, you're probably right. I don't suppose they have much of a moral compass.'

Bex walked with Heather to the front door. 'Thanks for dropping by – especially as you've enough to cope with without taking on our problems too.'

'It was nice to have something else to think about – even if it was only for a few minutes.'

Bex let Heather out and then returned to the kitchen. 'She's right.'

'Are you sure?'

Bex nodded and hugged Megan. 'As she says, it can't make anything worse and if it makes things better, all will be well.'

Megan shook her head. 'I hope you're right.'

36

'Got a few bits and pieces to get in town,' Joan told Bert on the Monday morning.

'OK, dearie,' he replied. No you ain't, he thought. You're off to the doc's.

He went to the sitting room window and watched her walk across the road and in through the back gate to the park. Then he gave it another five minutes before he followed her. When he got to Dr Connolly's surgery he peered through the glass door at the waiting area and saw Joan, sitting with her back to him, reading a magazine. He hovered by the door, glad that the weather was dry as he waited for her to be called in for her appointment. Ten minutes later he saw her get up, chuck her magazine back on the table and go through the door to the doctor's consulting room. Bert let himself in and took the seat she'd vacated.

He tried not to worry like he'd tried not to over the weekend but the problem was he was feeling sick with concern. Chest pains were never trivial, were they? Supposing his Joan was really poorly? He couldn't bear the thought of life without her. What would he do with himself with no Joan? As he sat there and contemplated the uncertain future he found himself close to tears. Fifty years they'd been together. Fifty! That was a long time in anyone's book.

And he'd always assumed he'd be the one to go first. Men

did, didn't they? He'd always said to Joan that, after he'd gone, she was to make sure she kept herself busy, she wasn't to mope. She'd be comfortable enough, what with his pension and her state one.

'Bert?'

He looked up. 'Hello, Joan.'

'What the blazes...?'

Bert stood up and they headed for the door. 'I think I ought to be the one asking the questions,' he said, holding it open for Joan.

'But...?'

'I overheard your phone conversation on Friday. I forgot my twine and had to come back in. Why didn't you tell me you've been poorly?'

The pair headed up the high street.

'I didn't want to worry you.'

'Like I'm not worried sick now. So, what's been going on?'

'I've had a couple of turns. The last couple have been while I was cleaning the church.'

'Bad?'

Joan nodded.

'Why didn't you ring me? I'd have brought the car down, come and got you.'

'The Reverend was there. And they didn't last. Nasty sharp stabbing pains but then they eased off. Anyway, the Reverend made me promise to see the doc.'

'You should have told me,' grumbled Bert.

'I was going to, when I got home.'

'And?'

'It's nothing too serious. I've got pericarditis, he says.'

'Sounds serious to me.'

'The doc said it's nasty but not desperate. I've got to take anti-inflammatories and go for some tests but the doc is sure I'll be as right as ninepence in no time.'

'Is this the truth?'

Joan nodded. 'Honest.'

'You gave me such a scare.'

'I'm sorry, Bert, me love. I didn't mean to. But there's something the doc mentioned and we need to talk.'

'What?' Bert's worry came crashing back.

'It's about you and me.'

'What about us?'

'About us not being married.'

''T'ain't no one's business but ours. Besides, after all this time we're common-law man and wife.'

'That's the thing, the doc says common-law marriage is a myth. He said that if we're not properly spliced we don't have no rights.'

'Get away.'

''Tis true.'

'Then maybe we ought to do something about it.'

'Maybe.' Joan chuckled. 'Mind, after fifty years is a bit late to start shutting the stable door. That horse ain't only bolted, he's probably died of old age.'

Later that morning, John Smithson, the school head, stopped Megan in a corridor as she was on her way to the canteen for lunch.

'Could you pop into my office for a second?' he asked.

Megan nodded – she could guess what this was about. She followed Mr Smithson, aware of curious glances from other pupils, although she'd already been the object of stares and whispers for the first four periods of the morning – hardly surprising given the accusation on Friday.

Mr Smithson led her into his office and shut the door.

'I've had a word with Mrs Simmonds.'

Megan nodded.

'She tells me you're OK with her idea of putting your side of the story to your year group's assembly.' He smiled at Megan encouragingly.

She nodded again. 'Not much of a choice, though, is it, sir?'

'Sadly no. I'd hoped that all that unpleasantness might be left behind in London but it seems that someone in your tutor group has made it their business to dig it all up. Do you know who it might be?'

Megan had a pretty good idea but she didn't think that dobbing Lily right in it would help matters. 'Not really.'

'I imagine you're into Facebook and WhatsApp like everyone else. Has anyone had a go at you, bullied you on the internet?'

'No. To be honest, sir, I've not made that many Facebook friends here since I've arrived. My stepmum suggested I didn't rush into things because of what happened before.'

'Very sensible.'

'I'm friends with Ashley Pullen but only in real life and I know it's not him.'

'Anyone else?'

Megan looked at the floor and shook her head.

'What about Lily Breckenridge?'

Megan glanced up. Did she tell the truth or answer with a barefaced lie?

Before she had to make the choice Mr Smithson said, 'OK, I won't keep you.'

With a whoosh of relief she fled and almost cannoned into Ashley who was hanging around in the corridor.

'Was that about…?' said Ashley. 'I heard he'd hauled you in. Are you OK?'

'He was checking I'm OK about what Mrs Simmonds is going to do. You know, what I said this morning, about the assembly.' Ashley nodded. 'I suppose I have to be, don't I – not much choice, is there?' She stared at Ashley. 'Thanks for caring though.' She cracked a wan smile. 'Especially as it's not cool for boys to hang out with girls at this school.'

'Shit, no,' said Ashley.

The pair walked towards the canteen. 'Smithson asked me if I knew who'd done it. Then he asked if I was connected to Lily on Facebook.'

'Do you think it was her?'

'Dunno. I just wonder about being her friend on Facebook. I mean, I said to you that I wasn't sure about it... She could have gone back through my timeline and sent friend requests to kids at my old school.'

Ashley looked at her. 'But why would she? I mean, she wouldn't have any idea about what happened at your old place so how would she know to ask questions? It doesn't make sense.'

'No, you're right. I mean, apart from you and the head, no one here knows anything about that.'

'And it wasn't me,' said Ashley.

'But someone knows something. Someone found out, didn't they?'

While John Smithson was interviewing Megan, Bex found that news of Alfie's escape was the talk of the pub. Word had got around in no time about Jacqui's rant at Bex.

'I don't know how he managed to open the gate,' she told Belinda.

'Obviously a right little Houdini.'

'I'm going to have to get a bolt put on. I can't risk him doing that again.'

'Would you like Miles to do it? He's pretty handy at that sort of thing.'

Bex thought about how much she'd irritated him by being useless. Surely such a request would only irritate him further. 'No, I am sure I can manage it.'

'Don't be ridiculous.' And before Bex could stop her Belinda had barrelled into the pub kitchen and put Miles on the spot.

'No – honestly, I'm sure I can do it,' she protested, trailing after Belinda.

'Shhh. Miles? What do you say? How about you pop round with your Black and Decker...'

'Of course. No problem.'

Did he really mean that or was he just being polite? Bex couldn't tell which, but she felt embarrassed that poor Miles was being made to cope with her ineptitude again.

'Sorted,' said Belinda. 'You buy the bolt and Miles here will fix it.'

'Thanks,' mumbled Bex. She didn't dare look Miles in the eye and rushed back to the bar.

Heather Simmonds stood on the stage in the assembly hall and stared out at the kids from Year Ten. A hundred and fifty faces stared back at her as she got into her stride with her themed talk. Some looked engaged but some looked bored to snores and some were staring at their laps. Heather would bet a pound to a penny they were messing with their phones. No matter – she ploughed on.

'That's the thing with fake news,' she said. 'If there's enough of it, no one knows what to believe after a while, do they? No one knows who are the good guys, the ones telling the truth, and who are the scammers, the criminals and the liars. Besides, if you hear something often enough, it's difficult to believe it not to be true. It's like advertisements on the telly – the product being promoted is always better than all the rivals, but they *all* say that, so who do you believe? Of course, it's worse with rumours. Rumours that are based on someone's opinion, a half-truth, something heard or seen but misinterpreted. Most rumours are harmless but some are damaging and downright plain nasty.

'There's one doing the rounds, right here, in this school, about a child at another school who had a tragic and terrible accident.' Suddenly the level of interest rocketed. Naturally – they all knew by now about the accusation on the whiteboard and so this talk wasn't about elections or international news or boring stuff like that, this was about a kid they all knew. 'In fact, if that girl hadn't stolen another pupil's prized possession and run away with it, the accident would never have happened. Because she was running, she tripped, she fell, she hit her head. A ghastly accident. It was witnessed by other pupils but some, *some*, chose to believe that it was the fault of the pupil for bringing the object, her very precious possession, into school in the first place.' Heather's gaze traversed her audience. 'Which one of you hasn't brought in something that is precious to you to show to your friends? Maybe it was a toy, when you were at primary school. Or a new phone. We've all done it, haven't we? Wanted to share something we're proud of. In this instance it was a notebook. A notebook containing pictures and memories of the other girl's father – a father who had died very suddenly. A notebook that was irreplaceable.'

There was another sea change amongst her audience. Heather had heard from other members of staff that after Megan had fled from the school the sole topic of conversation amongst the other kids had been the graffitied accusation on the board. And no wonder, thought Heather. The expressions of the majority of faces had gone from prurient interest to discomfort as they realised that their gossip and speculation about what Megan had done might have been very misplaced. 'If it had been your book, how would you have felt if someone had nicked it and run away with it? What the thief did was cruel and unkind but her friends didn't blame *her* for taking the book but the girl who brought the book to school. I don't know about you, but I think that's a pretty mean and unfair attitude. And now, someone here has chosen to believe this ugly rumour and to spread it around here – saying that Megan Millar was responsible for this death. A vile lie.' She glared down at the children. 'Fake news,' said Heather. 'Fake news. Please, next time you hear anything that you don't *know* to be true, question it. Ask where the story has come from. Don't believe everything you hear or read or see on the TV. Be more responsible, be less accepting. And never, ever, spread rumours. Thank you.'

As Heather sat down she could see all the teenagers looking at their neighbours in their tidy rows of chairs, shifting uncomfortably, and quiet muttering filled the air. One girl stared stonily ahead, her face bright red. Lily Breckenridge. Beside her, Summer Ashworth sniffed into a tissue.

Mr Smithson, along with other members of staff, strode off the stage and headed for his office as the pupils filed out of the hall by another door. There the head teacher picked up his phone and dialled the number for Giles Breckenridge.

'Giles,' he said when it was answered. 'Is this a convenient moment?'

'It's fine,' he was assured.

'I have a problem...'

Five minutes later, when he'd put the phone down, he buzzed through to his secretary. 'Can you get a message through to Lily Breckenridge in Ten Blake and tell her I want to see her tomorrow afternoon, in the break?'

'Yes, Mr Smithson.'

In her tutor room the pupils crowded round Megan.

'Did she really die?'

'Was it awful?'

'Were the cops called?'

Megan tried to answer as many questions as she could while Lily and Summer glowered at her from a corner.

Mrs Blake came in and clapped her hands. 'That's quite enough of that,' she said, her voice raised to be heard over the hubbub. 'Yes, it was all very distressing for poor Megan but we need to move on and put it behind us now. I think we can all be agreed that Megan saw something unfortunate and she doesn't need to have it all raked over again so I don't want to hear any mention of this again. Do I make myself clear?'

'Fat chance of that,' whispered Ashley from behind Megan.

'Do you want to share what you've got to say with the rest of the class?' questioned Mrs Blake.

'No, miss,' he mumbled.

'Right – sit down, all of you, and I'll take the register.'

Mrs Blake ran down the list of names and the kids answered 'present' as they heard their own being called and, as soon as Mrs Blake had dismissed them and left the tutor room herself, everyone crowded around Megan again.

'Was there a lot of blood?'

'Did she scream?'

Megan pushed her way through the press of her fellows and began to head for the door and her next lesson. 'I wasn't very close to her when she fell.' She couldn't bring herself to describe the sickening crack when Stella's head hit the corner of the wall.

As the tutor group began to stream out of the class behind Megan, one of the sixth form appeared.

'Lily Breckenridge,' the lad called above the chatter and clatter of thirty pupils. 'Lily Breckenridge?'

The chatter eased off as Lily answered.

'Message from Mr Smithson – he wants you in his office, in afternoon break, tomorrow.'

Lily's face flashed red before the colour drained from her cheeks. She stared defiantly at her classmates. 'What are you lot looking at?' she snapped as she pushed past everyone and strode along the corridor.

Ashley looked at Megan. 'I wouldn't want to be in her shoes,' he said, *sotto voce*.

'Do you reckon...?'

Ashley nodded.

'How did Smithson know?'

'Search me, but it kind of adds up. You all right? I mean, that must have been a pretty tough thing to have to sit through.'

Megan shook her head. 'It was but, like Mrs Simmonds said to me at the weekend, it'll probably be a seven-day wonder.'

When she and Ashley arrived in the next classroom, ready for their English lesson, Megan found a group of girls had saved a seat for her in the middle of where they had chosen to sit. Usually, whatever the subject, Megan found herself pushed to the front, under the teacher's nose, so this was quite a change. Suddenly it seemed all the girls wanted to be her friend. Megan wasn't sure how long this wave of sympathy and friendship was going to last but she decided she might as well make the most of it while it did. She smiled at everyone.

'If you want to sit with us, that is,' said one of the girls.

'Yeah, thanks,' Megan said. She smiled at Ashley as she plonked down. Maybe not as much as a seven-day wonder – maybe more like a seven-*minute* wonder. Mrs Simmonds had been right.

37

The next day, Olivia was at home, tidying up a few things ready for the arrival of Amy after she'd finished at the post office. She had another meeting with Heather about the church fête which was looming on the horizon. Given everything else she had to cope with now, she wasn't entirely sure she wanted this commitment and was wondering if, even at this late stage, she could possibly pull out of helping. If she and Nigel had to sell the house, and there was no way around it in her opinion, then she ought to be worrying about contacting estate agents and making sure the house was in tip-top condition rather than wasting her energies on sorting out who was baking for the cake stall or badgering the townsfolk for prizes for the tombola.

She looked at her massive living space with a visitor's eyes. If she put away some of clutter and, maybe, got some new cushions for the sofa, then the first impression would be OK. The kitchen was state-of-the-art and all the bedrooms, with the exception of Zac's, were perfectly acceptable. No, she decided, the house would do – or it would when Zac's room had been fumigated, again.

The click in the lock brought her back to the here and now.

'Afternoon, Amy,' she said as her cleaner let herself in. And that was another thing... the continued employment of Amy was an issue that was going to have to be addressed. Nigel had said that

Amy would have to go – one more expense that they could no longer afford. Olivia had argued that, with Amy to help keep the house in pristine condition while they sold it, they might realise a bigger price for it than if she had to sort it out on her own. It was, she'd said, a false economy to let Amy go just yet. But sooner or later Amy would have to be sacked and Olivia didn't fancy breaking the news.

'Hello, Mrs L. Shocking news about the vicarage, ain't it?'

'What news?'

'They got done over.'

'No!'

'Yeah. Someone broke in while they were at church. What sort of low-life does that?'

'That's dreadful.'

'Yeah, Bex was telling me about it when I did for her yesterday. She said that Mrs S had been round hers just afterwards – Sunday afternoon – and was really calm about it all. I suppose you have to be, if your husband's the vicar. Aren't they supposed to turn the other cheek and all that malarkey? I blooming wouldn't,' said Amy as she pulled open a cupboard and got out her box of cleaning things.

'No, I don't think I'd be like that either.' Olivia sighed. 'It's certainly a worry that so much of this sort of thing is going on.'

Amy walked over to the big dining table, squirted it with spray polish and began to rub it with a duster. 'And what's this I hear about you buying one of those new places?'

Olivia might have guessed that Mags would tell her daughter.

'I thought,' continued Amy, 'that you were dead against all the new houses going up. You've changed your tune, haven't you?'

Olivia was tempted to tell Amy that it was none of her business but decided that such a response would be a bit harsh. 'I was just looking around. I think the sales girl might have got the wrong end of the stick.'

Amy looked up. 'Oh yeah?'

Olivia decided to ignore Amy's sceptical tone of voice. 'Yes,' she said firmly. 'Now, I've got to go out a bit later. I've got a meeting about the church fête at the community centre.'

'Oh, yeah. Will Mrs S want to go ahead with that meeting, given what's happened?'

'She hasn't phoned to say any different.'

'Just saying.' Amy resumed her polishing.

'I'll let you get on – I've got work to do.' Olivia went upstairs to her bedroom and shut her door. She needed to phone some more estate agents and the last person she wanted to overhear the telephone conversations was Amy Pullen.

Forty minutes later she'd made her calls and picked up her jacket. She called to Amy as she trotted down the stairs.

'I'll put your money on the counter.'

'OK, Mrs L,' came Amy's voice from the downstairs cloakroom.

Olivia picked up her handbag from the kitchen counter and opened her wallet. She blithely pulled out thirty quid and then looked at the thin wad of notes that was left. She pulled it out and counted what remained. What the hell? Only fifty and she knew there should be seventy in there. She thought back; she'd got a hundred from the ATM after she'd paid for her coffee on Saturday with change from her purse and she hadn't spent a bean since. So, unless the ATM had short-changed her – which was unlikely – twenty quid was missing. Definitely.

Olivia sat down on a kitchen chair with a bump. She tried to think if she could have left her handbag lying around anywhere that a pickpocket might have been. But then, if she had, wouldn't a thief have taken *all* the cash? It didn't make sense. Maybe Nigel had taken it? Maybe that was it, but given he had his own bank card and he passed a cashpoint on his way to the station, was it really likely he'd help himself from her wallet without asking or telling her? What about Zac? No, of course he wouldn't steal from his own mother, what a ridiculous idea.

Which left Amy. Surely not? But Olivia knew that she didn't earn a massive amount and she'd witnessed Mags bailing her out only a while back so it wasn't completely unlikely that she might be tempted to filch a few extra quid. And, if she were honest with herself, this wasn't the first time she'd found that she didn't have quite as much cash on her as she'd thought. Maybe Amy had been pinching the occasional note, here and there. And if it was Amy, how the hell did she go about tackling the problem? Olivia put on her coat, slapped the money on the counter for her cleaner – not, she thought as she did so, that Amy deserved it if her suspicions were correct – and made up her mind to ask for Heather's advice when she saw her at the meeting.

'Bye, Amy,' she called as she headed for the front door.

Amy popped her head round the cloakroom door. 'See you Thursday.'

If I haven't had to sack you by then, Olivia thought. On the other hand, it would solve the problem of how she was going to let Amy go.

She got her bike out and cycled decorously down the hill, through the town to the community centre. The other members of the church fête committee were starting to gather as she arrived.

'Good afternoon,' said Olivia as she opened the door and went in. She was about to shut it behind her when she saw Heather approaching.

'Heather – I've just heard the news. How terrible.'

Heather nodded. 'I know. And as a result I'm going to have to ask everyone if we can postpone this meeting till later. I've got to go over to the police station and give them some more details about the things that got nicked.'

'What a nuisance.'

Heather stepped into the building and clapped her hands. 'Ladies, ladies…' she waited for hush to fall. 'You've probably all heard about the break-in at the vicarage on Sunday.' A few people nodded sympathetically and a couple looked startled. 'So I've just had a phone call from Leanne and they want me over at the police station in a little while to give them more details. I asked if they could make it later but our local police, as you are all only too aware, are stretched pretty thin and it's not possible. So, would you mind frightfully if this meeting got pushed back till later this afternoon?'

Everyone shook their heads and there were murmurs of 'fine' and 'of course' or 'no problem' around the room.

'In which case,' said Heather, 'I'll see you all later. How about four?'

Everyone nodded. She left again and Olivia followed her out to unchain her bike, trying not to look too put-out by the change of plan.

She cycled home and headed for the front door. She stopped before she put the key in it. She could hear voices. What the heck? First there had been the missing money and now Amy seemed to have invited people round.

Olivia opened the front door and stamped in. The TV was on. 'Amy!'

There was her cleaner, feet up on *her* sofa, watching telly with a glass of what looked *very* much like a gin and tonic in her hand.

Amy jumped so much at getting caught red-handed that the drink slopped over the edge of the glass.

'Mrs L! What are you doing back?'

Olivia glared at Amy. 'What on earth do you think you're doing?'

'I... I... just a bit of a break. Ten minutes, honest.'

Olivia stormed across the carpet and snatched the glass from Amy's hand. She took a swig. No wonder their gin bottle had been going down at an alarming rate. This was the last fucking straw.

'Out,' she shouted.

Amy stumbled out of the house, tears running down her face, the money she was owed left on the counter. She thought about ringing Billy; she needed a shoulder to cry on, but she reckoned he'd shout at her for being stupid. Like she didn't know that already.

What was she going to do? That was sixty quid a week she was going to lose. She and Ash had managed on less before – like when the old owners of The Beeches had gone – and it hadn't been easy. She didn't want to go back to scrimping and saving. She wondered if she could ask Billy for some cash. When she'd invited him to live with her over the weekends she hadn't mentioned money, and there was no denying he didn't mind spending money on her for treats. Whether he'd be as keen to help out with the housekeeping was a whole other issue.

She was scared of pissing him off, that was for sure and, God help her, it was easily done but she might have to risk it because she couldn't afford to feed another adult even if it was only a couple of days a week.

She raced down the hill and onto the high street. Ahead, she could see her mother's salon. Maybe her mum would have some advice, although she knew she could expect a chewing-out first. She played with the idea of not telling her mum the whole truth but there was no point. Olivia was bound to tell— Oh, holy shit! If Mrs L told other people, would everyone else she worked for sack her too? And Olivia had already made it plain that she wasn't the forgiving sort, and what better way to get her own back than by spreading the news that her cleaner had been helping herself to the gin? No one wanted a cleaner who wasn't completely trustworthy. Amy felt herself go hot and cold with fear as the full awfulness of her situation hit her. She stopped dead in her tracks.

Ought she go back up the hill and grovel to Olivia? Should she apologise and say she knew she'd been very stupid but that she'd learned her lesson and it wouldn't happen again? Should she get the first blow in and tell her other ladies before Olivia could – give them her side of the story? But, even as she thought about that last option, she realised that her side of the story was still pretty unattractive – she pinched her boss's booze and she could hardly plead extenuating circumstances; 'fancying a tipple and having no gin at home' was hardly going to cut it.

Or should she keep everything crossed that Olivia wouldn't tell? Immobilised by indecision, Amy stood stock-still in the middle of the pavement.

'Are you all right, my dear?'

Amy spun round. Heather.

'Yes... no... I mean...'

'You look like you've seen a ghost.'

Amy, so rubbish at keeping other people's secrets, couldn't help blurting out her own. 'Mrs L's just sacked me.'

'Oh, Amy. Why on earth?'

'She caught me drinking her gin. It was only a little one and it was only the one...'

'But even so,' said Heather.

'I know, I know,' said Amy, miserably. 'I was stupid and I shouldn't have. But I fancied a change from tea.'

Heather grinned wryly. 'Don't we all.'

'What am I going to do, Heather?'

'Let me think about it. I can't right now as I've got to go and see the police, but I will later, promise.'

'Oh gawd, yes, the break-in. I was so sorry to hear about that. I mean, you and the vicar of all people.'

'Thank you, Amy. It wasn't our best day. Rather unsettling, to be honest.'

Amy nodded.

'But an apology to Olivia start with – a really heartfelt one – would be a step in the right direction.'

'Humble pie,' said Amy as she nodded.

'I'd leave it a while if Olivia was very cross. Give her space to calm down. Life isn't easy for her at the moment.'

'Oh, you mean Zac and his drugs.'

A look of total surprise flitted across Heather's face before she said, calmly, 'Indeed. Now, I must go. Can't keep the boys in blue waiting.'

38

Lily Breckenridge and her father waited for Mr Smithson in his secretary's office. A buzzer on the desk sounded and the secretary switched her gaze from what she was doing to Giles Breckenridge.

'Would you like to go in?' she said.

Lily forced a nervous smile at her father as he got up and went through the connecting door, which he shut behind him. Lily knew what this was about, although she'd told her father that she didn't. Why, she didn't know, because what she'd done was about to be exposed – big time. She could feel her heart hammering in her chest and she felt slightly sick. It didn't help matters that her best mate was absent from school. If she was going to get an earful from old Smithson, she wanted to have Summer's sympathetic shoulder to cry on afterwards – but that wasn't going to happen.

She had to wait for five minutes before her father came out, looking thunderous, and she was summoned. There was no time to exchange more than a nod with him, before it was her turn to enter the head's office. Her knees were shaking so much that she could barely walk but she stared straight ahead and held her head high as she swapped places with her father.

'I'll come straight to the point,' said Mr Smithson. 'I know it was you who wrote that dreadful message. Your friend Summer Ashworth confirmed it last night.'

'S-S-Summer?' Lily was stunned. How... why would Summer betray her?

'Yes, I went to visit her after school yesterday. I had a suspicion but I had to confirm it. Only the governors knew about what had happened to Megan Millar at her old school – the staff here knew she'd had problems but nothing specific. So I surmised that, maybe, you had heard something from your father. When I questioned Summer she confirmed what I'd thought and she told me exactly what had gone on – about how you'd inveigled Megan to be friends on Facebook. About how you'd coaxed information out of her friends in London.' Mr Smithson stared at her coldly. 'As a premeditated bit of bullying, yours takes some beating. I asked her not to contact you before I had a chance to see you and your father. I told her that if she did, she would suffer the same repercussions as you.'

Lily swallowed. Repercussions? Her worries about her own skin suddenly outweighed her sense of betrayal by her so-called friend.

'I will *not* have bullying in my school,' barked Mr Smithson. 'And, as I have said, this was no spur-of-the-moment unkindness; this was planned and coldly carried out.' He stared at her with disdain. 'How could you?'

Lily didn't have an answer. Or rather, she did but she didn't think that telling him she was jealous of Megan's exotic beauty was going to help her case. She shrugged by way of a response.

'You are suspended for a fortnight. On your return you will be in a different tutor group, well away from Summer and Megan. I will not have this sort of behaviour in my school. Do you understand? If there is any sort of repeat episode I will take steps to have you permanently excluded.'

Lily nodded.

'You may go.'

She fled.

'Let's go home,' said her father as they left the secretary's office. Lily nodded again, not daring to speak. She thought if she did she'd break down completely. Suspended. That happened to the losers – not the cool kids like her. And if it hadn't been for Megan Millar this wouldn't have happened. She loathed Megan even more.

They got to where her father had parked his Jag.

'What were you thinking?' said her father, the anger in his voice cold and bitter. He eyed her across the roof of the car before he unlocked it and got in. Lily slid into the passenger seat beside him. 'I've had to resign as a governor. You've disgraced me.' He slammed his door then turned to her as he switched on the engine. 'How could you? And stop snivelling.'

'I am so sorry,' said Miles, coming out of the kitchen, shortly after Bex had started her shift at midday.

'Why?' Bex felt completely bewildered. Wasn't she the one who generally cocked up and needed to apologise?

'Because I promised to fix your gate and I haven't been round to do it.'

'Oh, please don't.' Crikey, Bex didn't want to give him another stick to beat her with.

'But I promised.'

'It doesn't matter. And I'm sure I can do it.'

'Really?' Miles raised his eyebrows. 'Look, it's no trouble and if I don't Belinda will make my life hell.'

Belinda? Really? 'Well...'

'Exactly. I'll pop round later. Anyway, how did Megan get on at school yesterday?'

Bex was surprised that he cared. 'OK, I think. She's a teenager so she sometimes isn't terribly communicative but, yes, I think her problem is solved.'

'That's good. I'm glad.' He sounded like he really meant it which surprised her even more.

A group of businessmen came in and, suddenly, Bex was rushed off her feet. The men picked up the bar menu and, with orders for food looking imminent, Miles disappeared back into the kitchen.

Then two women that Bex recognised from the school playground came in. If they recognised her there was no sign as they ordered a glass of Chardonnay each and then took the bar snack menus over to a table near the bar. Bex began to unload the glass washer.

'Have you heard about Olivia Laithwaite?' said one woman.

Hearing the name of her friend, Bex stopped putting glasses on shelves and openly eavesdropped.

'What's she done now?' asked the other mum.

'It's what she hasn't done, more like. She ought to have stopped those other houses that are going to be built, down on the ring road. She's on the council to make sure that sort of stuff doesn't happen to the town and then she does sod all about it.'

'Really?'

'And she's been seen at the show house by the station – more than once. Looks like she's going to buy a place at Beeching Rise. Buy-to-let, I've heard.'

'Bloody hell. Mind you, I suppose if you're that rich you've got to spend it on something.'

'You could give it to charity.'

'Huh – she's the sort who thinks charity begins at home.'

'And, do you know what else I heard about the Coombe Farm development?'

'No.'

The first woman put her menu down and leaned across the table. Bex had to strain to hear what was being said. 'That her husband has something to do with it. I was told he's some big noise in finance. Got his fingers in lots of pies, apparently. It wouldn't surprise me if he didn't have something to do with the developers. I mean, you know what these city-slicker types are like.'

Her companion nodded.

'That makes sense. Talk about greedy.'

Bex wasn't sure about the logic of the argument – working in finance didn't necessarily equate to being in cahoots with the housing developers – but it wasn't her place to butt in and say so. What she did know was that the speculation was almost certainly slanderous. And more than anything she wanted to tell the pair that Olivia was thinking about downsizing and buying to let was the last thing she was about to do – but she could hardly do that, either.

'I never did like that woman. Too much of a busybody if you ask me. And she's bossy. Oooh, look at this, they've got wild garlic soup on the menu. I'm going to have that.' And with that, the conversation veered away from Olivia, much to Bex's relief who was feeling increasingly uncomfortable about hearing her friend bad-mouthed by people who knew nothing about her.

As the lunchtime rush gathered momentum, Bex had to call on Belinda to lend a hand.

'I don't know how you coped on your own,' said Bex in a brief lull.

'It takes a bit of practice,' said Belinda.

Which reminded Bex of what Miles had said about her being completely inexperienced.

'You should have hired someone who knew what they were doing.'

'Don't be ridiculous,' said Belinda as she put a pint glass under the Guinness tap and opened it while she simultaneously measured out a large glass of Merlot. 'I hired someone I *like*. That's far more important. Anyway, you work with me, not Miles, so his opinion doesn't count.'

Bex felt that it probably did. The pair worked in silence for a few minutes while they dealt with the queue.

'One thing I need to mention,' she said in the lull. 'It's half-term soon.'

'I know. And you'll want the week off, won't you.'

Bex wrinkled her brow as she nodded. 'I feel awful asking but I don't think it's fair to ask Megan to look after the boys on her own. I know I'm only next door, but she'll have schoolwork to do over the hols and it's an awful lot of responsibility to land on her.'

Belinda served another customer. 'Nine pounds fifty, please,' she said. Then, 'I knew this would happen and I really don't mind.'

'But I feel as if I'm letting you down.'

Belinda took a tenner, rang it up on the till and handed over the change. 'You take the week off. We managed before, we'll manage again. There's a chance that one of the girls who help out in the evenings might be able to take a shift but you're not to worry.'

As she drank a cup of calming camomile tea in her kitchen Olivia felt her blood pressure start to return to normal. Maybe catching Amy red-handed had been a blessing in disguise because it gave her a copper-bottomed reason to get rid of her. She really didn't want to sack her but Nigel was insistent that it was an expense they could do without once they moved into somewhere smaller. Olivia had been dreading the conversation.

She finished her drink and wondered how Heather had got on at the police station. She glanced at the kitchen clock. Maybe she'd go along to the meeting a bit early and call in on Heather on the way. Until then, she had to work out how far Amy had got with the cleaning before she'd helped herself to the gin, and try and finish the job. Olivia sighed. She hated housework.

At three-thirty, Olivia shoved the hoover back in its cupboard and, once again, cycled down the hill. If Heather happened to be out then she'd decided to take a walk in the nature reserve till the meeting – she would check up on that den in the thicket, make sure the council was keeping it litter free. She parked her bike against the wall of the vicarage and rang the bell.

'Come in, come in,' said Brian when he opened it. He sounded pretty jovial which was unexpected considering that until recently he'd sounded anything but, and then he'd had that funny turn in the pulpit, and to cap it all his house had been burgled.

'Afternoon, Brian,' said Olivia. 'How are you?'

'OK, thanks. I expect you've come to see Heather.'

Olivia nodded.

'In the kitchen – go on through.'

Olivia made her way along the hall while Brian dived back into his study.

'Is this a good moment for a quick chat?' said Olivia as she reached the kitchen door.

Heather looked up from some papers she was reading at the table. She pushed them away. 'Fine. Tea?'

'I won't, thanks. I'm so sorry about the break-in. I was livid when I heard. Even Amy thought the people that did it had to be utter scum.'

'So, was that before or after she got caught drinking your gin?'

Olivia was dumbfounded. 'How...?'

'I met her in town on my way to the police station. She looked rather upset.'

Olivia snorted. 'As well she might.'

'So, I asked her what had happened and she told me. It was only a gin,' said Heather.

'It wasn't only the gin. I think she might have pinched twenty quid from my purse, too.'

'Amy? Surely not.'

'Someone has. I *know* how much was in there and, when I went to pay Amy today, I was twenty quid short.'

'It doesn't mean it was Amy.'

Olivia was about to respond when the doorbell rang again. Once again it was answered by Brian and a minute later the pair was joined by Bex who was carrying a large pot plant.

'Hello,' she said. 'I didn't mean to interrupt, but I brought you this, Heather, to say thank you.' She thrust the plant at Heather. 'It's from Megan and me.'

'It was nothing.'

'It was a great deal,' corrected Bex. She turned to Olivia. 'Megan was having some trouble at school and Heather sorted it. She came home from school yesterday so much happier than she has been of late.'

'Bullying?' asked Olivia.

'Kind of. There'd been some trouble at her old school and – oh well... it's all behind her now.'

'And you know Mr Smithson knows who was responsible,' said Heather.

Olivia looked from one woman to another, dying to know the details but not quite having the brass neck to ask.

'Megan said. I gather Mr Smithson is seeing the girl today. Anyway, I can't stop, I've left Megan in charge of the boys and I *must* get some more baking for the PTA fête done.'

'Ah,' said Olivia. 'Did you know the church fête is a fortnight later?'

'Erm... should I?'

Olivia thought she should but didn't say so. 'Heather and I are about to go to a meeting about it but we're always looking for people to help.' She looked expectantly at Bex.

'I don't mind producing a couple of cakes, if that's what you're after?'

'That'd be perfect.'

'Fine. I'll get the school fête out of the way and then I'll do some for you. And now I'll leave you in peace. I'll see myself out,' she said as she headed for the front door.

Heather glanced at the clock. 'I think we should go too.'

Olivia agreed.

They gathered up their things and followed Bex after a minute or so, with Heather pausing at Brian's study to tell him they were off out and not to forget to lock up properly if he had to leave the house.

'I won't,' he reassured his wife.

Heather banged the door shut behind her. 'Now, about Amy…' she said as they headed down the path.

'Look,' said Olivia, 'It has to be her who took the money. First the gin, now the twenty quid. And I'm starting to worry about the burglaries. You *and* Jacqui… *and* she's got keys to both your houses *and* there was no sign of a forced entry.'

'But think about all the other houses that have been broken into, houses that Amy has had nothing to do with.'

'Huh.'

Heather stopped on the pavement that ran beside the cricket pitch and turned to her friend. 'I heard something today. I've been in two minds whether to tell you or not but I think you ought to know.'

Olivia didn't like the sound of this. 'What?'

'When I was talking to Amy she asked me what I thought she ought to do. I said that if nothing else she ought to offer you a really heartfelt apology but I suggested she ought to wait a while to give you a chance to calm down. And I don't know why, but I added that life wasn't very easy for you right now.'

'You did what?' screeched Olivia.

'I know, I know, but that was all I said and I'd have never gone into any details… I wanted her to know that you've got some stressful stuff going on, which was why you might have been more cross than under normal circumstances. And that it might take you longer to become more receptive to an apology.'

Olivia still didn't look happy. 'Given how I feel right now I think hell might freeze over first.'

Heather shook her head. 'It was only some gin.'

'And twenty quid.'

Heather shrugged. 'I can't see Amy doing that, really I can't. Gin is one thing, cash is something else.'

Olivia rolled her eyes. 'Really? Then I think you're in for a sad disappointment.'

'Anyway, to get back to what I want to tell you; in response to me telling Amy life isn't a bed of roses for you she said, "Oh, you mean Zac and his drugs."'

Olivia reeled. 'She said *what*! The little madam.' She was incensed. How dare Amy make an accusation like that?

'So there isn't any possible truth in this?'

'Of course not. Zac wouldn't do drugs. She said that out of sheer spite – anything to draw fire away from herself. That does it, I'm going to have it out with Amy Pullen once and for all.'

Heather put her hand on Olivia's sleeve. 'Please don't. I told you because I'm your friend. You have to ask, why would Amy say that?'

'As I said, spite. Besides, how on earth would she know?'

'Zac and Ashley are close. She didn't say it in a spiteful way – it was something she believed to be true that slipped out.'

'Huh – then I bet it's Ashley who's been experimenting but has blamed it on Zac. Zac wouldn't do drugs, that's why I sent him to St Anselm's so he wouldn't mix with the wrong sort. Fat lot of good that's done when the kids on the council estate hang around the skatepark where Zac spends his free time.'

'You're absolutely sure about Zac? You would swear he's not smoking pot or anything? No funny mood swings, no odd behaviour, not sleeping a lot?'

'Well… yes. But he's a teenager. They all do that, don't they?'

'I'm only saying, Olivia, that maybe Amy has heard something – maybe from Ashley – and she believes it to be true. But if I were you, I'd check everything out before I dismissed it out of hand. Lots of kids have a go – it doesn't mean they're mainlining heroin. But wouldn't it be better to find out whether or not Zac is taking illegal substances for sure? Because if he is, you might be able to nip it in the bud now.'

For a second Olivia thought about telling Heather to mind her own business but then a few little things began to bubble into her head; the overpowering smell of body spray in his room – was that to cover up the smell of something else? His apparently guilty conscience. The way he always looked a bit dopey… Maybe he was, literally. She took a deep breath. 'OK, you may have a point,' she conceded. 'Maybe I should ask some questions. And if you don't mind, I'd like to offer my apologies for the meeting. I think I want to go home and have a good look around Zac's room while he's still at school.'

Heather nodded. 'I sincerely hope you don't find anything and Amy is mistaken.'

'So do I.'

39

Once again, Olivia retrieved her bike and cycled up the hill back to her house. She had a while before Zac returned which, she thought, would be enough time to have a proper search.

She went upstairs and opened the door. Even in the twilight of half-drawn curtains Olivia could see the room was in a disgraceful state; clothes littered the floor, schoolbooks, DVDs and papers were strewn over the surfaces, the bed was unmade and there were half a dozen dirty mugs sitting on shelves and the bookcase and near his computer. Olivia picked her way through the mess and threw the curtains fully open and then followed suit with the windows. She turned and looked at the room now it was bathed in light. It was as if Amy had never had a go at it. She shuddered.

Where, she wondered, would a teenage boy hide stuff? She had a rethink. Where would *she* hide stuff? She began by pulling each one of his drawers open and checking right at the back and under everything. Nothing. She wasn't too fussed about leaving signs that she had moved his stuff, had a good rummage – how the hell would he tell, given the overall state of his room? She checked under the mattress, behind every book on his bookshelf, inside all of his shoes in his wardrobe, in the pockets of all his clothes hanging up… Nothing, nothing, nothing.

Olivia sat on the bed. So – maybe Amy was lying and Heather had been taken in. But she still had that niggle that all was not right with Zac. He'd been far more difficult than any of his siblings, he was moody, some of his outbursts were unreasonable, the room constantly smelt of that revolting body spray and yet, when she thought about it, he didn't. If he was smoking pot in his room he had to be doing it out of the window. She crossed the floor and peered out at the patio below. No dog-ends were visible. But then Zac wasn't stupid.

Olivia went downstairs, out of the French doors and pushed back the plants from the edge of the herbaceous border. Bingo. There, on the earth, was a half-smoked roll-up. She picked it up and sniffed it. Old and slightly soggy from recent rain it smelt of nothing except stale ash but she was pretty certain she knew what she was looking at. She might have been Miss Goody-Two-Shoes at uni but she hadn't gone around with her eyes shut. Of course there was no proof that it was Zac's but it certainly wasn't hers or Nigel's.

She returned to Zac's room and sat on the bed again. She still had few minutes. Think! Mindlessly, she stared at the carpet. There was an indentation left in the pile from the dressing table being moved about half an inch. Why? Why would anyone move the furniture?

Olivia stood up, grabbed it and tugged. It moved, reluctantly, over the thick carpet until it was about six inches from the wall. Olivia peered down the back. Yuck – it was filthy along the skirting board. And, eureka, there were a couple of resealable plastic bags, a packet of Rizlas and a disposable lighter. Olivia leaned against the wall. She felt disgusted and betrayed. How could he?

Her husband was a gambling addict and her son was a junkie. Her world was falling apart and what had she done to deserve it?

Zac had had a shit day at school. All the staff had had a go at him about his course work – like he cared about it or them, come to that – but he didn't want the teachers on his back. They kept saying bullshit, like his parents didn't pay out all that money in fees to see him plough his GCSEs. Well, if he was going to end up at a dump like the comp, what did it matter? Only he couldn't say that, because it was too humiliating to have to admit to them that his dad was such a loser. Ha! Loser. Wasn't he, though – in every sense of the word.

Zac got off the bus, swung his schoolbag over his shoulder and loped across the road and headed for his home. What he needed was a joint. That'd calm him down. He scrunched up the drive and unlocked the front door. His mother was sitting on the sofa, looking like she was waiting for him.

'Good, Zac, you're home. We need to talk.'

Shit, this was all he needed. No, he didn't want to talk to her. He'd had a rubbish day and now he wanted to chill.

'Not now, I'm going to my room. I've had a crap day and I'm not in the mood.'

'Frankly, I don't give a toss what sort of day you've had, we need to talk.'

Zac stopped in his tracks, startled by his mother's tone of voice. Had the school phoned her about his work? He wouldn't put it past them, the bastards.

Then he saw what she was holding in her hands, holding out for him to see. Oh, Jesus, she'd found his stash. He felt bile rising in his throat and swallowed down the sour taste. Maybe he could brazen this out.

'What's that, Mum?' He dropped into an armchair and sprawled, trying to look casual, uncaring.

'I'm not sure. I've had a look on the internet and I think this one might be skunk,' she shook one of the bags, 'and this one ketamine. Or do you call it Special K?'

Zac shrugged. 'Dunno what you're talking about.'

Olivia stood up and walked over to where he was sitting. 'Don't,' she said, a dangerous hiss in her voice, 'don't you *dare* lie to me.'

Zac was shaken. 'Where did you get it?'

'From behind your dressing table, where you'd hidden it.'

'I can explain,' he blustered, sitting up straighter.

'I very much doubt it.'

His mother dropped the packets on the coffee table and wiped her fingers on her trousers like she'd been contaminated.

'Those bags... they're Ashley's,' he blurted.

'Really? So why is his stuff in our house? Hardly handy when you want a quick spliff, is it?' She picked up an object from the table that he hadn't spotted – a roach. 'I found this in the flower bed, under your window.'

Zac remembered the time he'd almost got caught out and chucked it out the window instead of disposing of it in the gutter above his window. The one time he hadn't been careful. Bollocks.

'Ashley hasn't been round here for months,' said his mother. She gave him a look of utter disdain. 'It seems to me that not only are you a junkie and an utter waste of space but a liar as well.' She leaned over to eyeball her son, towering over him, making him feel vulnerable and scared. 'You disgust me, do you know that?'

Zac tried another attempt to push back. 'That's rich, coming from someone married to a loser like Dad.'

'Don't! Don't you *dare* talk about him like that. Yes, he may have made mistakes recently but how the hell do you think we ended up living in a house like this and with you at a private school? Huh?' She glowered at him. 'Tell me that. Whereas you... you are blowing money you have never earned on a habit you can't afford.'

Zac was tempted to point out to his mother that his father's habit had turned into an unaffordable one but he didn't quite have the balls.

'So,' continued his mother, 'how *do* you afford it?'

'My allowance,' he mumbled.

His mum eyeballed him again. 'And this month I stopped it.'

'I'd saved some.' He couldn't meet her eye.

'You're telling me you haven't been pinching money from my purse, then?'

'Course not.'

His mother returned to the sofa and flopped down. 'Why don't I believe a word you say?'

Silence fell for a few seconds, both of them lost in their own thoughts. Zac wondered how his mother had suddenly decided to go through his things. What had prompted it? He was burning up with curiosity. If she knew about his drugs, what else did she know? Did she know how badly he was doing at school? For his peace of mind he needed an answer or two.

He raised his eyes and stared at his mother. She was gazing at the ceiling – a look of despair on her face. Some primeval sixth sense must have told her she was being watched because, wearily, she turned to face him.

'How…?' he started.

'How *what*?' she snapped.

'How did you know there were drugs in my room?'

'I didn't, but it seems half the town seems to think you've got a habit and once I'd been let into the secret I decided to see if they were right or not.'

'Who? Who knew?'

'Amy, Heather.'

'Amy?' Zac was shocked. 'Did Ashley tell her?'

'I have no idea. So, he's another one in the know, is he? Who else, I wonder?' But it was said to herself. There was a pause. 'But not me.' His mother sighed. 'What else don't I know?' She sounded on the brink of tears but Zac wasn't fussed about his mother's misery; he wanted to have a word with Ashley. How dare he blab to his mum? How *dare* he?

He stood up and went towards the front door.

'Oh no,' said his mother. 'You're not going anywhere, you're gated.'

'Says who?' He opened the door.

'Zac!'

But if his mother had anything else to say on the subject it was lost behind the slammed door.

*

Rage seethed inside Zac as he stormed down the road. He was going to have it out with Ash – he was going to punch Ash's lights out and Ash had it coming.

It took him fifteen minutes to get to Ashley's house on the estate at the other end of town.

'Come out here, you bastard,' Zac yelled as he hammered on the front door. He pushed the bell several times and then hammered again. He stared at the closed windows. 'Are you in there? I want a word with you.'

A woman pushing a pram crossed over the road and shot nervous glances in Zac's direction.

'Oi, Ash.'

But the house remained silent and the front door closed. In frustration Zac hit the door hard with his fist and immediately wished he hadn't. As he walked away he rubbed his knuckles.

He headed for the skatepark – maybe Ashley was hanging out there. He loped through the gates and headed for the rear of the public space, passing mothers and kids picnicking on the grass in the warm sun. He spotted his quarry and broke into a run. Ash was standing beside one of the ramps as Zac approached. He had his back to him as he watched a kid trying to do a kick-flip. He had no idea that his nemesis was heading his way.

Zac grabbed Ashley by his T-shirt which ripped.

'Hey...' said Ashley as he spun round.

'You shit,' he yelled at Ashley as he threw a punch.

Despite being caught completely unawares, some instinctive self-preservation kicked in and Ashley ducked as Zac's fist flashed forwards. It caught his ear but no worse than that.

'Zac?' Ashley jumped backwards, nearly losing his footing as his heel connected with the edge of the ramp. He stumbled and recovered himself as Zac closed in again. But the surprise had been lost.

Zac swiped a punch again but Ashley dodged it easily and

grabbed Zac's fist. The pair wrestled as Zac tried to get out of Ashley's grasp. Pound for pound they were well matched but Ashley was leaner and fitter. The kids on the ramps had stopped their tricks and antics and were gathering to watch the fight. A group began chanting Ashley's name, siding with him, which riled Zac even more. He threw another uncoordinated punch. Again Ashley dodged it before he hooked his right fist upwards which connected with Zac's chin. Pain jagged through Zac as he felt his teeth rattle and tasted a ferrous tang in his mouth. He wiped his hand across his lips and saw blood. 'What have you told your mum?' he growled.

'About what?'

'You know what.'

'I've got no idea.'

'Me, smoking weed.' Zac circled Ashley, like a cat after a pigeon, working out where best to strike.

'You're kidding me, right? Why would I do that?'

'Because you wanted to get at me cos I'm richer than you. Because you're jealous. Because you're a sick loser who wants to ruin other people's lives. Because you could.'

'Fuck off, Zac.'

That did it. Zac stormed forwards, fists flailing, no direction, no game plan, just energy and rage. Ashley ducked under the fists and landed a punch in his solar plexus. The air whooshed out of Zac's lungs. He doubled up and tried to breathe in again but he'd been winded. He whooped and wheezed but the air wouldn't come. He felt panic rising. He collapsed to his knees and put his hands on the ground in front of him as he tried to inhale. His head swam and for a second he wondered if this was it. He'd never felt so scared in his life. The seconds ticked by as he tried to haul air in but he could only manage pathetic gasps. The panic rose as he thought he was going to die.

Then suddenly his diaphragm recovered and he was able to draw in a juddering, whooping lungful of air. He rolled sideways onto the ground, clutching his aching guts, not caring he looked defeated, not caring he'd lost the fight. He was just grateful to be alive.

Ashley looked at Zac on the ground. What had he done? Had he really injured him? His emotions were a mixture of fear and hatred. Right now he'd never hated Zac more but what if he'd done something really appalling? What if he was really hurt? Dying? God, he didn't want to go to prison. But then Zac stopped gasping ineffectually and Ashley saw him take in a breath and the colour return to his face. Winded – that was all. He'd just been winded. Ash sagged with relief but then his hatred for Zac returned. That shit had frightened the crap out of him, on top of having a go at him. Zac rolled onto his side, clutching his stomach. Serve him right.

He glanced again at Zac, still rolling on the ground, still pretending he was hurt worse than he was, still making a meal of it, and then he saw the local copper heading towards them. Time to go. Ashley raced off across the grass.

'Right then, what's all this about?'

Zac had no idea who this woman was who was talking to him and he didn't care. He was still concentrating on his breathing and the pain in his stomach from the last punch.

'You all right, sonny?'

Zac coughed.

'Should I call an ambulance?'

'No...no,' he mumbled, gasping like a landed fish. He opened his eyes. Shit, a copper. 'I'm fine.'

'Doesn't look like it to me.'

Zac managed to sit up. 'I'm fine,' he repeated. He was trying to convince himself because he felt far from *fine*.

'What was the fight about?'

'Nothing.'

The policewomen sat on the ground beside him. 'Yeah, right. Someone got a grudge against you?'

'No.'

'So what's your name?'

'Zac.'

'Where do you live, Zac?'

Zac was tempted to say 'none of your business' but he didn't think that would be wise when dealing with the law. 'The other end of town.'

'You going to be all right getting back?'

'Yeah.' Not that he was going to go back yet. The last thing he wanted was another earful from his mum.

'Off you go then.'

'In a minute.'

Zac staggered to his feet and stumbled over to the bench where he sat down heavily. He felt dreadful. His head throbbed, his lip was swollen, his stomach caned and he'd been humiliated by Ashley. Life was a pile of crud. He leaned back on the bench and shut his eyes. The policewoman sat beside him and Zac couldn't think of a polite way of telling her to get lost so he sat, in silence, and hoped boredom, or someone needing her assistance more than he did, would rescue him. As the seconds ticked by, neither materialised. Eventually Zac glanced at his watch.

'I'll be off home in a minute.'

'OK,' responded the constable getting up. 'You going to be all right on your own?'

Zac nodded. 'Yeah, I got a bit winded. I'm fine now.'

'Go carefully then. And no more fighting.' The constable went, leaving Zac on the bench.

40

After Megan had got home from school she'd got a text from some of her new school friends inviting her to meet them at the skatepark. Suddenly, it seemed, she'd become the cool kid to be associated with and, not wishing to jeopardise her new-found popularity, she'd abandoned her homework and legged it up there. There she'd been mucking around with the group, taking selfies, playing with WhatsApp and Snapchat, when they noticed a ruckus over the far side of the recreation ground, but it seemed to be a couple of lads having a tussle so they'd ignored it. But then the local copper had rocked up and one of the lads had hared off – and Megan had recognised Ashley. She yelled after him but he was so busy legging it he didn't hear her and she could see that whoever he'd been fighting was still on the ground. She reckoned she knew who it was.

Suddenly, what Ashley had been getting up to seemed more important than currying favour with her new friends so she excused herself and directed her steps to the incident where she saw Zac, clutching his stomach, his face still contorted, lying on the ground with a policewoman crouched down beside him. Megan hung back, in amongst the gaggle of skateboarders who were rubber-necking too. Finally, Zac got to his feet and lurched over to a bench, then after a while the policewoman seemed to be reassured that Zac was all right and disappeared. Zac leaned forwards, his elbows on his knees, and stared at the ground.

Megan pushed her way forward. 'Zac, Zac, what happened?'

Zac sighed and shook his head, not looking at her.

Megan hunkered down in front of him. 'What happened?'

Zac raised his eyes. 'Ash. Ash hit me.'

'I saw that, but why?'

'I had a bone to pick with him. We fought. He got in a lucky punch.' Zac coughed.

'You fought?'

Zac wiped his mouth. 'Is my lip bleeding?'

Megan peered at him. 'I don't think so,' she said. 'But why fight?'

'He's been spreading stuff about me around town.'

'Like the fact that you do drugs?'

'Ssssh.'

Megan looked around at the open, empty space around them. 'No one's listening, Zac.'

Zac nodded. 'He told his mum.'

'Ash did? Really?'

'He must have done, because she blabbed to Mrs Simmonds who told my mum.'

'And you know this for a fact, do you?'

'Mum said that Amy and Mrs Simmonds knew so it stands to reason Mrs Simmonds got it off Amy – everyone knows Amy can't ever keep her mouth shut. So Mum searched my room and found my stash.'

'Your stash? I thought you were going to quit. You told me, you promised. Why didn't you chuck it all out?'

'You're kidding me right? Throw it away? It's valuable.'

Megan glared at him. 'What? So, you lied to me. I lent you the cash because you promised you'd stop.' She was furious.

'No... I... I will, but not yet.'

'You're a total git, do you know that? You're contemptible and a liar.'

Zac face crumpled. He looked close to tears.

'Christ,' said Megan. She stamped her foot in frustration before she confronted him again. 'This is an awful mess and the only person who can sort it out is you.'

Zac nodded, his eyes dark with misery.

'And you can do it. People do. You can clean yourself up, you can get off the habit.'

'Maybe I don't want to.'

Megan stood up again. 'Then maybe you're even stupider than I thought.' She strode off, fed-up and angry that Zac didn't seem prepared even to try.

She was almost out of the gate when she heard feet running behind her.

'Wait.'

She spun round. 'Why should I?'

'OK, I will. I will try.'

'You've got to do more than try, Zac. You've got to do it.'

'OK.'

'And you need to go home, you need to talk to your mum. You need to get her to help you.'

'I... I can't.'

'Why not? Zac, you don't have a choice. Besides, she knows you do drugs, how much worse can it get?'

Zac didn't answer.

'Then you're on your own.' Megan strode off.

Lewis and Alfie were in the sitting room playing a game which involved their complete supply of toy cars and a great deal of noise while Bex was in the kitchen busy creaming sugar and butter together in preparation for making a Victoria sandwich. Over the racket from the sitting room, she heard Megan call hello as she came through front door.

'Hi, Bex,' she said.

'How was the skatepark?'

'Fine, it was fun. Really good.'

'That's great.' Hallelujah, thought Bex. She got busy with her wooden spoon again, thwacking it around the bowl to make the butter and sugar mix pale and floppy.

Megan pulled a chair out and slumped onto it. There was something about Megan's demeanour which didn't mesh with her words.

'What happened about Lily?' asked Bex.

'Lily?'

'Didn't Mr Smithson want to see her today?'

'Oh... yes.'

'And?'

'Someone said he suspended her.'

'Good, that should teach her a lesson.'

'I suppose.'

Bex stopped beating the mix again. 'So, why aren't you happy?'

Megan shrugged.

'Has something else happened?'

Megan shook her head and stared at the table.

Bex pulled out the chair opposite her stepdaughter and sat down. 'Megan, I'm not stupid and something is bothering you. School is OK now, isn't it?'

Megan looked at her. 'School is fine,' she confirmed.

'Then there's something else going on.'

'It's just...'

'Yes?'

'Bad things seem to happen to people who are around me. Daddy, then Stella, then Lily...'

'No! No, sweetie, you mustn't think like that. Daddy's death was a terrible accident and no one asked Stella to nick our memory book and no one suggested to Lily she ought to pry into your past. The things that happened to those two were nothing to do with you.'

'Maybe.' She didn't sound convinced.

'They weren't.'

Megan fell silent again. After a bit she said, 'I saw Zac at the skatepark.'

'So?'

'He and Ashley had a fight.'

'A fight? What about?'

Megan shrugged and stared at the table.

'I wouldn't worry about those two,' said Bex. 'Fighting is a boy thing.'

'I suppose.'

'And I could be wrong,' said Bex, 'but Olivia was talking about her husband wanting to move into a smaller house so things at Zac's home may not be entirely rosy. If Zac's miserable he may be on a short fuse, and lashing out is what boys do when they're like that. Or, some do anyway.'

'Yeah, I don't think Zac's very happy at the moment.'

'There you go then. But I don't want you worrying about other people. You've had enough to cope with recently without taking on other people's problems too.'

'Maybe.' She still sounded sad and thoughtful.

'Let's have a cup of tea.'

'I'll do it.' Megan got up from the table and filled the kettle. While she stood at the counter with her back to Bex, she said, 'Zac told me he's on drugs.'

The wooden spoon Bex was using clattered into the bowl, then she said, quite calmly, 'Really? Silly lad.'

'Zac told me his mum has found out.'

'Ah. Poor Olivia.'

'He's in a bad place, Bex.'

'I can imagine. And I don't expect things are much better for his mum.'

Amy arrived home from doing some shopping to find Ashley waiting for her but she was too busy getting her key out of the lock and putting it away in her handbag to pay him much notice.

'We need to talk, Mum.'

'Give us a mo, Ash. I've not even got me coat off yet or put the kettle on. I'm dying for a cuppa, me.'

It took her a couple of minutes to put away the shopping, hang her jacket up and have a quick wee before she turned her attention to her son. It also gave her a couple of minutes to try and work out how she was going to tell him that, after the morning's events, things were going to be a bit tight again – worse if Billy stayed with them at weekends and she had another mouth to feed.

'Now, what's so urgent...' The sentence died on her lips when she saw the state of her son's clothes. Her desire for tea and her need to break the news about their new circumstances evaporated with the rise of irritation at the damage. 'What the bleedin' hell have you been up to? That was a new T-shirt. That cost good money, that did.' And a replacement wasn't affordable – not now.

'Sorry, Mum.'

'Sorry? I'll give you sorry.'

'It was Zac – he tore it.'

'Then he can blooming pay for it. How did it happen?'

'He went for me. I was at the skatepark and he just went for me.'

'Really? Just like that?'

Ashley nodded.

'And you did nothing to start it?'

'Nothing, I swear. He came off worse though. He fights like a girl.'

'But why? Something must have rattled his cage.'

'He thought I'd told tales about him smoking pot because you know that he does and now his mum does too. How did you find out?'

'More's the point, how did you know? You've not been doing drugs, have you?'

Ashley shook his head vehemently. Then he said, 'He told me ages ago. I think he thought I'd be impressed.'

'Were you?'

Ashley shook his head again.

'Well,' said Amy, 'I found out when I came across his stash, hidden in his room when I was giving the place a good clean.'

'So that's how you knew.'

'Yeah. Master Laithwaite isn't half as clever as he thinks he is. But I never told his mum.'

'How come?'

'I was tempted, I can tell you, but...' Amy shrugged. 'Well, it was none of my business and I didn't reckon Mrs L would like me bad-mouthing her precious son. And then, if I'm totally honest, I forgot. I've got enough of my own worries to fuss over other people's.'

'You forgot?'

Amy nodded. 'Yeah, it's not like it's anything to do with me – or you, for that matter. Anyway, something else happened today and I need to go and see Mrs L. Maybe I'd better apologise for that an' all.'

'What else have you got to say sorry about?'

'Never you mind. None of your business. I'll pop over after supper.'

41

B ex finished mixing the cake and poured the mixture into two tins before she popped them into the oven and set the timer.

'Good,' she said to herself as she began to tidy up the kitchen, washing up the mixing bowls, putting the flour, eggs and milk away, wiping down the surfaces. After a while she checked on how the cakes were doing, turned them around to make sure they got an even bake and then filled the kettle and flicked the switch.

She could hear the boys still playing their game with their cars, still engrossed in something that seemed to involved lots of crashes and excited shouts and vroom-vroom noises. Then, over the racket, she heard the doorbell ring. As she crossed the hall to answer it she wondered who it might be.

'Oh!' Miles.

'Is this a good time?'

Bex realised she'd sounded less than welcoming. 'Yes, yes, come in. I've just put the kettle on.'

'Great.'

She led her visitor into the kitchen where the smell of baking filled the air.

'Baking?'

'Cakes, for the school fete.'

'You got nobbled?'

'You'd think that now I've got a stepdaughter who is in year ten I'd have learned to say no when the primary school PTA is looking for volunteers.'

'Next year, maybe you'll be more determined.'

'Fat chance. I managed to get caught for the church fête too.' Miles laughed. 'You're a lost cause.'

'Hopeless.' Bex made the tea thinking that at least Miles hadn't concurred with her self-assessment that she was hopeless – well, not out loud at any rate.

As the tea bags stewed in the mugs she got out the cake tin and opened it.

'Can I offer you a slice of Victoria sponge?'

'You certainly can.'

Bex cut a large slice for him, put it on a plate and then handed it to him with his tea.

'This is very good,' Miles said indistinctly with his mouth full.

'Thanks.' Praise indeed. She sat down opposite him.

'Excellent, in fact.'

'Good. Glad you're enjoying it.'

'You have hidden talents.'

'Except when it comes to bar work.'

'You're doing fine.'

Blimey, that was a change of tune. 'Now,' Bex added for him.

Miles didn't contradict her but ate some more cake. Across the corridor the boys' game got increasingly raucous so Bex got up and shut the door. She was about to sit down when the timer went. A gust of hot air and steam wafted out of the oven door as she opened it before she reached in and extracted two cakes, baked to perfection. Expertly she got them out of the tins and put them on a wire rack.

Miles finished his cake. 'Now then...' He reached down beside his chair and picked up a cordless drill. 'About that bolt.'

'Oh yes, this is so kind of you.'

'Hey – I'm going to be drilling a few holes, not donating a kidney.'

'Even so.' Bex walked into the utility room and picked up a carrier bag, lying on the counter. 'Here we go. I hope I got the right sort of thing.' She handed the cardboard and plastic packet to Miles and he examined the contents.

'I think this'll do the job very nicely and stop Houdini making a repeat performance.'

'Good. The chap in the shop said that everything needed is in the packet.'

'Great. So, if you're not planning on more baking, I'd quite like a hand with this.'

'Of course.'

The pair went out of the house and down the drive to the gate where Miles battled to release the bolt and the screws from the packaging. Finally he managed to tear off the plastic and everything sprayed out onto the gravel.

'Bloody hell,' he muttered.

Both Bex and Miles dropped to their knees to scrabble around and retrieve the various components. Bex managed to gather up half a dozen screws and held out her hand for the pieces that Miles had found. Their fingers touched as he handed her the two main bits of the bolt and Miles seemed to let his fingers rest on hers longer than seemed necessary. Suddenly Bex felt awkward and scrambled to her feet again.

'I think I've got everything.' she said, trying to sound casual, and wondering if she was misinterpreting the situation.

Miles pressed the trigger on his drill and the gadget whizzed into action. 'Let's do it then. Give me the bolt and I'll fix that on first. Then we can line up the bit it slides into.'

'"The bit it slides into"? Is that a technical term?'

'Absolutely. Can't you tell I'm a pro?' He grinned at her but she was still feeling awkward so she didn't smile back.

Miles positioned the barrel of the bolt against the oak of the five-bar gate and drilled through the screw holes. 'Hold it for me a sec.'

Bex did as she was told, not looking at Miles as she did it and making sure their hands didn't touch again as he got a screw-driver out of his pocket and began to get the screws in. Once the first couple of fixings were in place he managed on his own, with Bex handing him the remaining screws one by one. Five minutes later the job was finished.

Miles slid the bolt across. 'There,' he said. 'Job done.'

'You're a star,' said Bex. 'Hopefully it'll stop the little monkey from escaping again and dropping me in the shit with the locals. Thank you.'

'My pleasure.'

'I'd say I'd buy you a drink to say thank you properly, but what with running the pub and everything, I don't suppose you've got the time.'

'Funnily enough, Belinda and I have decided that we need help in the kitchen.'

'She hasn't mentioned it to me – although,' added Bex quickly, 'it's none of my business.'

'Dunno – you're part of the team but we've only recently found someone so maybe Belinda was going to tell you tomorrow. And, assuming this guy can be trusted to make bacon butties unsuper-vised, I may have more free time but I'm not sure I want to spend it in the pub.'

'Indeed.' So that was her hand-of-friendship rebuffed.

Amy cleared away the supper things before she headed up the main road towards Olivia's house. As she walked she couldn't help wondering if Olivia had already spread the word about the gin incident or if she would slam the door in her cleaner's face. She was going to find out the latter soon enough, she thought as she crunched over the gravel and rang the doorbell.

'Oh, it's you,' said Olivia, when she opened the door.

'I've come to apologise,' said Amy.

'Have you?'

'Yes, I was bang out of order and you had every right to be

mad at me.' She looked her employer in the eye and waited for the 'too-little-too-late' comment, or for the door, as she expected, to be slammed in her face.

'You'd better come in.'

Surprised, Amy stepped inside.

'Thank you for apologising,' said Olivia. 'It's decent of you.'

Amy felt even more gobsmacked. 'Hardly, I was the one swigging your gin.'

'Even so.' Olivia walked over to the kitchen and picked up something. She came back and handed some notes to Amy. 'I owe you this.'

'No, no you shouldn't.'

'You did the work – well most of it.'

'That's not the point.' But she stuffed the money in her bag anyway. She couldn't afford not to.

'I wanted to talk to you, anyway,' said Olivia.

'Oh, yeah, what about?'

'Let's sit down.'

Amy still felt a little wary as Olivia led her over to the sofa.

'Right,' said Olivia, 'two things. Firstly, I need to know how you knew Zac has a drug habit.'

'I found them in his room, that time you told me to clean it.'

'And you didn't think I ought to know.'

'I didn't know what to do, Mrs L. It's not like it's something I've ever come across before and it weren't any of my business, and you'd gone out and then, if I'm honest, it slipped my mind.'

'Did it.' Olivia sighed. 'Never mind, water under the bridge, and I know now.'

'I know you do.'

Olivia looked at her with raised eyebrows.

'Zac and my Ash had a fight. Zac accused Ash of blabbing to me about it cos Zac told Ash a while ago apparently.'

Silence descended.

'And the other thing?' prompted Amy. She didn't feel comfortable sitting here with her employer. It was one thing kicking back on the sofa when Olivia wasn't around – that was a bit of devilry – but now she was being treated almost like a guest, Amy felt quite awkward and wanted to get home, back to her comfort zone. 'Oh, yes. The thing is – and this has nothing to do with the gin – but I might have to let you go.'

'Let me go?' *Nothing to do with the gin?* Like buggery it didn't.

'It's not the sack, honest,' Olivia insisted. 'The fact is, we're going to have to move.'

'Move?' Gawd, she was like a parrot.

'Yes, we're downsizing – possibly to Beeching Rise.'

'*Bee*—' Amy stopped herself. 'Mum said she'd seen you down there.'

'Yes. The fact is we need to live somewhere smaller – we don't need a big place like this any more and... well... we need to make some economies.'

'Oh.' Amy longed to ask about the whys and wherefores as she was consumed by curiosity but even she didn't have the nerve. 'When?'

'I'd like to keep you on while the house is being sold – to keep it looking pristine.'

'Oh.' It was a crust she was getting thrown, she supposed, and not one she could afford to refuse. 'OK.'

'I'll give you a good reference.'

Which, under the circumstances, was more than she should expect.

'And,' said Olivia, 'I wouldn't be surprised if the new people wouldn't want a cleaner and I'd be sure to recommend you.'

'Thanks.'

'But I'd rather you didn't mention this to anyone.'

'What – that you can't afford this place?'

'Something like that.'

'As if, Mrs L. The soul of discretion, me.'

Olivia gazed at her. 'I know.'

★

Olivia leaned against the doorjamb after she'd let Amy out and wondered how she'd kept a straight face. *Soul of discretion.* Talk about delusional. And, dear Lord, she needed a laugh given how her day had panned out. She checked her watch; half past six and no sign of Zac. She sighed and went over to the kitchen counter and picked up her mobile. She pressed the buttons to call him. No reply. She tried again – this time it was straight to voicemail. 'Zac, we need to talk. I want to help you. I know I was cross – it was the shock. Please come home.' She took a deep breath. 'I know I said some harsh things but I didn't mean them. I do mean this, though… I love you, Zac.'

Zac sat in the park, hunched under one of the ramps, his chin resting on his knees, and thought about his situation. He wondered why he did drugs – it certainly didn't impress his friends. The idea that drugs were what the cool kids did was a total lie; Megan had called him a twat, he'd fallen out with Ashley, his mother was disgusted by him and Dan the dealer was a nasty piece of work who scared the shit out of him. If he thought his dad was a loser then he needed to think again. He was far worse – he'd stolen from his mum, he was about to crash his end of year exams, no one liked him… He wallowed in self-pity and misery as he thought about how he'd screwed up his life.

His phone rang. Mum. He killed the call and switched his phone off. He couldn't talk to her, not right now. He was too ashamed of what he'd done. Megan was right; he had to sort himself out but he didn't have a clue how. Maybe there was something on Google.

He switched his phone on again. The green light telling him had a voicemail flashed. He hit the icon and listened to the message. *'Zac, we need to talk. I want to help you. I know I was cross – it was the shock. Please come home. I know I said some harsh things but I didn't mean them. I do mean this, though… I love you, Zac.'* Zac burst into tears.

★

Olivia was sitting on the sofa, oblivious to the late evening May sunshine streaming through the big windows of her house. Where had she gone wrong? she wondered. How had she missed the signs? What was the way forward? Round and round went the questions in the head. Along with the *big* question – did she tell Nigel? She knew she *ought* to but he'd get so angry, he would shout at Zac so much that there was every danger Zac might light out and do something totally stupid. She had to keep Zac onside; if she could keep him close then maybe she could help him turn things round. Rows and recriminations weren't the way forwards.

Feeling bone-weary with worry, Olivia got to her feet and went over to the computer on the desk in the corner. She switched it on, then went to pour a glass of wine while it sorted itself out. She entered the password then clicked the Google icon. *How do you get off drugs?* she typed. A surprising number of sites scrolled onto the screen. Methodically she clicked on each one and began to read what was said.

She was alerted to Nigel's arrival home by his key in the lock. Guiltily she killed the page and shut down Google.

'Hello, how was your day?' she asked with a fake smile on her face.

'Knackering,' said Nigel. 'The commute was a nightmare and the boss wanted six impossible things done by lunch.' He dropped his laptop case on to the sofa. 'Good, you've got the wine open. Pour me a glass while I get changed. Did you have a good day?' he asked as he headed for the stairs.

'Oh – you know – the usual.'

She switched off the computer and went into the kitchen to sort out Nigel's wine and supper for everyone, although she wasn't the least bit sure if Zac was going to come home to eat it. And if he didn't, when did she tell Nigel the whole truth? Or call the police for that matter?

She was about to dish up a paella when Zac slunk in through the front door, still in his school uniform. Their eyes met and she gave him a half-smile. In return he looked totally shamefaced.

'Hurry up and change, darling,' she said breezily.

Zac flicked a glance at his father, lounging on the sofa, sipping his wine and watching some programme about buying houses and then looked questioningly at his mother. She gave him a tiny shake of his head and was rewarded with a look of sheer gratitude.

The meal was eaten in near silence and afterwards Zac shot back upstairs, muttering about his homework. Olivia cleared away, topped up her husband's glass and then followed her son.

She knocked on the door, surprised that she couldn't hear any music.

'We need to talk,' she said quietly when it was opened.

Zac nodded.

Oliva shut the door behind herself. 'So?' she said.

Zac sat on the bed and put his head in his hands.

'Zac, this is a mess, isn't it?'

He looked up at her and nodded.

'I've been doing some reading up,' said Olivia. 'We can sort this out but you've got to want to.'

Zac nodded again.

'Do you?'

'Yeah. I'm so fucked up, I've got to.'

Olivia sat next to her son and put her arms around him. 'We can do this, we can do this together. It's not the end of the world but you have to promise me that you'll give it your best shot. And I have a plan.'

42

May drifted into June and all the kids in town were off for the half-term holiday, although for Megan, Ashley, Zac and other kids their age they might not have school but it didn't mean they escaped schoolwork. They knew that on their return to their classes the next week they'd be faced, almost immediately, with tests and exams so their respective schools would be able to gauge their likely performance in their GCSEs that they'd be facing the next year.

It didn't help matters that the weather was glorious, so the incentive to stay at home swotting was non-existent and Megan found her little half-brothers very useful in providing an excuse to go to the play park at least once a day.

Besides, she told herself, all work and no play...

She glanced at her phone to check the time – half eleven – stacked her books up on her desk, grabbed her mobile and stuffed it in the back pocket of her shorts and trotted down the stairs. As she reached the ground floor she could hear voices coming from the kitchen. Out of curiosity she headed across the hall to see who their visitor was. Miles – what did he want?

'Oh, hello, Megan,' said Bex. 'Miles has come round to see if Alfie has been successfully caged.'

'OK,' responded Megan, although she couldn't think why Miles should be that interested.

'Did you want something?' said Bex.

'I came to see if the boys wanted to go to the park – or the nature reserve. I'm fed up with revising and the weather is so nice.'

'That's a lovely idea. Tell you what, why don't I make up some sandwiches and you could have a picnic out.'

'Yeah, why not.'

'And I've got some cold sausages in the fridge. Give me five minutes and I'll make you a proper feast.'

'Cool,' said Megan.

'I'll give you a hand,' said Miles.

Megan poured herself a glass of water and sat on a chair while she watched the pair work. Her dad, she remembered, had always been pretty hopeless in the kitchen. Beans on toast was about the limit of his skills. He'd been brilliant in other ways; she remembered how he'd taught her to swim and ride a bike, how they'd gone kite-flying on the beach one summer holiday and how he'd made her a go-kart. But cooking? Nah.

Miles got one of Bex's big knives and expertly shredded some cabbage, celery and carrot. The blade flashed through the vegetables.

'You'll have to teach me how to do that one day,' said Bex, smiling at him.

'I'd be delighted to,' responded Miles. 'It's a useful skill to have. In fact, there's no time like the present.'

'Let's finish making the picnic first, hey, so the kids can get off out and enjoy the sunshine. You can give me a lesson when we're on our own.'

'I'd love to.'

Did Megan imagine it or was there something going on between them? No, she'd imagined it, she told herself. Miles was just being friendly. 'I'll go and tell the boys we're going out, shall I?'

'Please,' said Bex, busy buttering bread and slapping some tinned tuna onto the slices.

Megan wandered out into the garden and found the boys in the sandpit making sandcastles.

'We're off out for a picnic lunch,' she told them. 'Mummy's making sandwiches right now.'

'Can we go and see the diggers?'

Lewis rolled his eyes and scowled.

'I thought we'd go to the nature reserve and see how many bugs we can find.'

Alfie's face crumpled.

'But we can see the diggers on the way home,' she added, trying to avoid a meltdown.

'Must we?' whined Lewis.

'And we can go to the swings if you like.'

Lewis continued to look grumpy.

'We won't spend that long at the building site, promise. And perhaps I'll ask Mummy for some money for ice lollies.'

That clinched it; smiles broke out on both the boys' faces.

Bex came to the back door holding a bottle of suntan lotion. 'Slather the boys in this, would you?'

'Of course.'

Bex threw the bottle gently in her direction and Megan caught it. 'Tops off, lads,' she ordered.

By the time she'd got her half-brothers and herself protected against the summer sun, Bex had returned with a backpack filled with goodies.

'How long are you planning to stay out?' she asked.

'An hour or so – I dunno, really.'

'Make sure you've got your phone in case of an emergency or anything.'

Megan patted the back pocket of her cut-offs.

'Good, have a nice time, and boys, you're to do as your sister says, understand?'

Lewis and Alfie nodded.

'Let's go,' said Megan, hefting the rucksack onto her shoulders.

'Oh… I sort of promised the boys a lolly.' She looked hopefully at Bex.

'Of course.' Bex dived back into the house and re-emerged

with a ten pound note. Megan stuffed it into her other pocket then led the way out of the garden and along the road, Alfie's slightly sweaty hand held tightly in hers.

It didn't take long to reach the lane that led to the reserve and with an exhortation not to go too far, Megan told the boys they could run on ahead. It was, she thought, like letting dogs off the lead. The lads scampered off and then dived into the long grass in the big meadow causing an air-burst of butterflies to fly upwards. Megan followed more sedately feeling slightly wilted in the summer heat.

She kept track of the boys more by sound than sight as she walked along the footpath towards the stream. Every now and again they bounded out of the grass to check where she was before diving back in again. She found a place on the bank in the shade of a willow and near the bridge which she decided was perfect for their picnic. She dropped the rucksack off her shoulders and pulled her T-shirt, damp with perspiration, away from her back then headed off to tell the boys where to find her.

When she got back to her chosen spot there was a border collie sniffing at the rucksack and pawing it.

'Oi, shoo,' she yelled at it.

'Oscar's not doing any harm.'

The voice was familiar. Megan spun round. 'Oh, it's you.' She was still mad at him for fighting Ashley and lying about dealing with his drug problem. He didn't look that well; his skin was pasty and he had spots. Well, that's what you got for being a junkie, she supposed. 'What do you want?'

'Nothing, I'm out for a walk with Oscar.'

'I didn't know you had a dog.'

'No, he's new. He's a rescue dog.' Zac called the collie to come to him and the dog trotted over. Zac slipped the lead he was carrying onto his collar.

'Cool.'

'Mum got him for me.'

'Why?'

'You were right, Megan. I was a stupid twat and I needed to sort myself out.'

'And are you?' She wasn't sure she believed him – not judging by the way he looked.

Zac nodded. 'That why I've got Oscar. Mum read that people coming off drugs need something else to do. So she thought a dog might help me.'

'Does it?'

'A bit. It's still shit though and I feel like crap some of the time, really lousy. Honestly, I've never felt this bad.'

That explained the way he looked. Megan was almost inclined to feel sorry for him. Almost.

'But looking after Oscar,' said Zac, 'means I'm not thinking about myself all the time. And walking him is an excuse to break away from my old habits.'

'Is that why you haven't been to the skatepark?'

Zac stared at his feet. 'Dogs aren't allowed there. And I don't want to see my dealer either.'

'I can imagine,' said Megan. 'You ought to talk to Ash and apologise to him, though. It wasn't him who told your mum.'

'Really?'

'No, he told me his mum found some stuff in your room when she cleaned it.'

'OK, so I was out of order blaming Ash.'

'You were out of order trying to punch the living daylights out of him. You were out of order doing drugs.'

Zac nodded and sighed. 'Look, I've said you were right so there's no need to bang on about it.'

Megan eyeballed him. 'As long as you owe me money I've got every right.'

'Be like that then. I've got enough shit going on without people like you adding to it.'

'Piss off, Zac, and stop feeling sorry for yourself. All of this is your own fault.'

'Come on, Oscar,' said Zac. He tugged at the lead and stormed off.

'Be like that then,' Megan shouted after him.

The boys came bounding out of the grass, pink and glistening with perspiration.

'Is it lunchtime yet, Megs, we're starving,' said Lewis.

She knelt down by the bag and unzipped it, before handing out fat sandwiches to her half-brothers.

'Who was that?' asked Lewis.

'No one,' said Megan. 'A nobody.'

The boys, clutching their food, ran back into the long grass and left Megan staring after the fast disappearing figure, wondering if she ought to have been less harsh. She knew what it was like to feel friendless and alone with others ganging up on her and now she was doing it to Zac. Maybe, next time she saw him, she'd try and be more sympathetic. But only if he was still clean.

'Oughtn't you be getting back to the pub?' said Bex after Megan had left. And she was a tad concerned at the way he'd found an excuse to visit her and then had found an excuse to stay longer. For some reason, she felt less than comfortable in his presence.

'I thought you wanted me to teach you some knife skills.'

'Not if that means Belinda blaming me for you being late.' Or blaming her for Miles paying her more attention than she felt he ought.

'Jamie can cope for a minute or two. All the prep's been done and it's quite early for punters to want lunch.'

'Really?' said Bex. 'You seem to forget that I work there too and I've taken orders for food this early.'

'Do you want to get rid of me?'

'I've got things I ought to be getting on with,' she lied.

'More baking?'

She nodded.

'Another time, then,' said Miles. 'Maybe when you're back at work, next week, if we have a quiet lunchtime.'

'Maybe.' Or maybe not.

'As you're obviously busy, I'll be off.' His voice sounded chilly. Maybe he hadn't liked being rebuffed like that.

'Bye then,' said Bex.

Miles walked out of the kitchen and she heard the front door shut. She sagged onto a chair. It was for the best.

43

'Fancy a drink tonight?' said Billy as he let himself into Amy's little house. He walked into the kitchen and put his arms round her waist before he gave her a peck on the cheek. Ashley, who was helping himself out of the biscuit tin, scowled. 'It's Friday, after all. I've been paid and I feel like a night out.'

'Yeah, that sound like a plan,' said Amy. 'You'll be all right on your own, won't you, Ash?'

'I'm almost sixteen, Mum.'

'Almost old enough to leave home,' said Billy. 'Or get a job.'

Ashley stared at Billy. 'That's what you want, is it?'

'Just saying,' said Billy. 'It's what I did. I was earning a decent wage when I wasn't much older than you.'

'Bully for you.'

Amy glanced from one to the other. 'Now then, lads, if I'm going to get out I need to get supper on the table.'

'Don't bother for me. I'm going out,' said Ashley.

'But Ash…'

Too late, he'd stormed off and the front door slammed by way of an answer.

Amy turned on Billy. 'Now look what you've done.'

'If he were mine I'd give him a bloody good hiding for cheeking me like that.'

'It wasn't really cheek.'

'He should respect his elders and betters, if you ask me.'

'But he does; Ash is a good kid.'

'If that's what you want to think. You're too soft on him.'

Amy was about to ask Billy what business was it of his, but she didn't feel quite brave enough. 'Let's not argue, Billy. Tell you what, there's some beers in the fridge. Why don't you have one while you wait for your dinner.'

'What is it?'

'Macaroni cheese.'

'Mac cheese? Where's the meat?'

'It's the end of the week, and I had bills to pay. Things are a bit tight.' She didn't add that he was the main cause of her current financial problems, what with her needing to keep some beers in for him, to say nothing of the extra food.

'Would this help?' Billy pulled a wad of notes from his pocket and peeled off a couple of twenties which he threw on the kitchen table.

'I can't take your money,' she said, although she dearly wanted to grab it with both hands.

'You can and you will. And I want a nice piece of steak for my supper tomorrow. None of this mac cheese shit, understand.'

'It's all I've got for tonight.'

'Then Ashley can have it when he bothers to come home again. I'm not going to eat that muck.'

'But...'

'We'll eat at the pub.'

Amy grabbed her oven gloves, switched the oven off and took out the bubbling pasta dish. Much as eating out would be a treat, macaroni cheese was one of her favourites and she'd been looking forward to it. Never mind – she could heat up what Ashley left for their supper on Monday, when she didn't have to worry about what Billy would or wouldn't eat.

The pair strolled along the high street towards the pub in the warm evening sunshine, Billy's sour comments about her food forgotten. The town was busy with people also enjoying the summer weather.

'Shame the pub's not got a garden,' said Amy. 'It'd be nice to sit out to eat on a day like this.'

'Yeah, and get skin cancer.'

'Gawd, you're a right misery-guts, ain't you. What's rattled your cage?'

'I'll tell you what, watching that layabout son take you for granted.'

'He's not a layabout,' protested Amy. 'He works blooming hard.'

'No, he doesn't. Like I said, schoolwork isn't proper work.'

'Don't let's argue, let's not spoil things.'

'You're the one who's arguing,' said Billy.

Amy almost told him it took two to argue but, once again, she bit her tongue.

'What you drinking?' said Billy as they turned into the pub.

'White wine and lemonade,' said Amy. 'Lots of ice too. Thanks, darling.'

'See if you can get a table – I'll bring the drinks over.'

A few minutes later Billy pushed his way through the other customers, who were crowded into the little bar enjoying a start-the-weekend drink, towards Amy who'd managed to find a table in the corner. With him he also brought a couple of menus which he plonked down along with the drinks.

'Cheers,' said Amy, clinking her glass against his. She perused the menu as she sipped. 'Cor, this is nice. What are you thinking of having?'

'I think I might have the chicken and chips. You?' Billy took a long slurp of his drink and then wiped his mouth with the back of his hand.

Amy considered the choices for a few more seconds. 'I might have that too.'

Billy went to the bar to place the order and returned with more drinks.

'I've not finished this one yet,' protested Amy.

'Saves queuing again in a minute, doesn't it.'

'Are you trying to get me tipsy?'

'Maybe.' He grinned at her.

'You don't have to. I'm yours for the taking, you know that, Billy?'

'And talking about being mine...' Billy put his hand in his pocket and brought out a small box. 'I bought this at a car boot. It's a pukka bit of kit, mind. Worth a bit, if I'm any judge, and I thought you might like it. It's not an engagement ring or nothing, but, I thought that seeing as you're my girl now, you ought to wear something to show you belong to me. I don't want other men sniffing around you... know what I mean?'

Amy's heart, which had begun to beat wildly at the sight of the ring-box, settled down at the words *it's not an engagement ring or nothing.* And dropped still further at the notion that he was chaining her to him. She knew she ought to be pleased that he cared about her that much but there was a faintly sinister and threatening undertone that she didn't much like.

He opened the box and showed her the ruby eternity ring.

'That's pretty,' she lied. It was the sort of thing her gran had worn and she thought it was clunky and old-fashioned but hey, Billy said it was worth a bit. Shame she wasn't going to be able to flog it – she'd rather have the cash.

'Go on then, put it on.'

Amy took the ring and slipped it on her middle finger on her right hand. It was a bit tight. That wouldn't be coming off again in a hurry.

'There.' She held her hand up to admire it and then showed Billy. 'Thanks, babe.' She leaned over the table to give him a kiss and managed to topple over one of her glasses of wine. It deluged over him in a tidal wave.

'You stupid bloody cow,' he yelled at her as he leapt to his feet, his shirt and trousers drenched and dripping. He raised his hand and for a second Amy was convinced he was going to hit her.

The pub fell completely silent as everyone turned to see what the commotion was. Belinda rushed over with a towel from behind the bar and handed it to Billy. His face was thunderous as he mopped himself.

'Cancel my order. I'm off.'

'Billy!'

'You can stay and eat if you want. I need to get changed. Stupid bitch,' he spat as a parting shot before he shouldered his way through the silent drinkers and stormed off.

Amy began to cry and slowly the conversation level in the bar began to crank up again.

Belinda put her arm around Amy's shoulder. 'What do you want to do, hon? Shall I cancel your order too? I can give Billy his money back next time he comes in.'

Amy nodded. 'Don't feel much like an evening out on my own, now. Yeah, please do.'

'It was an accident. These things happen.'

'Maybe. And he'd just given me this, an' all.' She showed Belinda the ruby ring. 'Not that we're engaged, but he wanted me to have it. Well... he did.'

'That's lovely.'

'I suppose he'll want it back now.'

'I'd wait till he calms down to see which way the wind blows.'

'He was ever so cross, wasn't he?'

Belinda nodded. 'It may take a while for him to get over it, yes.' She went to the kitchen to cancel the food while Amy drained the drink she hadn't spilt and then made her way home.

Bex had enjoyed the half-term week and it was hard to get back into the routine of getting the kids out of bed and off to school. Furthermore, she wasn't entirely looking forward to running into Miles – not after pissing him off. But she couldn't let Belinda down and, besides, she liked it there. She liked listening to the regulars, chewing over the town's goings-on, she liked the buzz of the place if it got busy, she liked working for Belinda, she liked Miles... No, she didn't.

She finished making the beds and tidying up the boys' toys before she locked up and took herself next door to start her shift. Regarding Miles, she told herself to pretend nothing had happened and to be cool, calm and collected. Don't apologise, don't explain, she told herself firmly as she knocked on the pub door and waited for Belinda to unlock it and let her in.

'Hi, Bex,' her boss greeted her as she locked the door again. 'Did you have a nice break with the kids?'

'Yeah, it was grand. We were lucky with the weather, I suppose, so they spent most of their time out in the garden or at the building site watching the diggers.'

'What is it with your youngest and heavy plant?'

'Search me,' said Bex. 'At least he can't try and wander down there on his own – not since Miles fixed my gate. Right, what do you want me to do first? Bottling up?'

'Sounds great. I need to change a barrel; one of the beers ran out a couple of minutes before closing time and I couldn't be bothered to do it last night.'

Belinda went down to the cellar while Bex checked the stock of mixers under the bar and in the fridges before following her to collect more of the things they were low on.

'You missed a bit of a kerfuffle on Friday,' said Belinda as she pulled up the lever on the coupler.

'Really? What happened?' Bex started putting a selection of bottles into an empty crate, ready to lug back up the steps

'Your Amy had a row with her bloke.'

'Is that Billy?'

'Yeah, he's a car mechanic at the garage out on the Cattebury road. I think him and Amy have been an item for a bit. Anyway, on Friday they came in for supper and she managed to tip a large spritzer into his lap. He went ape. A couple of the regulars thought he was going to belt her one.'

Bex stopped moving the bottles. 'It doesn't sound as if he's much of a catch.'

Belinda shook her head as she reconnected the coupler to a new barrel. 'I've never liked him. I've always thought he's a bit shifty – a bit fly, if you know what I mean. But I suppose he must be fond of Amy because she told me that before she managed to throw her drink all over him he'd given her an eternity ring. Now, I don't know much about jewellery but this was obviously worth a bit.'

'Lucky old Amy.'

'Yeah, only I'm not sure the ring is worth being stuck with Billy.'

'So they're engaged?'

'She says not.'

Bex picked up the crate with an *oof*. 'And he may not be as bad as you think.'

'I suppose – except you hear of people that get stuck in abusive relationships and I'm fond of Amy. I'd hate to think of her being in that position.'

Bex began to climb the stairs. 'On the other hand, it's not really our business, is it?'

'No, you're right. And maybe Billy's reaction was a heat-of-the-moment thing.'

'I sincerely hope so.'

44

When Bex finished her shift and returned home, Amy was busy mopping the kitchen floor.

'Hi, Bex,' she said in her usual cheery way.

'What's this I hear about you trying to drown your boyfriend?'

'Oh, that... Yeah, bit of a disaster. Who told you?' Amy didn't sound thrilled that, for a change, she was the subject of gossip, not the purveyor.

'Belinda.'

Amy concentrated on her mopping and didn't respond.

'She says your bloke was really cross.'

'Who wouldn't be, getting a half pint of wine and lemonade dumped in their lap? He had every right to be cross – I made him look like he'd wet himself.'

'Oh dear.' Bex suppressed a grin. 'These things happen, though.'

'True.'

'Has he forgiven you?'

Amy looked up sharply and dumped the mop in the bucket. 'I wouldn't know, would I? He didn't stay around at mine like he was supposed to this weekend.'

'Oh, dear.'

Amy wrung out the mop. 'It might've been for the best if he was going to be arsey about what happened.'

'Distance makes the heart grow fonder,' murmured Bex.

'Yeah, and out of sight out of mind,' shot back Amy. 'On the other hand, I thought he was going to want this back.' She put out her hand for Bex to admire the ring.

'Blimey.' So that was the ring. Bex was genuinely impressed.

'But as he wasn't around to get it back I'm hoping it's mine for keeps. He says he bought it at a car boot. No idea what it's worth.'

Bex took Amy's hand and had a closer look. 'If those are rubies and not garnets I think you should get it properly valued and insured.'

'You reckon?'

'I would.'

Amy looked at her new ring again. 'Do you think whoever sold it to Billy knew it's worth a bomb? Cos I can't imagine Billy spending hundreds, can you?'

'Not ever having met Billy...'

'And maybe I shouldn't wear it to work but it's probably safer on my finger than at home, what with all these break-ins. Anyway, I can't stand here gassing if I'm going to finish everything, and you ought to be off to get the kids.' She returned to her mopping.

Olivia was, once again, going through the bank statements and the credit card bills, trying to balance the books. The first of the estate agents had been round that morning to give her a valuation and had been full of gloom and doom about downturns in the market and a slump in the price of houses and negative equity. She suspected the guy was preparing the ground for them getting less than what she hoped for – or needed; less than the sum he'd told her the house *might* be worth. Which left her trying to work out what was the minimum she and Nigel *could* accept and still manage to pay off his debts and afford another house in Little Woodford.

Her eyes began to glaze over as she studied the figures and she threw down her pen. Sod it, she needed a walk to clear her head. Oscar was in his basket, his head resting on the edge of it, his eyes closed, the epitome of a happy dog – a dog that knew he had fallen on all four paws when they'd selected him from the dogs' home. Mind you, he hadn't had a hard life before, since he'd had a very loving owner – but an owner who'd had to go into a nursing home and had been unable to take Oscar with him.

'Walkies,' called Olivia.

The dog reacted in a split second; out of the basket, eyes open, tail wagging.

How could any living thing go from *sleep* to *lively* in that space of time? wondered Olivia as she grabbed the lead and her keys from the hook behind the front door. It was something Zac could do with copying – although he was better than he had been, when it came to being prised out of bed in the mornings. She clipped the lead to Oscar and the pair set off into the sunshine towards the nature reserve. As she walked down the hill she thought about other changes in her son, changes that were now a sign of his recovery, and wondered how she'd missed the other, sinister signs that he'd been on drugs. He still suffered from mood swings – one moment he'd be reasonably normal and then, at the least thing he'd be raging and angry and almost out of control, and he was still a grouch first thing in the morning, but he didn't look half asleep most of the rest of the day. And his room didn't smell of that revolting body spray now he wasn't trying to disguise the smell of weed. Once again she asked herself how she could have been so naive. She also wondered why the school hadn't spotted anything but she didn't think it would do Zac any favours by confronting them, retrospectively, over their failure – given their zero tolerance, it wasn't beyond the bounds of possibility that they'd take punitive action, which was hardly going to help matters. It was one thing if they had to take Zac away from St Anselm's for financial reasons; it would be quite another thing if he got expelled for drug-taking.

Once they reached the open space Oscar was released and he

bounded off into the long grass. Olivia strolled along a path and followed the black and white feathery tail that was all that was now visible of the dog. Unusually, there didn't seem to be anyone else in the reserve. Olivia supposed it was because the stay-at-home mums were busy with the school run, everyone else was at work and the regular dog-walkers had taken their pooches out first thing and it wasn't yet time for the last walk of the day. Maybe she ought to come down at this time more often – it was certainly very pleasant.

She crossed the stream, taking time to gaze into the water and see what aquatic species she could see. Not a lot, as it turned out, and then she strolled up through the meadow to the little copse to check if the council was keeping the littering under control there. Oscar lolloped along, bouncing through the grass, revelling in the smells that only his nose could detect while Olivia listened to the twitter of numerous birds including a lark, high in the sky and out of sight, which was singing its little heart out. Butterflies flitted around the spikes of rosebay willowherb and clumps of ox-eyed daisies and it was, thought Olivia, an English summer meadow at its best.

She approached the coppice. She could hear voices – two men, by the sound of things. And also, as she got closer, two men who were arguing.

'Come off it. What do you know about risk? You've had keys to half of them.'

'Two, Billy, two. I've had the keys to two places.'

'And I've had to get rid of the gear. It's risky.'

'Risky? No one checks where the stuff comes from at a car boot sale. When was the last time you saw the fuzz prowling round the pitches?'

'But if they do, I'll be the one who gets nicked. Which is why this is all I'm going to give you. The rest – I'm keeping that as danger money.'

There was a pause and silence as Olivia strained to work out what was going on.

'Two grand? Is that all?'

'It's all I'm giving you.'

'In which case, Billy-boy, I might have to change my fence.'

'Do that, Dan, do that. And good luck, because I don't think anyone else will touch your stuff with a ten-foot bargepole. Not around here.'

Olivia backed off, her heart thumping like crazy, then she turned and headed swiftly back towards the stream. That was a conversation she was sure she shouldn't have overheard. When she was a good fifty yards from the trees she turned and looked round and saw one of the men heading off in the opposite direction to her, either ignoring her presence or oblivious to it. She breathed a sigh of relief; it seemed she'd put enough distance between them and her to be dismissed as a middle-aged dog-walker and not someone who had been earwigging their very dodgy conversation – a conversation she thought Leanne Knowles might want to know about.

Billy and Dan – she mustn't forget those two names. She repeated them to herself and wondered who they were.

Brian was on his knees but not praying – this time he was leaning over the beds in the vicarage garden and pulling up weeds from between the flowering plants and shrubs. The soil was warm under his fingertips and the mid-afternoon sun hot on his back and beside him a robin hovered around hopefully, darting in now and again to snaffle some little trifle unearthed by Brian's trowel. Above him, the same skylark that Olivia had heard was soaring and singing, filling the air with its beautiful, warbling trill. Brian eased his back and sat back on his ankles. He felt, he realised, content.

'God's in his heaven and all's right with the world,' he murmured to himself. Beside him, the robin cocked his beady black eye at him as if in agreement.

'You think that too, do you, fella?' He stared at the robin, which, unconcerned and emboldened by the supply of food Brian had been unintentionally supplying, eyeballed him back. Brian looked at the rest of nature that surrounded him: the spikes of the foxgloves with a couple of fat bumblebees crawling in and out of the pink bells; the campanula, buzzing with honey bees; a couple of red admirals basking in the sun on the ivy on the fence, lazily opening and closing their glorious wings; the roses – blowsy and heavy with petals, and suddenly he wanted to give thanks for it all.

He hauled himself to his feet, making the robin flutter off a couple of yards, and brushed down the knees of his trousers before he set off, purposefully, down the path to the church.

A minute later he'd pulled his heavy bunch of keys from his pocket, unlocked the ancient oak door and pushed it open. The deep peace of the empty church enveloped him but this time he didn't feel as if he was in a vacuum but wrapped in a blanket. He could have sworn he felt warmer in the cool air of the church than in the heat of sunshine outside. It was... comforting. Very comforting. He walked up the aisle and took a seat in the choir stalls and let his mind drift as his thoughts ranged from the beauty of nature to the mystery of creation and, as they did, so too came the realisation that he had reconnected with his certainty about there being a God. He shut his eyes and leaned back against the hard oak of the pew. Bizarrely, he had the feeling someone was resting a hand on his shoulder. The feeling of being at ease, of being loved and cared for, grew.

'Thank you,' he said out loud. 'Thank you.'

'Blimey, Reverend, you made me jump.'

Brian snapped his eyes open. 'Joan!' Joan Makepiece was standing near the lectern with a box of polishing clothes and an industrial-sized tin of Brasso clutched in her hands.

'What are you so grateful for, then?' she asked.

'Everything,' said Brian, joyfully. 'Everything.'

Joan eyed him as if he'd lost his marbles but Brian grinned at her like the proverbial Cheshire cat.

'It's a glorious day and everything is just fine. Don't you feel it, Joan?'

'I do. And I ought to tell you, those pills the doc gave me have worked a treat. I feel so much better.'

'Oh, Joan, I am delighted. Yet more things to give thanks for.' He beamed at her.

'If you say so, Reverend. Although, I could do with the Good Lord sorting out my arthritis if He's got a mind to. I'm a martyr to it and the doc says there's bugger all he can do – pardon my French – it's cos of my age. Now, if you'll excuse me, these brasses won't clean themselves.'

45

Olivia let herself back in to her house and slipped off Oscar's lead. The collie padded over to his water bowl and drank noisily for a few seconds before flopping back into his basket and shutting his eyes. Olivia looked at him with envy. If only life was so simple for her, she thought – sleep, eat, walk, play. No worries, no money problems, nothing. Bliss. But this wasn't reporting what she'd recently overheard to the local police. She went over to the desk, picked up the phone and rang the non-emergency number.

'It's about the break-ins that have been happening around Little Woodford,' she began. 'I think I may have some information…'

It was gone five when Leanne appeared on Olivia's doorstep.

'You'd better come in,' said Olivia. 'Tea?'

'No, you're all right.'

Olivia led Leanne over to the sofa. 'Take a seat.'

Leanne sat, took off her uniform hat and got out a notebook. 'So, I've been told you overheard two men talking, Dan and Billy, and they seemed to be referring to stolen goods. Is that right?'

Olivia nodded.

'But you have no idea who these two are.'

'No, not a clue. But one of them said something about the other having to look for another fence and there was also a mention of keys.'

'Keys?'

'Yes.' Olivia thought back. 'One of them said something like...
"what do you know about risk – you had keys to half of them."
And then the other said, "only two."'

'I see.'

There was a noise from upstairs and then the sound of footsteps.

'Oh,' said Zac from halfway down the staircase. He looked
worriedly at his mother then at Leanne. 'What's the matter?'

'It's all right, Zac,' said his mum. And the little sod might well
look guilty, she thought, given what he'd been up to recently, but
he wasn't in the frame this time. 'I heard something today which
might have a bearing on the burglaries. Leanne's come to talk to
me about it.'

'Like what?' asked Zac. He still looked wary.

'I overheard a couple of guys talking, that's all, up at the nature
reserve, at the lump of woodland in the middle of the meadow
– where the drugg—' Olivia stopped. She remembered that
amongst the drug paraphernalia had been bottles of Malbec and
that she'd blamed the council estate kids for nicking it from the
local supermarket when, now she knew what she did, she realised
that it had probably been *her* son nicking it from *her* wine rack.
'Where some of the local youths hang out,' she said.

Zac reddened. 'Yeah, well...'

'Do you know anyone in the town called Dan or Billy?' asked
Leanne.

'Dan?' There was a pause. 'Er, no.'

Leanne stared at him. 'Really?'

'No, why? Should I?' He sounded defensive.

'No.'

Zac loped off to the kitchen and poured himself a glass of
water before calling Oscar. The collie bounded out of his bed and
trotted over to Zac, his tail wagging.

'I thought I'd take Oscar out for a quick walk.'

'What about your homework?' said Olivia.

'It's revision – I need a break. And exams don't start till next week.'

'Don't be too long.'

'I won't.' Zac grabbed the lead off the hook on the back of the door and headed out.

Leanne stared at Olivia. 'I know he's your son but when I mentioned Dan's name... do you think Zac's answer was the truth?'

Olivia pursed her lips into a thin line. 'I don't know.' She sighed. 'The thing is... the thing is, Zac's had some problems recently.' She stared at her hands.

'Like?'

'Like he's been getting up to stuff I don't approve of.'

'Like?'

Olivia raised her eyes. 'Drugs. But he's promised me he's trying to kick it now.'

'He won't be the only one in town, as you know yourself.'

Olivia nodded. 'I think it's been going on for a while but I keep kicking myself for not spotting anything.'

'He's hardly likely to have gone round with a placard announcing what he was up to, though, was he?'

'Even so.'

'I think lots of kids get up to stuff their parents know nothing about. Didn't you?'

Olivia thought back. 'No, no I don't think I did.'

'Really? Blimey. No misspent youth?'

Olivia shook her head. 'I must have been so prim and boring.'

'Not getting into trouble isn't something to be ashamed of.' Leanne grinned at her. 'Unusual, though.'

'And it has made me spectacularly naive about my own kids. So... this Dan bloke – might he be someone Zac associated with, someone on the drugs scene?'

'Dan's not an uncommon name – so it doesn't mean there's a connection. I'll have a quiet word with one or two people.' Leanne stood up. 'Thanks for getting in touch. It may be that nothing comes of what you heard but you never know.' She put her hat back on and headed for the door. 'I'm glad Zac's seen the error of his ways.'

Olivia nodded. 'After I found out, he realised he was in a mess. To be honest, I think he knew he was ruining his life and wanted to stop but he didn't know how. He's finding it tough, though.'

'It *is* tough coming off drugs – horrible.'

'He says he feels miserable a lot of the time.'

'If he sticks with it it'll get better. Trust me.' Leanne gave her a significant look.

'You?'

'Oh yes. But it was a long time ago now and I'm not proud of it.'

'At least you're not utterly clueless like me. Maybe having a misspent youth isn't such a bad thing.'

'Maybe. Right,' as she opened the front door, 'I'm off. And thanks for coming forward. Let's hope it leads somewhere.'

Zac and Oscar walked down the hill towards the town centre. He was fed up with staring at his books and he wasn't sure how much good trying to revise was going to do after several terms of doing the bare minimum. And he dreaded his dad's reaction when the results came out. Life was such a mess, he thought. He was such a mess. Beside him trotted Oscar, oblivious to Zac's turmoil. They reached the bottom of the hill and the gate to The Beeches. The sound of happy shrieks wafted out of the garden, audible even over the steady stream of cars that trundled up and down the road.

Zac stopped to look over the gate. At the side of the house was a paddling pool and Megan's brothers were having a water fight with super-soakers and buckets. As he watched, Megan walked into view and caught sight of him.

'Hello,' called Zac tentatively.

Megan walked over to the gate. 'Hi. Have you apologised to Ashley yet?'

'Not yet. I haven't seen him.'

'You mean, you haven't made the effort.'

'Don't be like that.'

'You could go round his right now, couldn't you?'

'I suppose.'

'Like I said, all of this is your fault and you're the only one who can put it right and until you do and until you apologise to Ashley I'm having nothing to do with you. And I want my money back.'

'But I can't – my allowance has been cut.'

'Then get a job.'

'When – when can I work?'

'Saturdays, after school. Lots of kids do, why shouldn't you?'

'Because—'

'Sort it out, Zac.' Megan turned her back and walked off.

'Megan!'

But she went into the house and shut the door.

Nigel got home from work around seven.

'Hiya, Ol... Olivia,' he said as he dropped his briefcase by the front door. 'Good day?' He went over to Oscar's basket and patted the dog, who got up, stretched and licked Nigel's hand in appreciation.

'So-so. Had an estate agent round.'

'Oh yeah?' Nigel loosened his tie and took it off, shoving it in his jacket pocket. 'And?'

'Well, he wasn't very upbeat. Apparently there's a slump in the housing market and, while he's happy to put it on the market for one point three million, he thinks we'll be lucky to make that. We're far more likely to get one point one.'

'Oh. Well... that's all right, I suppose.'

Olivia shook her head. 'No it's not. We can buy somewhere else and clear your debts but your pension pot will remain empty, we'll have nothing left for emergencies and, without the income we used to get from your investments, we'll struggle with Zac's fees. And we can't afford to hang about and wait for someone to give us the asking price, we need a quick sale.'

'I'm sorry,' said Nigel.

Olivia was tempted to snap that so he bloody well should be, but what good would it do? 'So am I,' she said. 'Gin?'

Nigel nodded. 'I suppose we ought to cut out luxuries like that,' he said.

'We've given up holidays, we're giving up this house but I draw the line at gin and wine. We may have to live in reduced circumstanced but I'm not going to be miserable too.'

Olivia thought about telling him that, since she'd caught Amy knocking back their drink, the bottle was lasting longer than it had before. And, as their son had stopped nicking money from her handbag, the housekeeping was stretching a bit further too. But she reckoned that Nigel's reaction to such news would be to sack Amy and yell at Zac, which wouldn't help anyone.

She sloshed out the gin and added ice and lemon. 'So...' she said as she handed Nigel his drink, 'how's it going?'

Nigel snorted. 'You'd think it would be easy, wouldn't you, to walk past a betting shop and not go in, or to go into a pub for a drink and not put money in a machine but it's not.'

'And have you? Weakened, that is?'

Nigel shook his head and took a gulp. 'I've taken to going for walks in the park in my lunch break because the others always go to the Ship. They think I'm on some kind of fitness drive.'

'The office doesn't know.'

Nigel shook his head. 'Given that I work in the financial sector I think they'd have a pretty dim view if they found out.'

'Maybe. But it's ironic, isn't it? It seems to me most high finance is gambling.'

'Ha. But only on their terms. They're not keen on employees gambling with their own money – not if it gets out of control.'

'But it isn't, not now.'

'But it *was*. That's all that matters. They turn a blind eye to drinking – even snorting coke seems to be the norm – but losing one's own money in one's own time, well… close the door quietly on your way out.'

'Have you done drugs?'

Nigel looked up. 'Shit no. That's for real losers.'

Even more reason, thought Olivia, for Nigel not to find out about Zac. She felt that the last thing Zac needed, on top of the misery of kicking his addiction, was to have a massive showdown with his father.

She went into the kitchen to start cooking supper. Before she did, she opened a tin of dog food and then called Oscar in for his dinner.

Nigel got up and wandered over. He leaned on the counter. 'What I don't understand is why, given that things are now tight, you suddenly decided to get a dog?'

'I did it for Zac.' Which was true. 'I didn't think he was getting enough exercise – now he has to walk Oscar he has to get out and about.' Which wasn't entirely correct but was plausible. 'And what's more, because dogs aren't allowed at the park, it stops him going to that wretched skatepark all the time. I don't like the kids that hang out there.' Which she knew Nigel would completely swallow. 'And he's a nice dog.' Also true.

'I worry,' said Nigel, 'that Zac doesn't seem to have many friends. He never seems to bring anyone home these days.'

Olivia began to rummage in the fridge. And if Nigel knew the types Zac had been associating with he'd understand the reason why. 'There aren't that many kids in town that go to St Anselm's.'

'Maybe he'd be better off at the comp; at least all the local kids go there.'

'I very much doubt it,' said Olivia with a sniff. 'And let's hope,' she added firmly, 'it doesn't come to that.'

46

Amy made her way over the smart, newly raked gravel of Olivia's drive and let herself in. In the corner of the front garden were two estate agents' boards advertising the house was for sale. That'd get the town talking, she thought. Mrs L might have asked her to keep quiet about the sale – which she had done, apart from telling her mum, but that didn't count, did it? – but now the For Sale boards were up everyone was going to know.

'Coo-ee.'

'Morning, Amy,' replied Olivia from the kitchen. Amy could see she was adding ingredients to what she supposed must be a bread machine only she'd never seen it being used before. 'We've got a viewing this afternoon,' continued Olivia.

'So you're making bread.'

'Exactly. Every little helps.'

'What, people buy houses because they smell nice?' Amy was astounded.

'First impressions, Amy, first impressions. People aren't only buying a house, they're buying a lifestyle.'

Yeah, right. 'If you say so.' Amy shrugged off her cardigan and put on her apron. 'Where do you want me to start?'

'Lots of polishing, please.'

'Let me guess – so it smells nice.'

'And I'm going to pop into town and buy some flowers as soon as I've got the bread on.'

Olivia whirled around the kitchen finding the ingredients for her loaf and then as Amy got started in the sitting room came the rhythmic whump-whump of the bread machine mixing the dough.

'I'm going out now – back in a few minutes.'

Olivia sped out of the house leaving Amy grafting. She considered taking her bike but decided that, because she had so much to do, it would be quicker by car – assuming she could find somewhere to park, which wasn't a given at this time of day. She jumped into the driver's seat and two minutes later she was trawling the car park for a vacant spot. Finally, she struck lucky and pulled into the bay.

She grabbed her bag from the passenger seat and headed to the florist's. She knew that a bunch of flowers might be cheaper in the little Co-op but the selection generally only ran to carnations or maybe some roses but invariably they never smelt of anything and Olivia wanted *scent*. And lots of it. Freesias, she thought, as she opened the door with a ping.

'Hello,' said Belinda, who was standing by the counter.

'Belinda. What a surprise.'

'It's my great-aunt's birthday,' said Belinda. 'And what do you get a nonagenarian who lives in Edinburgh?'

'Flowers?'

Belinda nodded and tapped the Interflora catalogue on the counter which she'd been browsing. 'Mind you, given what this bouquet is going to cost it might be cheaper to fly up there and wish her a happy birthday in person.'

'But she'll love the thought.'

'I know. What are you getting?'

'Oh, only some flowers for the sitting room. Nothing wildly extravagant.'

'And what's this I hear about you moving?' asked Belinda.

'Seeing there are two estate agents' boards outside my house I can hardly deny it.'

'But you love it here.' Belinda was astounded.

'We're not moving away – we're getting something smaller.' Olivia faked a bright expression. 'We're rattling about in that big house now most of the children have left home. Soon it'll be only me and Nigel and we don't need all those rooms.'

'Even so,' said Belinda. 'What are you looking to buy instead? There's a fabulous cottage down near the church up for sale – you know, the one by the cricket pitch.'

Olivia knew it very well indeed. She also knew that it was going for much the same price as she was hoping to get for her place. And what was the point of telling a half-truth – everyone would know her new address soon enough. 'No, we're going to Beeching Rise.'

Belinda's eyes actually goggled for a second before she composed herself. 'Oh.'

The florist appeared from a back room. 'Sorry to keep you, ladies. I had to take a telephone order.' She looked brightly from one to the other. 'Now, who's first?'

When Olivia got back she noticed that Amy was whizzing through the downstairs and doing a terrific job. Making up for swigging the gin, she thought, cynically. She put the big bunch of flowers on the counter in the kitchen and opened one of the wall cupboards to get out a vase. She could see the one she wanted on a high self – a big cut-glass one that had been a wedding present. She stood on tiptoe to reach it, pressing on the work surface with her left hand to steady herself, while she managed to get the fingertips of her right hand to reach it. But the vase was heavier than she was expecting, her balance wasn't perfect and as she lifted it down, it slipped from her grasp and hit the counter, shattering. Razor-sharp splinters of glass flew everywhere and the crash reverberated through the entire house.

'You all right, Mrs L?'

No, she wasn't. She stared at her left hand. The back of it

had a deep cut right across it – for a split second she could see the white edges of the skin before blood filled the gash and then flowed out onto the counter. She felt sick and dizzy and felt herself swaying. Hands grasped her and led her to a chair.

'There you go Mrs L,' said Amy, as she sat her down. 'Hold your hand in the air while I get a cloth.'

Still feeling very faint, Olivia did as she was told, feeling the warm, slow, viscous trickle of blood make its way past her wrist to her elbow then, a few seconds later she felt something cold and damp being wrapped around her hand.

'I don't know much about first aid but I think that needs stitching,' said Amy.

'I'm sure it'll be fine,' said Olivia.

'No, it bloody won't be,' said Amy. 'It's a bad cut. You should get yourself to the doc's. If Dr Connolly can't sort it he'll get you to A&E, who can.'

Now Olivia was sitting down and the original shock was wearing off she began to feel stronger. She opened her eyes and looked at Amy who was crouching down beside her – all around her, all over the floor, were sparkling shards of lead crystal.

'I haven't got time, Amy. I've got people coming to view the house, remember.'

'Not till this afternoon. And I can clear this up and finish off.' Amy grasped Olivia's uninjured right hand with hers. 'I'm going to ring Bex and see if she can't run you over to the surgery.'

Olivia looked down at Amy's hands gripping hers. 'Maybe you're right. And apart from anything else I think I want some decent painkillers.' She gave Amy a weak smile. 'As the kids say, it's proper caning.'

'Right, I'm going to make that call. And if Bex can't I'll try Heather. There'll be someone who can help, I'm sure.' Amy crunched over the broken glass to find her mobile. 'And never you mind, Mrs L, I'll get all this glass sorted as soon as you're fixed with a lift.'

Olivia slumped back in her chair and tried not to think about

the agonising throb in the back of her hand as Amy began her
search for a Good Samaritan.

Bex put down the phone and picked up her car keys. Five minutes
later she pulled into Olivia's drive and, not bothering to lock the
car, ran to the door. Amy had it open before she had a chance to
ring the bell.

'Thanks for being so quick,' said Amy.

'Where's the patient?' Bex looked past her and saw Olivia, her
hand still in the air and a tea towel, stained with blood, wrapped
round it. 'You did the right thing,' she said to Amy.

'It's a bad cut.'

'I think straight to A&E, don't you?'

Olivia overheard. 'I'm sure that's not necessary. Besides, you
always have to wait so long and I haven't time.'

'It's a weekday morning,' said Bex firmly. 'I'm sure you'll be
straight in.'

Olivia looked sceptical.

'I'm not taking no for an argument. Are you all right to walk
to the car?' said Bex.

'Of course. I'm not an invalid.'

Amy and Bex exchanged a look. 'Come on then,' said Bex.
She picked up her car keys and Olivia's handbag and helped her
friend to the car.

Olivia was almost silent on the trip to Cattebury General. Bex
glanced at her occasionally and saw that Olivia's mouth was set
in a thin line.

'Does it hurt?'

Olivia nodded.

'Won't be long now,' said Bex as she pulled away from a set of
traffic lights. Ahead was a big sign for the hospital, with the red
A&E symbol pointing to a left turn. Bex swung the car round the
corner and straight into the car park. She drove right through it,
to the door to the hospital.

'Will you be all right to go to reception while I park the car?' Olivia nodded.

Bex dropped her off and was back in a few minutes, clutching the parking ticket. Her sandals squeaked on the polished floor as she made her way to the right department. Olivia wasn't in the waiting area. Had she been whisked off somewhere else?

'Can I help you?' said the receptionist there.

'I'm with Mrs Laithwaite,' she said.

'She's in triage.'

'Blimey – that was quick.'

'It's not all bad news with the NHS,' said the receptionist, tartly.

'No, no, I know.' Chastened, she took a seat in the almost empty waiting area and picked up an ancient and dog-eared magazine from the pile on the table. She was flicking through her third edition of *OK!* when the double doors to the A&E department opened and Olivia came out with a serious bandage on her hand.

Bex put the magazine down. 'You done?'

'Not yet. It needs stitching properly but I've got this dressing on in the meantime. More hygienic than the one I arrived with.'

Bex thought about the state of her tea towels in her kitchen and nodded. 'Do they know how long it'll be?'

'Do you need to get off? I can get a taxi home if you do.'

'Don't be silly. If it's any length of time I'm sure Belinda can cover for me. Let's face it, she ran that pub on her own for an age before she took me on.'

'I suppose.'

'How's the pain?'

'Better, thanks.'

Silence fell for a while and Bex looked at some pictures of a soap-opera celeb flaunting an engagement ring on her left hand and looking adoringly at a bloke who, while undeniably handsome, also looked completely gormless. Olivia, next to her, glanced across at the pages.

'Is Amy engaged?' she asked out of the blue.

'Engaged? I don't think so. Why?'

'I was sure she was wearing a ring, rather a nice one, when she was sorting me out. The trouble is, I wasn't really with it. The shock...'

Bex remembered. 'Oh that – yes, the ring her bloke gave her, but according to Belinda, it's not an engagement one. A gift, apparently – from her bloke.'

'Only... it's...' Olivia frowned.

'It's what?'

'Nothing. Pretty damn generous gift, though, if her bloke is not planning on marrying her.'

'Maybe it's paste.'

'Maybe. I always thought paste tended to be big and showy; that ring is quite tasteful.'

'And possibly antique,' said Bex.

'Exactly the sort of thing my mother used to wear.'

'When she showed it off to me I was a bit surprised – I mean, I don't know anything about Amy's Billy—'

'Billy?!'

'Yeah, he's her boyfriend. Why, do you know him?'

'Mrs Laithwaite?' called a nurse from the door to the A&E ward. 'Would you like to come through?'

'Told you it'd be quick,' said Bex, thoughts of Billy and why he'd not given Amy a more contemporary ring evaporating as she returned to her magazine.

When Olivia got back home, Amy had finished and had left a note saying she hoped Olivia's hand would soon be better. *And don't worry about the money, you can pay me next time.*

'There may not be a next time,' said Olivia under her breath.

She put her bag down on the counter in the kitchen and had a quick look around. She had to admit the girl had done a good job and she couldn't see a trace of glass or blood. The bread had finished and Amy had managed to remove it from the machine and put it on a rack to cool and she'd also put the flowers in water. They needed proper arranging but at least they hadn't been left to die.

And the house smelt as she wanted it to – clean, fresh, homely; perfect. Olivia glanced at the clock. She still had an hour before the expected viewing. Her hand was starting to throb again as the local anaesthetic and the painkillers wore off but she had to find out something first before she stopped and took an analgesic. She walked over to Nigel's desk and took out his keys then opened up the filing cabinet. There was her jewellery box. So that hadn't been pinched. She opened it. At first glance it looked like it was all there but then she remembered her other boxes, the ones containing the individual items like that eternity ring. She rummaged under the bank statements... the pearls, the emerald brooch, some other minor bits and pieces. But no antique ruby eternity ring.

Of course not, it was on Amy's hand.

Heather was pottering about her kitchen, listening to the early evening news programme and preparing vegetables for their supper, when the doorbell rang.

'I'll get it,' she called to Brian as she put down her knife and wiped her hands on a cloth. She glanced at her husband as she passed his study and saw him leaning back in his chair, deep in thought – but contented thoughts if the expression on his face was anything to go by.

'Hello, Joan,' she said when she saw who was on the doorstep. 'What can I do for you?'

'Can I come in?'

'Of course.'

'I won't be long – Bert dropped me down here and he's only gone to the cricket pavilion to check up on the fixtures list so he'll be back to collect me in a couple of minutes.'

'OK. Come through and take a seat.'

Heather led the way into the kitchen and flicked off the radio. 'Now, what is it?'

'Amy's been arrested.'

'What?' The word came out as a strangulated screech.

''Tis true.'

'But Amy? What for?' Heather lowered herself onto a chair.

'Something to do with the break-ins.'

'No. Not Amy. Surely not.' Heather rested her chin on her hand as she tried to make sense of the revelation.

'I was having my hair set when she phoned her mum. Mags was in a terrible state.'

'She would be. I still can't believe this.'

'But think about it – you and the doc's wife both had burglaries, *and* Amy cleans for you both.'

Heather shook her head. 'Coincidence. There've been plenty of other burglaries.'

Joan leaned back in her chair and folded her arms over her ample bosom. 'I'm just saying...'

'Saying what?' said Brian from the doorway.

Heather repeated the accusation and revelation and Brian looked increasingly baffled and concerned.

'Where is Amy?' said Brian. 'Maybe I should go to her.' He turned to Joan. 'Do you know where she is? Is she home?'

Joan shrugged. 'No idea. Mags may know.'

'Perhaps I'll give her a call. Do you have her number?'

'No, only the one for her salon,' said Joan.

'Me neither,' said Heather. She sighed. 'It's all very well everyone having mobiles these days but it makes the old phone book useless.'

'Do you know anyone who might?'

'Belinda? Olivia?' offered Heather.

'I'll try them.' Brian returned to his study.

A horn sounded outside the house. Joan heaved herself to her feet. 'That'll be my Bert. Sorry to be the bearer of bad news but I thought you ought to know. Let's hope this'll lead to you getting some of your stuff back.'

And, while Heather would have loved to see her mother's antique clock again, she didn't want it if it came at Amy's expense. 'I think I'd rather Amy is found innocent.'

Although she also knew that whatever the outcome, Amy's reputation, in a little place like this, was going to take a very long time to recover.

47

Amy, feeling horribly nervous, stood on the doorstep of The Beeches and rang the bell. Normally, she'd have let herself in with her key and got on with the cleaning but, under the circumstances, she wasn't sure Bex was still going to want her.

'Oh,' said Bex as she opened the door. 'Lost your key?'

Amy shook her head. 'I wasn't sure you'd still want me.'

'Want you? Why on earth not?'

Bex shut the door behind Amy and led her into the kitchen. The table was covered with sponges and fairy cakes that she'd got out of the freezer, all awaiting dollops of butter cream and icing which Bex had ready in two large mixing bowls.

'School fête tomorrow. I got asked to make some cakes.' She smiled at Amy, proud of her handiwork.

'Great.' Amy sounded as if it was anything but.

'So, what's all this about?'

'You've not heard.'

'Obviously not.'

'I got nicked by the police.'

'You got…? No!'

Amy nodded. 'I did.'

'But… but why?'

'You know that ring?'

It was Bex's turn to nod.

'Turns out it was Mrs Laithwaite's.'

'No!' Bex sat down. 'But you were given it... I mean, you didn't take it.'

'No, but I've got the keys to her gaff. And Jacqui Connolly's and Heather's.'

Bex frowned. 'But you didn't... you haven't... you're not a burglar.'

'Course I ain't. But it's not looking good, is it?' Amy sounded as if she were close to tears.

'No, I don't suppose it is. But the other burglaries?'

'Search me.' Amy gave a hollow laugh. 'Which they have, of course, and they found nothing except Mrs L's ring.'

'But Billy gave you that.'

'Oh, they've nicked him and all.'

'No!'

'He's denying everything. He says he bought the ring legit, at a car boot.'

'Did he?'

'Of course.' Amy looked hurt.

And everyone knew that stuff at car boot sales was always squeaky clean. Yeah, right. But it didn't make Billy a thief, thought Bex.

'And they had to release him without a charge too,' continued Amy.

Bex thought for a second. 'For what it's worth, I trust you, and I still want you to clean for me.'

'Really?'

Bex nodded. 'Quite apart from anything else, I can't imagine anyone would be so stupid as to pinch stuff from the houses they work in. And, if I'm any judge, Amy, you're not stupid.'

'Thank you – I think. You'd better know something, though, cos you're bound to hear sooner or later.'

'What?'

'I got caught by Mrs L, swigging her gin.'

Bex snorted a laugh. 'You what?'

Amy looked shamefaced. 'You heard.'

'How? Why?'

'She always tells me to help myself to tea or coffee when she's not there but one day I saw the bottle and I fancied a G and T instead. She caught me.'

Bex giggled. 'Not a hanging offence though, is it? Although I imagine Olivia was a bit cross.'

'She went bat-shit.'

Bex had to suppress another giggle at the incongruous thought of Olivia going 'bat-shit'.

'I'm surprised she didn't tell you,' said Amy.

'I think Olivia can be very discreet.'

'I would have done, in her shoes,' said Amy.

Yes, well... but Bex kept quiet. 'Anyway, this isn't getting my house clean or the PTA's cakes finished. And I'll be glad when they've all gone and I've got my freezer back. Although, on Monday, I'll be starting again doing another batch for the church fête.'

'You're mad, you know. Potty.' But Amy grinned as she said it then went to the kitchen cupboard to get her cleaning things and the polish. 'The usual?'

'Please.' Bex went back to icing her cakes.

Not surprisingly, the hot topic in the pub was Amy. Poor kid, thought Bex. But there was something ironic about the town gossip now being the focus of the town's gossip.

'Do you believe she's innocent?' asked Belinda.

'Totally,' said Bex. 'In fact I left her cleaning my place to come here.'

Bert, nursing a pint near the window, looked over to the bar. 'Was that wise?' he asked.

'I think so. Besides, I like Amy.'

Bert considered this. 'Yeah, she's a good'un. And her son Ashley is too. Better than that Zac Laithwaite, for all that he lives in a posh house. And why's that up for sale?'

Speculation in the pub shifted away from Amy and onto the Laithwaites with Bex avoiding joining in the conversation, knowing what she did about the family and the reason behind the sale. The pub got busier and the hubbub of voices was such that it was difficult to hear individual conversations.

'Amy said Billy got that ring at a car boot sale,' said Bex to Belinda quietly and out of earshot of the customers.

'Wouldn't be surprised. I hear Billy often does car boot sales.'

'I did one once,' said Bex. 'Me and the kids did it to get rid of old toys they'd grown out of. Never again.'

'That bad?'

Bex shuddered at the memory. 'All those people who swarm round while you're trying to set up your pitch, grabbing stuff, wanting to know how much, it was horrible; like being picked at by vultures. And then, after that, you have several hours of standing in a field, trying to look pleasant and being grateful to get offered fifty pence for something you know you paid twenty quid for.'

'Well, Billy's obviously got a different view because I think he does them most weekends.'

'And finds bargains, if that ring is anything to go by.'

'Not that it was such a bargain now it turns out it was nicked.'

'Indeed.'

Friday afternoons in Little Woodford were always busy, thought Leanne as she wheeled her bike along the crowded pavements and then chained it to the bike rack behind the town hall. She wasn't in her normal summer get-up of stab vest, white shirt, tie and black trousers but a bright floral skirt and a red T-shirt. With her hair down she looked like any other of the town's citizens, most of whom seemed to be out and about on this pleasant June day. Leanne had popped into town to post a couple of letters, pick up a few things from the Co-op and, maybe, have a coffee. She also thought that she might take a stroll up to the skatepark and chat to some of the kids who would be bound to head there after school seeing as it was both sunny and a Friday. She liked chatting to the kids; it was, she knew, part of the job. If the kids liked and trusted her they would be more likely to see the police as people who could help them rather than a force to be wary of. Not that the public in a small place like Little Woodford saw the police as the enemy like they did in some inner-city areas in other parts of the country.

She'd almost finished everything she needed to do in town when she saw the Laithwaite boy and his dog walking towards her.

'Hi, Zac,' she said.

Zac looked at her, bemused. 'Err, hello,' he mumbled.

'You don't recognise me out of uniform, do you?' She could see the penny drop as she fell into step beside him.

'Oh, yeah, you spoke to me after that fight.'

'And I hope you haven't done any more of that,' said Leanne. Zac shook his head.

'And I saw you in your house. I asked you about Dan or Billy, asked if you knew them.'

She saw colour flood into Zac's face. 'Did you? I don't remember.'

'Really? You told me you didn't know them.'

Zac shrugged.

'But you know Dan, don't you?'

Zac stopped dead and tugged on the collie's lead. 'I don't know what you're talking about.'

'Oh, I think you do, Zac, because you and I both know you used to do business with him.'

He shook his head.

'I've seen you with him, Zac.' Leanne knew she was lying but Zac didn't.

'Can't have done,' he blustered, not looking at her.

'Have it your way. Except your mum has also told me that you used to do drugs.'

'She *what*?'

'She also said she thought you were clean now. She said you knew you were in a mess and you've quit. Well done.'

'She had no right to talk to you.'

'She's your mum and she was worried.' Leanne changed the tone of her voice to a less brisk one. 'I did drugs once,' she said, cheerfully.

'It's a mug's game.'

'Yup – we both know that now. Have you ever nicked anything to pay for the gear?'

'No!'

'Just asking. People do.'

Zac growled.

'I did,' said Leanne. 'Proper little toerag, I was. I even nicked off my mum. Nicked the housekeeping. Of course, she caught me at it one day. Blimey – the row.'

Zac stayed silent.

'OK,' said Leanne. 'I believe you.' She didn't. 'So, if it wasn't you who nicked your mum's ring that Amy got caught wearing, it must have been her. We just need to prove it now.' She stared hard at Zac.

Zac stopped again. 'You think Amy stole Mum's ring?' He looked startled and worried in equal measure.

'It looks like it. She had the keys to get in the house and she's been caught wearing it.'

Zac shook his head slowly. 'You really think it's Amy?'

'I do,' lied Leanne. She knew Amy and she knew Amy would never steal off anyone. 'Right,' she glanced at her watch. 'I've got things to do, places to be. Bye, Zac.'

She was pretty sure now she knew exactly how Amy had got the ring. Zac had nicked it, sold it to Dan who'd sold it to Billy. She wondered what other business Billy and Dan did together. She'd heard a rumour that Billy was dealing in all manner of gear – she'd bet her bottom dollar that the pair had something to do with the robberies. Time for the real coppers to get involved.

48

Alfie was having a total meltdown and Megan had no idea why. She suspected he was overtired; he'd had a long week at school, the day had been warm and all the kids at the primary school were completely overhyped at the thought of the school fête the following day. Maybe, she thought, as she dragged a screaming, sobbing child along the street, taking him and Lewis to the park hadn't been such a good idea after all. She passed Zac and his dog but didn't have the energy to say more than a cursory 'hi'. Besides, if he was still being a git about apologising to Ashley she didn't want to talk to him.

She finally managed to haul her stepbrother as far as the gate and then hoisted him, kicking and struggling, onto her hip as she unbolted the catch and then thrust him inside. With a sigh of relief she leaned against it to recover while Alfie, still bawling, ran into the house, no doubt to tell Bex how horrible his sister was. Megan took a deep breath and followed on, Lewis walking beside her.

'That was fun, wasn't it?' she said looking down at him.

'Alfie was very naughty,' said Lewis.

Megan nodded. 'You can say that again.' She let herself into the house and followed the sound of Alfie's wails into the kitchen.

Bex was crouching beside him, pushing his fringe out of his eyes. 'What's happened?' she asked.

'I didn't do anything,' she said.

'She didn't,' agreed Lewis.

'It's Alfie being Alfie,' said Megan, having to raise her voice to be heard over Alfie's tantrum.

It took the best part of thirty minutes for Alfie to calm down enough to be taken up for an early bath and then have his supper in his pyjamas. He was pale under the tan the recent good weather had given his skin, and he had rings under his eyes.

'You need an early night,' said Bex as she served up high tea of sausages, mash and beans.

'I don't have to go to bed too, do I?' asked Lewis.

'No, hon, you can stay up. Only if Alfie is going to enjoy the school fête I think he's going to need his sleep.'

'Don't wanna go to—' But the last bit of the sentence was lost as Alfie yawned prodigiously.

The next morning Alfie tumbled out of his bed at just after six o'clock. He trotted across the landing to Bex's room and clambered onto her duvet.

'When are we going to the fête?' he said, shaking her shoulder to wake her up.

'Later,' mumbled Bex, rolling over and eyeing the clock radio. It was 6.05, the luminous green display told her. So early – what she'd give for a decent lie-in once in a while. Mind you, Megan had gone from being a lark to night-owl-teen in a heartbeat. Bex felt there must have been a weekend when she'd woken up at a normal time instead of at dawn or at mid-morning but maybe she'd blinked and missed it. She rolled back and smiled at Alfie. 'Sleep well?'

Alfie bounced up and down on the bed, utterly rejuvenated. 'I want to go now.'

'It won't be ready till this afternoon. After breakfast, if you and Lewis are very good, you can help me take all those cakes I baked up to the school. And then we'll need to come home for lunch before we go back at two.'

'But that's ages and ages,' said Alfie. 'Can I go to the diggers till then?'

Bex pushed herself into a sitting position and arranged her pillows to support her. 'We won't have time this morning. We'll be too busy.'

'Megs'll take me.'

'She can't take you all the time. She might have plans.'

Alfie's lip started to tremble.

'You can ask her,' said Bex. But given the way Alfie had behaved the previous afternoon, Bex didn't hold out much hope that Megan would jump at the chance.

An hour later Zac was also awake and staring at the ceiling. He could hear someone moving around downstairs. On a weekend his mum always made a cup of tea for herself and his dad but maybe today it was his dad performing this ritual, given how badly cut his mum's hand was. It was unusual for Zac to be awake at this hour on a Saturday and hear the sounds of the kettle being boiled, the tea being made, but he'd hardly slept as guilt and worry had refused to let him drift off.

He knew that sooner or later it would come out that he'd stolen his mother's ring and he dreaded what his parents' reaction would be. He thought he would be able to cope with the fury that his dad would no doubt unleash. But his mother... He'd been so vile to her all the time he'd been on drugs and she'd loved him unconditionally. He didn't know why because he hadn't deserved it. But he couldn't imagine that would continue when she found out he'd thieved off her. It wasn't just the ring, it was the money too, and he had no idea how much he'd taken over the last couple of years... hundreds, maybe much more because his allowance certainly hadn't covered his habit. And when she found out she'd be devastated. Zac didn't think he could bear the disappointment he'd inflict on her. Looking back, he couldn't understand how he'd ever thought he'd get away with it. And when the full truth of how appalling his behaviour had been his siblings would probably never talk to him again either. He would be an outcast, a pariah.

And that was before his dad realised how much money had been wasted on his education, because he knew as soon as the results of the end of year exams came in that was going to be horribly obvious. His dad was going to go mental. Well, he'd deserve the bawling out but it didn't make the prospect any less scary. Zac put his hands behind his head and breathed slowly as panic began to rise again.

Was this the result of coming down or was this fear of the future? Zac didn't know but what he did know was he was scared – terrified. And how he felt was entirely his own fault; no one to blame but himself. He'd fucked up his life, his exams, his family, his friendships. As he lay on his back the feeling of desperation grew and grew, as did his feeling of self-loathing. He'd let himself down, his family down... he disgusted himself. He was scum.

There was only one solution, as far as he could see. Maybe it was the coward's way out but he had to escape from facing the consequences of his actions and the only thing he could think of doing was to run away. He had a vague plan forming in his head; he'd get a train to London. He'd have to make sure he didn't get caught travelling without a ticket because he didn't have the fare but once he got to the big city he could disappear. He had no idea how he'd live but other people managed it. He'd have to hope something would turn up.

He'd wait till his parents had gone to bed then he'd load his rucksack up with some bits and pieces so he could survive for a few days and then he'd light out. He'd have to leave them a note telling them not to worry, owning up to everything, so they'd understand why he'd left and why they'd be better off without him.

He got out of bed and padded over to his dressing table, pulled a notepad towards him and began to make a list of things he'd need. And, on another page, he started to draft a note to his parents. He didn't want them to worry.

★

Brian lowered the *Guardian*. 'It's the school fête this afternoon,' he said, his voice muffled slightly by a biscuit he was eating with his mid-morning tea.

'Yes, dear, I know.'

'Are you coming with me?'

Brian, as a school governor, was expected to be there but Heather herself didn't really have an association with the primary school, not now, not since her children had long since left it. On the other hand she knew that Bex had been baking a whole mountain of cakes and it would be nice to have a home-made sponge or fruit loaf for tea without the faff of having to make it herself. She glanced out of the window. And the weather was perfect. Besides, if Bex was there, Megan might be too and it would be nice to see her on neutral ground and see how things were after that assembly. What with half-term and one thing and another she hadn't had a chance for a chat with the child since.

'Yes, I think I will.'

'Good. And what are your plans till then?'

Heather shrugged. 'I thought I might go and see Amy.'

'Do you think that's wise?'

Heather put her toast back on her plate. 'She can always tell me to go away.'

'But I phoned her and told her we believe in her innocence.'

'And I think that a visit – as a friend – is also in order. Goodness knows what people are saying about her.' Although she could guess.

'If you must, then,' said Brian. He returned to his paper.

'I'll be back in time to make lunch.'

Half an hour later Heather walked through the town to see her cleaner. As she passed The Beeches she saw Bex's car in the drive, boot open, with trays of cakes and buns already loaded into it. The sound of children playing wafted to her from somewhere in the garden. It seemed to Heather as though, despite their recent troubles, the family was settling in well.

The pavements were surprisingly busy as she walked along the high street. Maybe people wanted to get their chores out of the way before the fête or maybe they were out early because the weather promised to be hot later but whatever the reason, Heather loved the fact the town was bustling; all the locals enjoying themselves, shopping here rather than in Cattebury, with the lure of the big superstore. They went no further, though, because the centre was a dump – far too many tacky pound shops, bookies, payday loan offices and *Big Issue* sellers to tempt people to the few national chain stores scattered about.

Heather turned into Amy's estate and walked past front gardens, many of which had children's toys and bikes scattered on the lawns when they'd been dumped by kids out enjoying the glorious weather. On the road and pavement other kids were out in gaggles – girls walking about arm-in-arm, boys kicking footballs, a group of teens taking selfies as they perched on a wall. It was, thought Heather, lovely to see so many happy kids and a testament that, despite the best efforts of the Lilys of this world, the local schools did a good job.

Outside Amy's house was parked a shiny red roadster. It looked like Amy had a visitor, thought Heather as she walked up the path to the front door. She rang the bell.

'Oh, it's you,' said Amy. 'Come in.'

'Who's this?' said a man coming out of Amy's little sitting room dressed in a vest and jeans and with slicked back hair. Heather disliked him on sight.

'This is Billy,' said Amy. 'Billy, this is Mrs Simmonds. I do her cleaning once a week.'

Billy gazed at Heather. 'Nice to meet you…?'

He left the sentence hanging with a rising inflection to prompt her into divulging her Christian name. Usually she wouldn't hesitate but there was something about this guy… No way did she want to be on first-name terms with him.

'And nice to meet you, too,' she said, sidestepping the issue.

'I hope this is quick,' said Billy. 'Ames and I are planning on going out.'

Heather gave him her coldest stare before she turned to Amy. 'I came to see how you are. I heard what happened.'

'I'm OK. Apart from the fact that ring was confiscated.'

'Cost me a mint,' added Billy. 'The silly cow shouldn't have worn it to work.'

'But you gave it to me, Billy. I thought you wanted me to wear it, not stuff it in a drawer. You said you didn't want other blokes—'

Billy glowered. 'Never mind what I said.'

'And they're not pressing charges,' said Heather.

Amy shook her head. 'Billy bought it at a car boot. As I said to Bex, it was all legit. How was he supposed to know it was nicked?'

'Indeed.' Yes, antique ruby rings were bound to be all totally above-board at a car boot sale. Heather changed the subject. 'Are you going to the school fête?'

'Thought I might.'

'You're joking me,' said Billy. 'Why d'you want to spent an afternoon doing that?'

'It's fun,' said Amy. 'I used to love them when Ash was a kid there. There's loads of bargains and lots of my friends'll be there.'

Billy sighed and shook his head. 'Friends who'll avoid you like the plague cos you've been nicked by the police.'

'No they won't, they're proper friends who know I never did nothing.' She turned to Heather. 'Are you going, Mrs S?' asked Amy.

Heather nodded. 'I hear Bex has been baking.'

'Regular production line she's got going. I dunno how many she made but I reckon the cake stall will never have had as many as they're going to get today.'

'Excellent. That's tea sorted then.' Heather smiled at Amy. 'And I'm glad all is well.'

Amy nodded. 'And thanks for coming over to see me. I was

afraid there's them who'd have nothing to do with me now. You know... give a dog a bad name.'

'Let's hope not in this town.'

'If that's all?' said Billy impatiently.

Heather raised her eyebrows at him and Billy dropped his eyes.

'I'll see you at the fête, maybe.'

'Maybe,' said Amy.

But not if Billy has a say, thought Heather. She disliked him even more.

'OK, boys, you run off and play,' said Bex as she parked the car up in staff car park.

The boys unclipped their seat belts and climbed out of their car seats as Megan and Bex opened the rear doors, releasing them like greyhounds out of traps. The boys sped off around the back of the school where the happy shrieks and yells of overexcited kids drowned out almost all other sounds, from the rumble of traffic going down the hill to the birds singing in the trees.

'Right,' said Bex, as she opened the boot. 'Let's start unloading this lot.'

Megan eyed the rear of Bex's estate car, piled high with tins, boxes and disposable plastic plates covered with cling film. She picked out a couple of plates. 'Where do these need to go?'

'It's all being set up on the playing field – round the side of the school.' Bex picked up a pile of cake tins. 'Follow me.'

The pair set off to the field and soon found the long trestle table where they dumped their contribution before heading back to the car. It took a dozen journeys to empty the boot. On their last trip they were accosted by Jo, the PTA chair.

'I've been told what you've brought. That's fantastic. You are *such* a star.' She smiled at Bex with genuine warmth. 'I can't tell you how rare it is to find someone who promises the earth and who then delivers. Like you have.'

Bex shook her head. 'It's nothing.'

'It's a very great deal,' corrected Jo. 'And on top of all this you're going to run the tombola this afternoon.'

'I like to help out.'

'You've done more than that.'

Bex smiled shyly and shifted the weight of the cake she was carrying.

'Sorry,' said Jo, 'I'm holding you up, but before you go, two things: one I'm having a barbecue to say thanks to the helpers next weekend – Saturday lunchtime – and I'd like you and your family to come along, and secondly, would you consider joining the PTA?'

'I'll need to check about the first, make sure there's nothing else on,' said Bex, 'and may I think about the second?'

'The PTA is good fun. Truly.'

Jo's smile led Bex to think it might be. 'OK, I'm in.'

'Great.'

Bex walked on towards the stall.

'Hey, Bex – being invited to join something. That's good isn't it?' said Megan.

Bex nodded. 'I think so, yes. I mean, I know I've been to the book club but I think, judging by the PTA at the boys' school in London, the membership for this sort of thing is pickier.'

'Get you – in with the *in* crowd.'

Bex put the last of cakes down and eased her shoulders. 'Go and round up the boys, would you? We need to get a quick lunch before we get back here ready to finish setting up before the gates open. I need to make sure my stall is all ready to go.'

'Would you mind if I don't come to the fête?' said Megan. She looked at the hoards of small kids racing around in the play-ground.

Bex put her arm over Megan's shoulder and gave her a squeeze. 'Course not, sweetie. You see enough of small children at home without having to cope with them when you're out too. Where will you go instead? The skatepark?'

Megan nodded. 'I thought I'd grab a sandwich and head on down there. I expect there'll be people from school there.'

'Not just your mate Ashley?'

'No.'

'So I'm not the only one getting integrated.'

'Looks like it's not.'

49

Zac checked and double checked the contents of his rucksack. He'd have to wait till his parents had gone to bed before he could finish off his packing with food from his mother's cupboards. More stealing, he thought wryly, but he didn't think that cheese and ham and some tins of beans were in the same league as a ruby ring.

He felt restless and he couldn't settle. He'd made a plan and he wanted to be off now but he had hours to wait before he could go. He'd taken Oscar for a walk, he'd tidied his room – he didn't want to leave it for his mum to do. He knew it was a tiny gesture that wasn't going to make up for all the other shit that he'd done but it was one way of trying to make amends and say sorry. And he'd written a farewell note to his parents telling them not to worry. There had to be something else he could do to pass the time – maybe he'd go to the skatepark. Dan wouldn't be around at this time and maybe he'd see Ashley and Megan and apologise to them for being such a total arsewipe. Yeah, he'd do that.

He ran down the stairs two at a time, loped past his parents who were reading the weekend papers in the sitting room and skidded to a halt by the front door.

'I'm going out,' he announced. 'Don't wait lunch for me.'

'But what will you have?'

Zac shrugged. 'I'll be fine.'

'But sweetie—' started his mother.

'Don't fuss,' interrupted his father. 'The boy is old enough to make his own mind up.'

And if you knew the decision I've just come to… thought Zac. 'Bye,' he said, as he pulled his trainers on and slipped out of the door.

He walked down the drive, carrying his skateboard, and saw that the primary school opposite was heaving with activity as the parent-helpers sorted out the last-minute preparations for the fête. He remembered the fêtes he'd been to when he'd been a pupil there and the fun he and his mates had had – life had been so much simpler then, back when he hadn't messed everything up. A whoosh of self-pity enveloped him. How – why – had he got it so spectacularly wrong? Ashley hadn't. As far as he knew, his schoolfriends hadn't. Why him? Because he was weak and stupid and couldn't recognise a wrong decision if it came with flashing neon lights. He dropped his board at his feet on the pavement and scooted down the hill into the town. And even though it took him some minutes to get to the recreation ground, he was still feeling sorry for himself when he reached it.

The place was heaving, unsurprising given that it was a sunny Saturday, but the buzz and the sight of so many people out having fun failed to lift his spirits. Zac zipped along the path on his board to the skate ramps, keeping his eyes peeled for his mates. Well, they *had* been his mates – he wasn't so sure now. And who was to blame for that? he asked himself. Ah, there was Ashley, standing on the top of the half-pipe.

Zac jumped off his board and climbed up to join him. Ashley eyed him coldly.

'I'm sorry I hit you the other day,' said Zac.

Ash shook his head. 'You didn't. You fight like a girl.'

'OK, I'm sorry I *tried* to hit you.'

'And, let's get this straight – I didn't tell my mum about your habit.'

'No.'

'It's not what mates do.'

'No.'

'You're an arse, Zac.'

'I know and I'm sorry.'

'You should be.'

'I've stopped doing drugs.'

Ashley looked at his mate. 'Really? Or are you just saying that?'

'I've stopped. You and Megan were right, I was a twat.'

'Did you stop because your mum found out?'

'Partly. But it was all getting too heavy.'

'It was your own fault for getting involved in the first place.'

'I know. Tell me something I don't know.'

'Was it tough?'

'It sucked. Still does but it's getting less shit.'

The pair lounged against the safety rail in silence.

'How's your mum's bloke?' asked Zac.

'A git. He's trying to persuade Mum that I shouldn't go to uni.'

'Uni's not the be-all and end-all.'

'Says someone who doesn't live on the council estate. I don't want to be a car mechanic or a labourer. I know Billy's flush with cash but there's better jobs out there than that.'

'I won't be going to uni,' said Zac.

'Daddy won't fund it?' said Ashley.

Zac dithered with telling Ash that he wouldn't be finishing school either but he didn't think signalling his immediate plans was wise. Instead he said, 'I'm glad you don't hate me any more.'

Ash looked at him and grinned. 'I wouldn't go as far as that,' he said. And he swooped off down the ramp, up the other side and then back.

'Git,' said Zac, smiling, on his return. But he felt glad he'd sorted out that situation before he left. He didn't want to go away leaving things as they had been.

★

When Megan arrived at the skatepark Ashley and Zac were josh-ing like old times. Good. And Zac looked better, definitely less spotty and ill; more alert. Presumably he was still off the weed and whatever else he took. Maybe he'd be able to pay her back out of that stonking great allowance his parents gave him each month. She made her way over to the bench by the ramps and sat down to watch the kids doing their tricks and stunts and to enjoy the warm sunshine. She couldn't see any of her other new friends hanging around but then it was lunchtime. She pulled her sandwiches out of her pocket and nibbled on one of them. It was a bit squashed but it still tasted fine.

The boys looked over to her and waved and then slid down the slope and came to join her. They dropped their skateboards on the ground then Zac sat beside her and Ashley squatted on the parched grass.

'Give us a bite,' said Zac.

Megan tore her second sandwich in two and shared it between them.

'Looks like I'm always giving you stuff,' she said to him.

He blushed. 'Yeah, I know. I'll pay you back, promise. It's just it's going to be a while.'

'Bloody hell,' said Ashley. 'It's only a sandwich.'

'It's more than that,' said Megan.

'Megan gave me money to pay off my dealer,' admitted Zac.

Ashley turned to Megan. 'You did what?'

'I was desperate,' said Zac. 'He had a knife. He was going to use it if I didn't give him what I owed.'

Ashley's eyes widened then he shook his head.

'I know,' said Zac, defiantly. 'I don't need you to spell it out to me too. And I'm going to make it up to everyone but it's going to take a while.'

'Just as long as you do,' said Megan. 'I'm not going to forget.'

Zac looked from one to the other. 'I won't either, I promise. You have to trust me, I'm sorting it out. Whatever happens...'

He stopped and shook his head.

'Yeah?' said Megan. 'Go on.'

'No, nothing,' said Zac.

'It doesn't sound like nothing,' said Megan.

'Maybe it isn't. You'll find out.'

'Look,' said Ashley, 'either spit it out or shut up. I can't be arsed with you playing games.'

'Fine. I'll shut up then.'

'Good.'

The two boys glared at each other then Zac stood up. 'I expect you'll find out soon enough,' he said. He picked up his skateboard and headed off.

'What's he up to?' asked Ashley.

Megan sighed. 'I don't know. I've got this awful feeling it's not good. Anyway, enough of him. More importantly, how's your mum? Bex told me she ended up with a ring stolen from Zac's mum.'

'It was awful. It really shook her up when the police came round and Billy got mad with her for wearing it. How was she to know it was nicked?' His voice was thick with indignation.

'My mum say she's totally certain Amy is innocent.'

Ashley got off the ground and sat next to Megan. 'I know. That means a lot to my mum.'

'So if she didn't pinch it, who did?'

The two looked at each other. 'You don't think Zac...' said Megan.

'He might be a twat,' said Ashley, 'but even Zac wouldn't stoop that low.'

'No, no you're right.'

When Megan got back home the house was quiet. Presumably Bex and the boys were still up at the school.

She wandered into the kitchen and made herself a cold drink and a slice of toast – having shared her lunch with Ashley and Zac she was still hungry. Taking her snack she went into the study to look at her bank book. She wished now she'd not lent him the money – forty quid was a lot of money to her. Maybe not to spoilt and privileged Zac but Bex and her dad had taught her that money had to be earned, valued, and the stuff in her building society account was for her future; for driving lessons, or maybe to help her through uni...

She caught sight of the memory book and hesitated before she picked it up again. The last time she'd touched it had been immediately before Lily had written that poisonous message on the tutor room board – the message that had got her suspended. And the time before that had been the day that Stella had had her accident. Coincidence, Megan told herself. She picked it up and then dropped it again. Oh shit, supposing it wasn't *coincidence* and another awful thing would be triggered? Zac – supposing he did something drastic, *really* dramatic? He'd been in a really funny mood up at the skatepark and teenage boys did that sort of thing when they were troubled; she'd read about it in the papers. They had had talks about it at school.

Megan stared at the notebook. Don't be ridiculous. No way could their lovely memory book have some sort of evil associated with it. Defiantly she picked it up again and her worries about Zac were subsumed as all manner of memories of her dad flooded back. As she flicked through it, tears pricked at her eyes. She sniffed and told herself that her dad wouldn't want her to be sad. He'd tell her that she might have lost him but she still had Bex and the boys and her grandparents. She was making friends, she was doing OK at school. She needed to get a grip and count her blessings. She sniffed and dried her eyes, put the memory book and her bank book back and shut the drawer.

It was late afternoon when Bex and the boys got back and, once again, Alfie was having a meltdown.

'Too much sugar, too many additives, too hot, too tired, too much excitement,' said Bex after she'd carried her kicking screaming son into the house and deposited him, sobbing, on the sofa.

She tottered into the kitchen and slumped onto a chair. 'Put the kettle on, sweetie. I'm all in.'

'Apart from Alfie, did everyone have fun at the fête?' said Megan as she began to make the tea.

'Oh, Alfie had a ball, right up till the moment when I said it was time to go. And the fête was a massive success – helped in part by the weather. Jo thinks they raised nearly three grand.'

'Brilliant.'

'How was the skatepark?'

'Fun, mostly.'

'Mostly?' Bex raised an eyebrow. 'No one was horrid to you, were they?'

'No, nothing like that. I'm worried about Zac.'

'Still on drugs?'

'No. He says he's clean. I think he is. He's looking better.'

'That's good. So why are you worried?'

Megan shook her head. 'I don't know – just a feeling. Something's going on with him.' She shrugged. 'I don't know. Maybe I'm imagining things.'

'Maybe not.'

'Why do you say that?'

'Look, you're not to say anything to anyone – you promise me you won't repeat this.'

'Promise.'

'They've got money problems.'

'Money?' Megan ignored the fact the kettle had clicked off and went over to the table and sat down opposite Bex. 'How? Why?'

'Olivia told me that her husband is... *was*... a gambler. He's lost a fortune and they've got to sell up and move to somewhere smaller.'

Megan's eyes widened and she shook her head. 'I knew Zac had had rows with his parents but I kind of assumed it was all about his drug habit. I had no idea. Blimey.' As she thought about her mother's bombshell she returned to making tea.

'You don't think,' she said as she brought two mugs over to the table, 'that something like that could make Zac do something stupid?'

'I couldn't say, I don't know him. How stupid?'

Megan couldn't bring herself to voice her fears. 'Nah, I'm probably overreacting. And maybe Zac is being a drama queen.'

'Do you want me to have a word with his mum?'

Megan shook her head. 'And say what? That I've got a funny hunch about a boy I know vaguely from the skatepark?'

'Put like that…'

50

Zac put his phone on his pillow and tucked the note he'd written to his parents under it then dropped his house keys in the middle of the duvet. He took one last look at his room before he tiptoed out. He stopped on the landing and listened. He could hear the ticking sound the old timbers made as they cooled down from the heat of the day and the soft noise of one of his parents snoring. He crept down the stairs and across the living room to the kitchen. Oscar's eyes snapped open but Zac was focussed on his plan. As quietly as possible he opened the fridge and took out a packet of ham and some mini pork pies and a bottle of mineral water which he shoved in his bag. Then he went to the cupboards and dropped a couple of tins of baked beans in too. He checked the tins didn't need an opener but the tuna he pinched next, did. He rummaged in a drawer for one. Then he saw Oscar looking at him from his basket, his head cocked and his tail thumping softly. Zac went over and rubbed the dog's ears.

'Stay,' he commanded the dog.

Oscar's head dropped onto the side of his bed and his tail stilled.

'Good dog,' said Zac. Earlier he'd considered taking Oscar with him but had decided against it. It would be hard enough surviving in London without the responsibility of a dog too.

Finally he raided the fruit bowl for some bananas before he headed to the front door which he eased open.

Outside, the night was refreshingly cool after the warmth of the day and the sky was dark apart from the pinpricks of light from the stars. Gently, Zac eased the door shut behind him and then slung his rucksack onto his shoulder. He jumped across the path onto the grass; he didn't want the sound of his trainers crunching over the gravel to disturb his parents. He checked his watch and then slid his other arm into the strap on his rucksack to put it on properly. He had just enough time to get to the station to catch the last train. He hurried over the front lawn and then jogged down the hill towards the railway, hanging onto his backpack straps to stop it thumping uncomfortably against his spine. He checked his watch again when he got to Megan's house. Plenty of time. He dropped his pace down a gear or two and walked the rest of the way to the station. He glanced through the automatic doors at the departures and arrivals display board. No! The last train was cancelled due to a signal failure down the line. Bollocks!

Zac slumped against the wall of the station. Now what? He couldn't go home – he had no way of getting in. He'd have to wait till the morning and catch the first train. But by then it would be light and there'd be more people about and he was more likely to be recognised on CCTV, and there be more chance of getting nicked travelling without a ticket. And furthermore, there was a chance – admittedly a slim one – that his parents might find his note before he caught the train. This was a disaster.

A sudden hot gust of wind came out of nowhere and whipped up the dust and a few scraps of litter. It swirled around before subsiding. Then came a distant rumble of thunder and another gust. As Zac leaned against the wall of the station and tried to work out his best course of action, the gusts began to morph together into a breeze, a breeze which strengthened and chilled by the minute. Zac looked at the sky and saw the stars begin to be extinguished as the clouds gathered; there was a storm coming.

How long it would take to develop properly and how bad it might be were questions Zac couldn't even begin to answer but he was pretty sure that, at some time during the night, it was going to pour down.

Zac walked away from the station – he had to find somewhere to spend the night. He needed to get undercover or risk getting soaked through. As if to emphasise things there was another flickering flash over near the horizon and then a while later a low grumbling rumble. To his left was the building site. Surely there had to be a way in and once there he would be able to find no end of places to shelter, out of the storm. He walked along the perimeter fence, glancing up at it, trying to judge if he could scale it, but it didn't look that strong and he didn't want to bring it down and risk not only a fall but also make it obvious that someone had broken in. He grabbed the fence and shook it to gauge its strength. The section in his left hand sagged and moved away from the section in his right. The breeze block into which the fence uprights were inserted was cracked right through, allowing the panels to move. Zac gave the breeze block a hefty shove with his foot and the uprights parted company further. There was now a definite gap. Zac hunkered down and looked at it and decided he ought to be able to squeeze through it. Maybe there was a God.

Alfie was woken by the storm. He didn't mind thunder; Megan had once told him it was the people who lived on the stars playing bowls across the sky and he quite liked that idea. When they'd lived in London they'd once gone to a bowling alley and he remembered the rumble of the balls as they'd rolled towards the pins and the crashes and bangs of the falling skittles. And the fun they'd had, and the burgers they'd eaten. Yes, bowling was good. He felt wide awake as he sat in his bed and pulled his curtains back so that he could see the flashes of lightning better, although the sky was quite light so it wasn't as spectacular as some storms he'd seen. He pressed his nose against the pane to see better and spotted his digger in the middle of the lawn. And then the rain started.

No! Dougie shouldn't get wet, Mummy said so. Mummy said his paint would go funny and peel off.

Alfie clambered out of bed and went downstairs. What with the dawn light coming through the windows and the occasional flashes he could see his way quite well. When he got to the kitchen he dragged a chair across the back door, clambered on it and used both hands to turn the big old key in the door. Then he jiggled the bolt under the lock till it slid back. Climbing off the chair again he pushed it backwards before he turned the handle and opened the door.

With the door open a waft of cool air rushed into the house along with the rushing, hissing sound of the downpour. Alfie stood in the doorway watching the curtains of raindrops as they got swished around by the swirling breeze. He wasn't so sure about rescuing Dougie now – he was going to get cold and wet. As he lingered on the threshold he noticed the rain start to ease off slightly. Maybe he'd wait another minute or two. He pottered back into the kitchen, found his wellies in the utility room and stuffed his feet into them. He returned to the doorway. The rain was definitely lighter. He sat on a chair, stuck his thumb in his mouth and, with the door open, watched the storm ease off. Slowly the torrent of falling water moderated and the cacophony of the storm lessened to be replaced by the sound of a blackbird singing its heart out. Suddenly sunshine burst out from behind the cloud, casting long shadows across the garden and lighting up all the raindrops.

Alfie scrambled off the chair and went to the door. Everything sparkled, including his digger. He went outside to collect it.

'Silly, Dougie,' said Alfie. 'You're not allowed out in the rain, Mummy said. You're not like the big diggers.' He picked up the heavy Tonka toy and carried it back into the house where he put it by the Aga. 'You can dry out here,' said Alfie to his toy.

He gazed at the open door and at the early morning light. He knew it was early – too early to go and wake Bex, and Lewis wouldn't want to play. He could go into the sitting room and watch the TV or... or he could go and see the real diggers. No one would know. Alfie went to the door and out into the garden then he walked around the front of the house. He tried to open the gate but it was bolted fast, so he squeezed between the bars. The main road was completely empty – not a soul around. Further up the high street a cat trotted across the tarmac but that was the sole sign of life. Alfie hitched up his pyjama trousers and set off up the road.

He was tired when he got to the building site and his feet hurt. One of his wellies was rubbing a blister on his heel and he was cold too; his pyjamas were only made of thin cotton. He walked past the station and over to the building site where he hung onto the fence and gazed at the diggers. There were only a couple that he could see and they weren't doing anything. His little excursion, which had seemed a good idea, was turning into a rubbish outing. He wanted to be back home but the only way was to walk and his foot was really sore and he was cold, and miserable and hungry. A tear trickled down his face.

Olivia had been lying in bed, wide awake since the storm had struck, worrying about their future, about selling the house, about Zac, about the state of the world, about everything and anything and she'd seen the dawn break and the sun rise and, although it was far too early to be up and about on a Sunday, her hand ached and she wanted a painkiller. On top of that, she also wanted a wee and a cup of tea. Beside her Nigel was snoring as if he didn't have a care in the world. How could he, she wondered, given that many of her worries were as a direct result of what he'd done? She sighed. Blame and recrimination weren't going to help.

She slipped out of bed and padded down the stairs. As she

reached the ground floor, Oscar got out of his bed, shook himself vigorously and trotted over to her, his claws click-clacking on the floorboards. She patted him and he accompanied her to the kitchen where she fed him a couple of gravy bones while she made her tea. She picked up her mug and carried it back to her room, Oscar following her.

'Do you want to see Zac?' she asked the dog as they got to the landing. 'Go on then.' She opened the door to her son's room. The curtains were drawn back and the room was tidy. Really? Zac? This wasn't like him.

Then she saw the bed was empty. There was a note on the pillow.

The hand holding her mug slackened and tea dribbled, unnoticed, onto the carpet as Olivia made her way into the room and picked up the note. Shakily she put her mug down on the bedside table, sank onto the bed and began to read.

Dear Mum and Dad,
I've decided that the only way to make up for all the shit I've caused you is to go away. Please don't look for me, you'll be better off without me. I've left my mobile so you can't contact me and I don't want you to worry. I'll be fine where I am going.

Not worry? She was beside herself already. And, that phrase 'better off without me'... he wasn't... he couldn't be planning...? Dear God, no. She read on.

I know you know about the drugs but you need to know that it was me that stole the ring as well as money from your purse. It wasn't Amy.
I'll be alright and one day I'll make it up to you both.

No, that didn't sound like he was thinking about suicide. But even so...

I love you and I am so sorry for being a disappointment.

Zac

xxx

Tears rolled down Olivia's face and her hands shook as she lowered the sheet of paper onto her lap. Unsteadily, she got up and went to her own bedroom.

'Nigel.' Nothing. '*Nigel!*' She pummelled his shoulder

There was a grunt and a snort and he rolled over.

'Wha...' Blearily he opened an eye. 'What time is it?'

'Seven o'clock. Zac's gone.'

'Seven? What?' Nigel still sounded dopey.

'Zac's gone.'

'Gone where?'

'Gone. Run away.'

'You're kidding.' He was wide awake now.

'Jesus, Nigel, would I joke about something like that?' She thrust the note under her husband's nose. He took it, sat up and read it.

'Drugs?' He looked horrified.

Olivia nodded.

'Why the fuck didn't you tell me?'

'Because Zac told me he was going to stop. I knew you'd be angry and would yell at him but if he'd really did stop there was no need for the row.'

Nigel's hand clenched, crumpling the note. 'I had a right to know. I am his father,' he shouted.

'I think I had a right to know about your gambling but you didn't tell me about that till you were so far in a corner you had no way out,' Olivia shouted back.

Nigel stared at her. 'Has he stopped – the drugs, I mean?' He sounded sulky.

'Yes. It was one of the reasons I got him Oscar, so he had something to focus on, something to do. It made him get out in the fresh air, do some exercise, stop him lying around in his room smoking weed or snorting ketamine or whatever his substance of choice was.'

Nigel shook his head. 'And you're sure he's gone? Sure he's really left?'

'Nigel, you've read the note. Do you think he'd have written that if he was going to play hide and seek?' Worry was making her snappy and shrill. 'I'm going to phone the police.'

'Now?'

'No, in a couple of days. Of course *now*.'

'Yes.' Nigel looked at his wife. 'Where do you think he's gone?'

'Your guess is as good as mine.'

Olivia walked around the bed to the telephone on the table by her side. She picked it up and dialled 101. 'I'd like to report a missing person...'

51

Bex rolled over and looked at her clock. Half seven – that was a nice lie-in. Alfie must have been tired because generally he'd have woken her up ages before this. She could hear the TV downstairs; presumably the boys were watching cartoons. She stretched luxuriously and then swung her feet out of bed. She padded downstairs and into the sitting room.

'Morning, Lewis. Sleep well?' She looked around the room and saw that Lewis was on his own. 'Alfie not awake yet?'

Lewis shook his head, his eyes glued to the shenanigans on the screen.

'I'm going to make myself a cup of tea. Do you want anything?'

Lewis shook his head again.

Bex pottered into the kitchen and saw the back door was wide open. She froze. Burglars? Then she saw Dougie sitting by the Aga. It definitely hadn't been there last night when she'd gone to bed. She went into the garden and called her son's name. Silence.

Maybe it had been Lewis who had opened the door. She dashed back into the sitting room.

'Lewis, have you been outside this morning?'

Lewis sighed heavily and turned around. 'No.'

'What about Alfie?'

'I've not seen him.'

Bex took the stairs two at a time and charged into her youngest son's room. His bed was empty. Her heart began to hammer wildly and it wasn't from the exertion of racing upstairs. She went onto the landing.

'Alfie? *Alfie?* ALFIE?'

Megan came down the attic stairs, yawning. 'Bex?'

'The back door's open and I can't find Alfie.' Bex turned and raced back downstairs and called for her son in the garden again. Megan followed her. 'Not again,' she said.

Bex couldn't trust herself to answer. Her anxiety was making her very close to tears.

Megan raced to the front and checked the gate. 'The gate's still bolted,' she reported to her mum. 'He's got to be here, somewhere.'

Megan returned to the house and went through every room while Bex searched the garden, looking behind all the shrubs in the herbaceous border.

After ten minutes of scouring the whole place they met in the kitchen. 'I'm going to ring the police,' said Bex.

'And have you got a recent photo?' said Leanne Knowles.

Olivia stood up and walked across to a side table under the big window where she picked up a photo frame, took the back off and extracted the picture. She passed it to Leanne. 'There. It was taken at Christmas this year.'

'Any reason why he might have left?'

Olivia picked up the rather creased note and handed it to Leanne. She read it in silence then said, 'That pretty much explains it. Get out before he's found out.'

Olivia nodded.

'OK. So, what do you think he might have been wearing?'

'Hard to say. I've gone through his wardrobe and there's a grey hoodie missing and some jeans – black ones. And his trainers. And he's taken some food – a few tins, some fruit, a couple of pies. Not much.'

'OK, I'll start by circulating this to all our units in the area. We'll contact the Missing Persons' Bureau and I'd suggest you'd get hold of all his mates and see what they can do with social media.' Leanne's radio crackled into life. 'Excuse me,' she said to Olivia.

She walked outside to take the message.

'A missing person had been reported,' she was told.

'Yes, I'm on it. I'm with the family now.'

'Another one.'

'What?'

'A five-year-old. Reported by his mother, Mrs Bex Millar of The Beeches. Two kids from the same town. As far as we know there isn't a connection, although Mrs Millar's oldest child does know Zac Laithwaite but the missing boy, Alfie Millar, has gone wandering through the town before on his own.'

'OK, I'll go there straight from here. Can you get another officer here to stay with the Laithwaites? Oh, and I want any CCTV camera footage from last night reviewed.'

Leanne returned to the house. 'We're on the case and we're going to look at the CCTV footage. I'm sure we'll have Zac back in no time. I've got to go to another incident but a case officer is being assigned to you and will be here shortly. Try not to worry – I know it's easy for me to say but in the vast majority of cases we find the kids very quickly.'

Olivia, white with anxiety, nodded.

Zac woke up from a short and uncomfortable doze and was, for a second, disorientated. He was cold and stiff and his shoulder ached from sleeping awkwardly. He took in his surroundings: the rough concrete he was lying on and the unplastered brick wall a few feet away – ah yes, a half-built house. Slowly, easing his aching joints as he moved, he sat up and yawned.

Running away, he decided, sucked; so did being homeless, but at least he'd found shelter and had been kept dry when that storm had finally struck. And now he was hungry, he was bursting for a pee and he needed to get to the station to find a train. He stumbled to his feet and brushed cement dust off his jeans. He already looked a mess and he'd only been gone one night. He ran his tongue over his teeth and wondered if his breath smelt. He tugged on the zip of his rucksack and picked out a mini pork pie which he ate in a couple of bites. He washed it down with a swig from his water bottle, almost choking as the bubbles went up his nose, then he put the bottle back in his bag and zipped it up.

'Time to go,' he said to himself. He wondered when the next train was as he went through the gap in the wall that one day would be the front door. He then picked his way across the detritus of the building site, the broken bricks, the empty cement sacks, the puddles in the uneven ground, to the newly built road that snaked past the houses. He found a thicket of under-growth that had yet to be bulldozed or landscaped and had a swift pee into the bushes. He was glad he only needed a pee – he didn't fancy doing the other out in the open, although he'd better get used to living rough, he told himself as he did up his flies and set off again. He ducked behind some garages as he neared the show home and then raced along behind a row of terraced houses, worried that someone from the developers might be around to see him even though he knew it was unlikely, this early on a Sunday morning. He got to the gap in the fence and glanced around to make sure that he wasn't being observed. Quickly he slipped his bag off his shoulder, shoved it through and then crawled after it. He breathed a sigh of relief that he was back on the public highway and couldn't be done for trespass. He picked up his kit and began to walk towards the station. Further along the pavement he could see what looked like a bundle of clothes and contemplated his mother's likely reaction if she knew someone was fly-tipping. He then wondered if his mother had found his note yet and felt a pang of guilt because he knew what angst it was going to cause.

Zac approached the bundle and he could now see it was no such thing, but a small child dressed in pyjamas and a pair of wellingtons. He ran the last few steps, hunkered down and tentatively put his hand on the boy's face. It was warm. He was asleep not... Zac felt relief wash through him.

The kid opened his eyes and looked up at him. Zac thought he looked vaguely familiar. Maybe he'd seen him around the town – after all, Little Woodford wasn't a big place.

'Hey, buddy,' said Zac, gently. 'What are you doing out here?'

The kid's lip trembled and tears welled up in his eyes. 'I'm cold and I'm hungry and I want to go home,' he wept.

'Sure you do.' Zac could sympathise with all of that. 'You're a bit young to be out here on your own, aren't you?'

'I came to see the diggers.'

'Does your mum know you're here?' The boy shook his head and the tears flowed faster.

Zac stood up and then picked up the lad to set him on his feet. The child howled. 'Owwww. My feet hurt,' he sobbed.

Zac knelt on one knee and sat the child on his other one. 'What's your name?'

'Alfie.'

'Then, Alfie, is it OK if I take your wellies off?'

Alfie nodded.

Zac tugged the boots off causing Alfie to squeal again. He had a look at the kid's feet. The back of one of his heels was rubbed raw and the other had a fat, puffy blister. He looked at the station and considered his options. He could abandon the lad here and catch his train as planned. Or – and he knew this was the only real choice he had – he could take the kid back to his home and dump him on the doorstep. Zac sighed. His escape to the city would have to wait a few minutes. He had to hope that he wasn't going to get spotted by anyone who might recognise him, and that his parents hadn't yet found his note and come out looking for him. He made the only decision he could; there was no way he could leave the kid here, alone on the street. He'd take the boy home, ring the doorbell and run away. Job done.

'OK. How about a piggyback?'

Alfie, his face wet with tears and sobbing quietly, nodded.

Zac stood Alfie on his bare feet while he slipped off his rucksack, stuffed the boots in it and then swung the child up and onto his back. He grabbed his bag and set off towards the town. 'Where do you live then?'

'Past the play park.'

Like that narrowed it down. 'OK,' said Zac. 'And I'm Zac, by the way.'

'Thac,' lisped Alfie.

He headed towards the park along a still quiet main road. A car swished past on the wet tarmac and Zac kept his head down, hoping his face wasn't visible if anyone in the car bothered to look at him. He reached the park gates. 'Now where?'

Alfie pointed dead ahead. Zac trudged on.

Ahead he could see the fluorescent yellow and blue of a police car driving towards him. He pulled his hood further forward. The car pulled up beside him. Fuck.

Zac pushed his hood back as Leanne rang the doorbell at The Grange.

'You did the right thing,' she said to him.

Zac shook his head as the door opened.

'Zac!' said his mother. 'Thank God. Where was he?' She threw the door wide and gazed at her son, swallowing down tears of relief as he crossed the threshold.

'He was walking along the high street. He'd found Alfie Millar who had also gone walkabout and was taking him home.'

'I'd have been on a train if it hadn't been for that,' said Zac.

'Then, thank God for Alfie,' said Olivia.

'Welcome back, Zac,' said Nigel. He came over to his son and sighed.

'Don't,' said Olivia, shooting him a look.

'You frightened the crap out of us,' said Nigel. 'I'm so relieved you're back.'

'I'm sorry,' said Zac.

'The main thing is you're safe and well. That's all that matters in the long run,' said his father.

'But the other stuff...'

'It doesn't matter,' said Nigel.

Zac looked bemused. 'But Mum's ring...?'

'That you sold to Dan,' said Leanne. 'Your dealer? Danny Nightingale?'

'How did you...?'

'I told you, Zac, I'm a copper. I know this stuff. I think he needs a visit.'

'You won't tell him I said anything?' said Zac.

'Said what?' Leanne tugged at her stab vest, pulling it down and adjusting her belt. 'I'm off then. And don't run away again, Zac. It's always better for everyone to face the music rather than run away from your problems. Truly.'

Zac nodded.

52

When the doorbell rang, Bex wasn't entirely sure she was ready to see anyone. If she'd been frightened for Alfie's safety the first time he'd run off it was nothing compared to the second time. And as for the relief that had engulfed her when he'd been returned safely... All the emotion had wrung her out and, despite the fact it wasn't even time for elevenses, she felt almost ready for bed again. Lewis was still glued to the cartoon channel, semi-oblivious of the near-awfulness of what had happened, Megan was up in her room blaming herself for not having followed up her premonition that Zac about to do something drastic, and Alfie was in his, having a nap because he obviously hadn't had a proper night's sleep and he was exhausted.

The doorbell rang a second time and Bex gave a sigh before she headed out of the kitchen to answer it.

'Miles.'

'I had to come round. Belinda said there was a police car parked in your drive. You haven't been burgled, have you?'

Bex shook her head. 'No, Alfie went walkabout again.'

'No! How? Didn't my bolt work?'

'Fine, as far as I know. He managed to squeeze between the bars.'

Miles shook his head. 'I know I called him Houdini but it was meant as a joke. I didn't expect Alfie to follow quite so closely in his footsteps.'

Bex shook her head. 'It was so awful. I woke up and he'd gone. I had no idea...' Her voice caught in her throat as she relived the shock of finding the back door open and Alfie's bedroom empty.

'Come here,' said Miles, opening his arms and enveloping Bex in a massive hug. Her emotions and tiredness got the better of her and she leaned her forehead on his shoulder as sobs began to wrack her. His arms tightened around her and the feeling of being safe and wanted increased. She relaxed, sagging against him, allowing him to support her. She felt his lips against her hair.

No!

She pushed away from him. 'Stop.'

'Why?' he murmured into her curls.

'Because... a million reasons because. Because of Belinda, because it's wrong, because what sort of example am I setting for my kids?' Bex pushed harder and out of his grasp. Panting, she took two steps back.

'But...?' said Miles.

'There's no "but" about it. How could you? What about Belinda?'

'What about her?'

'She's your partner.'

Miles began to laugh.

Bex looked at him in exasperation. 'It's not funny,' she snapped.

'Oh, yes it is. Yes, she's my partner; she and I have half-shares in the pub, but that's it. That's all it is – business.'

'Business? You mean you're not...'

'Romantically involved?' Miles raised an eyebrow. 'Shagging?'

Bex felt her face flare. 'Well...'

'No, we're not. We did, we have, but we decided that we're completely wrong for each other and if we were to make a success of the pub it was strictly business only.'

'Really?'

'Really. We get on fine as working partners – but live together?

We'd kill each other before a week was out. Check with Belinda if you don't trust me.'

Bex looked up and stared at him. Did she believe him? Did she call his bluff and ask Belinda? She hadn't been married to Richard for so long as to have forgotten the way men could lie if they wanted to.

Miles was smiling at her. 'At least that explains why you worried about me coming round here and jumped like a scalded cat if I got close to you. And there was me thinking it was because you didn't like me much.' He shook his head. 'I can't tell you how unhappy it made me to think I didn't have a chance.'

Bex was lost for words. 'Oh,' was all she managed to get out.

'So, do I? Have a chance?'

'Maybe. I don't know...' She smiled at him. It wasn't an abhorrent idea, far from it, but the thought of it made her feel unfaithful to Richard. And what about the kids? How would they feel? Megan especially. 'I'll think about it, promise.'

'As long as there is a ray of hope.'

Bex nodded.

Leanne leaned against her locker at the police station and began to unzip her stab vest. What a day! Normally, a Sunday shift was a total doddle; a patrol or two, maybe a domestic to deal with, sometimes a drunk-and-disorderly in the summer... but two missing kids and then a couple of raids. It was probably more excitement than Little Woodford had seen in a decade – the local paper would have a meltdown. They'd had to get back-up from Cattebury to get enough manpower to deal with the simultaneous searches of Danny Nightingale's gaff, Billy Rogers' place, plus his locker at the car dealership, which Mr Silver, the owner, had been less than pleased about, search warrant or no search warrant.

'Looks bad,' he'd protested.

It had looked a lot worse when they'd started removing bags of nicked stuff that Billy had stored there. A couple of customers had been agog with curiosity, as had Mr Silver, as they'd carried out laptop after laptop, cameras, jewellery and some nice antiques.

'What was Billy up to with all this?' he'd asked.

'No good,' was the response.

Leanne had to admit it had been a great day as far as results were concerned; both kids found, Billy and Danny nicked for theft and possession of stolen goods, a number of items recovered that could now be returned to their rightful owners, and a stop put to the recent crime-wave that had been the scourge of Little Woodford. But now she couldn't wait to get home and put her feet up. She hadn't become a PCSO in a place like this to deal with criminals like Dan and Billy – proper nasty they were, and when they were behind bars the law-abiding residents would be able to breathe that much easier.

Although it made her wonder what Amy had seen in Billy in the first place. As far as Leanne was concerned, Amy was well out of her relationship with him, assuming she wanted out of it, that was. And if she didn't... well, she deserved everything she got. Mind you, thought Leanne, since she and Amy had been at a school together she'd known that Amy had had a dodgy taste in men. That boy that had knocked her up just before she took her GCSEs had been a waste of space and hadn't even hung around to do the decent thing. As soon as Amy had told him she was in the family way he hadn't been seen for dust.

Leanne hung her uniform in her locker, shoved her shirt in her bag to wash at home and locked the door. She felt bone tired as she made her way out of the station and took herself home. As she walked down the high street she wondered how the Laithwaites and the Millars were dealing with their errant children. She suspected Alfie would be smothered in kisses while Zac would have to do a lot of explaining.

Zac's *explaining* was on hold while he recovered from his night of rough sleeping. He knew he was going to have to talk to his parents at some length and he was worried and concerned about their reaction but, after tea and toast, exhaustion had completely overwhelmed him and he'd been asleep moments after getting into bed, leaving his parents to worry about his motives and where they might have gone wrong.

'Was it our fault?' said Nigel as he and his wife ate roast lamb, neither of them enjoying their food but going through the motions of Sunday lunch regardless while Zac slumbered upstairs.

'But the other kids were fine.'

'That's what I mean.' Nigel laid his knife and fork on his plate. 'Maybe we got complacent.'

'But we had no reason *not* to think we were anything but good parents.'

Olivia was going to add that maybe, if Nigel had been home earlier these past few years instead of never getting through the front door before eight at the earliest, he might have bonded better with his son, got to know him, spotted that he was going off the rails. But as she was about to challenge him she realised that she was as much at fault, what with the council and committees and the WI and the book club and all the other things she did to occupy her endless free time. She could hardly cast the first stone.

She took another mouthful of lamb and redcurrant jelly and chewed. 'I think,' she said, 'I ought to spend more time with the family.'

Nigel glanced at her. 'You sound like a politician who's about to resign.'

Olivia nodded. 'That's about the size of it. I think I need to give up all my committees and clubs. I'll get the church fête out of the way and then I'll resign from everything.'

'But you love that stuff.'

'I love Zac more.'

'But what will you do all day? You'll go stir crazy.'

'I could get a job – part-time, like Bex. Then I'd be around when Zac is home from school. Let's face it, any extra money would help. We haven't had an offer on the house yet which tends to make me think the estate agent was right and we might have to be prepared to accept less than we'd like.'

'You think?'

'We haven't the luxury of holding out for the full price – you know as well as I do that the debt collectors are starting to get impatient, to say nothing of the way the interest is accruing.'

'What would you do?'

'Bex found employment.'

'But you told me she works at the pub.'

'So? Work is work. After lunch I shall look at what's in the Sits Vac in the local paper.'

After lunch Bex asked Megan to keep an eye on her half-brothers, who were playing in Lewis's bedroom with the contents of the dressing up box and a den made from the clothes horse. She was amazed by the resilience of her youngest who had woken up at midday and bounced down the stairs almost as if nothing had happened. He'd complained about having sore feet but a dab of Savlon on each heel and a sticking plaster had solved that. However, he had listened solemnly to Bex's lecture about never, *ever* wandering off again and had nodded in understanding when she'd explained that he'd been lucky that one of Megan's friends had brought him home and not someone bad – very bad, who might have taken him away so he'd not have been able to see Megan or Lewis or his mummy again.

'Or Dougie,' added Alfie.

Bex had had to suck her cheeks to kill a smile. Obviously being separated from Dougie was the critical issue. But at least she felt that she'd been able to get across to Alfie the seriousness of what he'd done without frightening the little mite to kingdom come and giving him nightmares.

Telling Megan she'd only be half an hour, she'd slipped out of the house and up the road. She had with her a large bunch of flowers she'd cut from the garden. It wasn't much, she thought, but there was nothing she could buy or produce that would say thank you adequately for what Zac had done for Alfie.

As she walked up the hill she wondered how to phrase her gratitude. It was tricky because Zac had sacrificed his plan of running away to take Alfie to safety so, despite the fact that Olivia's son had done a good deed, it had all been brought about by the fact that he'd planned to bring some serious heartache to his family. Bex reckoned that whatever she said would be better than saying nothing.

She rang the bell and a man answered the door.

She smiled and said, 'Hello, you must be Nigel. I'm Bex – Alfie's mother.'

'Ah, Bex. Come in.'

Nigel opened the door fully and Bex stepped in to the house. Olivia was seated on the sofa – she looked exhausted; Bex could sympathise with that.

'Hi, Olivia,' she said, holding the flowers out. 'I brought you these.'

Olivia got up and took them. 'You shouldn't have,' she said as she inhaled the scent of the roses and admired the jolly ox-eyed daisies, the aquilegias and the spikes of white delphiniums.

'Totally inadequate given what happened and I am sure Zac won't be the least bit impressed but I didn't know what else to say or do. If it hadn't been for him...' Bex stopped as a sob threatened to well up.

Olivia nodded, then she stepped forward and hugged Bex. 'And if it hadn't been for Alfie, Zac would probably be in London by now and I dread to think how that might have turned out.'

'Kids, eh?' said Nigel.

Olivia went to the kitchen and got a vase which she filled with water and put the flowers in. 'These are so lovely,' she murmured as she arranged them.

'I think the previous owner of my house had green fingers.'

Olivia moved the flowers to the middle of the coffee table in the sitting room. 'I shall miss this garden when we move,' she said. 'I try and tell myself that it'll be fun planning a new garden but...' She stopped. 'So how is the wanderer?' She sounded falsely bright.

'He's had a nap, he's had a lecture about not doing it again and I'm going to make our gate completely childproof. I shall ask Miles to put netting on the inside so Alfie can't climb through it or up it. But he's fine. I don't think he's got any idea of what might have happened and I think it's for the best I keep it that way. How's Zac?'

Olivia shook her head. 'He came home tired and hungry and a bit shamefaced.'

'Which he bloody should be,' said Nigel, 'given what he owned up to in his farewell note. Drugs, stealing—'

'Stealing? Not Zac doing all those burglaries?'

'God, no,' said Olivia. 'Thank God. No, it was just from us. Although I say "just from us" – I mean, that's pretty bad.' She looked bleak.

'It was the drugs that made him do it,' said Bex. 'Megan says he's clean.'

Nigel nodded. 'Apparently.'

Olivia gave him a look. 'I think he is and I think he's learned his lesson. And his punishment is our lack of trust in him because that is going to take years to win back.'

Nigel didn't look convinced.

'And I don't think what you said to Leanne,' continued Olivia, staring at him, 'was terribly helpful.'

Bex was agog to know what it was but couldn't ask.

'I don't see anything wrong with a public flogging, personally,' muttered Nigel.

'And I don't think you're in a position to suggest it. People in glass houses...' snapped Olivia.

'It was a joke,' said Nigel.

'I must be going,' said Bex. She stood up. She knew it was worry and the subsequent relief and exhaustion that was making this couple bicker but she didn't want to be a witness or a referee.

'I'm sorry,' said Olivia. 'But I am so glad Alfie is safe. And I'm kind of glad Zac had something to do with it – it's something he can be proud of. He's made a lot of wrong decisions recently and that was most definitely a right one.'

'It was,' said Bex. 'Truly, a right one. And I must get home. I had to say thank you and I want you to tell Zac that I am unbelievably grateful, I always will be. What he did, to muck up his own plans and rescue Alfie, was pretty noble. I know it doesn't make up for the rest but I think it shows he's got a good heart. The other stuff...? We all make mistakes.'

'I suppose,' said Nigel.

'Thank you,' said Olivia. 'I think everyone is entitled to make mistakes – as long as they only make them once.' She looked at Nigel and smiled and he gave her a tentative smile back.

Bex felt that Olivia might not have quite got around to forgiving her husband but was on the path to it. Maybe the awful events of the previous night had happened for a reason.

53

A fortnight later, Lewis and Alfie were haring around the vicarage garden while Megan manned the Aunt Sally stall and Bex, aided by Heather, dispensed tea, home-made scones and cakes in a large tent, borrowed from the local scout group, pitched on the lawn and decked out with picnic tables and chairs and bunting. It was, thought Bex in a short lull between hungry and thirsty customers, the epitome of what a church fête in a little place like this ought to be.

'Need another two cream teas,' said Amy, pushing her way between the chairs and the customers.

'Coming right up.' Bex began to pile a cake stand with scones, a pot of jam and a tub of clotted cream, plus a couple of slices of cake and a selection of delicate brown bread sandwiches. She dumped it on a tray and then added a pot of tea and a jug of milk which Heather handed to her.

'Ta,' said Amy. She bustled off.

'I'm surprised Amy volunteered,' said Bex quietly to Heather after her cleaner was safely out of earshot. 'I wouldn't have had her down as a do-gooder.'

'What, like the rest of us mugs who find we can't say no when we're asked to chip in?'

'Pretty much.'

'I think she's trying to make up for what that awful boyfriend of hers did.'

'But he didn't actually do the burglaries, did he? I thought he was the fence.'

'Apparently he got hold of Amy's keys – the ones we've all given her so she can get in to clean. He got them copied and handed them over to Dan. And, according to Leanne, Billy was always encouraging Amy to tell him about the posh houses where she worked.'

'I wouldn't imagine he'd have to encourage her that much,' murmured Bex.

'Well... no...'

'Still, knowing about the place before you actually broke in must have been quite handy. No wonder Amy has got a bit of a guilty conscience.'

Bex was rearranging some of the cakes, topping up the piles of scones from boxes hidden under the table, putting slices of cake on almost-empty plates together to free up some space, flicking crumbs off the tablecloth. When she'd finished she looked up and saw Jacqui Connolly bearing down on her.

'Oh, hell,' she whispered to herself.

'Something the matter?' asked Heather, quietly.

'Tell you later.' Louder she said, 'Jacqui, what can I do for you?'

'I came to apologise.'

'Really?'

'For having a go at you about your son.'

'No, it's fine,' said Bex. 'Water under the bridge.'

'But it wasn't fine. I said some awful things. It was just... it was Lisa's birthday that day and I was upset.'

'It must be so difficult for you.'

'But you know what it's like. You've lost someone.'

Bex nodded. 'Yes, I have.'

'Anyway, I've come to a decision.' She looked at Heather.

'What's that, Jacqui, my dear?'

'I'm clearing out Lisa's room. I need to move on. She's gone, she isn't coming back, I need to accept it, go back to work, sort myself out...'

Heather reached across the table and put her hand on Jacqui's arm. 'As long as you are sure that's the right thing.'

Jacqui nodded. 'Frankly, I don't know how David has put up with me.' She glanced from Heather to Bex. 'It hasn't only been not being able to let go... I may have been drinking a bit much.' She smiled. 'There, I've said it. Don't they say admitting things like that is the first step to recovery?'

'You drank?' said Heather.

Bex awarded her an instant Oscar for best actress. She really had sounded as though Jacqui's revelation had come as a total surprise and given that anyone who employed Amy had to be fully aware of it, that was a pretty laudable reaction.

Jacqui nodded, sadly. 'Yes, and it doesn't help.'

'Everyone copes in their own way,' said Heather. 'There's no right or wrong.'

'Thank you,' said Jacqui. 'Thanks for not being judgemental.'

'Let he who is without sin cast the first stone,' quoted Heather.

'Maybe.'

Amy bustled back up. 'Two cream teas, two lemon drizzle and a pot of tea for four,' she commanded. 'Hello, Jacqui, you all right?'

'Fine thanks, Amy. And I must be on my way. You're busy and I mustn't hold you up. I'll see you at the book club maybe, or the WI.' She turned to Bex. 'You ought to join.'

'I'll think about it,' she promised.

But she already thought she might. Getting involved with the town's activities had given her more to think about than the loss of Richard. She'd made some good friends already; OK, it had taken a couple of months, but these things couldn't be pushed and now she felt as if people in the town cared about her and her little family – Heather and Olivia, and Belinda and Miles... Jo from the school, and now the other mums on the PTA.

An hour later she and Heather cleared up the last of the plates and cups at the tea tent, piled them onto trays and took them over to Heather's kitchen to wash them up.

'Actually, let's leave it for a few minutes. I'm knackered and I want a sit down and a cuppa first.'

Bex nodded. 'Good idea. I'll just pop back out to tell the kids where I am and make sure Alfie hasn't made another bid for freedom.'

'He wouldn't, would he?'

'I don't think so. We had quite a long chat about what might have happened.'

'Good.'

Bex went back into the garden to tell her kids where to find her and was back in Heather's kitchen before the kettle had boiled. They had been joined by Olivia.

'Great fête,' said Olivia.

'Thank you,' said Heather. 'And thank you both for everything you two did to help.'

'A pleasure,' said Bex.

Heather made the tea and brought it over to the table.

'Nigel and I have had an offer on the house,' announced Olivia.

'That's great,' said Bex.

'It's a bit curate's egg. I mean obviously we need to sell but I'll be so sorry to have to move out. And I expect I'll get used to living on an estate in a modern box. At least we'll have a roof.' Olivia tried to look positive. 'The main thing is that we'll be staying in the town. I think if we'd had to move away I wouldn't have coped.'

Bex nodded. 'I know what you mean about this place. I can't imagine living anywhere else now. I love it here; I love the people, the sense of community... I even love the gossip. All those secrets, which aren't, because no one seems to be able to keep anything quiet.'

'Well, that's Amy for you!' said Olivia. 'Mind you, she doesn't know everything. She hasn't found out about Nigel yet and his little – ahem – problem.'

'I doubt if she will – I mean,' said Bex, 'who would tell her?'

'She knows we're moving and making economies but she doesn't know why.'

'She won't hear it from me,' promised Bex.

'Nor me.'

'Then I think it'll be the only secret in Little Woodford Amy won't be privy to,' said Olivia.

Brian came into the kitchen with a carrier bag containing the takings from the various stalls. He dumped it on the table. 'I think we might have broken records this year,' he said, cheerfully. 'I'm going to join you for a cuppa and then go to my study to count it. And talking of Amy,' he said, 'which you were, I have to tell you that you are wrong. There's another secret that she doesn't know about.'

'Really?' chorused the three women.

'Are you at liberty to share it?' asked Heather.

'I certainly am. In fact, tomorrow I've got to make it public from the pulpit.'

'And?' asked Bex.

'I've got to read the banns for Bert and Joan Makepiece. Or rather Bert Makepiece and Joan Downing.'

'But they've been married fifty years. Even I know that,' said Bex.

'They've been *together* for fifty years. Anyway, he's decided to make an honest woman of her.'

'Blimey,' said Olivia, 'who'd have thought it? How on earth did they keep that under their hats for so long?'

'Probably because Amy doesn't clean for them,' said Bex. 'But how come? I mean, I'd have thought people of that generation would have tied the knot rather than risk the scandal.'

'Well,' said Brian, 'it seems Bert met Joan when he was doing his national service and brought her home to meet his mum. According to Joan, she loved the place so much she got a job here and Bert's mum took her in as a lodger. Then Bert's mum died very suddenly and well... she moved out of the spare room into Bert's. Everyone round about thought they'd been married up in Catterick where Bert had been based and Joan and Bert didn't see any reason to confirm or deny the story.'

'But why now? I mean,' said Bex, 'after all this time, why bother?'

'Because they've just discovered that there is no such thing as a common-law marriage.'

'Isn't there?' said Bex.

'No. So if anything happens to either of them, the other is left in a really dodgy position. They decided that even though it means revealing the secret that they've been living in sin for half a century they ought to sort out their affairs.' Brian chuckled. 'Mind you, I think Joan is rather looking forward to setting tongues wagging. Underneath that butter-wouldn't-melt exterior I think she can be quite mischievous.'

'Bless her,' murmured Bex.

'Oh,' said Olivia, 'and talking of secrets... what's this I hear about you and Miles?'

'What?' said Heather and Brian, together.

Bex could feel her face flaring. 'It's nothing, honest,' she mumbled.

'That's not what Belinda told me. She said Miles has been finding any excuse to,' Olivia raised her hands and made imaginary quotation marks in the air as she said, '"pop round" to your place to help you out.'

'Well, you know... the gate needed to be made Alfie-proof.'

'And?' prompted Olivia.

'There was the tap washer that needed replacing.'

'And?'

'I needed to borrow a stepladder to replace a light bulb.'

'And?'

'Oh, OK, I *like* Miles.'

Olivia looked smug.

'I have been trying to be a bit discreet, you know, keep it quiet,' said Bex.

'Keep it a secret, in a small town like this?' crowed Olivia. 'You have to be joking!'

Acknowledgements

To be honest, 2017 didn't start off well and, as a result, writing this book ended up having to take second place to real life. Because of that I want to thank the Head of Zeus team – in particular the wonderful Rosie de Courcy – for their endless patience and kindness, which allowed me to get back on track in my own time. And the same goes for my indefatigable agent, Laura Longrigg, who was equally understanding. I also need to thank Kirsty Falconer for reading the parts of the book and making sure I didn't get too fanciful. And a big thank you to my friends and family for the support, encouragement, cups of tea, kind words, glasses of wine, gin... It made all the difference.